About the

Laurie Benson is an award-winning historical romance author. Her novel *An Unexpected Countess* was voted Mills & Boon's 2017 Hero of the Year. She began her writing career as an advertising copywriter, where she learned more than you could ever want to know about hot dogs and credit score reports. When she isn't at her laptop avoiding laundry, Laurie can be found browsing museums or taking ridiculously long hikes with her husband and two sons. For more info go to: lauriebenson.net

Regency Secrets

Regency Secrets:
Secret Lives of the Ton

LAURIE BENSON

MILLS & BOON

First Published in Great Britain 2023
By Mills & Boon, an imprint of HarperCollins*Publishers*
1 London Bridge Street, London, SE1 9GF

www.harpercollins.co.uk

HarperCollins*Publishers*
Macken House, 39/40 Mayor Street Upper,
Dublin 1, D01 C9W8, Ireland

ISBN: 978-0-263-31881-4

MIX
Paper | Supporting
responsible forestry
FSC™ C007454

AN UNSUITABLE
DUCHESS

I'll always be grateful to my wonderful editor, Kathryn Cheshire, for giving me this opportunity and for helping me bring Julian and Katrina into the world. Thanks for your guidance and support. You're the best! And thank you to everyone at Mills & Boon Historical, especially Linda Fildew, Nic Caws and Krista Oliver, for all that you've done for me.

Thanks Courtney Miller-Callihan, for having my back and for just being you.

To the history bloggers and the people who answered my historical questions – thanks for making research fun.

Lori V. and Lisa D. – this book might not have been written if it weren't for the two of you. Thanks for encouraging me to put this story to paper and for not running the other way when I asked you to read it – a number of times. I love you both!

To Jen, Mia, Marnee and Teri – thanks for riding this rollercoaster with me and for being such great friends.

Thanks, Mom, for teaching me that I could do anything if I put my mind to it. To my boys – you mean the world to me. Thanks for never complaining when deadlines have had me ordering takeout for dinner. And thank you to my husband for always believing in me and for proving that love at first sight really is possible.

Finally, thank you, kind reader, for picking up this book. I hope this story makes you smile, and that you enjoy this brief armchair vacation in Regency era London.

Chapter One

Mayfair, London, 1818.

Katrina Vandenberg had come to the conclusion that the ballrooms of London were rather dangerous places.

As she stood under a glittering chandelier in the Russian Ambassador's ornate drawing room she rotated her sore foot beneath her gown. It didn't help. Anticipating its tenderness, she held her breath and gingerly lowered her slipper to the red and gold rug.

'Why does Lord Boreham continue to ask me to dance?' she groaned as her foot began to throb. 'Each time we do he stumbles through the steps and blames it on me being American and not knowing the movements. This time he stepped on my foot so many times I stopped counting.'

'Perhaps he is enamoured with you,' replied Sarah Forrester, the daughter of the American Minister to the Court of St. James.

'Perhaps he's waiting for me to issue a war cry in the middle of the dance floor and wishes to have an excellent view.'

The friends laughed and a number of the finely dressed gentlemen and ladies looked their way. One of them was their hostess, the Russian Ambassador's wife, Madame de Lieven.

'I suppose you could wear boots under your gown to protect your feet from clumsy partners,' Sarah whispered, hiding her amusement behind her fan. 'Although it would not be very fashionable.'

'I do not believe even that would help. But perhaps I could pretend the orchestra is too loud and I cannot hear them speak. Then maybe I could avoid listening to them boast about how important they are or prattle on about some ancient relative's great accomplishment.' Katrina nodded towards a group of gentlemen. 'One day I wager one of them will show me his teeth in an attempt to impress me. London would be lovely if it weren't for the men.'

When they laughed again Madame de Lieven narrowed her eyes and gave them a chastising shake of her head.

Katrina took a deep breath and shifted her gaze. 'I do believe our hostess is attempting to inform us that ladies in London do not laugh out loud during entertainments such as this.'

How she wished there was somewhere she could go to avoid the constant scrutiny. And that smell! Had someone forgot to bathe?

She rubbed her forehead and a drop of wax hit the embroidered forget-me-nots on her white silk glove.

Evenings like this were always so tedious.

This evening could not become any more tedious.

Julian Carlisle, the Duke of Lyonsdale, didn't know how Lady Morley and her daughter Lady Mary had cornered him. And that bloody chandelier! He was certain his valet would have an apoplexy when he saw how much wax was falling onto his new black tailcoat.

Tonight's crush was so great it had become difficult to

raise his glass of the Russian Ambassador's fine champagne to his lips. If he tried he might inadvertently brush his hand over the front of Lady Mary's dress. It would be interesting to see her mother's reaction to *that*. Most likely Julian would find himself embroiled in the scandal of the evening, with a wife he did not want.

He would stay thirsty.

'And so I told her,' continued Lady Morley, 'that if Madame Devy moved back to Paris we simply would not know what to do. She is the best in London. She makes all of Mary's dresses. Not that she needs any help to show as well as she does. Has the bearing of a duchess, I always hear.'

Thirty-three. Thirty-four. The peacock feather in Lady Morley's turban bobbed with every nod of her head. Julian continued counting. The unique sound of soft feminine laughter floated from behind him and he wished he were part of that conversation instead of this one. He made a conscious effort not to sigh.

Before he could school his features into his usual bored expression he wrinkled his nose. What was that smell? It reminded him of his gardeners in the heat of summer. A man's sweat should not be mixed with an abundance of flowers and sold in a bottle.

Julian managed to down the remainder of his champagne in one gulp. The bubbles tickling his throat were a welcome distraction. 'I understand cards are being played across the hall. Is that where your husband is this evening?' he asked, with no real interest.

Lady Morley blinked at his sudden interruption. 'Oh— oh, yes, I believe it is.'

'I'll be off, then.'

Both ladies curtsied to Julian, and he began to attempt a shallow bow. He bumped into something soft. As he turned to excuse himself high, soft breasts met his hard male chest.

A startled woman with pleasant features and a pair of deep blue eyes looked up at him. Then her gaze travelled slowly down to his waistcoat and back up to his face. When her white teeth tugged at her lower lip, he had a strong urge to lick and soothe that lip. Mentally shaking himself, he tried to gain control of this unexpected yearning.

Her eyes widened, and a faint blush swept across her cheeks. 'Please forgive me, my lord,' she murmured.

Nine years had passed since anyone had addressed him simply as 'my lord'. Everyone knew he was the Duke of Lyonsdale and should be addressed as 'Your Grace'— even if he didn't care to know *them.* 'I assure you no apology is necessary. I believe the fault is mine.'

She bobbed a shallow curtsey and turned away from him. As he watched her make her way through the crowd something inside him shifted. Suddenly he was striding across the room, not even aware of the parting of finely dressed people before him.

Stepping onto the terrace, Katrina closed her eyes and filled her lungs with fresh night air. For a brief time, at least, she would not have to be conscious of her every action.

The amber glow of candlelight, shining through the tall windows and doors of the large brick house, streaked this outdoor haven. In the far corner was an unoccupied area that called to her. It would be an ideal place to escape inquisitive stares and pointed whispers.

The stone of the marble balustrade felt cool against her gloved hands and was a welcome contrast to the warm crush inside. Peering out into the dimly lit garden, she gradually began to relax, enjoying her first bit of solitude all evening. It was wonderful to finally be alone.

'We are fortunate the evening air is so pleasant and there's no rain,' rumbled a deep voice to her right.

Resisting the urge to push the intruder over the railing, Katrina held back a sigh. 'Yes, we are quite fortunate,' she said, in what she was certain was a bored tone. She kept her eyes fixed on the landscape below, hoping it would discourage further conversation.

'The quality of the Ambassador's garden is well noted. Have you walked through it yet?'

'No, I have not. Fortunately for us there are lanterns placed along the pathways so we can enjoy the beauty from up here.' He would soon learn she was not a woman who dallied in the shrubbery. Perhaps he would move on.

When Katrina glanced over at him, she was surprised to discover the handsome gentleman she had clumsily bumped into a few minutes before. He was standing tall, facing the garden, in formal black evening clothes, with the moonlight shining on the waves of his neatly trimmed dark hair. She studied his profile with its chiselled features and square jaw. He must have noticed, because he turned his head towards her and their eyes met.

It happened again. The ground seemed to shift, and this time their bodies hadn't even touched. Deciding it was best to focus on the flowering shrubs and manicured lawn, she diverted her attention away from the man at her side.

Julian closed his eyes and clenched his jaw. Was he actually reduced to discussing the weather and gardening with this woman? When had he become this dull? And he was certain she had just dismissed him. No one *ever* dismissed him.

For the first time in his life Julian felt the need to capture a woman's attention. 'Are you new to town?'

In whose world was this captivating conversation?

'I suppose. I have only been in London for a few weeks.'

'Your accent escapes me.'

She crossed her arms under that pair of lovely small breasts and turned towards him. 'I'm American.' When he remained silent, she tilted her head and studied him. 'Pardon me, but have we been introduced?'

He shook his head, amused at her candour. 'Not that I recall—and I am fairly certain you are not someone I would forget.'

'Then speaking with you would not be proper.' She glanced at the French doors, as if she expected to see someone. 'Did you follow me out here?'

Julian never followed women, and he never acted improperly. He had needed to get away from Lady Morley, and that smell had been unbearable. There had been no reason to consider it further.

'We must have had the notion to step outside at the same time.'

'And you just happened to find yourself standing next to me?'

He shifted under her sceptical expression. 'It appeared to be a pleasant spot.'

She narrowed her eyes momentarily before she turned her attention back towards the garden and began to drum her fingers on the stone.

Below them, a figure walked in and out of the shadows, along one of the garden's gravel paths, as the flames inside the lanterns flickered. Julian traced the figure's movements. 'You wouldn't happen to be hiding from someone, now, would you?'

She looked at him with a curious glint in her eyes. 'Why would you think that?'

'When a woman as striking as you is alone at a ball teeming with men, one must conclude that her solitude is by choice. Are you attempting to avoid a foolish suitor?'

Her lips twitched. 'What makes you believe I have foolish suitors?'

'Ah, I said suitor. Apparently there is more than one.'

'Perhaps I was simply seeking a breath of fresh air.'

'Then I would say any man who wasn't wise enough to accompany you out here to take the evening air was foolish.'

The silk of her ice-blue gown shimmered in the moonlight as she turned her body to face him. 'And why is that?'

He had the strongest urge to step closer. She smelled like lemons. 'Because in this secluded spot he has left you free to be charmed by another man.'

'Are you attempting to charm me?'

'Do you find me charming?'

'Not in the least,' she replied, even though her expression said the opposite.

'Then I suppose your suitor is safe in his position of favour.'

A soft laugh escaped her lips before she quickly pursed them together.

'Or perhaps not,' he amended, revelling in the odd satisfaction that she found him amusing.

'My purpose in coming out here was simply to enjoy a bit of solitude.'

'And I have intruded on your privacy—not well done of me at all. Perhaps we might enjoy the solitude together?'

'Then it would not be considered solitude.'

'Semantics,' he replied with a slight shrug. 'So, why are you seeking solitude?'

She looked down at her slippers and appeared to give her answer great consideration. 'I grew weary of people telling me how important they are.'

He wondered if he was like that. He didn't think he was. Nevertheless, it was probably best not to let her know how important he really was. 'A bold admission.'

'An honest one. And what brings *you* out here? If you were planning on having a clandestine meeting, I fear you are keeping some lady waiting,' she said with a teasing smile.

'I'm not. Perhaps I too grew weary of spending time with people I have no interest in.'

'Than we are of a like mind.'

'It appears we are.'

Her lips rose into a full smile and for the first time in his life Julian forgot to breathe. 'You are lovely,' he admitted, before he could stop himself.

'Thank you, but I have been told I am much too expressive.'

'Not to me.'

'You're trying to charm me again.'

'Am I? I thought I was simply being honest. I appreciate a true smile. I find the false ones maddening.'

What in the world had got into him? Perhaps her candid speech was infectious. Her unguarded manner and their frank discussion should not appeal to him, yet he found her entertaining.

She shifted her stance, and her skirt rustled as if she was shaking out her foot. 'Well, it appears that you, my lord, are not a typical member of the *ton*.'

If she only knew.

It was as if he was being pulled to her by some magnetic force. His heartbeat quickened as he stepped even closer. Her lips looked so soft. As his gaze travelled down to the small swell of her breasts his fingers instinctively curled. He needed a distraction.

Turning back towards the balustrade, he focused his attention on the stars. He had never attempted to count them before. For a moment longer he could feel her watching him. Then she turned and tipped her face up to the inky night sky.

* * *

Katrina wondered at the sudden change in her companion's demeanour. There must be some unspoken rule of English Society she had unwittingly broken. During their brief encounter he had managed to make her forget she was a stranger, navigating uncharted waters. But his silence spoke volumes. She would have to peruse *The Mirror of Graces* again tonight before she fell asleep, to find some clue as to her *faux pas*.

Their engaging conversation had improved her mood, and she was determined to hold on to that feeling for as long as she could. 'It appears as if every star in the heavens is out,' she mused, testing the waters for his response.

'Do you enjoy stargazing?'

She glanced at him and smiled at his friendly, inquisitive expression. 'I have been known to occasionally look upon the stars, if that is what you mean.'

'But can you identify the constellations? Do you know their names?'

She shook her head.

He leaned closer and his sleeve brushed her arm. 'See that grouping of stars over those trees? That's the constellation Cassiopeia.'

It took her a moment to attend to what he'd said, with his body so close to her. 'That's the name of an ancient Ethiopian Queen.'

He nodded. 'And that is her constellation. What do you know of her?'

'Only that her excessive pride in her daughter Andromeda angered Poseidon so much that he commanded the Queen to sacrifice Andromeda to him.'

'Very good. In fact Andromeda is over there.'

She took note of the stars he pointed to.

'It is said Poseidon was enraged because Cassiopeia's sacrifice was not completed,' he continued. 'As punishment, he placed the Queen on her throne in the night sky. Do you remember what happened to Andromeda?'

Katrina could feel him watching her and she shifted her gaze back to him. 'She was rescued by Perseus, whom she married.'

'She was. Now, Perseus is over there.' He leaned across her and pointed to another grouping of stars. He smelled wonderful—like champagne and mint.

Their faces were mere inches apart. His lips looked so firm and smooth. For a moment their breaths mingled. Suddenly he jerked his head back, and unwelcome cool night air blew across her face.

She needed to shift her attention away from his lips and recall what they were discussing. 'Is that truly Perseus, or are you attempting to appeal to my sense of the romantic?'

'That truly is the constellation Perseus. It is said that Athena placed Andromeda next to Perseus in the night sky when Andromeda died.'

'Oh, that *is* romantic.'

He wrinkled his brow as he stared at the stars. 'I suppose some might consider it that way.'

'But you do not?'

'I never gave it much thought until now,' he replied with a slight shrug.

Their eyes met, and it was as if every part of Katrina's body was straining to get even closer to him. She needed to get away before she did something embarrassing, such as caress the arm that was now pressing against her own.

Taking a deep breath, she clasped her hands together. They were safer that way. 'Well, I should return. My party will wonder where I have disappeared to and hopefully the air inside will have cleared.' She smiled at him and moved away from the balustrade. 'Thank you for showing me the stars. I can truly say I was not bored in the least.'

He bowed, and when he raised his head she caught the

laughter in his eyes. 'I am glad. I was not bored either. I hope you will find some pleasure in what is left of your evening.'

She curtsied in return and walked to the doors leading back to the drawing room. As she reached the threshold she couldn't help glancing at him over her shoulder. When their eyes met she lowered her head, and attempted to hide her satisfied smile.

From the moment she'd left his side it had been impossible for Julian to look away from her. If he had looked away he might have missed that one last glance she'd given him before she entered the house. It didn't matter that she had caught him staring like an untried boy. That last look had told him everything. She wanted him just as much as he wanted her.

Pulling his shoulders back and crossing his arms, he tried unsuccessfully to suppress a grin. The novelty of knowing that this woman desired him without knowing his prominent position in Society was exhilarating. Her lemon scent lingered in the air, and Julian took in a deep breath while leaning his lower back on the balustrade.

This night was turning out to be far from tedious after all.

'Now, that's quite odd. It almost appears as if you are smiling. But I know that can't be, because while *I'm* returning from a pleasurable time spent in the garden *you*, my friend, are all alone.'

Lord Phineas Attwood, the Earl of Hartwick, sauntered up the terrace steps. He was dressed all in black except for his crisp white shirt. The knot of his cravat appeared askew, and a lock of black hair was draped over his right eye. He ran his fingers through his hair, attempting to comb the lock back into place. It was no use.

Stopping next to Julian, he also crossed his arms over

his chest and followed Julian's gaze to the French doors. 'Does she have a name?'

'Who?'

'Whoever she is that has caught your interest.'

Julian closed his eyes and with an exasperated sigh turned his attention from the doors to his friend. 'What makes you think it's a woman?'

Hart raised both brows. 'Come, now, I always tell you what has put a smile on *my* face. We can compare notes. I'll tell you about my lady, and you tell me about your lady.'

'There is nothing to tell.'

'Very well—I'll start. Margaret has the most amazing mouth. She can—'

'You were in the garden with Lady Shepford?' Julian closed his eyes. 'You are mad. Not two hours ago you took over two hundred pounds from Shepford at cards, and now you take his wife.'

'Exciting, isn't it?' Hart replied, adjusting his cuff. 'I can't help if she finds me irresistible, and he is positively unlucky tonight. It was impossible not to win his money.'

'One day some husband is going to challenge you, and I have no desire to be your second.'

'I am aware that you believe widows are preferable, but I'm not you. Married ladies are infinitely preferable to unmarried ones. At least they aren't fishing for a title. Honestly, you worry for nothing. My coach is always at the ready, and I'm very competent with pistols and swords.' He pushed himself off the balustrade. 'I'm bored—let's go to White's. Stop scowling. You look like my old tutor.'

Julian shook his head. There was no reason to stay. He would have enjoyed spending more time with the American woman. Had she been a member of the *ton* he would have re-entered the Ambassador's townhouse and immediately sought an introduction. Unfortunately, with the responsibility of his title, a relationship with an American was not possible.

When he married again it would be to an English-woman of prominent lineage—just as his ancestors before him and just as he had done before. Respectable English noblemen did *not* marry American women.

Why was he even thinking of marriage? Hart was right. It was time to leave.

Chapter Two

Reading the *Morning Chronicle* should not be so difficult. Katrina had done it every morning since she and her father had arrived in London a few weeks ago. However, today she was finding it impossible to read even one article—and it was all because of that English gentleman she had talked with out on the terrace the previous evening.

The dining room in the house her father had leased in Mayfair was quiet except for the occasional tinkling of a Wedgwood cup hitting a saucer and the crinkling of paper as her father turned a page of the document the American Minister had sent over.

Feeling frustrated by her lack of concentration, Katrina pushed the newspaper aside and reached for a piece of toast from the silver rack in front of her. As she began spreading honey on the bread she couldn't help but smile recalling their conversation for the hundredth time since last night.

Why couldn't she stop thinking about him? She was not attracted to Englishmen—at least she hadn't been until last night. Most of those she had met since arriving in London had been proud, patronising and too self-possessed for her taste. But this gentleman had appeared to be none of those things. He hadn't even made any foolish comments about her being American. On a night that had begun so poorly he had managed to make her laugh and forget about the pain in her foot. And she couldn't deny that being close to him had made her heart race.

Honey began to drip through her fingers, and Katrina shook her head as she licked away the sticky sweetness. How long would it be until she saw him again? Once he obtained a proper introduction they'd be able to speak openly, and she would finally know his name. He might even ask her to waltz.

While she had no desire to tie herself to an English gentleman, spending time in that man's company during the various social engagements she was obligated to attend while she was in London would be an excellent diversion.

Smiling to herself, Katrina returned her attention to the newspaper and tried to concentrate on reading it one last time.

In another part of Mayfair, in a much larger house, Julian walked out of his suite of rooms and rubbed his pounding forehead. He needed more sleep. Several times during the night he had awoken from vivid dreams about the American woman. Now this lack of sleep left him very irritable—and very frustrated. What he needed was a quiet, peaceful morning.

From the sounds drifting out through the doorway of his breakfast room, there was little hope of that happening.

Crossing the threshold, he noted his mother and grandmother were deep in conversation at the elegantly set table. Grasping at his last few moments of peace, Julian passed the livery-clad footmen on his way to the mahogany Sheraton sideboard and filled his plate. The smell of ham made his stomach growl, making him realise how hungry he was. The moment he sat down coffee was poured into a porcelain cup.

Just as he was about to bring the aromatic liquid to his lips, the chatter around him stopped. His mother's sharp eyes were focused on him, and Julian cursed himself for not taking breakfast in his study.

'Good morning, Lyonsdale,' she said, while refolding a note that had been lying open next to her plate. 'How was the Ambassador's ball?'

'It was a crush, as usual, but surprisingly tolerable.'

'And Lady Wentworth? Did she enjoy the evening?'

Julian had been trying to keep his association with the widow discreet. Obviously he needed to try harder. He blew into his cup and decided to be evasive.

'She was not there.'

'Then who held your attention for so long on the terrace?'

Julian's fingers clenched the handle of his cup before he carefully placed it down on the saucer. He was one and thirty. Was it too much to ask for some privacy? He needed to speak to his secretary about seeing what could be done to hasten the renovations of his mother's townhouse.

'Pray tell, how is it possible that you possess such information?'

His grandmother Eleanor, the Dowager Duchess of Lyonsdale, paused in spreading butter on her toast. 'Your mother has already received a note this morning from Lady Morley. Isn't that correct, Beatrice?'

'Your friend has written to you about what I did last night?' Julian asked indignantly.

'She has only commented on your actions because she says you left rather abruptly and she had thought you were about to speak with her husband regarding their daughter.'

'Why would she assume I intended to approach Morley about her?'

His mother trailed her slender finger around the gold

rim of her cup and raised her pointed chin. 'She, and every other member of the *ton*, is aware that you are in need of an heir. It is obvious that Lady Mary is a suitable choice. Her father is an earl, and she is the niece of a duke. And you have spoken with her. Your conversation confers distinction upon any gel you single out.'

'I have not spoken with her.'

'You must have. You've danced with her. Surely you had *some* manner of discussion on that occasion.'

Had he? Julian tried to recall any remnant of conversation, but he could not. Nothing about Lady Mary set her apart. All the chits who had recently entered Society resembled one another, twittering behind their fans and taking measure of him when they thought he wasn't looking. They were all so young. He must have spoken to her, but he honestly could not recall doing so.

'I may have also mentioned to Lady Morley that you might consider their daughter.'

Julian had stopped listening to his mother moments before, but that declaration caught his attention. The pounding in his head increased. He would not let her dictate which woman he would marry—*not* this time.

'It was not your place to speak for me,' he bit out.

'I made no promises, but surely you see you cannot keep wasting your time with Lady Wentworth. That woman is an unacceptable choice. Her family is of no true consequence. It is time you secured this line. If Edward hadn't been foolish enough to race his horse that day we would at least have had him as your immediate heir. But with his death the line falls to your grandfather's incompetent nephew, should you perish, and he will destroy our good name.'

A familiar hollow feeling opened in Julian's chest—which was why he never wanted to think about Edward. The way his mother had so callously mentioned his dear brother's death fuelled the anger welling up inside him. Was there ever a time that she thought of either of them as more than a necessary part of fulfilling her own duty to bear an heir and a spare?

'You have avoided marriage long enough,' she continued. 'It's high time you fulfil your duty to marry again and finally bear an heir. Lady Mary will make us a perfect duchess. You should be thanking me for saving you from the trying task of finding you a suitable wife.'

'Thanking you?' he sputtered. 'You chose a wife for me once. It did not end well. You will not dictate my choice to me again.'

His mother appeared hesitant to say more, and the tension eased somewhat in his shoulders. Maybe he would be lucky enough to have her abandon the conversation entirely.

'At least *consider* Lady Mary.'

Or maybe she would continue to pester him till he lost his appetite completely!

He swallowed a mouthful of tepid coffee and pushed the cup away in disgust.

Before he could reply, his mother rushed ahead. 'She is from a prominent family, has been trained from birth to assume such a title, is accomplished, and appears strong for breeding. You could not possibly require anything else.'

But he did. He felt it. Only he wasn't certain what it could be. He simply knew he could not continue this conversation while he was still suffering from lack of sleep. This decision was too important—and his coffee was cold.

'You never did say who you were with last night on the Ambassador's terrace.'

'No, I did not.'

His mother held out her cup for more tea. A footman immediately appeared at her side. She wasn't leaving the table any time soon. Julian rose from his chair and dropped his napkin onto the table.

His grandmother glanced at his untouched plate and looked at him with soft, sympathetic eyes. 'You have not eaten a thing. Surely you must be hungry? Would you like Reynolds to fetch you something else?'

Her genuine concern softened some of his anger. 'No, thank you.'

'I could have a tray sent to your study. Surely we can find something to tempt you?'

'There is no need. I believe I have lost my appetite.'

Hart's breakfast room was blissfully quiet. No one was pestering him to make a decision that would affect the rest of his life. Julian knew he needed to marry soon. He couldn't keep delaying the inevitable. The longer he waited, the younger the girls would be. However, each time he considered marrying again his stomach would do an uncomfortable flip. This time was no different.

Why couldn't he find a woman among the *ton* like the American woman who had captivated him last night? Staring sightlessly at his plate, Julian gave a slight start when Hart's butler cleared his throat.

'Is there anything else you require, Your Grace?'

'Actually, Billings, would you see if His Lordship has any lemon curd?'

The butler exited the room as a sleepy Hart wandered in, wearing a black brocade dressing gown. A lock of hair covered his heavy-lidded blue eyes. Hart's gaze followed his butler as Billings re-entered the room and placed a Wedgwood bowl before Julian.

'So this is what my breakfast room looks like,' Hart said through a yawn. 'I was told you were here, however, I didn't believe it.' He dropped into his chair and stared in horror at his friend's toast. 'What has happened to the butter?'

'It's lemon curd.' Julian took a bite of toast and closed his eyes, savouring the flavour.

'I've never seen you eat lemon curd before. I did not even know I *had* lemon curd—and why the bloody hell are you putting it on your toast?'

'I have no idea.' Julian took another bite and wiped his lips with his napkin. 'I woke with the oddest desire for lemons.'

Hart accepted a cup of coffee from Billings and reclined in his chair. 'So what has brought you to my door at this ungodly hour of the morning?'

'It's past ten—hardly ungodly.'

Hart stilled, his cup halfway to his lips. 'In all the years you have known me, and with all you know about me, do you *really* think I rise anywhere near this hour?'

'Point taken. Your coffee is quite good. I do not believe I've tasted it before.'

'That's because you knew enough not to come here for breakfast. Now, enjoy this pot. I do not expect you to bother me for breakfast again any time soon.'

Julian continued to eat his toast. *Lemon curd on toast was exceptional.* He licked his lips, wondering why he hadn't thought of eating it before.

'What does bring you here?'

Perhaps if he talked about it with his friend he might release some of his frustration. Leaning back in his chair, Julian took a final sip from his cup. Billings was at his side in an instant, refilling it. Hart eyed his butler and the man retired from the room, closing the door quietly behind him.

'She wants an heir.'

'Who?'

'My mother.'

'That's no secret. She has made it quite clear that you have been remiss in fulfilling your duty. Is that why you are here at this hour? You have run away from your mother?'

Julian flung a piece of toast at Hart.

'I say, that was quite undignified of you.' His friend picked the toast from his chest and bit into it. 'This is quite good.' He licked his fingers. 'Has she selected another simpering chit for you?'

'Yes, but this time she has spoken to the family, indicating that I have an interest. She has gone too far.'

'And who is this paragon of the *ton* she has so carefully chosen to bear the next Duke?'

'Lady Mary Morley.'

As if he was trying to recall her name, Hart momentarily shifted his gaze. 'Could be worse. She has the most delicious-looking breasts I've seen. They're so full and tempting. Here—pass the lemon curd over.' He picked up the bowl from Julian's hand, dipped his spoon in and licked it clean. 'See…now you've done it. I will not be able to look at Lady Mary's delectable breasts without recalling this taste.'

'Would you please focus?'

'I am!' Hart took another scoop of lemon curd.

'On my problem, dolt!'

'I would if I saw one! You've told me you need to marry again. She is a better choice than any of the other chits your mother has favoured. She's a prime article, appears biddable, and those breasts—'

'Can we please not focus on Lady Mary's breasts?' Julian bit out through clenched teeth.

'Maybe *you* can stop focusing on Lady Mary's breasts. I, on the other hand…'

The pounding in Julian's forehead was back. The fact that he could not recall any conversation with Lady Mary was not promising, and the thought of educating a girl as young as seventeen about marital relations made his stomach roll.

'I did not come here to listen to you tell me what an excellent choice Lady Mary would be. Believe me, I am well versed in her virtues.' He ripped off pieces from a slice of dry toast, trying to hold on to his composure. 'I've danced with her before, but I cannot recall any of our conversations. And I do not believe I've ever seen her smile. I mean a genuine smile, not a false one. Have you ever seen her smile?'

'Can't recall…probably not. Most of them don't.' Hart took a sip of coffee and studied him. 'I was not aware that smiling was a requirement of yours.'

'I am simply stating that a woman should be able to smile if she wishes.'

'I suppose…' Hart said hesitantly. 'I don't understand why you're so angry. Do whatever you wish. You could run through Almack's naked, drink brandy for breakfast, wear puce—it would not matter. No one ever questions you. Actually, the brandy sounds like a splendid idea. Do you think I have any in this room? I honestly don't know the last time I was in here.'

Hart scanned the room for a decanter of amber liquid and turned back to Julian. 'If the chit is not to your liking, do not pursue her. But I am curious. Why do you continue to say you need to fulfil your duty and find a bride when it appears you do everything in your power to discount all the choices? You do realise the sooner you choose someone, the sooner your mother will stop casting you in a dudgeon.'

He scooped some lemon curd onto a slice of apple and popped it into his mouth.

Why did Hart have to be so insightful? Julian knew he needed to marry soon. As it was, he was thirteen years older than most of these girls—fourteen, in Lady Mary's case. In a few more years he might be bedding someone young enough to be his daughter.

Julian rubbed his chest. He wished he had more time.

Lady Mary was as good a choice as any for his duchess. Lineage was important, and the Morley family could trace their blood back to the Tudor courts. So why did Julian feel sick each time he thought of marrying her?

Suddenly clever blue eyes and a warm smile filled his thoughts. If only Lady Mary was like the American he wouldn't think twice about marrying her.

Shaking his head, he resumed slathering his toast with lemon curd.

Chapter Three

Later that evening Drury Lane buzzed with a multitude
of voices as a large crowd awaited the evening's performance. Katrina found the theatre impressive in size, with
three rows of boxes above orchestra level and two additional rows of open seating above. Chandeliers were
suspended from each box, illuminating the theatre and
making it easy to see its occupants.

Scanning the colourful attendants, Katrina found her
gaze was drawn to a box close to the stage in the row
above her own. She adjusted her opera glasses to get a
better view.

'I thought English gentlemen were more discreet in
their intrigues. Lord Phelps appears rather bold,' she whispered to Sarah as they sat together in the Forresters' box.

They both watched as a tall blonde woman turned adoringly to the portly older gentleman as he slid her mantle
from her shoulders. Katrina's eyebrows rose as the cut of
the woman's dress was revealed. The last time she'd seen
a dress cut that low, she'd been in Paris.

'Perhaps that woman is his daughter,' Sarah said,
clearly not believing her own suggestion.

'What do you think possesses a man to seek a mistress?'

'Lack of contentment, I suppose,' replied Sarah with a slight lift of her shoulder. 'It appears much more common here than it does back home. Most of these *ton* marriages seem to be for convenience and not love. That may explain why there are so many indiscretions.'

Katrina's gaze drifted back to Lord Phelps, who appeared to be introducing another older gentleman to his mistress. 'I am grateful joining the ranks of the *ton* is not to be my fate. I would never want my future tied to a man who would likely have liaisons.' She turned to Sarah and her spirits lifted. 'Hopefully when I return home I will find an honourable man who will think me so captivating he will have no choice but to offer for my hand.'

'Hopefully he will be handsome, as well as honourable,' Sarah said with a grin.

Before Katrina was able to respond her father sat down in the vacant seat on her other side. 'And how are the two of you enjoying the evening thus far?'

'We have been admiring the sights,' Katrina said as she smiled affectionately at him. 'It appears a number of boxes are garnering quite a bit of attention, and it's lovely not having stares and whispers pointed in *our* direction for once.'

But in a box across from where Katrina sat in comfortable conversation a man *was* staring—a very surprised man.

Julian narrowed his eyes and studied the woman in pale pink satin. He lifted his spyglass for a better view. She had rich golden hair, delicately curved shoulders, and her face moved with animation as she talked with the woman to her right. There was no mistaking it: this was the American he had spoken with on the de Lievens' terrace the night before—the same one who had plagued his thoughts throughout the day.

The older gentleman sitting next to her smiled indulgently, and Julian had an unnatural urge to drag her away from her companions. What the hell was wrong with him?

'I believe you have not heard a single word I've said for the last five minutes,' Hart complained with annoyance as he flipped a guinea in the air and caught it.

'Of course I have. You were discussing one of your latest liaisons.'

Hart let out a deep-throated laugh and leaned back in his chair, tipping it precariously. 'Not unless her name was Royal Rebel. Which, come to think of it, would be an exceptional name for a princess I am intimately acquainted with… I was speaking of the race I attended this afternoon and the amount of blunt Royal Rebel brought to my pockets. Came from behind and all. It was quite exciting.'

Julian was unable to keep his gaze from returning to the American, even though he tried to focus on his friend.

'What's her name?' Hart asked, flipping the guinea again.

'Whose name?'

'Whomever the lady is who has your attention—attention, I might add, that should be focused on *me*. It was sporting of you to invite me out this evening, but you really are an abominable host.'

Julian glanced at this friend. 'What makes you think it is a lady who has my attention?'

'Foolish of me. I suppose you are studying the folds of some gentleman's intricately tied cravat?' When Julian gave no reply, Hart shook his head. 'You realise it will not take me long to determine who has captured your attention?'

Placing the coin in his pocket, Hart took his spyglass and openly scanned the boxes across the way. 'There is the Montrose box—nothing new in there. Rothschild has some guests, but unless you are interested in *much* older women I think we can safely say your attention was not focused there. Then there is the box with the American delegation… Hmm…potential there. Next we have—'

'You know that box?' Julian closed his eyes, praying his friend hadn't heard the inane question.

Hart laughed softly and arched a cocky brow. 'So your thoughts were of a political nature?'

He didn't have to look so smug.

'Oh, very well, Julian. The gentleman and lady seated to our far left are Mr and Mrs Forrester, the American Minister and his wife. The other gentleman in the front row is Mr Peter Vandenberg, an American author who has recently arrived in London and will be one of the American representatives at the Anglo-American Conference. Surely you have heard of him? My understanding is that he has been welcomed all over the courts and drawing rooms of Europe and has lived for the past eight months in Paris. It's interesting that President Monroe has entrusted him to successfully negotiate the treaty between our countries.'

A mischievous sparkle flashed in Hart's blue eyes. 'Sorry to say I am not acquainted with anyone else in the box. Are you disappointed?'

'Dolt.'

'I can make some enquiries if you like.' Hart smirked and eyed Julian with open curiosity.

'No need. I am simply enjoying the view.'

Julian wondered if Peter Vandenberg was the American woman's husband. They were obviously well acquainted, considering the way she occasionally touched his arm when she spoke. He was too old for her, but Julian knew of many marriages arranged between young women and much older men. If he did not give proper attention to spending time with Lady Mary, his marriage might eventually resemble that one.

It hadn't occurred to him when they spoke that she might be married. Crossing his arms tightly over his chest, Julian forced his jaw to unclench. Why should he care if she was married?

The orchestra struck up its opening chords and the red velvet curtains of the stage parted. The narrator stepped out, and Julian was grateful for the distraction. However, when the interval was announced it annoyed him that he noticed the exact moment when the American woman left her box.

Once the performance had ended Julian couldn't help searching for her as he prepared to enter Hart's carriage. He turned towards the people still exiting the theatre and scanned the crowd for a pale pink gown. Not far away, to his left, he saw her standing next to Vandenberg while the man spoke to a coachman.

As if some strange force of nature had tapped her on the shoulder, she turned his way. Their eyes met. Recognition mixed with pleasure lit her features and the commotion around them faded away.

She pulled her mantle closed, appearing to hold off a chill. There were a number of interesting ways *he'd* like keep her warm. Her head tilted slightly, as if she was trying to read his thoughts, and then her lips rose into that alluring warm smile.

There was movement by her side, and Julian's gaze darted to the older gentleman next to her. When Vandenberg's hand moved to her elbow Julian's grip tightened around the gold handle of his walking stick. Meeting her eyes once more, Julian tipped his hat to her before climbing into Hart's coach.

'Where shall we go next?' Hart enquired as he settled himself on the green velvet bench and adjusted the cuffs of his black coat. 'Shall we try White's for cards?'

'Have your driver take me to Helena's. I promised I would make an appearance at her card party this evening.'

'I still do not understand this attraction you have to Helena. She, my friend, is the devil. Tell me she is nothing more than a passing fancy.'

'I do not understand why you are so against my association with her.'

Hart leaned forward across the carriage. 'She wants to improve her rank.'

'As do most women of the *ton*.'

'Tell me you are not thinking of marrying her.'

'It hasn't crossed my mind. You are mistaken about Helena. She has informed me that she has no wish to marry again.'

'And you believe her?'

'She has not given me a reason to doubt her.'

He and Helena shared a mutual physical attraction. She was the widow of the Earl of Wentworth and missed her marriage bed. She told him she enjoyed her independence. It was the perfect arrangement. Julian would never pay for sex. He wanted shared desire.

Hart opened his mouth to say something, but then turned and looked out of the window. 'Mark my words: Helena is trouble. You'd best remember that.'

However, at that moment Julian was having a difficult time remembering anything about Helena at all. His thoughts kept returning to a warm smile and a pair of lovely eyes.

Chapter Four

For days Julian couldn't seem to rid himself of the pull the American woman had on him. Suddenly she seemed to be everywhere. Each time he saw her their eyes met briefly, but he refused to pursue an introduction. Any enquiries he made about her would lead to speculation. He did not need members of the *ton* thinking he was panting after some American, even if that was exactly what he was doing. She was too tempting—and all wrong for a man who needed to live up to the Lyonsdale title.

The crackling and popping of the fire broke the silence in the library, where Julian and his grandmother faced each other over a chessboard. Absently twirling a glass of his favourite brandy on the Pembroke table, Julian wondered if the American would be attending the Langley ball later that evening.

'Your mother went to a musicale at the Morleys' tonight. I assume you were invited as well? You had no desire to attend?'

'I had already accepted another invitation,' Julian said as he slid one of his black pawns along the board.

'You do not like the girl?'

He gave a careless shrug. 'I have not spent enough time with her to form any opinion of her character.'

'You have danced with her recently.'

'She is a rather quiet partner. Do not fret. I am aware of her family's history and I know she is an appropriate choice.'

'It matters not to me if she is the one you will choose. I will not be marrying her. She does show quite well, though. I wouldn't think it a hardship to produce an heir with her.'

Julian jerked his head up. 'This is hardly a topic you and I should be discussing.'

'Why not? You're a grown man. We have both been married. I doubt there is anything you could say that would shock me.' She arched a challenging brow.

His stomach gave a queasy flip. 'You are my grandmother.'

She took a sip of her sherry and waved her glass in the air. 'Is that the best you can do?'

'It was not meant to shock. Discussing my marriage bed with you is unsettling, to say the least.'

'I am mentioning it because I know how important finding a suitable partner in bed can be for a happy marriage. Your grandfather and I had a happy marriage. Did you?'

Every muscle in his body turned to stone. She knew he hated discussing Emma. It was too painful.

He shifted his attention back to the board, trying to blink away the wretched image of his wife's lifeless form lying on the bloody sheets of her bed. He'd been holding her hand when she had slipped away. Offering her comfort at the end had been the least he could do, since it had been his fault she would never see her twentieth year.

'I had a satisfactory marriage,' he bit out, moving a random chess piece.

His grandmother's attention was back to analysing her next move. 'You were never cruel to Emma, however, I always had a sense that you were indifferent to her presence.'

He forced his jaw to unclench. 'And you think I was wrong in that?'

'I suppose it depends on what you want in a marriage.'

He rarely lost his patience with his grandmother, but she knew as well as he that what he wanted in life for himself did not matter. His parents had chosen his bride for him when he'd been away at Cambridge. When he had returned home one Christmas he had been informed that he would be married to a girl he'd never met. It had made him ill, but he'd understood that his needs and desires did not come before his duty. What mattered above all else was the legacy he left to the Lyonsdale name. He had known that to be true then, just as he knew it to be true now.

'I accepted my responsibility,' he said, looking his grandmother in the eye and raising his chin.

'Yes, you did—quite well, I might add. To my knowledge you never questioned your father's decision.'

'You know I could not cry off, even if I had wanted to. A man does not break an engagement. It is not done.'

She leaned in. 'But would you have done so if you could?'

If he had, Emma would still be alive today.

He took a large swig of brandy. 'I knew how important it was to have an exemplary woman share the Lyonsdale name. Father made an appropriate choice in Emma. There was no reason to protest.'

'And yet even though you accepted their choice the spark in your eyes you had as a child went out when you made your vows, and it has not returned since. You need to find that spark again.'

She made it sound simple, but Julian knew that honouring the responsibility of his title meant he would be bound, yet again, to a marriage of convenience. The only sparks that mattered were the ones he could fire off in his speeches at Westminster.

'Why am I certain you are about to tell me how I can regain what I have lost?'

His grandmother gave a slight shrug. 'I was fortunate. I married your grandfather and we fell in love. Your father was not as fortunate. We were certain your mother would be a rose in his pocket, but she had thorns. Being married to her killed something precious inside him, and he became consumed with politics and Westminster.' She leaned across the table and levelled him with a pointed stare. 'There is more to life than that. It did him no good.'

His father had been the very model of what an English duke should be. Nine years had passed since he'd collapsed and died while delivering a speech to the House of Lords, and to this day people continued to tell Julian how much they had admired him. If only Julian could be half the man he had been.

'I disagree. He helped this country achieve great things.'

'And it cost him his life. No one will convince me that his heart did not give way because of the strain of his political career.' She drained her glass of sherry. 'We were wrong in preventing him from choosing his own bride, and he was wrong when he did the same to you. Life is too brief, Julian. Trust someone as old as I. Do not waste your life tied to someone you do not want.'

If only it were that easy. Out of an entire ballroom of girls the only one he had been drawn to wasn't an appropriate choice—to say nothing of the fact that she was probably married to a man old enough to be her father. The point of taking a wife was to produce an heir. His father had told him many times that it wasn't necessary to like the person you married. You just needed to tolerate them.

Thankfully his grandmother's attention was back on the chessboard. 'Oh, and Julian...? I seem to have misplaced my edition of *A Traveler's Tale* by that American author—Vandenberg. Would you mind purchasing another one for me the next time you are near Hatchards?'

The Vandenberg name should *not* follow any conversation about marriage. He needed to concentrate on finishing this game of chess. Soon Hart would arrive, and they would be off to the Langley ball. However, tonight, he vowed, he would not search for the American at all.

Only the flutter of shuffling cards and the soft murmur of voices could be heard in the card room at Langley House. Footmen stood along walls that were hung with yellow silk damask, ready to refill crystal glasses at the mere lift of a hand. Purposely removed from the hubbub of the ballroom and the front public rooms, this drawing room was located near the end of a long hallway. Serious gambling was always done at the Langley ball, and serious gambling required concentration. It was the ideal place for a man who needed to keep his mind occupied. It didn't even matter to Julian that he was losing miserably.

'Perhaps a new table is in order?' Hart suggested as he collected his winnings.

A new table would not change his luck, but Julian surveyed the other seven tables for open seats anyway. As his gaze skimmed past the doorway he caught sight of Helena, in a jonquil satin gown, its bodice cut to accentuate her womanly curves. With an air of confidence she scanned the room until her grey eyes landed on him.

The beginnings of a smile tipped the corners of her full mouth as she made her way to his side. 'Do not tell me luck is against you tonight,' she said in a silky voice.

'It definitely is now,' mumbled Hart, low enough for Julian to hear.

He shot Hart a look of reproach and turned to her. 'I've had better luck,' he replied congenially.

'Have you been to the ballroom yet? The orchestra is exceptional.'

The American woman was probably in the ballroom—dancing with some braggart. 'The ballroom does not interest me tonight. Perhaps I'll try another table.'

She cocked her head to the side, exposing the pale skin of her neck. 'Perhaps we could play together,' she whispered.

'Perhaps we could.' He should have found the smooth skin of her neck enticing. He had before. However, looking at it now, he found his body surprisingly unaffected.

They were about to search for an open game when a footman approached him with a request for his presence at the Duke of Winterbourne's table. He felt an unprecedented sense of relief in having to leave Helena's side to join his friend.

Excusing himself, Julian followed the footman across the room.

Helena watched Lyonsdale walk towards the table full of his friends who were playing whist. As he leaned over to whisper into Winterbourne's ear Lyonsdale's black tail coat stretched across his broad shoulders. It was a pity the tails covered the outline of his muscular legs and his firm backside...

She could feel Lord Hartwick's eyes on her. For the last five years he had never once attempted to hide his hatred of her. It was perfectly reasonable, considering what she had done to him. However, watching the drama unfold around her at the time had been so entertaining she refused to feel any remorse. Her only regret was that she had believed his father's lies. He had told her that he would marry her if she helped him with his plan—a plan that she was certain had devastated the man's son.

Why hadn't Hartwick walked away when Lyonsdale left?

He tossed a lock of hair out of his eyes and pulled back his shoulders. 'He will never make you his duchess. I will see to that.'

Although he was splendid to look at, his confidence grated. 'Do not imagine you will be able to dissuade him.'

'But I find I rather like the idea, and I don't believe it will take much effort on my part. I suggest you search elsewhere for that elevated title you so desperately seek.'

The foolish man thought he could best her. 'I do not follow suggestions—least of all from you.' She shook out her fan and pasted on a sly smile, glancing pointedly across the room at the woman she knew to be Hartwick's current conquest. 'You should tell your friend she should not wear emerald. The colour does nothing for her complexion.'

Hartwick turned his head and followed her gaze. His lips pressed together as he took a glass of champagne from the tray of a passing footman. 'Maybe in this instance you should follow my suggestion. I hear Ponsby is on his last breath. You might want to try him. You'd have better luck.' He did nothing to hide the sarcasm from his voice.

Why would she want a decrepit duke when she could have a handsome, virile one? 'It appears you are worried for your friend. Do you believe I will damage him?'

'Your excitement is stirred by breaking people. You won't be able to do that with him.'

'You mean like your Lady Caroline? It's a pity she is no longer with us. Your father enjoyed her immensely.' She arched her brow and anticipated his reaction.

He brought his glass to his lips and his nostrils flared. 'I see you have no remorse for your part in bringing an innocent woman to his bed.'

Why should she? The foolish girl hadn't been forced to accept every glass of champagne Helena offered her. She hadn't poured them down the girl's throat.

Recalling that entertaining night brought a smile to her lips, and she leaned close to Hartwick, purposely pressing a full breast into his arm. 'You might not want to discuss this here, where someone may overhear us,' she whispered into his ear. 'You don't want them to guess the truth about her death, now, do you? Tell me…did she choose poison, or was it something more dramatic?'

His jaw clenched, and his athletic body stiffened against her breast. If they had not been in a drawing room, with a good number of the *ton* around them, she might just have provoked him enough to strike her.

She couldn't help but smile. 'I do believe I have found a weakness of yours, Lord Hartwick. Everyone has at least one, and it is so delicious whenever it is discovered.'

'I warn you—if you cause any problems for Lyonsdale you will regret it.' He moved from her side, downed the remainder of his champagne, and strode across the room to join his friends.

It was amusing that he thought he could stop her. She deserved that title, and all the wealth and power that went with it. She should have had such an advantageous marriage the first time. Instead, due to one minor indiscretion, she had found herself married to a gambler and a drunkard.

Hartwick's father had promised to make her his marchioness and laughed at her when she'd reminded him. No one made a fool of her. It would be her turn to laugh when she became Duchess of Lyonsdale.

Near a corner of the Langleys' ballroom, in front of a large potted palm, Katrina was learning that she was not the only one who regretted dancing with Lord Boreham.

'I do so wish I did not have to agree to dance with everyone that asks me.' Lady Mary Morley pouted as she stood beside Katrina. 'On that last turn Lord Boreham managed to elbow me quite hard in the stomach.'

'How was that even possible?' Sarah asked, staring at the area in question, which was covered in elaborately embroidered white muslin.

'I can assure you it's possible,' Lady Hammond commented dryly while fanning herself. 'He once knocked heads with me during a quadrille.'

They began to laugh, and Lady Mary immediately covered her mouth to stop herself. The diamond bracelet on her wrist sparkled in the candlelight.

'Surely there must be a way to avoid him,' Sarah said.

Lady Mary shook her head. 'Mother says one should have a full dance card if one is to be considered an incomparable, and if you decline even one offer to dance you must decline all the others.'

Katrina found that rule of social conduct one of the hardest to accept. She suspected she was not the only woman in the ballroom who felt that way. 'That hardly seems fair.'

'That might be. However, it is the way of things. Mother says if one is to catch a duke or a marquess one needs to rise above all the other girls vying for such a title and become an incomparable.'

'And how does one become an incomparable?' Sarah asked with amusement.

Lady Mary was not as naïve as she appeared. She tilted her head coyly. 'I suppose if everyone knew the answer to that, no one girl would stand out.'

'Well done, Lady Mary,' Sarah said with a smile, glancing around the crowded ballroom. 'And are there many dukes and marquesses for you to choose from?'

'I'm afraid there are very few, and I don't think I'd like

to settle for an earl.' She turned to her friend and offered Lady Hammond a genuine apologetic smile. 'Sorry, my dear. I didn't mean anything against your Hammond.'

Lady Hammond waved her fan carelessly in the air. 'I'd much prefer a young earl to an old duke.'

Both Lady Hammond and Lady Mary appeared to be a number of years younger than Katrina, and she wondered just how old the girl's husband was.

'Isn't your father an earl?' Katrina couldn't help pointing that out to Lady Mary.

Lady Mary adjusted her bracelets. 'He is. However, my uncle is the Duke of Ralsteed. I was born to be a duchess. I do not have to settle for an earl.'

Lady Hammond let out a delicate sniff. 'You'd change your mind if Lord Hartwick made an offer for you. With his looks and those blue eyes, you'd forgive him his title.'

A blush spread across Lady Mary's cheeks, making her appear even younger. 'That might be true. However, my sights are focused on one specific duke—even if he does make me nervous.'

'Being nervous around a man can be a good thing,' Sarah offered helpfully. 'It might mean you find him very attractive.'

'Oh, I do,' Lady Mary agreed, nodding vigorously before she caught herself. 'I do think he is very handsome... except he is a bit old.'

'He is the same age as Lord Hartwick,' Lady Hammond said with exasperation.

Lady Mary looked as if she was fighting the urge to stamp her foot. 'Well, he appears older.' Stepping closer to Katrina and Sarah, she shook out her fan to cover her lips. 'He comes from one of the most respected houses and has great influence in Parliament. His manner is very formal, and each time I am in his presence I find him austere and imposing. He seldom speaks. I don't believe he needs to. He can fluster people with just the lift of his brow.'

He sounded like a bore to Katrina. 'And this is the man you would like to marry?'

Lady Mary nodded again, with excitement in her eyes. 'Just imagine the respect his duchess will be granted. And he's rich. He is a man who does not need to marry an heiress. Should we marry, we might very well be the wealthiest family in Britain.'

'Which would be wonderful,' Sarah remarked, 'as long as you can stay awake long enough to enjoy it.'

'Sarah!' Katrina chided her friend with what she hoped was a stern expression.

These two girls had been nothing but kind since being introduced to them by Madame de Lieven. They were eager to hear about America and about Katrina's time in France. She didn't want Sarah's unchecked honesty to ruin a pleasant discussion.

'I am simply stating that should a man be that...flinty, it might be difficult to stay awake in his presence,' Sarah explained.

Lady Hammond let out a small laugh before she pressed her lips together. 'I can't imagine anyone falling asleep in His Grace's presence.'

He was sounding more and more like everything Katrina didn't want in a husband. She turned to Lady Mary. 'But if you were married to him, eventually you would fall asleep beside him.'

The rosy colour drained out of the girl's face and she glanced about the room, as if this fine specimen of an English nobleman might overhear them and curse them with an arched brow. 'I could never do that. I am certain he would never approve.'

Yes, this duke was definitely someone Katrina was grateful would not be part of *her* future. 'Could it be possible that you might forgo this favourable duke and marry someone for love?'

Lady Mary and Lady Hammond looked at one another with confusion. There was no way to know for certain, but from her perplexed expression Katrina would guess that Lady Hammond's marriage had been an arranged one. There still might be hope for Lady Mary.

However, she now addressed Katrina as if she were a small child. 'I imagine that is an American way of thinking. Why would I marry for love when I could marry a duke?'

She would never understand the English. But there was no sense in filling the girl's head with romantic notions. Katrina had spent some time this evening in the presence of the girl's mother. It hadn't taken her long to see how determined she was to promote her daughter for an advantageous match. Good luck to the man who married into *that* family!

While Katrina had been contemplating what it would be like to be married to a man such as Lady Mary's duke, the discussion had turned back to life in America. It was making her feel nostalgic for her friends back home. As Sarah was regaling them with tales of life in Washington, Katrina excused herself, to slip away for a few minutes to the ladies' retiring room.

She was about ten feet from the end of the long hall when she almost walked directly into the last person she had any desire to see. It was that self-important Englishman from the Russian Ambassador's terrace, who appeared to be too proud to associate openly with an American.

She hadn't been aware that he was in attendance, and he seemed just as surprised to see her. His green eyes widened momentarily with recognition, but as usual he said nothing—no greeting at all. Not one to be intimidated,

Katrina looked directly at him and waited. Even without seeking an introduction it would be a great insult if he completely ignored her this time. Now she would see how high in the instep he really was.

This was the closest she'd been to him since the night they'd talked under the stars. He'd nodded acknowledgement to her one night at the theatre, but each time she'd seen him after that he had avoided making eye contact. A number of times she'd caught him staring at her, but he had always diverted his gaze so quickly, she'd been certain he must be giving himself a headache with each sudden shift of his eyes.

And now he was standing less than five feet in front of her, impeccably dressed in formal black evening attire, with candlelight shining on the chestnut waves of his hair.

Perhaps it was because they were so close, or maybe he had had too much to drink, but this time his gaze roamed over her body. The hallway was growing very warm, and she shook out her fan to cool her heated skin.

He gave her a polite nod. 'Pardon me.'

That was it? That was all he would say?

It was quite obvious from his demeanour that he had no intention of saying more.

He must be great friends with Lady Mary's duke.

They wouldn't be able to continue down the hall unless one of them moved to the side. Katrina was tempted to take both her hands and push him over, but instead she inclined her head and swished around him, doing her best to ignore the fluttery feeling she'd got from hearing the rumble of his deep voice.

Chapter Five

The next morning Julian could barely finish his paper-work. His attention kept drifting to the American. He'd been astonished at the sense of longing he'd felt when she had walked past him last night. While she hadn't exactly given him the cut, her brief response to his apology for almost knocking into her for a second time had been any-thing but friendly. They hadn't spoken since the night of the de Lievens' ball. What could he possibly have done to warrant the daggers she had thrown at him with her eyes?

He was angry with this woman he didn't even know for turning his life upside down. Thoughts of her popped into his mind at all hours of the day, and each time he saw her his body immediately snapped to attention. He hadn't bedded Helena in weeks, and as of late his blood was only stirred by thoughts of the American. How could he get any work done?

He needed sex. His lack of release was playing havoc with his mind—that must be why he was so fixated on a woman he'd barely spoken to. He needed to see Helena.

Walking into the entrance hall of her townhouse, Julian handed her butler his hat and walking stick. The sound of footfalls on the wooden staircase caught his attention, and he watched Helena make her descent, her curves straining against a blood-red dressing gown. He should have felt like dragging her somewhere and bedding her for hours. He didn't.

Perhaps it was because they were in a very public area of the house, with her butler not far away. Julian shifted his eyes to her drawing room door, giving her a wordless command. As they entered the sparsely furnished room Helena closed the door and locked it. She always had been good with discretion.

Before she could utter a word Julian pushed her up against the door and kissed her. He needed her to help him forget the American right now. But the kiss felt all wrong—awkward and unpleasant. He closed his eyes, willing his body to react. Her lavender scent filled his nose.

Why did it suddenly seem so overpowering and unappealing?

He pulled his head back and looked down at her inviting expression. She was one of the most beautiful women in England. *Wasn't she?* He'd used to think so. His brow wrinkled as he studied her delicate features. The outline of her breasts was not even enticing him to undress her.

Helena slid her hand up his chest and combed her fingers through the hair by his temple. 'We could retire to my bed.'

That would be the ideal place. However, he could barely kiss her, let alone bed her. He turned away from her eager expression and glanced towards the settee. 'This room will suit our purposes.' He placed distance between them and took a seat.

'Would you care for some brandy?' she asked.

His body was tied in knots of uncomfortable tension. If only he could relax... He nodded, and when she sat down he felt her right thigh push up against his left. He took a long draw from the glass. The warm liquid eased some of the tightness in his shoulders and he shifted his thigh so it was no longer pressing against her leg.

She sketched circles on his knee with her finger and avoided his eyes. 'You are quieter than usual. Have I done something to displease you?'

'No. I find I have much on my mind today.' He forced himself to smile reassuringly. It was not her fault his body wasn't co-operating. He took another drink.

'What has brought you here? You've never called on me during the day.'

Unable to voice the real reason, he shrugged. 'I needed to see you.'

That seemed to satisfy her, and she attempted to hold back a smile. 'I see.'

She was giving him time to elaborate, but how could he? He had no idea why his body wasn't responding to her. He kissed her again, more demandingly this time. In his mind he saw magnetic blue eyes and a warm smile—so he squeezed his eyelids tighter. He told himself that Helena could do amazing things with her mouth. It was no use. He wasn't even remotely hard.

Julian released her and drained the contents of his glass. The burn washed away the taste of their kiss. This visit had been intended to cure him of the affliction brought on by the American. Instead it had made him want her more. He was out of ideas on what to do. He needed advice.

Helena watched Lyonsdale swallow the remaining contents of his glass. When he was finished, the glass landed on the table with an audible thud.

He stood rather abruptly. 'Pardon me, but I have matters I need to attend to today.'

Without giving her a chance to reply, he walked out of the room.

Picking up his discarded glass, she ran her tongue over the rim where his lips had been. He never called on her during the day. Surely this was the sign she had been looking for. She had finally caught him. This time all her plotting and planning would land her the title she so richly deserved. He might even have left to make arrangements about asking for her hand.

How she wished she could be there when her brother heard she would be the next Duchess of Lyonsdale! Her new title would trump his title of earl. Finally she would be above him. He and that puritanical wife of his would regret the day they had said they wanted nothing more to do with her when she had become obligated to marry Wentworth. They could beg all they wanted—they would never dine in Lyonsdale House!

She poured herself a small splash of brandy. No longer would she have to sell items from her home to purchase this fine vintage. It was exhausting, hiding her financial situation. Soon that would all be a memory. Soon she would dine at Carlton House with the Prince Regent and his set while she wore the Carlisle diamonds.

Not far away, Katrina was preparing herself for an onslaught of advice as she was escorted down the hallway of Almack's towards the assembly room where Madame de Lieven was waiting. When she'd received her note, requesting a meeting regarding a matter of the utmost importance, Katrina had been curious as to what the summons could possibly mean. Could she be about to enter into a lengthy discussion about the consequences of not following the strict rules of English etiquette? Or was Madame de Lieven about to inform Katrina in person that she was revoking the vouchers she had granted?

Katrina wished she had someone besides her maid,

Meg, to accompany her. Madame de Lieven was known to be quite commanding. There would have been safety in numbers.

Stopping before a set of double doors, Katrina raised her chin and took a deep breath, reminding herself to remain polite no matter what the woman had to say.

Light poured into the cavernous room from the large windows, brightening the white walls and gold trim. In the very centre of the room sat Madame de Lieven, at a white linen-covered table set for tea. Closing the book she had been reading, she motioned Katrina forward.

'I am pleased you accepted my invitation, Miss Vandenberg. I realise it is a bit early in the day for making calls, and the venue is unusual, but I do have my reasons.' She turned her head to the doorkeeper. 'Please see that Miss Vandenberg's maid is taken care of downstairs, Mr Willis, while we settle things here.'

That didn't sound very promising. As Katrina watched Meg trail Mr Willis out of the large ballroom she wished she could follow them. Shifting her gaze, she accepted the chair that was offered.

Madame de Lieven was a woman of strong self-importance, who moved with ease among the leading political figures of London. She had a way of influencing the people around her. Katrina was certain she wanted to keep her eye on 'the Americans', and that was why she'd offered to sponsor Katrina and the Forresters at Almack's.

She handed Katrina a cup of tea with milk and sugar. 'You intrigue me, Miss Vandenberg. I have noticed that you are a woman very much like me—a fish in a different pond.'

Katrina steadied herself under Madame de Lieven's intense gaze. 'Forgive me, I don't understand.'

'Since I am also a foreigner here, I am aware that it is not always easy to adjust to English customs. You have shown yourself to be a woman of intelligence and diplomacy. Two qualities I admire.'

'I see no reason to hide the knowledge I possess, but I try not to appear too forward in my opinions.'

'You should be aware that you have impressed me enough that I believe together you and I could accomplish great things here.'

Katrina's brow furrowed. 'I do not understand,' she said again.

Madame de Lieven placed her cup on the table. 'Let us be American and speak plainly.'

Katrina bristled at the insinuation. Anticipating what Madame de Lieven might say or do had kept Katrina amused since she had arrived in London. This time she sensed the next thing she said would cause her orderly life to be changed in ways that wouldn't be pleasant.

'I have noticed that you can be a bit too honest with your emotions at times. However, you possess a keen mind. Your presence is a refreshing change for me, and I have decided I will find you a husband here in London, so you can remain even after your father's negotiations are settled. It is the reason I extended the vouchers for Almack's to you. Our assemblies will prove helpful in finding you a husband.'

'A husband?' Katrina placed her cup down on the table and clasped her hands together on her lap. What had she ever done to give Madame de Lieven the impression she was looking for a husband? Whatever it was, Katrina knew she needed to stop doing it. 'I do not want a husband.'

'Of course you do. Every woman wants a husband. A husband provides a woman with…security.'

'What I mean to say is I do not want a husband here… in England.'

Madame de Lieven appeared sceptical.

Katrina continued. 'I will return to New York when my father's work here is finished. I plan to marry an American.'

'Nonsense,' Madame de Lieven said, appearing appalled. 'I can help you secure an excellent match. There are a number of rich, untitled Englishmen who would be pleased to marry an attractive woman with knowledge in the art of diplomacy, regardless of your background. You could live in wealth and splendour. Besides, you do not have many more good years left. You are almost on the shelf.'

Katrina was not about to tell her that all the luxury in the world couldn't compensate for a wandering, haughty husband. 'I appreciate your thoughtfulness,' she managed to say evenly, 'but we also have wealthy gentlemen back home. And, more to the point, money will not figure prominently in my choice of husband.'

Madame de Liven gave her a dubious look.

'Of course it is desirable to live comfortably,' Katrina amended. 'But you should be aware that, while I appreciate your offer to assist me in finding a husband, I intend to follow my heart.'

'You are referring to love?'

'Yes.'

'You are so very American. Love has no place in marriage. No one of consequence marries the person they love. They marry the person who is in a position to provide the best life possible.'

'And by "the best life" you mean one with wealth and privilege?'

'What else is there?'

'Companionship, humour, trust—'

'That is what your friends are for.'

Katrina rubbed her lips together, trying not to show her

frustration. 'Although I appreciate your interest in finding me a husband, it is not necessary.'

Madame de Lieven smiled regally, then let out a low sound that was almost a laugh. 'I believe finding you well settled here will be highly entertaining. I expect I will see you at tomorrow night's assembly. We can begin our search then.'

Katrina opened her mouth to protest again, but before she could get the words out Madame de Lieven motioned someone forward with her hand.

Mr Willis approached the table and bowed. 'The musicians are ready,' he informed her.

Clapping her hands together, Madame de Lieven motioned to the balcony and soft strains of music began to drift through the room. 'I've asked you to meet me here today because Mr Willis believes he has found us a new orchestra and I am to determine if they will suit. I will be interested in your opinion of their abilities.'

Katrina was grateful for the change in subject. She had no desire to marry an Englishman, and she hoped she would be able to convince the persistent Madame de Lieven to let the matter rest.

Julian should have been reading the latest reports from his steward in Hertfordshire. Instead he had sought out Hart at Tattersalls. Luckily, his friend was predictable. Hart was inspecting the horses that were to be auctioned off tomorrow. He did little to hide the surprise in his greeting, but after a few minutes they fell into companionable silence while they watched three horses parade around the paddock.

'That black thoroughbred looks very fine. Perhaps I will bid on him tomorrow.' When Julian didn't reply Hart watched him from the corner of his eye. 'Although I am considering purchasing a mule instead. Do you think that would do?'

'Yes…' Julian murmured, while he considered once again his time at Helena's. When had he stopped feeling the desire to bed her? They had agreed to a relationship based on satisfying each other's physical needs. If he no longer desired her was there any reason to continue visiting her?

'Splendid. I will send the bill to your house.'

'Of course.'

Hart yanked him to a stop. 'Julian, you have just agreed to buy me a mule. What the devil is wrong with you? All week your mind has been elsewhere.'

It took Julian a few blinks before Hart came into focus. Turning away from his friend's inquisitive gaze, he looked out towards the horses. 'Apologies, I've been woolgathering.'

Hart placed his booted foot on the lower rung of the fence enclosing the horses and leaned his arms on the upper railing. 'You don't say? Will you tell me what has you so distracted?'

Julian stepped closer to his friend and crossed his arms over his chest. He hoped he would not come to regret this. 'You know women…'

Hart grinned. 'I like to believe I do.'

Taking a deep breath, Julian watched the horses as they ambled around the pen. If anyone overheard them it would stir up gossip. He moved closer to Hart and lowered his voice. 'I went to see Helena this morning.'

'A daytime visit—that's a bit unusual,' Hart said slowly.

'I'm baffled. She's a beautiful woman, but the entire time I was in her company my thoughts were elsewhere.'

'On another woman?'

'Yes.'

Hart rubbed away a small smile with his gloved hand. 'Who?'

'I don't know her name,' Julian said, in a low, forceful voice that did nothing to hide his frustration.

'I don't understand.'

'She is new to London and we haven't been introduced.'

'So seek an introduction.'

'It would only lead to more speculation on my affairs. It would not do for people to think I have an interest in her.'

'Why not? It's just an introduction—unless you're planning on seducing her on the dance floor?'

That thought had crossed Julian's mind—more times than he would care to admit even to himself. 'It is not amusing. I have not been able to get her out of my head. I search for a glimpse of her whenever I am out. I think I hear her voice in crowded rooms. *This* is not normal.'

'Maybe not for you, but at least it explains your odd behaviour.'

'What do I do? How do I remove her from my thoughts?'

Hart shrugged his shoulders with careless ease. 'Why would you want to? It's evident that you want her, so end this association you have with Helena and pursue this woman.'

If only he could. 'That is not an option,' Julian replied, squeezing the bridge of his nose.

Hart faced him and crossed his arms. 'What hold does Helena have on you?'

Julian let out a snort of disbelief. No woman directed his actions, and he would find a way to forget this American. He just needed to determine how to do that. 'Helena has no hold over me.'

'Prove it. End your association with her. If your interest lies elsewhere, follow it. You are making this more complicated than it needs to be.'

'With this woman everything is complicated.' Julian's

gaze drifted to the horses. 'Besides, nothing could possibly come from an association between us. She's an American.'

An indecipherable look flashed in Hart's eyes. 'So? Do you believe all Americans are cannibals, perform war dances, and run around with hatchets when they get angry? Make certain you do not call out another lady's name while bedding her. She might scalp you.'

'Very amusing.'

'Don't let her nationality prevent you from pursuing her. I imagine American women are quite uninhibited in bed.'

'Well, I'm not going to find out.' And it was driving him to distraction.

'You need to stop being so bloody proper. I cannot see one benefit to not doing what I want, when I want. End what you have with Helena. It's obvious your attention has shifted elsewhere.'

'It is not that easy.'

'Of course it is. You say, *Helena, I am finished with you.*'

'Truly? Have you ever ended a relationship with a woman?'

'That's beside the point. We are discussing you. I know you too well. You, my friend, are boringly monogamous.'

'Let it alone, Hart.'

'Very well. Then continue to tup Helena while you imagine a certain miss who shall remain nameless.'

The statement left him unsettled and guilty. There was only one thing to do.

Chapter Six

Julian was not looking forward to seeing Helena before leaving for Westminster the next day. He might have sent her a note. It would have been far easier and much less painful on his part. But he could not be so callous. It wasn't her fault that he'd met someone he couldn't stop thinking about.

This time when he knocked on her door her butler didn't appear surprised to see him. He was left to wait for her in the drawing room. The idea of sitting was not appealing, so he walked around the room to relieve his restlessness. A few minutes later Helena walked in, wearing her blood-red dressing gown.

'Forgive me,' he said. 'I did not realise you would be preparing for the evening.'

'I was resting, and didn't see the point of dressing when I heard you were here. This is a pleasant surprise. Would you care for a brandy?'

He would have liked the entire bottle, but that would just muddle his brain so he politely declined.

She trailed her fingers down his chest. 'Do you wish to retire upstairs? I could see to your comfort.'

No matter what room they were in, Julian knew he would not be comfortable. 'I believe I'd prefer to remain here.'

A questioning look flashed in her grey eyes as she gestured towards the settee.

Julian chose an armchair instead.

Prowling behind him, Helena skimmed her fingers along his shoulders before lowering herself into the slightly worn silk armchair closest to him.

'What brings you here today?' she asked, reclining back. 'You left rather abruptly the other day.' She tipped her chin towards the box on his lap. 'Is that your way of apologising?'

He handed her the blue velvet box. 'It is…for a number of things…'

A look of confusion crossed her face before she slid her hand up his thigh. 'I hope you will stay longer today, so I may thank you properly.'

The boldness of her gesture forced him to shift in his chair. He nodded towards the package in her hand, relieved to know that she was easily distracted by expensive objects. 'Open it.'

Her eyes sparkled with eager anticipation as she lifted the lid. Slowly she pulled out the long strand of pearls and arranged them between her breasts, which were suddenly exposed through her open dressing gown.

He wished he could tell her she was wasting her efforts on him. 'They suit you,' he said. It was as much of a compliment as he could muster.

'They are beautiful,' she said, more interested in the pearls than in Julian. 'They will go well with the new gown I have ordered from Madame Devy. Perhaps we could attend Drury Lane or Vauxhall, and I will wear them for you.' She finally looked up at him. 'I know how you dislike attracting attention, but I think we will turn some heads.'

Julian's jaw clenched as he studied his brown leather gloves. 'Helena, there is something I need to ask you.' He turned his attention to her expectant expression. 'You are aware that I have a deep regard for you?'

She smiled up at him. 'I am.'

'Well… I was wondering if you are content with the state of our friendship?'

'What are you trying to say?'

'When we began this liaison both of us knew it could not continue indefinitely the way it is.'

'That is true,' she said through a seductive smile. The scent of lavender filled the air as she leaned in closer.

'And we both entered into this with a mutual understanding that eventually we would part ways.'

Her mouth fell open. 'You are *ending* this?'

'While I have enjoyed our time together, surely you knew that it would not last?'

'I cannot believe you are doing this,' she whispered. The sound of her heavy breathing mingled with the ticking of the clock. She jumped from her chair and poked him in the chest—hard. 'Lord Hartwick is behind this.'

He pulled his brows together in puzzlement. 'He has nothing to do with this.'

'Then there is another woman.' She eyed him up and down in disgust. 'Have you offered for Morley's chit? Your mother acts as if an announcement will be made any day.'

'I have not offered for her. There is no other woman.' She didn't need to know the truth.

'Why are you doing this?' she demanded, clenching her fists at her sides.

'I did not think you would be upset. You told me you had no intention of marrying again,' he stated firmly.

'And you *believed* me?' she screamed. She stormed across the room with her head high, and then spun around. 'And you give me *pearls*? We have been together all this time and you give me *pearls*!'

'What is wrong with pearls? They are quite expensive.'

Her body visibly shook with rage. 'You are the Duke of Lyonsdale! You should be giving me diamonds!'

His sympathy for her was quickly diminishing upon seeing her greedy nature. 'I did not have to give you anything!' he bellowed.

'You selfish boor!' She picked up a silver candlestick from the table closest to her and flung it at his head.

He ducked just in time.

'I am worth diamonds—not pearls!'

Before his control slipped further he needed to leave. Striding across the room, he unlocked the door and didn't look back.

When he stepped outside the soft breeze cooled his heated skin. His body hummed with anger at her selfishness. Sitting in his carriage would do him no good. He needed physical exertion. He would walk home—but first he needed to make one more stop.

Chapter Seven

Descending the staircase in the centre of Hatchards, Katrina scanned the room below her. This bookshop was one of her favourite places in London. The soft whispers and the occasional sound of the turning of pages were welcome after spending the entire morning on social calls with Mrs Forrester and Sarah.

As she continued to search for her maid Katrina let her gaze skim over the few patrons who were selecting books from the dark wooden bookshelves that lined the walls. An older woman in an elaborately decorated black hat was comparing books with a younger woman dressed demurely in lavender. Near them a dandy dressed in a navy jacket and puce trousers stood in a studied pose, reading the book he held through his quizzing glass.

Scanning the room further, Katrina felt her heart skip a beat. Standing near her maid, at a table piled with books, stood a broad-shouldered, dark-haired gentleman in a finely cut bottle-green coat, buckskin breeches and top boots. Was her time in London destined to be cursed with the presence of the rude Englishman from the Russian Ambassador's ball?

Katrina hesitated on the staircase, wondering if she should turn around and go back upstairs before he spotted her. Suddenly he lifted his head, as if sensing her gaze, and their eyes met. She could not turn back now. Taking a breath, she gripped the wooden banister and proceeded to slowly walk down the stairs towards Meg.

Katrina picked up the first volume of *Frankenstein* and thumbed through the pages. 'Have you found anything of interest?' she asked Meg.

Her maid smiled and showed Katrina the book in her hand.

'I do not believe *Clarissa* is an appropriate choice for you,' Katrina said.

'I've heard it's scandalous, and I'm hoping they have it at the lending library. The heroine is told to marry an unappealing gentleman and then is tricked into running away by a rake. I bet there is a dungeon in the story. I love a story that takes place in a dungeon.' Meg sighed and then glanced inquisitively at the book in Katrina's hand.

Taking into account her maid's vivid imagination, Katrina quickly placed *Frankenstein* back on the table. 'I'm well aware of the plot. You do know you can borrow any of my books?'

'Do they have dungeons, kidnappings, evil earls or ghosts?'

'No.'

'Then why do you think I would want to read them?' Meg asked, wrinkling her brow.

There was a deep laugh from across the table. Keeping her head averted under the rim of her bonnet, Katrina blocked her view of the gentleman across the table. Searching for a more appropriate novel, Katrina spotted a copy of her father's book. As she reached for it her hand brushed against a strong hand encased in a brown leather glove. Startled, she looked up.

'We meet again,' the annoying Englishman said.

No, we don't, because you are too rude to seek an introduction!

Katrina took a breath to compose herself before she spoke. 'So it would seem.'

'Forgive me. I believe that is the book I have been searching for.'

'This book?' Katrina asked, holding it up to show him the title on the spine.

'Yes, that is it.' He reached for another copy and began to turn the pages. There was a hesitation before he looked up at her. 'I've heard it's a very good book. You would not happen to know anything about it, would you?'

'I can highly recommend it. The book presents the observations of a traveller and contains much happy humour.'

Katrina glanced around the shop to see if anyone was watching them. Meg had moved to a nearby bookcase, engrossed in *Clarissa*. What was the point of having your maid accompany you around the town if she walked away when the man you wanted to avoid began speaking with you?

He walked around the table and stood next to her, smelling of leather and fresh air. 'The account is humorous?'

'Yes, Lord Byron has said he knows it by heart, and Scott has said it is positively beautiful. I understand the book is selling rather quickly. You might wish to purchase one before they are all sold.' She looked closely at him, challenging him to actually buy it.

'You appear intimately acquainted with the book,' he commented, his eyes narrowing.

'I suppose I am. My father is the author.'

'You are Mr Vandenberg's daughter?' he asked in a rush of breath.

'Yes, my lord, I am.' She crossed her arms over her

chest. If he said one disparaging thing about the fact that her father was a writer she was leaving immediately. He would deserve the cut.

He tipped his head to her. 'Then I shall be certain to take your recommendation. My grandmother speaks highly of it as well.'

'Your grandmother?'

'Yes. My grandmother seems to have misplaced her copy. I came here today to purchase a new one for her.'

He was intending to purchase her father's book because his grandmother had lost her copy? That seemed rather...sweet.

Katrina caught herself before she smiled. *He wasn't sweet. He was rude!* Still, she couldn't help asking him if he was a doting grandson.

'I suppose I am.'

He smiled at her and he appeared even more attractive.

'She seemed truly distressed to discover it missing.'

He stepped a bit closer and inhaled. Was that some odd English custom?

Katrina eyed him and placed her father's book down. 'Did you just *sniff* me?' she whispered.

A small smile raised one corner of his lips. 'Now, why would I do that?'

'Why, indeed?' Katrina replied, narrowing her eyes at him.

She edged a little further down the table. The heat from his body somehow made its way over to her. This man had ignored her for days. Why couldn't her body do the same to him? She could practically feel his every breath. That slightly unsettling feeling was back.

'If you will excuse me?' she said, turning to leave.

He blocked her way with his body. 'You do not need to leave yet, do you?'

'I cannot stay. You must realise our speaking without

an introduction is highly improper.' It was easier not to look at him, and she picked unseen strings from her pale blue and white spencer.

He glanced around and edged closer to her. 'That didn't bother you before.'

'A momentary lapse in judgement.'

'No one here knows we have not been formally introduced,' he said quietly.

'*We* know we have not,' she chided. 'And you have done it again! You sniffed me.' She stepped away from him, feeling more than a little unsettled. 'I can assure you Americans do bathe.'

His lips twitched. 'Why do you smell like lemons, Miss Vandenberg?'

Katrina's brows drew together in confusion. 'That is irrelevant—and I refuse to carry on this conversation when I do not even know your name.'

'We could remedy that easily. I could simply tell you what it is.'

'Do you always flout the English rules of conduct?'

He appeared to ponder her question for a moment. Then he shook his head. 'Actually, I never do. However, I see no harm in it this time. But if you insist we will do this in the proper manner. I shall need to borrow your maid.'

'You'd like to borrow my maid?'

'I would.'

He walked to Meg, who was watching the interaction between her mistress and this perplexing Englishman. They bent their heads together, and a short while later both walked towards Katrina.

'Miss Vandenberg,' Meg said, trying unsuccessfully to hide her smile, 'may I present His Grace the Duke of Lyonsdale? Your Grace, this is my mistress—Miss Katrina Vandenberg.' She curtsied and watched them both closely.

The scoundrel! Katrina's eyes widened. 'You're a *duke*?'

A slow smile made his lips turn up invitingly. 'I am.'

'You are the Duke of Lyonsdale?'

'Yes, I believe we have established that.'

Meg, as if sensing her mistress's temper, smartly moved back to her place by the bookcase.

'Why didn't you tell me?' Katrina demanded.

'My name? I was going to, but you seemed to need a proper introduction so I had your maid do it.'

'That's not what I meant,' Katrina said as she shook her head. 'You led me to believe you were simply a lord.'

'How did I do that?'

'You did not correct me when I addressed you. You must have found my ignorance vastly entertaining,' she replied waspishly.

It had been bad enough when she'd thought he might be a titled gentleman, such as a baron, but he was a *duke*! In England, his station in life was so far above hers he probably would never have spoken to her again if it had not been for this accidental encounter.

She would not show him that it hurt.

'Miss Vandenberg—'

'I'll not be played for a fool. I'm sure you have enjoyed telling your friends how ignorant Americans can be. Well, let me tell you—'

'Miss Vandenberg,' he interrupted more forcefully. 'I didn't correct you because we had not been introduced. I had no opportunity to tell you my name or indicate my station.'

'You could have corrected the way I had addressed you.'

'And sound like a pompous fool? I think not.'

He certainly would have sounded like a pompous fool, but Katrina was not convinced he didn't have another motive for not telling her the truth. He must have had a great laugh at her expense.

'In any event, what you did was rude.'

Both his brows rose and he jerked his head back. 'I assure you, causing you any distress was most unintentional.'

Then his lips twitched, and she wanted to throw a book at him. The man was insufferable.

'You are laughing at me,' she said through her teeth. 'I believe I have spent too much time here today. I bid you good day—Your Grace.'

As she stormed out of the bookshop she wished she could restrict her engagements to those he would never consider attending.

Julian's encounter with Miss Vandenberg left him perplexed. No one had ever schooled him in proper behaviour before. No one would ever have dared. And yet this American had thought it necessary to inform him that he was rude.

He should have been insulted by the way she'd spoken to him, but she had been so certain in her conviction, so passionate about the way she deserved to be treated, he had not been able to fault her.

He was a man of strong convictions as well. When he had entered the shop it hadn't occurred to him that he would leave finding Miss Vandenberg even more desirable than he already had.

By the next day he was still reliving their discussion and anticipating when he would speak to her again.

Deciding to visit the woman who was indirectly responsible for their encounter, Julian sought out his grandmother when he returned home from his committee meeting. Upon entering her private sitting room, he found her resting in a bergère chair, with a book in her hand.

'Come in Julian,' she said, waving him closer. 'You truly have spoiled me.'

He walked across the gold and white Aubusson rug and sat down next to her. 'I see you are enjoying your book.'

'You were slippery, presenting me with that volume yesterday. The arrival of this copy was quite unexpected.'

'This copy?' he replied, perplexed.

'Yes—the one you had Mr Vandenberg inscribe.'

Julian gestured to the copy of *A Traveler's Tale* that she held in her hands. 'May I…?'

His grandmother placed a black ribbon between the pages and handed the book to him. 'It is a lovely inscription.'

He eyed his grandmother through his lashes and turned to the title page. He was speechless. Obviously Miss Vandenberg must have arranged this—but why?

When she had stormed out on him yesterday Julian had not known if he should go after her. No one had ever walked out on him before. What had possessed her to have her father inscribe a book for his grandmother?

'I did not do this,' he admitted, handing back the book.

'Of course you did. I have told no one else I misplaced my copy.'

'I believe Mr Vandenberg's daughter arranged this.'

'His daughter? How would she know?'

'I mentioned it to her yesterday, when we spoke at Hatchards.'

'How very delightful of her. You have never said that you are acquainted with the family.'

'I am only acquainted with the daughter.'

His grandmother arched her brow. That was not a good sign. 'Just the daughter? How unusual for you. How did you make her acquaintance?'

'A mutual friend,' replied Julian, picking a speck of lint off the sleeve of his navy tailcoat.

'I see. And is the lady in question married?'

'She is not.'

'And how long have the two of you been acquainted?'

'Not long.'

Her eyes narrowed, causing Julian to shift restlessly in his seat.

'Tell me about this girl.'

'She is not a girl.'

'How old is she?'

'I do not know. I thought it wasn't polite to enquire.'

His grandmother chuckled. 'When the lady in question is my age, it absolutely is not. But for a younger one I do not think it at all beyond the pale.'

'And a lady of your age would be how old, exactly?'

'You impertinent man—we are discussing your friend, not me.'

'And why exactly are we discussing Miss Vandenberg?'

'She had her father send me this lovely book. I am curious as to what kind of girl would do such a thoughtful thing. You say she did this completely without your influence?'

'I doubt the lady could be influenced into doing anything at my bidding,' he muttered.

'Nonsense—you are Lyonsdale.'

'At the moment that fact does not seem to be to my advantage with her.'

'Why not?'

'Miss Vandenberg is a little cross with me at the moment, due to my title.' He knew it was absurd, and saying it out loud made it appear more so.

'I do not understand. Does she not realise the significance of your station?'

'She does. However, I do not believe she cares.'

'Because she is an American?'

'Because she is Miss Vandenberg. In truth, I find at

times that she baffles me with her logic.' And his reaction to her mere presence baffled him more.

His grandmother tilted her head and he realised he'd said too much. Miss Vandenberg wasn't a woman he was courting, or even a woman he should be thinking of courting. And yet he'd told his grandmother more about her than he had about any other woman.

Knowing that she was annoyingly perceptive, he knew he needed to place distance between them before she started asking a litany of questions. He pushed himself off the chair and walked to the window overlooking Grosvenor Square.

'Would you take me to Almack's tonight?' she called to him.

Dear God, he should have just left the room. The last place he ever wanted to go was Almack's. He might as well place a notice in the *Morning Chronicle*, stating that he was shopping for a wife.

'Why in the world would you want me to do that?' he asked, trying to think of an excuse as to why he could not take her. 'You've been going there for years without me.'

'Yes, and it is about time you used those vouchers of yours. Each year you pay for them, and each year you never use them.'

He wasn't giving in. Her reasoning wasn't good enough.

She rubbed her knees and sighed. 'If I don't move these bones they may stiffen permanently.'

Crossing his arms, he arched a sceptical brow. If the woman hadn't been born into the aristocracy, she might have made a fine living on the stage.

'I do not have many years left,' she continued. 'Is it so wrong for me to wish to spend time with my grandson? I rarely see you any more, with all the time you are spending with Lord Kenyon's committee and other Parliamentary affairs.'

She blinked a few times, and Julian wasn't certain if he saw tears in her eyes.

Should he remind her that they saw each other most mornings over the breakfast table? He searched the frescoed ceiling for an answer, but the cherubs just laughed down at him. He allowed her to live with him in London during the Season because he cared about her, and knew they probably didn't have many more years left together. Perhaps it was time he hired her a companion and rented her a townhouse.

Letting out a deep breath, Julian knew he was going to regret agreeing to go with her. And yet he was unable to say no.

Chapter Eight

As Julian stepped into the cavernous assembly room at Almack's the large mirrors magnified the many women and men who turned to look. Heads poked around the gilt columns to his right, and some people even had the impudence to raise their quizzers at him. This was why he avoided mixing with the likes of the marriage mart. Their unabashed interest in him was tiresome.

He walked further into the room, with his grandmother on his arm and his mother at his other side. They left a buzz of voices in their wake.

'This is a testament to how much I care for you,' he whispered down to his grandmother. 'Do not expect me to escort you here again.'

She blinked up at him innocently and readjusted her hand on his arm. 'Evenings such as these have a way of turning unexpectedly. You may change your mind.'

'There is nothing in Christendom that would make me enjoy myself tonight,' Julian replied through a polite smile, knowing the people around them were trying to listen to their conversation.

His mother nodded regally at the Duchess of Skeffington and Lady Harlow. Julian knew his mother was not fond of the gossipy pair. He wasn't either, and had no qualms about pretending he did not see them.

'You are shocking people tonight with your presence, Lyonsdale,' his mother said from behind her fan. 'They see a man in search of a wife. Perhaps you might consider announcing your intentions and quelling their interest?'

'Madam, tonight I have no intention of announcing anything.'

His mother pursed her lips together and looked away. Julian was surprised she hadn't broached the subject of Lady Mary sooner. He assumed she was here somewhere. Lady Morley would not be remiss in displaying her daughter to the eligible men of the *ton*. There was no sense in delaying the inevitable. Tonight he would speak with Lady Mary and discover if he would be able to endure sitting across the breakfast table from her each morning.

Taking a deep breath, he inhaled the mixed floral scents and the body odour that permeated the room. There would be no escaping to the terrace for some cleaner air tonight. He scanned the room for Lady Mary and stifled a yawn. With all these masses of white spinning about the floor he would never be able to identify her unless she was standing directly in front of him.

He leaned over to his grandmother. 'Please tell me they have begun serving something more fortifying here than that insipid lemonade.'

'I wish I could—but that is what flasks are for, my boy,' she whispered, patting her reticule.

From the corner of his eye he spied Lady Morley, heading their way. Before he was able to summon an excuse to avoid having to speak with the woman his grandmother came to his rescue.

'Oh, look—I believe I see Lady Cowper,' she said. 'Will you excuse us, Beatrice?' Without waiting for a reply she tugged on Julian's arm and they began walking towards one of the patronesses who ruled Almack's.

'Now you see why I avoid these evenings,' Julian said, studying the crowd in front of them and trying to determine the least dangerous route to Lady Cowper. 'They can be most trying.'

'Chin up, my boy, I believe this night is about to become quite interesting.'

He glanced down at his grandmother. Why did he have the feeling she was privy to something he was not?

They approached the affable Lady Cowper, and the ladies exchanged pleasantries. Then she turned her full attention to Julian. 'What a pleasure to see you, Your Grace. It has been some time since you've been in attendance.'

'Yes, I suppose it has.'

'It appears we have caused quite a stir this evening,' his grandmother commented, glancing around.

'Yes, in fact I believe your arrival has surpassed tonight's latest sensation.'

His grandmother stepped closer and lowered her voice. 'Really, Lady Cowper? Do tell.'

'That American author Vandenberg is here, with his daughter. I understand the man is entertaining, and his daughter is quite accomplished.'

Julian's heart skipped a beat, and he fought the urge to scan the assembly room for her.

His grandmother's eyes widened a little too much. 'Really? They are here tonight? I would enjoy making the man's acquaintance. *A Traveler's Tale* is a most enjoyable read.'

'I am certain Madame de Lieven can introduce you. She has sponsored the family.' She leaned in close and lowered her voice. 'We were astonished when she promoted the Americans. However, I find they comport themselves surprisingly well.'

'Americans are not the provincials some imagine them to be,' Julian stated firmly, feeling an inexplicable need to come to their defence.

Both women stared at him in surprise, before Lady Cowper narrowed her gaze. 'Surely you're aware that we have seen very few American women in our circles? It was difficult to determine how they would behave.'

His grandmother began to cough, and Julian would not have been surprised if she had dramatically thrown herself on the floor to enhance the effect.

'My word, do you require assistance?' Lady Cowper asked with true concern.

His grandmother shook her head and the coughing miraculously stopped. 'A glass of lemonade should help ease the tickle in my throat,' she said, patting her chest. She grasped Julian's sleeve and gave it a subtle tug, leaving him no choice but to walk with her to the refreshment table.

He handed her a glass and held back a laugh when she poured in some clear liquid from a small silver flask. He wasn't certain what she had added, but as long as it was potent he didn't really care. Selecting a glass, he held it out to her, and she added a generous splash. The smell of gin reached Julian's nose as he raised the glass to his lips. If his father had been alive now the man would have had an apoplexy, knowing the matriarch of their family carried gin on her person. However, if it would help Julian survive an evening in the marriage mart he would not admonish her.

'Do you see her?' his grandmother asked as her gaze trailed over the room.

He had known she was up to something! He took a long drink. 'To whom are you referring?'

'Oh, I think you know.'

'What exactly are you plotting?'

'Why do you believe I am plotting anything?' she asked, arching an inquisitive brow.

'I am not dim-witted,' replied Julian, and he arched his brow in return.

'No, you are not.'

'That was not an answer.'

'What was the question?'

He momentarily closed his eyes. When he looked back at her the glass in her hand was empty. 'I'm trying to decide if it is wise to give you more lemonade.'

She reached behind him and took another glass. 'You do not need to attend to me all evening. You should look around. You might find someone of interest.'

Julian eyed his grandmother in annoyance. Why did the women in his life seem to have this need to meddle in his affairs? He stood near her, refusing to give any indication that he was in search of a wife. However, this time when his gaze travelled across the room he easily spotted Miss Vandenberg amid the whirl of white. He was transfixed as he watched her attempt to move gracefully through a quadrille with that idiot Lord Boreham.

'Are you going to dance with her?' the pest at his side whispered.

He glanced down at her. 'I have no desire to dance this evening.'

'Forgive me. I thought you had found something that held your attention. I must have been mistaken.'

'You most certainly were,' he replied, his eyes inexplicably drawn back to the dancing couple.

She lowered her voice even further. 'If that is Miss Vandenberg, Madame de Lieven will know if she has been given permission to waltz.'

Julian stared at his grandmother, aghast. 'I have never waltzed here, and I do not intend to do so now.'

However, if they did waltz together he would have her

undivided attention. She would not be able to leave the conversation when it was convenient for her, as she had each time they'd spoken in the past.

A smile tugged at his lips as he watched her walk off the dance floor.

When the quadrille ended Katrina returned to Mrs Forrester and Sarah, who were standing near one of the white gilded columns. She was grateful for the reprieve.

'You appear to have both feet intact,' Sarah teased. 'Perhaps Lord Boreham has taken dancing lessons.'

Fanning herself to cool her heated body, Katrina smirked. 'No, I have simply become adept at hiding my pain.'

'Did you hear about the caricature that was printed of him recently?' Sarah asked, staring questioningly into her glass of lemonade.

Most of these satires mocked political figures and the Prince Regent. Katrina knew there were others that were drawn of certain members of the *ton*, but since she was fairly new to London, and not well acquainted with too many people, she never paid much attention to them. However, now she was intrigued. 'What does it look like?'

Sarah glanced over at Lord Boreham, who was standing a few feet away with a group of young bucks. 'In it he is sprawled on the ground at the entrance to the Palace of Westminster. I do not recall the caption, but the image was memorable. A number of the dandies standing with him now were having a good laugh over it last evening.'

Although she was not fond of the marquess, Katrina felt sorry for him. It must be mortifying to have someone you didn't know make a mockery of your life.

'Katrina, if you persist in moving your fan so rapidly I fear the lady behind you will discover her peacock-feathered cap flying away!' advised Mrs Forrester.

Katrina slowed her hand. 'Pardon me, but it is so warm in here. I'm looking forward to stepping through the next dance just to create a breeze.'

'A waltz would do nicely,' Sarah said.

Katrina leaned in closer. 'I cannot believe we need permission to waltz here. I have been waltzing all over Europe, and now someone of no relation to me must give their consent.'

'Well, I find it unusual that men cannot wear trousers here,' Sarah said, scanning the stocking-clad calves of the men around them. 'What an odd rule.'

'Perhaps the patronesses are using their influence as an excuse to admire finely formed legs,' replied Katrina. 'What I don't—'

'Madame de Lieven, how wonderful to see you,' said Mrs Forrester, a bit too enthusiastically.

Katrina raised her fan to hide her laugh and turned. Her eyes widened when she saw the Russian Ambassador's wife on the arm of the Duke of Lyonsdale.

'It is lovely to see you, ladies,' Madame de Lieven said, inclining her head. She introduced Mrs Forrester and Sarah to the Duke, and then turned to Katrina. 'I understand you are already acquainted with His Grace?'

Katrina could feel the weight of his attention as she lowered herself into a curtsy. 'I am,' she muttered.

'Ladies,' he said, in that deep voice that reverberated through her body. 'I hope you are enjoying yourselves this evening.'

Mrs Forrester replied rather quickly—perhaps because she was wary of what Katrina or Sarah might say. 'Thank you, we are. I believe Almack's is an experience one must have in order to fully appreciate it.'

That was vague enough. Katrina bit her lip to keep from laughing.

'And what do you appreciate the most?' he asked them, with a knowing look in his eye.

'We've been discussing the fine dancing,' replied Mrs Forrester.

'And the fashionable attendees,' said Sarah as she glanced down at the Duke's muscular calves, encased in white stockings.

When Katrina coughed to cover her laugh, he narrowed his eyes at her. 'And, Miss Vandenberg, what have you come to appreciate this evening?'

Don't say finely formed legs!

Katrina knew he suspected their discussion had not been innocuous. Could she ignore a duke in the middle of Almack's and not lose her voucher? Probably not. She lowered her hand and stared directly into his green eyes.

He arched his brow.

She glared momentarily.

His lips twitched.

'I have been enjoying honest discussions with my friends.' She saw in his eyes that he understood what she implied.

Madame de Lieven cleared her throat and they both turned her way. 'Miss Vandenberg, His Grace has requested a waltz with you, and I have happily granted his request.'

Katrina stared at her and prayed she had remembered to close her mouth. 'How kind of you,' she managed to utter. Who was *she* to speak for Katrina? And that insufferable man knew she could not turn him down now.

'I believe the waltz is next,' Madame de Lieven noted, appearing pleased with herself.

Lyonsdale held out his arm and sent Katrina a challenging look. 'Then it is wise for us to proceed to the dance floor,' he said.

She glared at him while politely resting her hand on

his sleeve. They excused themselves and strolled through the crowd of people who parted for them. Watchful eyes followed their every step.

'I assure you I do not bite,' he whispered into her hair.

She chewed her lip to stop herself from telling him to go to the devil. Stepping on to the dance floor, he spun her around elegantly and placed his gloved hand on her back. Heat ran from his hand through her entire body. It was becoming difficult to breathe normally. A momentary sense of panic made her wonder how quickly the waltz would end. Maybe she could fake an illness in the middle of it?

He pulled her closer. She pushed her body further away.

'I have the distinct impression that you would rather be elsewhere,' he said. 'May I ask why?'

'No, you may not. I am still angry with you, lest you had not noticed.'

'I thought you might be. Does your anger preclude us from speaking?'

'It does. Angry people should not converse. It leads to further ill will.'

'Is that an American rule of conduct? What is the case when only one of the party is angry?'

'Then that person should remain silent. Usually the harshest statements are made in anger.'

He leaned his head closer. 'And you are angry with me because you feel I have deliberately deceived you?'

'Yes.' She would not give him the satisfaction of knowing she was also angry because he had previously ignored her.

'You say angry people should not converse, and yet here you are speaking to me. I really am becoming puzzled with your logic.' He inhaled slowly.

Katrina jerked her head away from his.

He had the nerve to grin at her. 'I am simply stating the inconsistency of our situation.'

'Do not patronise me,' she chided. 'And stop sniffing my hair. It is disconcerting.'

'For you or for me?'

'For me,' she replied in a low, forceful voice. 'If sniffing my hair leaves you disconcerted that is another reason you should stop doing it.'

'But there lies the rub. You see, where you are concerned I cannot help myself. I have become quite fond of lemons, by the way.'

'They can be sour and leave a bitter taste in your mouth.'

His gaze dropped to her lips. 'Yes, that is true. But they can also be refreshing, as well as tart.'

'Perhaps you would do better to seek out something bland, like lavender or orange blossom. I've noticed a great many women in London favour those scents. I am certain if you try you can find an alternative place for your nose,' she suggested with false sweetness.

His lips twitched. 'Oh, I can think of a few places my nose would care to be.'

The insufferable man! She was not as naïve as he might think.

'I am not speaking with you.' She raised her chin, annoyed that he had taken the upper hand in their discussion.

'So you said. You dance very well, by the way.'

'Do you always ignore other people's wishes?'

'Usually. They never seem to mind.' He gave a small shrug as he guided her gracefully into a turn. 'In any event, I was not ignoring your wishes. You stated quite clearly that you were not speaking with me. I, on the other hand, have never said I am not speaking with you. In fact I believe you are the one ignoring your own wishes. *You* are continuing to speak with *me*.'

She shifted her attention to the dancers behind him and let out an exasperated breath.

He leaned down slightly. 'That still might constitute speaking. It is a confirmation of your annoyance with me.'

Sliding her gaze back to him, she wondered how many more minutes she would have to be in his company. He sent her an amused look. Could she kick him during the dance without anyone seeing?

'Now, Miss Vandenberg, you do not want the entire assembly to know that you are cross with me. It might reflect poorly on you. I suggest you pretend to enjoy being in my arms.'

That was the problem. Being in his arms was distracting, and it was making her feel all…fluttery. She forced herself to appear bored.

He appeared smug.

Blast it all!

'Do you think every unmarried woman in this room wants you?'

'Well, since I am one of only two eligible dukes in England who are able to eat with their own teeth, yes, I believe that to be true.'

'I suppose that would matter were I English, but, you see, to me your title has little appeal. In fact, to me, your title is inconsequential.'

'How so?' he asked, tilting his head to the side.

'The other ladies in this room are shopping for a title and prestige, but I am not. I intend to return to America when my father is finished with his business here and I have no intention to marry you or any other Englishman. So, you see, your title holds no interest for me.'

Julian almost stumbled on the wooden floor. He didn't know how to respond. *His title was impressive!* There wasn't an available woman in the room who didn't want to be married to him. Except, it seemed, the woman in his arms.

Over the years there had been times when he'd wished he could find someone who would see him for the man he was and not his title. Now that he had his wish, he wasn't certain he liked the result.

Annoyed with the turn in their conversation, he knew he needed to regain the upper hand. He leaned forward and took a deep breath. Miss Vandenberg shot him a frustrated glare.

It was much too easy to get a reaction from her, and Julian wasn't ready to think about why that pleased him. Any reservations he'd had about asking her to waltz had gone the minute he held her in his arms and she began to speak. He wondered if she smelled like lemons everywhere…

'Please stop,' she whispered.

'The dance? I think people would notice, don't you?'

'Sniffing me.'

'Oh, that. If it truly bothers you I will find it within me to stop.'

'I would appreciate the effort.'

There was a brief silence. 'I do need to thank you, though.'

'For rinsing my hair with lemon juice? I assure you it has nothing to do with you.'

'No, not that. I want to thank you for sending my grandmother your father's book. It was quite kind of you.'

'It was no bother.'

'All the same, you made an old woman very happy.'

'Then, for her, I am pleased I arranged it.'

He thought he saw the faintest hint of a smile. 'Tell me how you knew it was the Dowager Duchess of Lyonsdale I was referring to in our conversation. It might have been my maternal grandmother.'

'Do you realise how commanding you are? Phrasing

requests as questions is much more polite.' She lifted her brows expectantly.

He, the Duke of Lyonsdale, had just been schooled in manners again by this American. It was absurd.

'It's a habit born of my title. In any event, I will heed your well-meaning lesson and try again. Would you please explain your exceptional deductive skills to me?'

This time a smile definitely tugged at her lips, and Julian found his question well worth the effort.

'I enquired about you and discovered the Dowager lived in your home. I assumed she was the lady in question and had the book sent there.'

'And how did you explain the request to your father?'

'I've been handling my father's correspondence while we have been abroad. I told him we had encountered each other at Hatchards, and that you told me your grandmother's tale of woe.'

'He did not question our introduction?'

She leaned closer to him. He could feel her breath on his ear, and he wanted to close his eyes to savour the sensation.

'I have a secret, Your Grace. In America, formal introductions are not an absolute necessity. Americans frequently meet each other in similar fashion.'

Leaning back, she met his gaze with a good-humoured twinkle in her eyes. Her voice had been low and husky. The heat from her breath had travelled through every part of him.

He lowered his lips towards her ear, wanting to prolong this playful turn in their conversation. 'What else do Americans do?'

The music of the waltz ended, and Julian was forced to let her go.

'I suppose you will have to continue to wonder,' she replied with an impish grin.

He held in a smile, wishing he could spend the remainder of the evening in her company.

Chapter Nine

Many a quizzing glass was raised as Katrina and the Duke walked through the parting attendants. Katrina could hear the whispers following them. Their sparring had been much too entertaining. She needed to remind herself that he was an arrogant man who had avoided her until their accidental encounter at Hatchards. Now, instead of leaving her when the dance was over, he was escorting her off the floor. Spending more time in his company would not be wise.

She began to slide her hand from his arm. 'I see my father is waiting for me. Thank you.'

The Duke held her hand in place, keeping her at his side. 'Would you be so kind as to introduce me?'

Would he act like an arrogant aristocrat towards her father? She slowed her steps before leading him to where her father was standing, not far from the dance floor. After introducing them, she waited for Lyonsdale's next move.

He gave a polite nod of his head to her father. 'I'd like to thank you for sending your book to my grandmother. Your kind gesture made her quite happy.'

'It was my pleasure. I am always delighted to hear someone has enjoyed my efforts.'

'I hear all of London is enjoying your efforts. I understand you are here in preparation for the Anglo-American Conference? I imagine your days are filled with information-gathering. Hopefully you will also have opportunities to explore more of London. I fear evenings such as this do not show us in our best light.'

The inconsistency in his behaviour was baffling, and it was difficult to form a clear picture of his character.

'And what would you recommend to the worldly traveller?' she asked.

He turned his head towards her. 'Vauxhall Gardens and Drury Lane for entertainment, Tattersalls for quality horses, Hyde Park for beauty and fresh air, and Gunter's for ice.'

He really did have lovely hair. It appeared thick and had some wave to it. And she realised she had memorised every detail of his chiselled features and square jaw.

Her father cleared his throat, drawing Lyonsdale's attention away from her. 'I believe you could easily write a guide to London and earn a few pounds, Your Grace.'

'I fear spending most of my life here has given me a skewed perspective on what others would find entertaining. Perhaps I presume too much?'

'I do not think you presume too much at all,' her father continued. 'Your very thorough list has intrigued me.'

Katrina tilted her head, taking in Lyonsdale's comfortable yet elegant stance. 'What would you recommend above all else? If you had only one day in Town, where would you go?'

There was a substantial pause, as if he was trying to recall what he found enjoyable. 'I would go to the British Museum and see the Elgin Marbles.'

She tried to recall ever hearing the name. 'I'm not familiar with them.'

'They are a collection of artefacts from Ancient Greece. You should try to see them before you leave.'

She found it a surprising answer, coming from a man so consumed by his work. 'And that is what you enjoy in London above all else?'

His lips rose into a hint of a smile. 'At the moment they are my preferred attraction.'

Her father cleared his throat again. 'I believe I was correct in my initial assessment, Your Grace. You could compose an admirable travel guide.'

Lyonsdale shifted his intense focus from her. 'Thank you, sir. I will keep that in mind in the event that I find I am a bit light in the pockets. However, I doubt it would be as entertaining as I hear your book is.' He smiled pleasantly. 'Please excuse me. I shall take my leave. It has been a pleasure.' He tipped his head to both of them and turned away.

She sensed her father's weighted stare.

'Let us find you some lemonade,' he suggested when Lyonsdale was far enough away. As they began walking towards the refreshment table he lowered his voice. 'This will not end well, my girl.'

'There is no story here, Papa. Do not look to write one.'

'That dance said differently. The man is a duke.'

'I am well aware of that.'

'Then you know you can have no future with him. He is destined to choose one of his own to marry.'

'His choice of a bride does not concern me. You know I do not wish to find a husband here. I will not be attached to a man who will commit himself to me in the eyes of God, only to cast me aside when it's convenient for him to do so. I know all about how Jerome Bonaparte deserted his wife because she was American. I have no desire to have that done to me.'

'Those might be your feelings at the moment, but feelings can alter when attraction comes into play. I have seen it happen before.'

'There is no attraction here. There is no game to be had.'

'You fool yourself if you think so. This room witnessed quite a display of mutual attraction this evening. I would not be surprised if you find yourself in the papers tomorrow. I am only saying this to caution you. Guard your heart, my dear.'

'It was a waltz. Two people have to grant each other their undivided attention. What you witnessed was a dance.'

'What the entire room witnessed were two people so absorbed with one another they did not notice when the music ended,' he said, handing her a glass of lemonade.

'Of course we did. We stopped dancing.'

She could not deny that she was attracted to Lyonsdale, but it wasn't as if he was irresistible. Ignoring the pull, she refused to scan the crowd to see who was receiving his attention now.

As Julian reached his grandmother's side he followed her gaze to the couples who were assembling on the dance floor.

'You were waltzing,' she commented, sipping her lemonade.

He lowered his head to keep their conversation private. 'We are not discussing this.'

'I am simply making an observation.'

'Well, please do not.'

'She is rather a pretty thing.'

'I said we are not talking about this.'

'Talking about what?' his mother interjected as she joined them.

'We were discussing the headache Julian has suddenly

acquired,' replied his grandmother as she smiled into the rim of her glass.

Julian straightened and pressed his lips together to keep from laughing.

'But you never get headaches. How long have you had this one?' his mother asked anxiously.

'Only a short while, I assure you,' he replied, locking his fingers behind his back.

'Is it severe?'

'Not at the moment, but that could change.'

'Do you require a physician?' she asked in a panicked voice, studying his face.

'A physician is not necessary.'

'Very well. I know I need not remind you that you must dance with someone else this evening. We cannot have people believing you have designs on your one partner.'

Julian knew his mother was right. He had only danced once this evening, and he was certain people were speculating about his attendance. If he singled out Miss Vandenberg as his only partner, people would assume he was courting her.

Studying the room, he finally spotted Lady Mary, moving elegantly through a quadrille. He would ask her to dance. It was time he put some effort into conversing with her.

Moving his gaze from Lady Mary, Julian momentarily caught the eye of the amusing Miss Vandenberg...

An hour later he collected Lady Mary for their dance. When he took her hand in his there was no consuming need to pull her into his arms. Was this what bedding her would feel like? Putting on his usual bored expression, he began to dance. He studied her small features, her round youthful face and thick auburn hair. Nothing inside him stirred.

'Is there something wrong, Your Grace?'

'No. Why do you ask?'

'You appear perplexed.'

'Not at all,' he replied, blinking away his thoughts.

They danced in silence for quite some time, and Julian tried to think of something they could discuss.

'Your family—are they well?'

'Yes, thank you. And yours?'

'Very well.'

The minutes ticked by.

He tried again, 'I expect your ride here was pleasant?'

'Yes. The roads were very smooth. We encountered very few delays.'

'Excellent.' Julian clenched his jaw.

Again, there was silence.

'Have you been enjoying your time here this evening?' Lady Mary finally attempted to keep the conversation moving.

'Yes, thank you. And you?'

'Yes, very much. I always enjoy a ball or an assembly. It is agreeable, seeing so many friends in one place.'

How was it possible that she could speak of enjoyment without really smiling? And why did her eyes appear so lifeless?

'What other things do you find enjoyable?'

'Well, I enjoy needlework, playing the pianoforte, helping my mother entertain, and riding through Hyde Park.'

Not once did he see a spark of excitement in her. 'But what is it that makes you truly happy?'

She looked confused. 'Forgive me. I do not understand.'

'If there was one thing you could do for enjoyment, what would it be?'

'It would be difficult to pick only one thing. What would *you* choose?'

Julian fought the urge to close his eyes in exasperation. 'I do not know. I wanted to know what you would choose.'

Lady Mary gave a false smile. 'Well, we have that in common. I am not certain what I would choose either.'

Chapter Ten

The next morning Katrina was still not fully awake as she sat in the dining room, having breakfast with her father. She took a bite of her toast, and her eyes alighted upon a few sentences in the *Morning Chronicle*.

The crunchy bread got stuck in her throat and she began to cough.

There was an account of an '*eligible Duke*' dancing with a '*foreign lady*' at Almack's. Speculation was that the '*eligible Duke*' was looking for a bride, and the '*foreign lady*' was attempting to gain a title.

Her father handed her his napkin. 'I was wondering when you would see it. All the newspapers have something to say about your dance. Apparently London has been eagerly awaiting any indication that Lyonsdale is interested in marriage, and if an eligible man attends Almack's it's assumed he is in search of a bride. One newspaper speculates that there might be a romance forming between you.'

'But he was there to escort his mother and his grandmother.'

'I doubt he would tell you if he was looking for a bride.'

Katrina pushed the paper away, feeling unsettled by the

attention. 'Then why dance with me? Obviously I cannot be under consideration.'

'That didn't stop the rumours that you are searching for a title.'

'I've danced with a number of titled gentlemen while we've been here. He is not the first one.'

'Yes, but you have not danced with an unattached man of his rank. A duke who never dances the waltz and suddenly does so with you will cause people to speculate.' He narrowed his eyes at her. 'Why do you think he asked you?'

That very question had kept her up most of the night, and she still had no answer. She would eventually return to New York, and he would remain in England—probably married to some dull daughter of another duke. Glancing at her toast, Katrina dropped it onto her plate. Her appetite was gone.

The moment Julian entered his breakfast room he knew something was amiss. Apart from the servants his mother was there alone, and there was already a glass of what he assumed was sherry in her hand. Just as he was about to take his first sip of coffee she slid the newspapers closer to him.

'Have you read them yet?' she asked.

'No. Why?'

'Because you are in all of them. You and that *American*.'

The servants didn't need to witness this discussion. He signalled for them to leave and searched for the gossip column in the paper closest to him.

'What do they say?'

'That you danced with her.'

It was too early to deal with his mother's irrational ranting. He pushed the paper aside and took a sip of his coffee. 'It was only a dance.'

'They are saying you are looking for a bride.'

'That should make you happy.'

'Having every Mayfair mother attempt to shove their daughter your way—hardly. They say she is looking for a title.'

'Miss Vandenberg? They obviously have never spoken to the lady.'

'Careful, Lyonsdale. She may seek to trap you.'

'Miss Vandenberg is the last woman in all of London who would trap me.'

'Then you have no designs on her?'

'Of course not. As I said, it was just a dance.'

And it was. Wasn't it?

Later that morning Katrina was composing a letter to her cousin John when she heard a carriage roll to a stop outside her home. Peering through the linen curtains of the drawing room, she tried to see who it was.

As she shifted her body and tilted her head further Wilkins knocked on the open door to inform her that she had a caller. He seemed to be standing a little taller. When she picked up the card from the silver salver she blinked twice at the Dowager Duchess of Lyonsdale's name.

It could not be a coincidence that she was calling on Katrina the very day the papers had printed gossip about Katrina and the woman's grandson. If only she had time for a glass of Madeira.

When the slight old woman slowly entered the room, Katrina dropped into a curtsy and felt the weight of the Dowager's studied gaze.

Drawing on her diplomatic experience, Katrina smiled politely. 'Your Grace, I am honoured by your call.'

The Dowager's eyes were sharp and assessing. With a slight lift of her chin, she held herself with a commanding air. 'Good day, Miss Vandenberg. I wanted to call on you to thank you for your generous gift.'

At least she hadn't demanded Katrina leave the country.

'Would you care for some tea?' Katrina offered, gesturing towards the settee and chairs near the fireplace.

'Tea would be lovely.' The Dowager perched her small, erect frame on the settee. 'Shall we wait for your mother?'

Katrina sat in one of the bergère chairs and nodded to Wilkins for tea. 'My mother passed away many years ago.'

The Dowager's eyes narrowed. 'My mother died when I was an infant. I have no memory of her.'

'Nor I. Mine died two days after I was born.'

A look of understanding passed between them.

The Dowager cleared her throat. 'I assume your father has hired a companion for you, while you are in London?'

Katrina shook her head. Her Great-Aunt Augusta, who had been more a mother to her than anyone, had passed away ten months before. She would have accompanied them to London. Having someone else living with them in her place would have been too painful a reminder of her loss.

'He offered, but I declined.'

'That sounds rather lonely. Surely you have someone to chaperon you when you are attending your social engagements?'

'I do not mind solitude. And the wife of the American Minister has been kind enough to chaperon me on most occasions. Other times I have my maid, who has been with me for many years.'

'I assume having other Americans around you has eased your adjustment somewhat?'

'It has.' Katrina could tell she was being measured by the Duke of Lyonsdale's grandmother. She just wasn't sure why.

'I find it surprising that your father will be involved in negotiating a treaty between our two countries. I doubt anyone here would ask Byron or Scott to do such a thing.'

'My father is a barrister as well as an author. He has presented cases to our Supreme Court and performed services for President Monroe.'

'I see.' The Dowager was silent as she openly took in her surroundings. 'Will your father remain with the American delegation in London after the negotiations are complete?'

'As yet he has not been asked to do so.'

How long did it take to make tea?

The Dowager nodded thoughtfully and clasped her hands on her lap. 'You must convey my appreciation to your father for the book he sent me.'

'I will let him know when he returns home today. Are you a great reader?'

The Dowager inclined her head. 'In my youth I read often. I fear that with age my eyes are not what they once were. Most days I have my maid read to me. It is easier on my eyes.'

Finally Wilkins entered with the tea tray. 'Will there be anything else, miss?'

Katrina had taken note of the Dowager's slight frame. 'Yes, Wilkins, I believe a nice log on the fire will do, on such a dreary day.'

The Dowager's body appeared to relax slightly as the cosy fire warmed the room.

'How would you care to have your tea?'

'With some milk and four lumps of sugar, please.'

Before she caught herself, Katrina's brows rose in surprise. Her Great-Aunt Augusta had enjoyed her tea very sweet, as well. Preparing the cup brought back fond memories of the times when she'd used to sit with the woman who had raised her. She had been her mother's aunt, and of a similar age to the Dowager. There was something in the Dowager's eyes that reminded her of her aunt.

'An extra sweet or two never hurt anyone,' the Dowager explained, with the faintest hint of a smile.

Katrina grinned and inclined her head. 'My Great-Aunt Augusta would certainly have agreed.'

'Then your great-aunt had exceptional taste,' she said with a sparkle in her eye. She accepted the Wedgwood cup from Katrina. 'I understand you are acquainted with my grandson?'

Knowing this was the true intention behind the unexpected visit, Katrina focused her attention on pouring herself tea. 'I am.'

'I assume you have seen the papers today?'

Katrina placed her cup on the table in case the Dowager's words left her with shaking hands. 'Yes, I have.'

'What are your feelings on the speculation, Miss Vandenberg?'

'His Grace showed a polite courtesy in asking me to dance. There is nothing more to it. The papers seek to sensationalise the mundane to sell copies. In truth, my only concern is how my actions reflect on my father and his work here.'

The Dowager's features softened and she took a sip of her tea. 'You'll have to acquire a thick skin to live among us. The papers have something to say about everyone. Do not let what they print concern you.'

'Thank you, but I believe my actions will not warrant comment in the future. I am not an outrageous creature to garner their attention.' And for that Katrina was grateful.

Her comment seemed to appease the Dowager, and the remainder of her visit was spent discussing their shared love of reading and Katrina's tour of the Waterloo Battlefield.

By the time the Dowager left, Katrina knew her to

be not only elegant in manner, but kind-hearted as well. She had extended an invitation to Katrina to call on her at Lyonsdale House, and even informed her that on Monday afternoons at two she was always at home to receive calls. She had also informed Katrina there was no need to bring a chaperon.

It would be rude not to return the call, and if Katrina was honest with herself she was curious to see Lyonsdale's home...

Chapter Eleven

Katrina stood at the front door of Lyonsdale House and studied the wavy grain of the polished wood. While this door was similar in size to the door of her own London home, this building was much larger. All she needed to do was lift the brass knocker. And yet she couldn't manage to raise her hand above her waist.

The Dowager had invited Katrina to call on her. She'd even specified a time that would be most convenient for her. And, while it wasn't exactly a normal calling hour, it did show she had been sincere in her invitation. Didn't it?

If Katrina didn't knock soon, the posy of violets in her hand would be reduced to a wilted mess. She glanced down and wondered if she should have brought them. Her Great-Aunt Augusta had always enjoyed it when Katrina had brought her flowers from the garden. It had seemed to brighten her spirits. But this woman was a dowager duchess. Maybe it simply wasn't done. She was about to toss the bouquet into a row of nearby boxwoods when the door suddenly opened.

Standing before her was a slim, grey-haired man that Katrina assumed was Lyonsdale's butler. He eyed her with a speculative gaze, before his focus dropped to the flowers in her hand. 'May I help you, miss?'

Katrina straightened her shoulders and gave him a polite smile. 'Yes, thank you. I was wondering if the Dowager Duchess of Lyonsdale is receiving.'

His gaze dropped once again to the flowers. 'Do you have a card?'

There was little question that she should have tossed the flowers. It was too late now. The man had made it a point to let her know he had seen them.

There was almost a look of recognition when he read her card. 'This way, miss,' he said, allowing her to step foot inside the hallowed hall of Lyonsdale's grand home. 'I will inform Her Grace that you are here.'

Katrina's footsteps echoed down the hall as she was shown into an ornately decorated drawing room. Gold cherubs flew along the gilded mouldings that ran along the high ceiling, and life-size portraits of past generations stared down at her from their lofty positions on the crimson silk walls. The room smelled of almond oil, no doubt from the freshly polished doors and furniture.

Not certain where to sit, Katrina decided on a bergère chair in the grouping of seats closest to the door. She stared at the portrait of an austere gentleman across from her, who wore a ruffled collar. From his perch on the wall, he didn't seem to like her flowers either.

She was beginning to believe the butler had forgotten about her when she was greeted by the warm smile of the Dowager.

'Miss Vandenberg, this is an unexpected surprise.' The Dowager took a seat opposite Katrina and her gaze dropped to the flowers. 'What do you have there?'

Katrina handed her the posy that had reminded her of home. 'These were growing in our garden. They were so lovely I thought I'd share them with you.'

The Dowager's eyes grew misty. 'My son would pick

violets for me when he was a small child. They bring to mind such cherished memories. Thank you.'

At least she hadn't committed another *faux pas*. 'You are most welcome. I'm glad they give you pleasure.'

Their conversation was interrupted when the butler entered the room, carrying a tea tray.

'I have grown accustomed to enjoying a cup of tea around this time,' the Dowager said. She handed the flowers to her butler. 'Reynolds, do see to these and bring them back here.'

The Dowager poured tea into two of three Sèvres porcelain cups, remembering that Katrina liked it with milk and only one lump of sugar.

Reynolds returned with the flowers in a small gilded vase, and the Dowager signalled to him to place it on the table closest to her.

'Have you had the opportunity to see more of London since we last spoke?' she asked, stirring her four lumps of sugar into her tea.

'I went with the Forresters to see the new exhibition at the Royal Academy yesterday. The paintings were lovely. I especially enjoyed one of fairies by a Mr Henry Howard.'

'Are you fond of art?'

'Yes, very much so.'

'Then I must introduce you to the Duchess of Winterbourne. Olivia is a lovely woman, and I believe the two of you might share some interests.'

There was something unidentifiable about the Dowager that continued to remind Katrina of her great-aunt. Both women had the ability to fill her with a sense of comfort.

She was about to respond when the sound of heavy footfalls drifted in from the entrance hall. Both she and the Dowager turned towards the doorway and found Lyonsdale standing on the threshold. He was dressed in a bottle-green tail coat, brown waistcoat, and buckskin breeches. And he appeared to be just as startled as Katrina to find themselves staring at one another.

'Do come in, my boy,' the Dowager said with a bright smile. 'I believe you're acquainted with Miss Vandenberg?'

There was a slight hesitation in his stride, and he narrowed his gaze at his grandmother. 'Of course. Good day, Miss Vandenberg,' he said, executing a perfect bow.

The sound of his voice left her with flutters low in her abdomen. 'Good day, Your Grace.'

The Dowager motioned to the chair next to Katrina. 'Would you care to join us? A nice cup of tea might be just the thing after your long committee meeting.'

Katrina found it difficult to determine if she wanted him to stay or if it would be better for him to leave them.

'I would not wish to interrupt your discussion.'

Horrid, fickle man!

'Nonsense. Miss Vandenberg and I were just beginning our visit. There is nothing to interrupt.'

He inclined his head and took the seat next to Katrina. Her heart turned over unexpectedly.

'You are back early today,' the Dowager continued.

'No, I return home at exactly this time each Monday when the committee is in session.'

So this was one of the ways a duke occupied himself during the day. 'Is this a Parliamentary committee?' Katrina asked.

He accepted the tea and shifted his gaze to her. 'It is.'

'What does your committee meet about?'

'We are investigating the effects of working conditions on child labourers.'

'You are?'

He lifted his chin, as if he was anticipating derision. 'I assure you it is a valid issue, and one that needs to be addressed.'

It wasn't necessary to point that out to her. She was simply surprised that a man of his substantial wealth had any interest in the children of the poor.

'I agree. It's commendable that your committee has taken up the cause for those who are frequently neglected.'

'We have just begun our interviews. Our aim is to ensure these children are neither exploited nor harmed.' His gaze drifted to the flowers. 'I see the violets are multiplying,' he commented to his grandmother. 'This is the first time you have seen fit to display them outside your rooms.'

The Dowager gave Katrina a warm smile. 'These are from Miss Vandenberg. She was kind enough to bring them to me.'

He did nothing to hide his surprise. 'You have brought my grandmother flowers?'

'I have. I found them beautiful and wished to share them with her,' she stated, annoyed with herself for feeling the need to explain her actions to him.

'I would have assumed you would favour orchids or some other rare, exotic bloom.'

'I am partial to simpler things. I do not need the world to confirm a pedigree for me to appreciate beauty.'

He studied her over his teacup, and she found the room was growing rather warm.

'They match your eyes.'

'I beg your pardon?'

'The violets—they are the same colour as your eyes.'

It was impossible to pull her gaze from his—that was until the Dowager gave a discreet cough.

'Miss Vandenberg, would you care to see our library?' she asked. 'With your fondness for books, I am certain you will find something of interest to borrow.' She turned to Lyonsdale. 'With your permission, of course.'

'That is a fine idea. Please, by all means, Miss Vandenberg. My library is at your disposal.' He sat back in his chair and took a sip of his tea.

Katrina now had an excuse to remove herself from his presence. Maybe it would relieve her of the restless feeling that hadn't gone away since the moment she'd laid eyes on him.

'That's very kind of you.'

'Capital,' the Dowager replied with a broad smile. 'I shall wait here while you escort her.'

'Me?' he spluttered, and appeared to be thinking up an excuse as to why he wasn't available.

'It is your library,' his grandmother explained. 'You know it far better than anyone else in this house. Besides, I've had a dull ache in my legs all day. I do not expect you will take long.'

If Katrina hadn't been paying such close attention to him she might have missed his hesitation before he turned back to her.

'Shall we, Miss Vandenberg?'

They entered the hallway in silence, walking side by side. After a few moments she turned to him. 'You do not need to remain with me while I make my selection. I am certain I will be able to find my way back to the drawing room.'

'Are you attempting to remove yourself from my company?'

'Not at all. I simply assume you have pressing matters that require your attention.'

'I find I can think of nothing at the moment that is more pressing than helping you obtain something for your enjoyment.'

This time when he spoke his voice was warm and friendly.

She had provided him with an excuse. If he chose not to take it, it was no longer her concern.

'Your grandmother called on me recently,' she said, as a way to explain her presence in his home.

'I assumed she must have.'

'She is a lovely woman.'

'That's debatable.'

'Come, now—she is quite affable.'

He shook his head. 'That is one word to describe her. I can think of others.'

'You are very fortunate to have her.'

Their arms inadvertently brushed against one another, and he placed some distance between them. After a few more steps he moved his hands behind his back as they continued down the long hall.

'If you had a grandmother like mine you might have a different opinion on the matter.'

'I did not know either of my grandmothers. They passed away before I was born.'

He lowered his head and looked at her with regret. 'Please forgive me. I should have thought before I spoke.'

He might not appreciate his grandmother, but she did. She gave him a reassuring smile. 'No apology is necessary.'

They strolled through an ornately carved archway and entered a long wood-panelled extension of the hall. To their right, tall windows with blue damask silk draperies brought muted light into the room. The opposite wall was covered with life-size portraits of men in various poses and attire.

Katrina paused and looked over the portraits of the men who were staring down at them. She advanced further and their superior gazes followed her.

'Who are they?'

He appeared to stand taller, if that was even possible. 'May I introduce you to the Dukes of Lyonsdale?'

Her eyes widened as she spun around. '*All* of them?'

He let out a soft laugh at her obvious amazement. 'We are missing one. However, every man in this room has held my title at one time. My ducal title is one of the oldest in England.'

In Katrina's dining room at their country home in Tarrytown her mother's portrait hung on the wall behind the chair where she had sat. Her father said it reminded him that she was still somehow with them. He also carried a miniature of her mother on his person. The only other portraits of her family were one of her father and one of his parents. Lyonsdale had many, many more.

Near the doorway they had walked through hung the portrait of a man with dark curly hair, wearing armour. His sword was raised in the air as he sat upon his steed. From his expression she gathered he would be happy to use that sword on her if she moved the wrong way. He was an intimidating sight.

Lyonsdale approached her. 'That is Edward Carlisle, the First Duke of Lyonsdale. He was awarded the title by King Henry the Seventh for service to the crown in battle.'

'Which battle?'

'The Battle of Bosworth.'

Well, that explained nothing. She continued to study the designs on the man's armour.

'The Battle of Bosworth took place during the War of the Roses.'

He might just as well have been speaking Italian.

'You *have* heard of the War of the Roses, haven't you?'

She shook her head while she looked up at the superior expression of the First Duke. 'Do you know when he was given the title?'

'Of course—in the year 1485, not long after Henry was crowned King.' He placed his hands behind his back and rocked on his heels.

Lyonsdale knew what his ancestor had been doing

in 1485. She knew little of her family's history past her grandparents. A bubble of laughter escaped her lips.

He appeared affronted. 'What have I said that you find so amusing?'

'All I know of my family is that my great-grandfather came to America from Holland and was proficient in building ships. That is how my father came to inherit our shipyard in New York.'

There was no telling if his shocked expression was at the lack of information she possessed or her ancestor's occupation.

'Surely you know more than that?'

'No. That is all I know,' she said with a shrug. 'My father may know more.' She knew nothing of her mother's family. It had never occurred to her to ask.

Lyonsdale appeared to be catatonic. He wasn't even blinking.

'Would you like to tell me about the others?'

It took him a minute to answer. 'What others?'

She gestured to the portraits with her hand. 'The other Dukes.'

He snapped out of his stupor and let out a deep breath. 'I believe you are simply being polite.'

'That's not true. Tell me more about your family.'

They walked from portrait to portrait and he recounted numerous accomplishments spanning hundreds of years. It was an impressive group of men. Had they all been in a room together it would have been difficult to choose one who stood out from the rest.

When they reached a gap between two of the portraits Katrina stopped. 'Where is this one?'

Lyonsdale cleared his throat and crossed his arms. 'The Fifth Duke was a disgrace. He was too concerned with his own pleasure and did not live up to the responsibility of his title. His portrait is not fit to hang with the others.'

Now, *this* sounded interesting. She stepped closer and lowered her voice to a conspiratorial whisper. 'What exactly did he do?'

He leaned his lips close to her ear and his warm breath fanned her neck. Her eyes fluttered at the sensation.

'I'll. Never. Tell.'

When he pulled his head back the cool air was a shock.

The proper thing to do would be to end this discussion, however much she wanted to know what the man had done.

'Was it something truly dreadful? I'll wager it was.'

He arched a regal brow, which gave him an expression closely resembling that of the Sixth Duke, who was looking down at them with disdain.

'Miss Vandenberg, it is not polite to poke into other people's affairs.'

She gestured to the empty wall. 'He is dead. He will never know.'

He spun on his heels and walked towards the far end of the room. 'I meant *my* affairs,' he called out over his shoulder.

She hurried to catch up with him. 'I was not talking about you. I was talking about the Fifth Duke. What was his name?'

'His history is my history. His actions reflect who I am. Hence it is my affair. His name is inconsequential.'

'That's a peculiar name.' She tried to hold back her smile but it didn't work.

He stopped abruptly and turned to her. Their eyes met and a smile tugged on his lips.

It felt like an odd little victory.

'I believe you were interested in my library?'

'I was… I am.'

What did one have to do to be removed from a portrait

gallery? Was he a gambler? A rake? Perhaps he enjoyed his brandy a bit too much?

'I can keep a secret.'

His dubious expression was the only response she was to receive.

Past his shoulder she spied Lyonsdale's own portrait. His face was fuller and younger.

'You appear astonished to find me here,' he said.

'Is it a requirement that none of you smile for your portraits?'

'The responsibility of this title is not a jovial matter. The portraits should imply that.'

She let her gaze drift to the men who were still watching them. 'I suppose... But none of you appear at all pleased with your illustrious accomplishments.'

'Would you have us laugh in our portraits?'

'No, but a hint of a smile would be refreshing. You are an impressive collection of English noblemen. However, I fear dinner would be a dour affair if you all were present.'

He looked insulted, which she found amusing. 'I believe, Miss Vandenberg, we were heading to the library.'

'Lead on, Your Grace. I will humbly follow.'

'You are a sauce-box. You are aware of that, are you not?'

It proved impossible to hold back her laugh.

She was about to respond when she froze at the sight of the library before her. The long oak-panelled room held more books than Katrina had ever seen in any home. All four walls were covered from floor to ceiling with rows of books, and at the far end two walls of bookshelves jutted into the middle of the room. She wished she might remain in this room for days.

'It may prove difficult to make your selection if you do not step inside,' he called out from inside the room, with a trace of laughter.

Warmth spread across her chest, up her neck and across her cheeks. Avoiding his gaze, she crossed the threshold and was met by the scent of old books and leather.

'This is lovely.' Her voice died away in the hushed stillness of the room.

'Thank you. You may explore it to your heart's content.'

'I'd caution against making such an offer. You may find me curled on the floor, surrounded by books in the early-morning hours.'

'One can only dream, Miss Vandenberg…one can only dream.'

Smiling at his teasing comment, she navigated around a grouping of well-used chairs and highly polished tables. As she walked along, scanning the shelves, she felt the heat of his presence behind her.

'Are you a great reader?' she asked. 'Or do you rarely frequent this room?'

'In my youth I would spend many agreeable hours here. That large chair by the fire was a particular favourite spot of mine. It is from there that I read about gods and adventures and pirates and kings. Unfortunately now my duties in Westminster keep me too busy to read for pleasure.'

That made her pause and turn to him. 'There is always time for a good book. Even if that time is before you close your eyes at night. A well-told story feeds the soul.'

'Spoken like the daughter of an author.'

He didn't have a true measure of her if that was what he thought.

'Spoken by a woman who knows the value of literature,' she replied, poking him in the chest. 'You should consider my words.'

'I consider all your words—much to my vexation.'

What man said that to a woman?

'You think I'm vexing?'

He crossed his arms and raised his chin. 'I think you provoke me to see the world differently.'

'Forgive me. I do not wish to inconvenience you,' she snapped, spinning around to prevent herself from saying more.

He took her arm and gently turned her to face him. 'Do you seek to purposely misread me? If so, you should be commended. You do a fine job.' He was wise enough to redirect their conversation. 'Now, tell me if you have any notion of which subject matter might interest you.'

The heat from his hand on her forearm warmed her entire body. She glanced about, needing to recall the purpose of their excursion. Intrigued by his ancestors, she was curious about the battle he had mentioned.

'Would you have any books on your country's history?'

'Are you certain I cannot interest you in a gothic novel?' A teasing glint sparkled in his green eyes. 'Perhaps one with a dungeon?'

She held back a smile and faked eagerness. 'Do you have any?'

'I honestly couldn't say,' he said dryly.

'Well, it matters not. I am interested in a historical read.'

He let go of her arm. 'Follow me. I will show you where to look.' He led her behind the last row of shelves. 'Is there anything about our history you have a particular interest in?'

It wasn't necessary for him to know that she wanted to learn more about his family. She was certain that would make him strut about for the remainder of their time together. He had mentioned a King Henry. She could start there.

'Since we have no monarchy in America, I'd like to read about yours.'

He slid the brass and oak library ladder towards her. 'You should look on the upper shelves.'

* * *

Julian picked up a book on Greek mythology and began skimming the contents while he waited for Miss Vandenberg to make her selection. He had read this book before, many years ago. From what he could recall he had enjoyed all the fantastical tales. Maybe he would read a few pages this evening, before he turned in for the night.

He should allow her to peruse his collection without hovering around her like some lovestruck youth. It would be the polite thing to do. But Julian had no desire to be polite.

'What do you know of King Henry the Eighth?'

She really did have a lovely voice. When he lifted his head, his reply caught in his throat as he found himself at eye level with the delicate curves of her breasts.

Her creamy skin was flushed with a warm glow as his gaze fixed on a small birthmark on the upper swell of her left breast. How he wished he could spend hours exploring that one small spot. How many birthmarks did she have? Did she have them in other enticing places?

The catch of Miss Vandenberg's breath broke his concentration. He quickly raised his gaze to meet her amused expression.

'Well?' she prompted.

That birthmark had caused the blood to rush from his head to his groin, and Julian had no recollection of their conversation. She rolled her eyes and lowered herself to the next step down. Her breasts were now out of his direct line of vision. He wasn't certain if he was relieved or disappointed.

'I asked what you know of King Henry the Eighth. There are a number of volumes of books on him here.'

Books. They had been discussing books. Would she think it odd if he banged his head against one of the shelves? Probably. He snapped the book on mythology closed.

'He ruled England during the sixteenth century and altered the course of our religious practices. You may find it interesting that he had six wives.'

Her shocked expression made him laugh. '*Six?* How could one man have six wives?'

'One died by natural means, he beheaded two, divorced two, and the last outlived him.'

'He beheaded his wives?'

'Two of them, yes.' He backed away from the ladder to give her room to step down. Curious as to the book she had chosen, he held the tome that was still in her hand and read the title. 'Excellent choice,' he informed her.

'Why would any man behead his wife?'

'It is said he found them…unfaithful.' This really was not a discussion one should have with a young, unmarried lady.

She stepped closer to him. 'So he killed them? I have heard of many instances of wives being unfaithful here. Are they still beheaded for it?'

'If that were the case there would be quite a few ladies missing.'

'I really cannot begin to comprehend you English.'

'And what puzzles you so?'

'Your ideas on marriage and what constitutes a good one.'

'And what constitutes a good marriage to an American?'

'Love, fidelity, friendship…respect.' She tilted her head to the side and a loose blonde curl caressed her long neck. 'Have you ever been in love?'

A duke did not fall in love. Duty came before personal interest. Everyone knew that. He shook his head.

She nodded, as if she understood. Since she was an

American, she would never have to concern herself with duty. This woman would be able to marry for love.

As an unmarried gentleman, he knew he should tread lightly in conversations of marriage. Yet she had been the one to broach the subject first. It would be poor form to end a discussion she was clearly interested in.

'Have you ever been in love?' he asked.

A wistful look crossed her beautiful face. 'I have not fallen in love yet, but I have witnessed it enough. Have you not seen two people so in love that it appears their hearts will stop beating if they are not together? That is the love I believe my parents had and what I wish for myself. I want to wake to thoughts of one gentleman and close my eyes to dream of him.'

'The sounds rather consuming.'

'I believe love is consuming—in the most wondrous of ways.'

'Now you are waxing poetical, Miss Vandenberg.'

'Laugh if you will. But I shall live my life in America, in a marriage of love and fidelity, happy to keep my head.'

The thought of her married to someone else and living far away disturbed him. He could not fathom why it should bother him. He did not believe her silly notions of love. He certainly did not want her to love *him*!

'And you, Your Grace—what is your idea of a perfect marriage?'

He had no idea. A knot formed in his stomach. His marriage had not been perfect. Even in the best of times it had felt awkward. His grandmother said she had been happy with his grandfather, but the man had died before Julian was born.

'I do not know,' he replied honestly.

'Maybe some day you will discover what it means to be happily married.'

'I doubt that.'

'For that I am truly sorry.'

She proceeded to walk past him, and he moved his arm across the aisle to block her passage. It was mere inches from her breasts. He didn't want her to leave. Not yet.

Their eyes locked and he lowered his head towards her, taking in her lemon scent. She was unaware of how captivating she was when she smiled.

'You think I'm vexing,' she said softly, with those tempting lips.

He lowered his head closer. 'I think you're enchanting.' Just one taste was all he needed. 'Katrina...' he whispered, testing the sound of her name.

'I don't know your name,' she said, their breaths mingling.

'Carlisle.'

'What Carlisle?'

'Julian Henry Michael Charles Carlisle.'

'That's quite a long name.'

'We English like to impress.'

When their lips finally touched he closed his eyes.

Almost instantly she pulled back and ducked under his arm. Reaching the end of the row, she paused and gave him a devilish grin. 'As impressive as your name is, I do not believe it is impressive enough to warrant a kiss from me.'

By the time he walked out from where they were hidden, he caught sight of her walking out through the library door. Crossing his arms and leaning against the bookcase, Julian chided himself at his own stupidity. Dreaming about her was one thing, but actually knowing the feel of her lips and the taste of her mouth would be a mistake. He suspected that if he ever did kiss her thoroughly, she would be impossible to forget.

Chapter Twelve

People from various classes and backgrounds were stroll-ing around the British Museum as Katrina and Sarah made their way from one marble statue to the next.

'I don't see what all the fuss is about. I understand they are quite old, but most of them are broken,' Sarah mused.

Suddenly both women stopped at a marble sculpture of a nude man reclining.

'On the other hand,' Sarah continued, 'I'm beginning to see what merit there is to these works.'

They both tilted their heads slightly, taking in the stat-ue's details.

'Do you think it is accurate?' Katrina whispered. 'Even the size?'

Sarah gave a gentle tug on her arm. 'If we have seen one naked man today, I am sure we will see others.'

Heat began to creep up Katrina's face and she low-ered her head. Still, the prospect of actually seeing what was inside a man's breeches was too great a temptation. She turned her head one last time before Sarah pulled her forward.

'I noticed the beautiful bouquet in your drawing room earlier,' Sarah said with a smile. 'I presume the roses were from Monsieur DuBois? He is very handsome, and he was attentive to you last night at the musicale.'

Katrina lifted her shoulder. 'He is passable.'

'Come, now, with his dark eyes and comely features, you must admit he is fine on the eyes.'

Katrina shrugged again.

Sarah looked surprised. 'He is not to your liking?'

'He is…in some respects. DuBois is pleasant company, and we have things in common…'

'But?'

Katrina wished she could explain it—especially to herself. Monsieur DuBois was a lovely man. She enjoyed his company. When they had first met in Paris, months ago, she'd fancied herself smitten with him. However, things had changed since she had arrived in London. Lyonsdale had tried to kiss her.

'He doesn't make my heart race.'

'I wasn't aware you thought requiring a physician was desirable,' Sarah said, laughing.

'I believe a man should make you feel something. When he kisses you it should feel like…'

'When he kisses you it should make you feel as if you can't quite catch your breath.'

'Exactly.'

'So kissing him does not make you feel like that?'

Katrina shook her head. 'We shared one small kiss in Paris. My breathing never altered.'

There was no reason that Sarah needed to know the kiss hadn't exactly been a small one. At the time she had thought it a great passionate adventure to be held in his arms and kissed deeply. Now she was trying to recall why she had thought it was so wonderful. Perhaps because it had been her first kiss. Lyonsdale had merely bushed his lips against hers and she had felt as if she would melt into the floor. There was no telling what would have happened if she had allowed him to actually kiss her.

'I think the next time you find yourself alone with Du-Bois you should kiss him again.'

'Sarah!' she chided, looking around.

'No one can hear. My mother is in the next gallery,' her friend replied dismissively. 'Perhaps he was trying not to offend your delicate feminine sensibilities.'

'Sarah, he is *French*.' Katrina rolled her eyes. 'And I am not going to kiss him again. Let's concentrate on the exhibition.'

'I think our discussion is infinitely more interesting,' Sarah countered, trudging behind her to the next group of statues.

Julian wasn't surprised that Hart had already moved on to the next gallery. When he finally caught up with him he found his friend lounging against the large doorway with his arms crossed, staring into the second room displaying the Elgin Marbles.

'You know, you might not grumble every time I mention coming here if you actually took the time to look at the pieces,' Julian commented, approaching his side.

'I believe the attendees are much more stimulating subjects.' Hart motioned with his head to the other side of the room. 'I have been watching them for the last ten minutes. They really are quite entertaining.'

Julian looked across the room and froze. This could not be happening. He had thought he might be making progress. He hadn't thought of her once since early morning. Fate truly was playing tricks on him.

Miss Vandenberg looked fetching in a small navy bonnet and a navy pelisse over a pale green dress, and she appeared to be enjoying the time she was spending with Miss Forrester.

'I understand you waltzed together.'

Julian was uneasy with the mischief in his friend's eyes. 'How do you know that?'

'I read the papers, like everyone else—albeit later in the day. What do you say you introduce me?'

'No.'

'I promise to behave.'

'No.'

'Windsucker.'

'Dolt.'

Hart tossed the lock of hair out of his eyes. 'Well, I think you're going to have to do something. It seems the lady knows you are here.'

The moment their eyes met every part of Julian's body reacted to the sight of her. When she gave him a small smile he managed to nod in return.

'Capital! You've been acknowledged. Now, go and speak with her.'

What could he possibly say to her when all he could think about was taking her to some remote area of the museum? Trying to kiss her had been highly improper. What if she was angry with him for his boldness?

He was at war with himself. Part of him wanted to go over to her and remain with her for the rest of the day. The other part of him knew that spending any more time with her would make him miserable with unfulfilled longing.

'Are you going to stare at her all afternoon?' teased Hart.

'The thought did occur to me.'

Katrina could actually hear the pounding of her own heart. She had spied Lyonsdale standing near the doorway and simply wanted to observe him. But he had caught her staring, and Katrina had been so embarrassed she had lowered her head so he wouldn't witness her blush. Now, because they had made eye contact, he would feel obligated to say hello.

With a confident stride he crossed the gallery with his companion and stopped a few feet in front of her. 'I hope you ladies are both well,' he said, inclining his head politely.

She struggled with the urge to finish the kiss he had started. 'Yes, thank you, and you?' she said, twisting her finger around the braided handle of her reticule.

'Quite well, thank you,' he replied, and then introduced Katrina and Sarah to his friend, Lord Hartwick.

'Have you both been enjoying the exhibition?' Sarah asked.

'He has,' replied Lord Hartwick. 'I must confess broken statues do not hold my interest—especially when most of them are of men.'

Lyonsdale eyed his friend sharply, and a silent communication passed between them before Lyonsdale turned back to Katrina. 'Has any particular piece caught your eye?' he asked.

Why was it that the only sculpture she could remember seeing was that of the nude man? Was Lyonsdale as muscular as the man carved out of marble? From the way the cut of his coat accentuated his frame, he appeared to be. There had to be another piece of art she could remember seeing...

'The horse's head,' she blurted out, grateful she had thought of such an innocuous piece.

'It is quite lifelike, is it not? I enjoy the friezes myself.'

Their almost kiss had muddled her brain. Katrina was beginning to picture *his* head upon the statue that had so intrigued her earlier. That odd flutter was back, low in her abdomen, and the air was growing thin. If she didn't distance herself from him immediately she was certain to make a cake of herself.

'Well, it was nice to see you again. I believe we will leave you gentlemen to your leisure and continue on.'

When Lyonsdale inclined his head and was about to turn away, his friend cleared his throat. Katrina caught the questioning look that crossed Lyonsdale's face.

Lord Hartwick tipped his head. 'I believe, ladies, that you could not have a better guide than His Grace. Perhaps you would be interested in having him explain the Marbles to you?'

Katrina eyed both men hesitantly. How could she possibly say no without insulting Lyonsdale? But if she spent any more time with him in a room full of barely clad statues she might tug him behind one and kiss him till he had trouble breathing as well.

'It is very kind of you to offer, however, we would not want to keep you longer than necessary with our pace,' she said, feeling Sarah's eyes on her.

'I assure you it would be of no inconvenience. Although I can understand you wanting to take your time with the exhibition,' Lyonsdale said, glancing at his friend.

'Well…thank you again for your offer,' she said, linking her arm through Sarah's. Hopefully the air was cooler in the adjoining gallery. 'Perhaps we will see each other again.'

When Miss Vandenberg and her friend were a good distance away, Julian rounded on Hart. 'What in the world possessed you to do that?'

'Well, pardon me for trying to extend the encounter.'

'Next time do not lend me your assistance.'

'Next time I won't. You are on your own, Romeo.'

'Do not call me that.'

Hart shook his head. 'You must be aware that the two of you produce an interesting display when you're together. It's like nothing I've witnessed with you before.'

'What display?'

'When the two of you stare at one other, one might expect you each to drag the other behind some grand statue in this room.' Hart glanced around. 'Possibly that one over there.'

Julian's eyes narrowed. 'She declined your offer to have me show her the Marbles. What in the world could possibly make you think she wants me?'

She had also refused his kiss, however, he was not about to state that fact. Her eagerness to leave just now told him how insulted she must be by his improper advance. He had allowed his passion to overtake him. Guilt churned in his gut.

'Oh, we are not playing the two young simpering misses, are we? If there is one thing I know, it's the look of a woman who wants to be taken. Now, don't expect me to give you an exact recounting of the number of times she glanced at you and the way her breathing increased when you drew close to her.'

None of this could be true. 'How do you know her breathing increased?'

'Her lovely little breasts rose most rapidly.'

Julian's right hand curled into a fist. 'What were you doing staring at her breasts?' he said through his teeth.

'Pardon me—have we met?' Hart crooked his lip. 'I'm curious. Have you called out her name yet when you're with Helena? If you have, please tell me she noticed.'

Julian tugged at the cuff of his sleeve. 'You'll be pleased to know I have ended my association with Helena.'

A broad smile broke out on Hart's face. 'You have been keeping secrets from me. Not at all sporting of you. Did she turn some tables?'

'She threw a candlestick at me, but I managed to save my head. She was offended that the pearls I gave her weren't diamonds. Apparently a duke should give diamonds when he ends a liaison. Did you know that? I didn't. Glad I never did give her any, though.'

'So now you are free to pursue the lovely Miss V?'

'She is an unmarried woman. I'll not ruin her.'

Hart eyed him closely. 'Perhaps you should marry her, then.'

'What? *You* are talking about marriage? *You* who repeatedly defile the sanctity of such a union all over Town?'

'Well, I am not talking about *me*. You are too honourable to have her any other way, and you have a disturbing need to get leg-shackled again. Why not now? Why not to her? Once you get over this obsession with her you can find amusements elsewhere.'

'She is an American.'

'She is hardly running around in animal skins.'

'So I should throw away centuries of the Lyonsdale bloodline to marry an untitled woman who isn't even English? How do they even raise their children in America?' Just the idea of it was making him sweat.

'Do you believe that if you marry her you will create green dwarf children with pointed ears? She is pretty, appears intelligent, and she comports herself well. I am sure her children will follow suit. If anything, she is the one who would be making a sacrifice. After all, your children could resemble you.'

'I am a duke. It's not done.'

Julian's eyes drifted to the doorway and he clenched his jaw. He wanted her—more than anything. But it was his lot in life that he could not have her.

'Very well. However, it makes no sense to me why you would want to remain this frustrated.'

'I am *not* frustrated,' Julian replied, more loudly than he had intended.

Hart grinned in triumph.

Spinning on his heels, Julian cursed his friend as he walked away.

Later that evening Julian sat at his desk and stared at the blurred writing on the paper in front of him. He should have been focusing on memorising the words he had written, since he would be delivering them to a chamber full of his peers in a few days' time. Instead he was continuing to mull over Miss Vandenberg's reaction to him at the museum. It had been apparent that she couldn't wait to leave his side. She was an unmarried woman, and he had tried to kiss her. Of course she had been insulted by his actions. Hart's assessment of their encounter had been all wrong.

Julian was not in the habit of apologising for anything. This time he needed to make an exception.

A low knock on his door broke the silence of the room. His mother stood in the doorway, dressed for her evening engagements. He motioned for her to enter and she took a seat across from him.

'You are working late, I see,' she said, adjusting her gloves.

'I am memorising a speech.'

'I hear you are expected to give an address this week. I hope the vote is in your favour.'

'Thank you.'

She shifted a little in her chair and glanced down at her hands, folded in her lap. 'You have brought nothing but honour to this family. I am very proud of the man you have become.'

'Thank you,' he replied, taken aback by her unusual praise.

'I'm aware that you do not appreciate me pestering you to find a suitable bride, but I only do so because I'm interested in what is best for you.'

'And you believe what is best for me is Lady Mary Morley?' He sat back and crossed his legs, knowing it was time to begin showing an interest in the girl.

'I do. She is from a prominent family, and she has been trained in how to comport herself as a duchess.' His mother leaned forward in her seat. 'Lady Mary is graceful, accomplished, and she appears robust. Since she is but seventeen, she should have many years ahead of her to bear you a number of children. She will be an asset to you—not a hindrance. Surely you must see she is an ideal choice?'

On paper, she was—but she wasn't someone who could stir his soul and make him ache when he had to leave her. She wasn't Miss Vandenberg.

He looked at his mother's hopeful expression and knew she believed she was guiding his actions for the benefit of the Lyonsdale name. And they both knew the family's reputation meant everything. He recalled what Miss Vandenberg had said in the library about the bond between her own parents. Was it possible he could eventually have that with Morley's daughter?

'Were you eager to marry my father?'

His mother's eyes widened momentarily before she caught herself. 'I beg your pardon?'

'When you were told you would be marrying, were you eager to do so?'

Julian didn't miss the uncomfortable expression that crossed her face. 'I do not recall. I am certain the thought of becoming a duchess in one of the most prominent families in England was pleasing. But I honestly do not recall being eager for anything in my life. I find such strong emotion rather base and vulgar.'

'Were you happy being married to him?'

She shifted again on the chair. 'I do not understand why you are interested in such things. People in our position do not concern themelves with happiness. We strive for contentment, and I was content being married to your father.'

Julian rubbed his chest, relieving some of the tightness that was gripping his ribcage. He glanced at the portrait of his father, visible beyond his mother's right shoulder. Had he ever heard his father laugh? Was that what being married to the wrong woman did?

He shook his head as he buried those questions in his subconscious. 'Was there something else you wanted to see me about?'

She took a breath and appeared relieved at the change in subject. 'Actually, there was. I heard from Lady Jersey that Finchley is reconsidering his vote. I thought that might be of interest to you.'

'I appreciate you taking the time to inform me. I shall speak with him tomorrow.'

'I understand he has been known to dine at White's.'

Julian wished that he could tell if she was interested in his affairs because she truly wanted to help him, or because she wanted another accomplishment of his to place in the family annals. It would have been nice to believe she did it out of a fondness for him.

'Thank you, Mother.'

She turned away. 'I am glad I could be of assistance.' When she'd reached the doorway, she turned back to him. 'I trust you to make the right decision. I will say no more about Lady Mary and defer to you.'

He watched her turn into the hallway before he sat back in his chair. Staring once again at the portrait of his father, he studied the pair of solemn green eyes that looked back at him. Since he was young, Julian had looked upon the life his father had led as a blueprint of the way a duke conducted himself. Once he'd died Julian had clung to the actions that had defined his father. There was no guidebook that came with becoming a duke. One went by example.

Had his father ever regretted marrying his mother? Had he been he content living with a woman who showed no affection and would rather jump into a pond than have an intimate conversation? Would he ever have admitted it to his son?

This was the life he was destined to lead. His mother had said that people in their position didn't concern themselves with happiness. Looking upon his father's solemn portrait, he was certain the man would have agreed. It was time that Julian stopped holding out hope for what could never be.

But then his thoughts turned to a pair of fine blue eyes. Simply thinking about Miss Vandenberg made him smile. She amused him, exasperated him, and excited him. She deserved an apology for his actions. He only hoped that this time when he saw her, he would be able to control his desire.

Chapter Thirteen

The next afternoon rain fell in sheets and thunder shook Katrina's house while she wrote letters home to her family and friends. Her concentration was broken when Wilkins presented her with the unexpected sight of Lyonsdale's card. A fluttering feeling settled low in her abdomen as she rose from her writing table and brushed out the wrinkles of her blue and yellow muslin gown. She needed to compose herself before he entered the drawing room.

'Good day, Your Grace,' she said, dropping into a curtsy. 'My father is not at home, but at the Chancery. I can relay a message to him if you wish.'

The sight of him in her home was making her babble.

'Actually, Miss Vandenberg, I came to call on you.'

Certainly she had misheard what he'd said. She glanced at Meg, who wasn't doing anything to hide her surprise at seeing the Duke of Lyonsdale in the cosy drawing room. When Katrina finally caught her maid's eye she gestured for her to return to her seat and continue mending.

Awkwardly Lyonsdale cleared his throat. He appeared to be waiting for something—her manners and proper etiquette, probably. He had her so flustered she couldn't even recall proper protocol.

Walking to the settee and the chairs by the fireplace,

she gracefully lowered herself into one of the chairs. 'Would you care to sit?'

'Thank you, I would.' A faint smile softened his features as he sat across from her, looking very masculine on the delicate settee.

When he accepted her offer of tea, she nodded her request to Wilkins. Her butler eyed Lyonsdale, before giving her a crisp nod and leaving the room without closing the door.

She turned her attention back to her guest. 'I'm surprised you have ventured out on such a dreary day. I must confess I've not heard many carriages go by all morning.'

He shifted restlessly on the settee. 'I had some important matters to attend to. While the roads are a bit treacherous, they are passable.'

The unlit fireplace seemed to hold his interest. When he looked back at her, the tension was palpable.

'I needed to see you to offer you my apology.' The words came out stilted, as if he hadn't said them often. He should have apologised for ignoring her weeks ago.

'Why are you offering me your apology?'

He leaned closer and they both stole a glance at Meg. Thankfully her maid appeared occupied with her mending. He licked his lips and Katrina almost slid off her chair, remembering the brief feel of those lips brushing against hers.

'I need to apologise for what occurred in my library,' he whispered.

There were many things this man could apologise for, and he was choosing to apologise for their almost kiss?

She was mortified that she had believed him to be as attracted to her as she was to him. It would be horrid to hear him admit he hadn't intended to kiss her. Dear God, maybe *she* was the one who had moved her lips up to his!

'Let us not speak of it again,' she whispered back.

His brow wrinkled. 'I fear I have offended you, and that was not my intention.'

'You have not.'

'Are you certain?'

This was torture. Did he have to go on? 'I assure you there is no need to speak of it.'

He lowered his chin and licked his lips again. 'Miss Vandenberg, I feel a need to be frank.'

'Please do not.' Could not the floor open up and swallow her, just this once?

He kept his voice low. 'I did not wish to insult you, but you stir something inside me.' A pained look crossed his face.

The breath she was holding was released with a whoosh, and she held her stomach to steady the butterflies inside.

'You wanted to kiss me?'

'I thought that was very apparent.'

'But you just apologised.'

'Because I insulted your honour with my action.' He rubbed the back of his neck and eyed her sideways. 'You pulled away from me in my library. Did you want me to kiss you?'

How could she answer that and not sound wanton?

'Did you?' he prodded.

She was struggling to find a response when Wilkins arrived with the tea tray. He placed the tray on the table between them and quietly left the room, once again leaving the door open.

'Oh, look! The tea is here,' she said.

'So it is.' He shifted in his seat and then straightened. 'How fortuitous,' he said dryly.

It was taking quite a bit of effort to hide her relief. 'Tea?'

'Yes.'

'Milk and sugar?'

'Neither, thank you.'

Katrina glanced at him in surprise.

'I don't enjoy my tea sweet,' he offered.

'Apparently,' she replied, handing him his cup.

He looked over at Meg and then back at her, and then placed his cup and saucer on the table. He kept his voice low. 'Aside from offering my apologies to you, I also have another reason for calling on you today.'

'Which is…?'

'While I was out this morning I saw this and thought you might enjoy it.' He held out a wrapped package she hadn't noticed he had been holding when he entered.

'You know I cannot accept it,' she said, pouring a splash of milk into her own cup.

'Please—think of it as a way for me to extend my thanks for the book you sent to my grandmother.'

'Or a peace offering?'

Amusement sparkled in his eyes. 'If you like.'

She hesitantly placed her cup on the table and took the package. As she unwrapped it her eyes widened. '*Frankenstein*. I want to read this.'

'I thought you might. You were looking at it the day we met at Hatchards.'

Her hands fell to her lap, still holding the book. 'You remember that?'

He leaned in closer and lowered his voice. 'I also remember your maid's love of gothic tales, so you might want to consider hiding it from her.'

Thunder boomed in the distance.

'That is probably a wise suggestion.'

'I thought so.'

'Have you read it?'

He shook his head and leaned back. 'No. However, I purchased a copy for myself as well and thought to begin it tonight.'

This time thunder shook the room, and Katrina glanced

at the closest window. Rain poured down the panes, obstructing the view of the street. 'It does appear to be an ideal day to read such a tale. It would be a shame not to take advantage of this atmosphere. Would you like to begin reading it now?'

'You mean together?'

'Certainly. Unless I am keeping you from a pressing engagement?'

'I'm intrigued by your suggestion. How do you propose we begin?'

'I suppose each of us could read silently, if you find that acceptable?' It might prove difficult to concentrate on the words if she had to listen to his deep voice read them.

He nodded, and then his eyes widened as she lifted her delicate chair and placed it next to the settee.

'I do not believe I have ever witnessed a lady moving furniture before. You *do* have other servants, do you not?'

'Of course. But I am fully capable of moving this chair, and it would have delayed our enjoyment if we'd had to wait for them.' She settled herself into the chair and smiled over at him.

'You do realise you could sit here on the settee with me? There is room for both of us,' he said.

Thunder boomed again. 'No, I do not believe that would be a wise idea.' He smelled heavenly—like clean soap and leather.

'You are next to me now.'

But this way there was no risk of her caressing his arm or making a cake of herself in any other way. 'I am already settled quite nicely here. Please—won't you open to the first page so we may begin?'

Lyonsdale arched his brow, appearing every inch the aristocrat he was. 'So I shall be the one to hold the book?'

'You are the man. I thought it was your chivalrous ob-ligation to hold the book while I read.'

'But I am a duke, so I thought you would be holding the book for *me*,' he said with amusement in his eyes.

'Yes, but I am an American. We believe that every man is created equal.'

His gaze raked her body. 'But you are not a man.'

'You've noticed.'

'It has not escaped my notice.'

Katrina found the room suddenly quite warm, and she smiled at him through her lashes.

He gave an exaggerated sigh. 'Very well. I will be your chivalrous bookstand.'

She handed him the first book of the three-volume edi-tion. 'I will be very grateful.'

'Will you show me how grateful?'

'What did you have in mind? I could make you more tea?'

'Not exactly what I was thinking.'

'I shall have biscuits sent up.'

By the time Wilkins arrived with a plate of biscuits Ka-trina was leaning over the armrest of the settee, her chin almost resting on Lyonsdale's shoulder. The Duke was ac-tually reclining back on the sofa in a most inelegant pose, with his legs crossed. Their heads were almost touching and they were reading from the same book, completely unaware of the butler's presence.

The two engrossed readers remained that way for over an hour. When they finally stopped reading for the day Lyonsdale closed the book and stared straight ahead, chewing his lower lip. It was proving impossible for Ka-trina to take her eyes off that soft skin.

'I must confess I have never read anything quite like that in my life,' he commented, still appearing very re-laxed in his reclined pose.

He twisted his head towards her and she rushed her gaze up to meet his. There was a twinkle in his green eyes, and she was positive he had caught her pining for his lips.

'Have you?' he asked.

'Hmm…' she managed to utter thoughtfully, not having any notion of what he'd said.

Lyonsdale grinned. 'I asked if you'd ever read anything like this. I certainly haven't.'

'No, I've haven't either. Thank you for purchasing it for me.'

The rain still pelted against the windowpanes and the room echoed with the soft ticking of the mantel clock. He leaned his head closer to her.

Oh, dear, he was going to kiss her!

Katrina's breath caught in her throat and she spun her head towards Meg.

Her wonderfully discreet maid still appeared engrossed in her needlework.

'Meg, perhaps you would like to get some tea for yourself,' she called out.

Raising her head from her mending, Meg shifted her gaze between her mistress and the Duke. She had been Katrina's maid since Katrina was fifteen and Meg twenty-six. They had been together almost ten years, and Katrina knew her well enough to see that Meg wasn't certain if she should leave Katrina alone with Lyonsdale.

Katrina gave her an encouraging nod and Meg placed her mending aside and slowly stood.

'I will not be long,' Meg said, curtsying and leaving the room without closing the door.

When Katrina turned back to Lyonsdale she noticed his satisfied grin. 'I simply sent her for some tea because she has been sitting by that window for hours. She needed a respite.'

He raised both his hands. 'I did not say a word.'

'Would you care for more tea?'

His gaze dropped to her lips. 'What I really want is to kiss you before your maid returns.'

Pointing her finger at him, Katrina let out an exasperated breath. 'I did not send her away so you could kiss me.'

His brow wrinkled in confusion. 'You truly do not want me to kiss you?'

She should never have sent Meg away. Lyonsdale was much too charming. Kissing him would be a great mistake. They had no future together. What if his kisses made her lose her breath? What would she do then?

With the tips of his fingers he gently raised her chin. 'Tell me now, before your maid returns. Will you allow me to kiss you?'

Oh, how she longed to know what his kisses would feel like. Losing her ability to speak, Katrina simply nodded her head. His lips curved into a slow smile as he traced her lower lip with his thumb. Then he lowered his head and kissed her softly.

The simple touch of his lips against hers left Katrina wanting more.

Julian knew from the moment he stroked Katrina's tempting lower lip that stopping at one kiss would be close to impossible. As it was, it took all his effort not to pull her on top of him after one innocent kiss. Shifting his head, he nipped her mouth until her lips parted. She tasted like sweet tea and something wonderful.

With her hand tentatively resting on his chest, she hesitated a moment before deepening the kiss. This was heaven.

She was kissing him back, gently exploring his mouth. His cravat was growing tight, along with his breeches. He needed to stop, but it was painful to think he had to release her from his arms. Reluctantly, he pulled his head back.

Her eyes were still closed, and her lips held a faint smile. He was about to kiss her again when her lashes fluttered open, revealing eyes that were his favourite shade of blue. Transfixed by the sensuous sight she made, Julian knew at that moment that he never wanted Miss Vandenberg to kiss anyone else.

'I thought you said just one kiss,' she uttered breathlessly.

'Forgive me. I will strive to do better next time,' he teased.

'I believe you are much too confident in your charms.' She smiled as she lowered her hand from his chest and placed it on her lap.

'Perhaps I am.' He picked up a loose tendril of her hair and rubbed the silky lock between his fingers before hooking it over her ear. 'It was a pleasure reading with you.'

'I enjoyed it thoroughly.'

That smile of hers warmed him even further. 'How long do you anticipate remaining in London?'

She gave a slight shrug. 'It is difficult to tell. A few months, I suppose. Hopefully the negotiations between our two countries will progress smoothly.'

The notion of her leaving and his never seeing her again was burning like acid in his gut. Soon he would approach Morley about his daughter. Then his life would be spent devoted to his responsibilities in the company of a woman he was indifferent towards. Deep down he knew he would never feel as happy as he did at this very moment with Miss Vandenberg. He didn't want the feeling to end. Not now, anyway.

'I have a proposition for you.' Even before the words were out of his mouth he couldn't believe he was actually going to ask her. He needed to spend less time in

Hart's company. 'Would you consider finishing the book with me?'

'You mean continue to read it together?'

'Yes. I realise it is highly irregular. But you were the one to originally suggest it. You once told me you have no intention of marrying an Englishman. And a man in my position must marry a woman from the highest levels of English Society. But you must admit we do enjoy each other's company. I see no harm in spending some more time together before our lives change course.'

She bit her lip. 'Even as an American I know it would not be proper. My reputation would be ruined.'

'I assure you we would see each other in secret. No one would ever know.' He took her hand in his and placed it over his heart. 'On my honour, I would not do anything to jeopardise your reputation.'

She leaned towards him and a mischievous sparkle lit her eyes. 'Then it would be our secret?'

He liked the idea of sharing something only with her. It felt…intimate. 'Yes. It would be our secret.'

This was an ideal solution to his problem. It would be easier for him to proceed with marrying Lady Mary if thoughts of Miss Vandenberg weren't floating through his head all the time. He'd wager that familiarity would lead to boredom. The more time he spent with her, the more quickly he would realise she was not that remarkable. It made perfect sense.

There was just one more thing that would make this arrangement perfect. 'And when we are alone together you can call me Julian.'

She eyed him sideways and he thought she was going to refuse, until another mischievous smile crossed her lips. 'Very well, Julian. Then you must call me Katrina.'

He knew in his bones that from this moment on she would always be Katrina to him.

Her body appeared to dance with excitement as she shifted in her seat. 'Do you promise not to tell a soul?' she asked.

They grinned at each other like two children conspiring to steal all the Christmas treats.

'I promise. And you? You must also promise not to share this with anyone.'

'My lips are sealed,' she said through a smile. 'Fortunately for you I have a strong desire to know how this story ends.'

Chapter Fourteen

Three nights later, Katrina noticed two things about the
Whitfields' impressive entrance hall. The first was that
her drawing room could easily fit inside it. The second
was that the large black and white marble floor resembled one large chessboard, which was appropriate since
the happenings of the *ton* always appeared to be a stra-
tegic game.

She had not seen Julian since he had called on her and
proposed their secret pact. It felt like weeks, although
she knew it had only been days. He'd said he would call
again when he was not busy with his affairs at Westminster. She did not want to interfere with his duties, but if
this continued it would take them over a month to finish
reading the book.

Sarah tapped her wrist. 'Do not look to your left,' she
whispered into Katrina's ear. 'Lyonsdale is standing by
the staircase and has eyed you very intently from your
slippers to your hair. You cannot tell me that man does
not have an interest in you.'

Katrina's heartbeat quickened and she had an urge to
adjust her hair. Reliving his kiss, she refused look at him,
certain she would blush. Surely Sarah would be able to tell
they were now more than passing acquaintances.

'Sarah, you have to stop. Someone might overhear you.'

'But do you not want to know that his eyes are still on you?' Sarah looked at Katrina with a wrinkled brow. 'Why will you not even acknowledge him?'

At this moment she couldn't acknowledge him. If she did, everyone around her would know they shared a secret. It would be impossible to hide it in her expression.

Katrina was saved from responding by the appearance of Madame de Lieven, who glided up to them on the arm of Mr Armstrong. It was the first time she could recall being happy to see the woman.

'Miss Vandenberg, Miss Forrester—how lovely to see both of you again. You remember Mr Armstrong?'

Katrina recalled the hawk-like features of the youngest son of Lord Greely. 'Of course. How do you do, Mr Armstrong?'

'Quite well. I had the opportunity to speak with Wellington at length earlier.' His chest was puffed out a bit more than usual. 'I am acquainted with him, don't you know?'

Katrina watched him raise his quizzing glass and observe the room. When his quizzer rested on her, Katrina raised her chin until he lowered the glass.

'Pray tell, Miss Vandenberg, have you found the time to explore Town yet? I am certain it's like no place you have imagined,' he said.

'I find London most diverting,' she replied politely.

His lips rose in a superior smile. 'I notice you were extended vouchers to attend Almack's. You dance very well for an American.'

How exactly should one respond to a comment like that? She was never certain. Glancing to her right, she noticed Sarah's attention was on her slippers, her pursed lips giving away her amusement.

'I understand you know how to waltz?' Mr Armstrong continued.

Oh, no. No. No. No. Why couldn't she have talked with him later in the evening, when her waltzes might have all been claimed?

'I do,' Katrina replied slowly, glancing at Madame de Lieven. She caught the knowing glint in the woman's eye.

'I believe that's the beginning of one now. If this dance isn't claimed, would you do me the honour of dancing with me, Miss Vandenberg?' He held his arm out to her.

She wanted to flee. If she waltzed with him she would have to spend time with him for longer than any human being should be required to be in his company. However, if she declined his invitation she would be forced to sit out every dance. That would lead to a very dull evening.

She had no choice but to take his arm. If only he were Julian.

Julian stood near the threshold of the ballroom and watched Lord Greely's whelp escort Katrina onto the dance floor. Even in the low light coming from the chandeliers above he had no difficulty tracing her graceful form as she moved through the waltz. She was a vision in white organza and blue silk. He could watch her all night...

'I would not wait too long to pursue her. She will be taken if you do,' Hart commented casually.

Julian took a sip of what he was certain was watered-down Madeira and wished he had borrowed his grandmother's flask. 'I don't need your advice.'

'Apparently Armstrong has no objection to the lady's nationality. Maybe he likes leprechauns...or would the children be wee beasties? I cannot recall.'

'What do you suppose he is up to?' Julian wondered out loud as he narrowed his gaze.

'Isn't it obvious? The man appreciates a pretty face and a lithe form. He might even enjoy dancing.'

'I've never trusted him,' Julian said, eyeing the couple over the rim of his glass.

'Really? You don't trust him with all things or with your Miss V?'

'She isn't mine, and I have never trusted him about anything. He is a sycophant and always has been.'

'You are aware there is a bet placed in White's about the two of you.'

'Me and Armstrong?'

'No, you dolt. You and Miss V.'

Julian's heart began to pound. He had only called on her that one time, and he had taken pains to walk to her house in the pouring rain with a rather large umbrella. How could someone know of their secret arrangement?

'How was I not aware of this?'

Hart shrugged. 'Do you really care? There are plenty of bets placed about me. I pay them no heed.'

A tic formed in Julian's jaw. 'What does it say?'

'The bet is on how long it will take for you to enter into a liaison with her.'

Julian had a sudden need to crush something—or someone. He consciously relaxed his hold on his glass. At least the bet was not about *if* he was having a liaison with her already.

'Who placed the bet?'

Hart resumed watching the dancers and crossed his arms. 'Don't recall. They really are stunning together... all that golden glory. I imagine their children will be very attractive. Unless, of course, they do take on the appearance of green beasties.'

'You're an ass.'

'So you have said—time and again,' Hart replied with amusement. 'Shall we play some cards? I have a hunting box in Scotland that Lord Middlebury must be missing. I am feeling generous and may lose it to him.'

* * *

Helena stepped to the edge of the dance floor and studied the woman who had captured Lyonsdale's attention. Could this be the woman who had somehow persuaded Lyonsdale to waltz with her at Almack's?

Elizabeth, the Duchess of Skeffington, approached her side. 'I am amazed we are listening to a quartet this evening. And the wine is positively insipid. It appears, Helena, that the Whitfields are not as prosperous as they once were. I would not be surprised if young Whitfield is hunting an heiress this very night.'

When Helena made no reply, her friend continued. 'That is a lovely gown she is wearing. I believe by the cut it's French. It certainly cannot be American-made.'

Helena shifted her gaze. 'To whom are you referring, Lizzy?'

'Oh, forgive me. I thought you were watching Miss Vandenberg—the woman dancing with Mr Armstrong.'

'Why would I concern myself with someone dancing with a mere third son?'

'Because she is the woman Lyonsdale waltzed with at Almack's. I was watching them that night. He appeared quite taken with her. I assumed you had heard. It was on everyone's lips the next day.'

Of course she had heard about his waltz. She paid attention to every bit of gossip in the papers. One never knew when it might be used to one's advantage. However, Lyonsdale had danced with the woman only once, and she had assumed it was for political reasons.

'You never said anything to me.'

'As I said, I assumed you had already heard. You know how much I loathe gossip. It was astonishing to see, though. He appeared to be smiling that night. I don't believe I have ever seen him do so with a woman.'

The American was still turning about the floor in her

waltz. Her hair was the colour of straw, and her lips were too thin. The gown she wore covered a form that did not possess breasts or hips that would bring a man to his knees.

'Who is she?' Helena asked her friend.

Lizzy's eyes brightened. 'She is the daughter of Mr Peter Vandenberg, the American author who is here on diplomatic affairs. One would think London was full of bluestockings, with all the talk of his book.'

They stood in silence, each watching Miss Vandenberg.

'It's fascinating,' Lizzy continued, 'that when Lyonsdale chose to waltz it was with an American. That's rather…humbling.' Lizzy eyed Helena over her fan. 'I've not witnessed you and Lyonsdale conversing tonight.'

An unwelcome flush crept up Helena's neck and she forced herself to appear relaxed. Was it possible that he had ended their affair because of a provincial colonial? What did it say about her that he had replaced her with an American? She stole a glance at the men and women standing around them. Were they discussing it behind their fans and casting judgement?

'Surely you haven't been watching him all evening,' she said to Lizzy, pushing her nails further into her gloved fist.

She needed to ensure no attachment was forming between Lyonsdale and the American woman before she found herself the subject of gossip in the papers for her smug brother to gloat over.

Chapter Fifteen

For a ball consisting of weak beverages and a poor choice in musicians, Katrina found there was quite a crush. Apparently the Whitfield name meant something to the *ton*. She excused herself from Sarah and Mrs Forrester to find a bit of a reprieve in the ladies' retiring room. When she crossed the threshold, she was relieved to find the delicate gilded chairs were empty and the sole occupant was a maid, who remained by the door.

Walking towards a wall hung with mirrors, Katrina peered at her reflection. She had a rosy glow, which sadly was the result of heat and not from the joy of dancing with her various partners. They hadn't exactly been horrible partners. They just weren't Julian. If she had been dancing with him her glow might have been from an amusing conversation—or from the way her body seemed to catch fire whenever he was near.

She missed him. She assumed he was keeping his distance so as not to cause speculation. It was an honourable action, but she didn't have to like it. How she wished he would ask her to dance. Then she could listen to that amusing deep voice that warmed her like a cup of chocolate.

Katrina was so absorbed in her thoughts that she almost didn't notice a woman in a Pomona-green silk gown walk up beside her. She was stunning, with perfect delicate features and a thick head of dark hair. The woman studied her own reflection and adjusted the curls near her temples before shifting her grey eyes to Katrina.

'Aren't you that American woman?'

Would there be one ball, one fête she would attend where she wouldn't have to face at least one ignorant comment about Americans?

Katrina held back a sigh, anticipating one of those conversations. 'There are a few Americans in London. Which one do you believe me to be?'

'The author's daughter,' the woman replied, raising her chin.

'By author, do you mean Peter Vandenberg? If so, I am indeed his daughter.'

The woman eyed Katrina critically, from her slippers to her hair. *Did she not realise Katrina could see her?*

'And who might you be?' Katrina asked.

'Oh, I am Lady Wentworth. I am a very dear friend of the Duke of Lyonsdale. I understand you danced with him recently at Almack's?'

That statement had not been uttered by chance. Katrina's muscles tightened like a bowstring. 'His Grace and I did share a dance.'

'He is a handsome man, is he not?'

'I suppose.'

If one liked men who had wavy dark hair, moss-green eyes, chiselled features, and cut a fine form.

Lady Wentworth let out a soft, disgustingly lovely laugh. 'Surely you agree? It's a pity you're American, and therefore could never become his duchess. I can assure you whoever he does marry will be quite fortunate.'

Her lips rose in a sly smile. She leaned close to Katrina's ear, and her hot breath scorched her neck.

'He knows how to do delicious things to make a woman quiver with need.'

She stepped back, looked Katrina directly in the eye, and cocked an arrogant brow. Katrina's stomach rolled and pitched. She would not give this horrid woman the satisfaction of knowing how her words had filled Katrina with a sense of betrayal. Could this be why Julian had not called on her?

After weeks of pretending that English aristocrats didn't bore her to sleep, Katrina had become quite adept at hiding her emotions. She smiled sweetly back at the witch beside her. 'One would imagine that since he is neither married nor publicly displaying a mistress he has yet to find a woman who makes him feel the same in return.'

There—that felt better.

Katrina forced her lips into the brightest smile. 'Do enjoy your evening, Lady Wentworth.'

As if she didn't have a care in the world, Katrina turned and breezed out of the room. Unfortunately the reality was that her world had just become a colder place. She would only be in London for a few months. It shouldn't matter to her that this woman was sharing Julian's bed—but it did.

She needed time away from the ballroom and the sight of Lady Wentworth.

Earlier in the evening she had a pleasant conversation with the Duchess of Winterbourne, who had mentioned there were some lovely landscapes hung along this long, deserted hallway. Now was the perfect time to view them.

The sound of confident footfalls had Katrina praying that the pompous Mr Armstrong had not found her. Turning her head, she was startled when Julian took her arm and tugged her through one of the open doorways into an oak-panelled room.

The sight of three large stuffed birds glaring at her in the moonlight from the round table beside them made her jump, and it took her a moment before she shifted her attention to the man standing a few feet in front of her. Lady Wentworth's comment echoed in her mind, and it occurred to her that all Julian had to do was look at her to make her insides quiver. She had to remind herself he was not the man for her.

'Are you trying to ruin me?' she demanded, placing her hands on her hips. 'What possessed you to drag me in here?'

He stepped closer, creating a cushion of heat between them. No man deserved to look that good in unremarkable formal black evening clothes.

'Of course I'm not trying to ruin you. My committee meetings have been consuming my days. I wanted you to know I have not forgotten about our promise.'

Once more she heard Lady Wentworth's voice.

'Please do not feel obligated to continue to read with me. You're a very busy man, and I'm certain you'd prefer to read the remainder of the book at your leisure.'

He lowered his gaze towards his shiny black dress shoes. 'On the contrary, I would rather read it with you.' As he looked back up at her through his thick lashes a look of confusion crossed his face. 'Do you no longer wish to read with me?'

He was not courting her. She had no claim on him. How could she tell him how she felt without sounding jealous? *Which she absolutely wasn't.*

'Do you really think this is an appropriate place to have a conversation? We should not even be in here together.'

'I had no choice—you would not so much as look at me.'

'I was trying to avoid speculation about us.'

Julian narrowed his eyes and tipped his head back. 'We have spoken before in public. I do not think it would shock people if we were to do so again.'

'And how would you have informed me that you want us to continue reading together with people around us?'

The faint, distant strains of the quartet drifted into the room through the closed door as he flashed her a devilishly handsome smile. 'That is why this is an ideal location for our discussion.' Sliding his hand around her waist to the small of her back, he pulled her to him. 'I cannot stop thinking about you and our kiss.'

Neither could she, and that was a problem. Before she fell asleep she thought about it, over and over. Even at odd moments in the day she would think about the feel of his lips and the taste of his tongue. She had wanted that kiss to go on for ever.

She placed her hands on his solid chest, intending to push him away. Her arms wouldn't move. How she longed to press her body further into his.

A look of what might have been tenderness softened his features. 'You are most unexpected.'

It would be so easy to lose herself in him, but according to Lady Wentworth he was one of many English aristocrats with philandering ways. She would not be one of his conquests.

He lowered his head to hers and his soft breath caressed her lips. This time she pushed against his chest, and he immediately let her go.

'I will not kiss a man who shares his affection with another.' It was said in such a rush she wasn't certain she had been coherent.

He jerked his head back and crossed his arms, his biceps bulging under the sleeves of his coat. 'Are you referring to me?'

She put her hands on her hips. 'Yes—you were the one who looked as if you intended to kiss me.'

'I did want to kiss you… I *do* want to kiss you. However, I'm not sharing my affection with anyone.'

Now it was Katrina's turn to narrow her eyes. 'Not even with your paramour?'

He let out a bark of laughter. 'My what?'

'Your paramour...or mistress. Or do you call her something else?' Katrina huffed. 'I would appreciate it if you would not find so much amusement in what I'm saying.'

'Forgive me,' Julian said, quietening down and trying unsuccessfully to stop smiling. 'I can truly say I have never met any woman quite like you.'

'Simply answer the question, please.'

'What was the question? Oh, yes—well, I don't call her anything because there is no one else.'

'But I thought... That is to say, aren't you...?' Katrina chewed her lip, feeling foolish. She knew she hadn't mistaken Lady Wentworth's insinuation. But who was she to believe? A horrid woman she didn't know or Julian—Julian who felt deeply about honour and duty?

'Do you really think we should be discussing this?' he asked, lowering his head and prompting Katrina with his eyes. 'You know gently bred ladies should not even be aware of such things?'

'Well, I am. I lived in Paris and I have witnessed open displays of indiscretion.'

She had even stumbled upon Comte Janvier and Madame Broussard in a garden once. The Comte's trousers had been down around his knees and Madame Broussard's skirt had been lifted so high Katrina knew exactly what occurred between men and women. However, it wasn't necessary for Julian to know the extent of her knowledge gained from that tableau.

'Are you are telling me there is no one you are sharing your affections with?'

'I have had women in my life in the past with whom I have shared my affections, but no longer. Now I find the only woman I want to share my affections with is you.'

Katrina's heart hammered against her ribs and the room grew unbearably warm. 'Only me?' she let out with a breath.

Slowly and seductively his lips rose into a smile. 'Only you.'

Staring into her eyes, Julian felt overwhelmed by his feelings for her. He lowered his gaze and found his attention riveted to her smooth skin and that enticing birthmark on the upper swell of her left breast. He hardened at the thought of trailing his tongue from that birthmark down to the nipple he knew was hidden under the white organza of the bodice of her gown. He wanted to suck on that nipple until he heard her groan—or moan.

Bloody hell, what would she sound like?

'I wish I knew what you were thinking,' she said, biting her lip.

'There are times when you make it very difficult to be a gentleman.' He pulled her close and crushed his lips to hers. Her mouth was warm and sweet. Best of all, she was kissing him back with as much passion as he felt coursing through his own veins. He could kiss her all night... Until she moved her lower body against his and his trousers tightened even more. Then the image of sliding himself inside her would not leave his brain.

'Say my name,' he said, trailing kisses along her jaw and having the oddest desire to hear his name on her lips.

'Julian...' It came out more like a moan as he softly bit her neck.

As much as he knew he shouldn't, he slid his hand up her waist over the soft fabric of her gown until he cupped her left breast. The weight of it fitted perfectly into his palm, as if she were made just for him. He gave it a gentle squeeze and felt her breath catch in his mouth. Her nipple hardened into a tight bud in his palm. With his eyes closed he broke the kiss, to trail soft nips down the long column of her neck. As he reached her collarbone he pulled on the neckline of her gown and kissed his way along the small swell of her breast, paying special attention to that beguiling birthmark.

Her fingers were digging into his shoulders, and it felt so good. When he swirled his tongue around her sweet, hard nipple she let out a throaty groan that nearly had him laying her down on the table that was next to them. He sucked on it and she softened in his arms. Every subtle response from her body increased his desire to drive deep inside her. The air was quickly leaving the room. It was torture that she was an unmarried woman he couldn't have. This was an urgency of passion such as none he had ever felt before. He needed to know she wanted him just as much as he wanted her. Even if he knew he could not take her.

He began to edge her skirt up and cursed his gloves, which would prevent him from feeling how wet she was. He let go of her gown and kissed her once more. Her eager response matched his. The pressure of her body moved against him, causing friction. He needed to stop before he disgraced himself.

It took a tremendous amount of discipline to pull his head away from her soft breast and step back. When he did, they were both panting hard.

She was a vision, with her lips still wet from his kiss and her left breast exposed. Much to his disappointment she adjusted her bodice and returned to looking like a very proper lady faster than he would have preferred. His body, however, was not showing any signs of softening. He closed his eyes and silently counted off the British monarchs in chronological order.

'Is anything the matter?' she asked. 'You appear to be in pain.'

He laughed at her innocent comment and cracked open one eye. 'I thought you'd lived in Paris.'

Her brows drew together in confusion, and then her expression cleared in some form of understanding. 'Is that why you stopped?'

'I stopped because had I not, I would have had to find some explanation for the state of my trousers for the remainder of the evening.'

He wasn't certain she understood. She opened her mouth to say something but suddenly the door opened—and Miss Forrester walked into the room.

His heart stopped in panic and he felt as if he had run a very long race.

It appeared she hadn't spotted him as she addressed Katrina. 'I cannot believe you are hiding...'

Her eyes darted to Julian and her lips parted. It was remarkable how quickly she composed herself and focused all her attention on Katrina, completely ignoring him.

'Considering how easy it was for me to gain entrance to this room, it might be wise for me to remain to lend you an air of respectability, should anyone else see fit to come in here,' she offered.

Katrina did not appear to be alarmed by Miss Forrester's presence. Hopefully this meant Miss Forrester could be trusted not to reveal their encounter. As much as he liked Katrina, he still had no desire to be forced into marriage. His heartbeat began to slow down.

Katrina's attention remained on Miss Forrester. 'Why were you searching this hallway?'

'Because my mother was concerned that you were taking an inordinately long time in the retiring room and I offered to fetch you. Lucky for both of you I did. I remembered how interested you were in those paintings the Duchess of Winterbourne mentioned, and thought you might be hiding from the remainder of your dancing partners.'

Katrina rubbed her forehead. 'How many dances have I missed?'

'Just one.'

Miss Forrester's presence had alleviated the pull on Julian's trousers and it was now safe for him to return to the ball. He would leave it to Katrina to find an explanation for her friend. But before he was able to excuse himself, the door opened again. This time Hart stepped inside.

If this kept up she was sure to be ruined!

Even in the moonlit room there was no mistaking the amused glint Julian saw in his friend's eye as he glanced from Miss Forrester to Miss Vandenberg and finally to Julian. Hart casually leaned his back against the door and crossed his arms. His smirk was not appreciated.

'I say...this *is* interesting.'

Miss Forrester stepped forward, as if to block Hart's view of Katrina. 'Miss Vandenberg and I entered the room just a few minutes ago. We were unaware that His Grace was already in here.'

Hart bit his lip and nodded sagely. 'I see—and what exactly drew you two ladies to this remote location?'

'Taxidermy.'

'Pardon?'

Miss Forrester raised her chin and crossed her arms. Apparently she was standing her ground. 'I said taxidermy.'

Hart rubbed the smile off his lips. 'I see. And what specimens drew you to this room, exactly?'

She waved her hand carelessly behind her. 'Birds.'

'So you have an interest in ornithology?'

'Ye-e-e-s,' she replied, drawing out the word.

'And what particular species were you interested in seeing?'

'Well, whatever species His Lordship has, of course.'

'Of course.' Hart tossed back the lock of hair that fell near his eyes.

He was having too much fun at Julian's expense. Hopefully he could convince Hart not to tell their friends about this.

Miss Forrester took a step forward, crossed her arms, and tipped her head to the side. 'And you, my lord. What brings *you* to this far corner of the ball? There is nothing of interest here.'

'On the contrary—I have an interest in birds as well,' he said through a smirk.

She looked as if she was about to reply.

Hart held up his hand. 'I assume you are finished with your studies in this darkened room, so we will say it's been a pleasure and allow you ladies to return to this evening's entertainments.'

Miss Forrester grabbed Katrina by the hand and pulled her towards the door. 'That's very kind of you. Good evening, gentlemen.'

Katrina glanced back at Julian one last time with a regretful look before she was dragged out through the door. He didn't even get a chance to say goodbye to her, or to kiss her one last time for the night.

Hart closed the door and locked it. Why hadn't Julian thought to lock the door earlier? Perhaps it was because he'd never needed to do so before. This was the first and only time he had ever stole away with a woman at a ball.

'You and I need to have a talk,' Hart said. 'And I know just the place to have it.'

They walked two doors down to the Whitfields' billiard room, and Hart racked up the balls without saying a word. Julian grabbed two cues from the rack on the wall, grateful for the short reprieve. Once the balls were set, they flipped Hart's lucky coin to see who would go first. Julian won.

He leaned over the Whitfields' billiard table and released his cue. He watched the balls scatter.

Shaking his head, he turned to Hart. 'How in the world did you find us?'

'As luck would have it I was supposed to be meeting someone there shortly. It appears you and I need to begin coordinating our appointments.'

Julian narrowed his gaze. 'That won't be necessary. What you witnessed was a mere coincidence.'

Hart walked around the billiard table, analysing the best angle for his shot. He looked as if he was trying to hold back a smirk. 'I see. We can move forward with that story if you like. But I will say it is fortunate it appears you have gained another ally in Miss Forrester.'

Julian rested his hand on top of his cue and watched Hart line up his shot. 'Why do you believe it is a good thing to have Miss Forrester as an ally?'

Aside from the fact that she wouldn't gossip about what she'd found when she had walked into the room.

'To gain the support of your lady's friend is always a good thing. Just think of all the ways we could use her.'

Julian sent him a stern look.

'I mean you. All the ways *you* could use her.'

'I will not be using anyone. Nor will you. And Miss Vandenberg is not my lady. It was an accidental encounter, nothing more.'

'If you say so,' Hart said, taking his shot.

Hart never agreed so easily. This was not a good sign.

Chapter Sixteen

The late morning sun warmed Katrina's garden as she sat
on a wooden bench with her box of watercolours. Peering
closely at a teacup filled with violets, she concentrated
on trying to recreate this small reminder of home. As she
swirled her sable-haired brush through the purple and blue
paint Julian's comment about the colour of her eyes when
they'd sat together with his grandmother drifted into her
thoughts. It made her smile.

Glancing down, she realised she'd muddled the colours together into an unusable mess. There had to be a
way to shove him out of her mind. She closed her eyes,
took a deep breath of the floral-scented air, and listened
to the birds chirp around her. If she tried hard enough she
could imagine she was sitting in her garden back home
in Tarrytown, overlooking the sparkling Hudson River.

It was peaceful there.

It was quiet.

'Have you managed to fall asleep like that?'

Katrina opened one eye and met Sarah's quizzical gaze.
And just like that her peaceful bubble burst.

'What were you doing?' Sarah asked, taking a seat on
the bench across from her.

Katrina cleaned her paintbrush in a glass of water. 'I was resting my eyes.'

'It is lovely here in the shade,' Sarah said as she untied the cinnamon silk ribbon of her straw bonnet and casually tossed it beside her. 'And what a charming bunch of violets. I have little skill with a paintbrush, much to my mother's displeasure.'

'Skill or patience?'

'Both, I suppose. How long will that take you to complete?'

Katrina shrugged and continued to add petals to the paper. 'I find the process soothing.'

Or at least it had been until Sarah began rhythmically tapping her foot on the gravel.

'Is there something you wanted, Sarah?'

'I was hoping you would accompany me to Bond Street.'

'We were shopping only yesterday.'

'I've reconsidered those slippers. You remember? The ones with the fine needlework?'

'I have no wish to move along with the crowds today. Could it possibly wait for another day?'

'I suppose it could, but— What is that?'

Katrina looked up to find Wilkins, walking towards them on the garden path, carrying a large vase of purple and yellow flowers. As he drew closer, she realised they weren't exactly flowers.

'Pardon me, miss. These came for you, and I was wondering what you would like me to do with this unusual arrangement?'

'Aren't those weeds?' Sarah asked, as she narrowed her eyes at the objects in question.

'I believe so, Miss Forrester,' he replied. 'Thistle and ragwort, if I am not mistaken. Would you prefer I place the stems in the garden for you, miss?'

Although they were indeed weeds, the arrangement had been created with obvious care. Katrina thought the contrast of purple and yellow to be rather striking. But why would someone send them to her?

'Did they arrive with a note, Wilkins?'

He handed her a folded piece of paper sealed with a blob of red wax.

True beauty resides in the most unexpected places.

When she read the message she knew they could only have come from one man—the only man who had ever told her she was 'most unexpected'. She folded the paper and brought it to her lips to cover her smile. He was clever. She would give him that. And, as much as she tried, it was difficult to remain unaffected by Julian.

When she directed Wilkins to place them in her bedroom he stared at her as if she belonged in Bedlam. The moment he was far enough away, Sarah jumped up and sat next to her.

'Who are they from? Did Mr Armstrong send them?'

'No, he did not. They're from an acquaintance.'

Sarah eyed her with open curiosity. 'If someone sent me weeds I do not believe I would be smiling. Unless—' Her eyes widened with realisation and she snapped her lips shut. She waited until Wilkins had disappeared through the terrace door before she continued. 'They are from Lyonsdale.'

Katrina looked away. 'What would cause you to believe so?'

'Because you only smile like that when he is near. What did the card say?'

'It is of little importance.'

'Why will you not tell me?' Sarah said, fisting her hands on her lap.

Katrina turned back to her friend. 'There is nothing to tell.'

'After finding the two of you together, I wish you would admit you fancy him.'

She could not allow herself to think such thoughts. If she thought too much about how she felt about him heartache would be her only reward. 'What good would it do? We have no future together.'

'The Duke's questionable taste in botanicals paints a different picture. Has he called on you?'

Katrina rubbed the tightness in her chest. She hated lying to Sarah, but she and Julian had promised not to tell anyone about their secret agreement. 'Of course not. The man is a duke and I am American. I possess no title and have no impressive heritage. And, I have heard rumours that he is carrying on a liaison with Lady Wentworth.' *Now* Sarah would stop pestering her about him.

'You are prettier.'

Katrina sent her an incredulous look. It was an admirable attempt on her friend's part, but Katrina knew how beautiful Lady Wentworth was.

'Well, you are more amiable, and probably much more intelligent.'

That made Katrina laugh, and she was grateful to have found such a good friend.

'Why do you believe he sent those…weeds?' Sarah continued.

Katrina shrugged and returned her focus to the violets. His cheeky gesture had made her smile.

'You cannot convince me you are indifferent to him, and he is obviously quite taken with you. Let me help you with this.'

'Oh, no,' Katrina said, pointing her paintbrush at Sarah. 'Do not do a thing. Do you understand, Sarah?'

'But I can help you. As you are aware, my presence

will add an air of discretion to your encounters, and it will also protect you in the event that you discover his taste in most things is consistent with his taste in botanicals. Please let me help you.'

'I said no. Do not misinterpret a fond regard for romance.'

'But he kissed you!'

'What?' Katrina glanced around in panic, her heart racing.

'At the Whitfield ball. You cannot tell me he did not kiss you. When I entered that room you looked like a woman about to swoon.'

She needed to stop the pounding of her heart. 'I do not swoon. I never swoon. And, more importantly, we did not kiss. There was no kiss.'

'Well, there should have been! You need to be around him more.'

'Sarah!'

'I am simply stating my opinion.'

Chapter Seventeen

The Forresters' barouche rolled through Richmond under a canopy of trees as a soft breeze blew. The coachman guided the team of four to a raised mound where trees and shrubs dotted a grassy lawn that sloped off in all directions. Sarah chose a shady area under an old cascading willow tree as the perfect spot for a picnic.

If Katrina had to spend a day without being near Julian, at least she was in a pretty place.

After setting a large wicker hamper on the white cotton blanket, Sarah's footman returned to the barouche.

'This really was a fine idea, and at this early hour I'd be surprised if we encounter anyone else for hours.' Katrina began unpacking the food from the hamper. 'I can't recall the last time I was on a picnic. Whatever made you think of this?'

Sarah gave a careless shrug. 'It came to me the other day when I was in Hyde Park. I was told this is an ideal place to pass the time. Spending the day away from London is a nice reprieve from all the calls we must make and the dull visitors we must receive.'

'Whatever would I do without you?'

Sarah's lips turned up in a mischievous grin. 'Trust me when I say you would be lost without me.'

* * *

Not far away, two riders were racing through a clearing at top speed. The coat-tails of the rider in front flapped in the wind behind him. A satisfied smile rested on his lips. The second rider clutched his horse tightly with his muscular thighs. His slightly long black hair whipped into his eyes as he angled his body lower, attempting to outrun his opponent. His face was set in an expression of pure determination, and he was oblivious to the scenery around him.

Julian kept his eyes fixed on the grove of trees that marked the finish line. 'You'll never outrun me!' he yelled over the pounding of hoofbeats.

'This race isn't over yet!' Hart yelled back as he pulled his horse directly to the left of Julian's.

Julian's horse was ahead by a neck when they reached the trees. As he pulled in the reins he spun his horse around and laughed. 'And that, my friend, is how you win a race.'

'You don't say? I would not have noticed you had won if you had been remiss in mentioning it.'

'That is why I knew it was my duty to do so.'

Julian had forgotten how much he enjoyed flying through the fields at top speed. He was glad Hart had suggested this outing. He could have called on Katrina today, but he had been shaken by the intensity of his need for her when they'd been alone at the Whitfields' ball. His carelessness at not locking the door had almost cost her her reputation. Fortunately Hart valued discretion. The next time he was alone with her, if they were not careful, they might not be so lucky.

'You realise I held back?' Hart said, breathing hard. He tossed his head to move the lock of hair that fell over his eye. The lock slid down again.

'Yes, you have the appearance of a man who took his time,' Julian replied, smirking.

'I do, don't I? In any event, it was a fine race. Let's find a spot in the shade to rest the horses. I do believe I have a flask somewhere on me.' Hart searched their surroundings and smiled. 'Maybe we could beg refreshment from those fair ladies sitting in the shade,' he said, gesturing with his head.

There was a large willow tree with a thick covering of branches swaying slightly in the breeze. It wasn't until a strong gust of wind blew the branches aside that he spied the women sitting under it. How was it possible that Katrina was sitting not far from him on the park-like grounds of Hart's estate? She was wearing a straw bonnet, a white and blue striped gown, and a blue spencer—and she was stunning.

Watching the men approach lazily on horseback, Katrina wondered why she had chosen this particular bonnet to wear today. She was certain there was a better choice in her wardrobe somewhere.

'I do believe that is Lyonsdale and Lord Hartwick,' Sarah said softly, smiling at the men as they rode closer. 'What a strange coincidence that they're here today as well.'

Katrina watched her friend with suspicious eyes. 'You couldn't possibly have known...could you?'

'How could I have known they would be here? It isn't as if I am a friend of either His Grace or Lord Hartwick. You look quite fetching, by the way. Your face has a bit of a pink glow.'

Katrina glared at her friend.

'I am simply stating my opinion,' continued Sarah.

By the time the men reached them Katrina could hear her heart pounding in her ears. She watched Julian pull his mount to a stop under the tree. The footman approached as well.

Sarah motioned him away. 'You may stand with the carriage. We will not be requiring your assistance.'

'Ladies, what a pleasant surprise,' Lord Hartwick said with a tip of his head. 'I was not aware that you were acquainted with this place.'

'This is our first foray here, my lord. It's quite picturesque,' Sarah replied in an overly pleasant voice.

Julian arched his brow at Katrina and she lifted her shoulder in a slight shrug. To her, he appeared to be a suspect in this 'chance encounter' as well.

'This is one of my favourite places,' Lord Hartwick said. 'The view from here is rather stunning. Have you had an opportunity to study the landmarks, Miss Forrester?'

'Why, no, I can't say that I have.'

Lord Hartwick jumped down from his horse and held his hand out to Sarah. 'Would you be interested in having me point them out to you?'

One might think there was a fire on the blanket, watching the speed with which Sarah stood. 'That is most kind of you, Lord Hartwick.'

Katrina suppressed the urge to trip her as they brushed the cascading branches out of their way and walked to the look-out with his horse trailing behind.

Julian slid out of his saddle and tied the reins to a branch. Patches of sunlight danced along his brown coat through the leaves.

He gestured towards the blanket with his hand. 'May I?'

She nodded as she took off her least favourite bonnet.

After he had accepted a glass of Madeira, he stretched out his legs. 'I only decided on this adventure last night. How did you arrange this?'

Katrina wondered why she had never noticed that his

legs were so long and powerful. She raised her gaze to meet his. 'I didn't arrange this. I assumed you did.'

They both turned to find their friends occupied with viewing the scenery through the trees. 'You do realise you are on his land?'

It would take a great deal of control not to trip Sarah at some point today. 'I was not aware. Sarah never said…'

'They believe they are quite clever.'

'I believe they are two people who should never be left alone together. In some ways they are far too much alike. Does he know?'

He appeared affronted by her question. 'About our arrangement? No, I vowed not to tell anyone. Does she know?'

Katrina shook her head. 'It was difficult not to tell her, but I too have kept our secret.'

He looked back at their friends. 'I wonder what they would say if we told them we might have been alone in your home if it weren't for their assistance.'

'I believe my picnic would come to a rather abrupt end.'

'And I believe my friend would suddenly remember an important meeting back in Town.'

The sight of Julian's soft lips curving into a smile left her mouth dry. While she had been attracted to him before, knowing what his kisses did to her was a complete distraction now. Did those kisses have any effect on him as well? Would he want to kiss her again?

She took a sip of Madeira. 'While we are waiting for them to stop pretending they are interested in the view, I was wondering if you might offer some assistance in a matter that has been troubling me.'

A look of concern crossed his face. 'Of course.'

'Recently I received a substantial bouquet of thistle and ragwort. Unfortunately the sender was remiss in signing the card. I don't suppose you would have any idea who in London might send such a thing?'

His brow creased, but he had a hint of a smile. 'Someone sent you weeds? How unusual. Does that happen often?'

'Never. I found the colour combination quite striking, and I wish to show my appreciation to the sender for their thoughtfulness. But, alas, I don't know who to thank.' She smiled innocently.

His gaze dropped to her lips. 'And how would you show that appreciation?'

'I don't believe it would be proper to divulge that to anyone but the sender. A pity, that…'

'Yes, a pity.' He shifted slightly. 'You can give me an idea, though?'

'No. I don't believe I can.' Katrina averted her eyes as she tried not to smile.

He leaned towards her. 'Not even a hint?'

She shook her head and took another sip of Madeira.

Julian swallowed hard.

She bit back a smile. Perhaps he did want to kiss her again. There had to be something they could talk about that did not conjure up thoughts of his lips on her skin. Her breasts began to tingle and she almost spilled her wine.

'Do you ride here often?' she asked, all in one breath.

It took him a moment to answer, as if his thoughts had been far from where they were. 'I haven't in an age. Although Hart and I have enjoyed racing up this mound for many years.'

'I assume from the familiar way you refer to him that you are great friends?'

He nodded. 'We are. I have known him all my life. Our family estates border one another, and we attended Cambridge together. And you and Miss Forrester—are you great friends?'

'I feel we are becoming so. I was introduced to her years ago in Washington, and now we share a similar circumstance in a foreign land. She has a good heart, and we have similar tastes in amusement.'

'Is Washington your home?'

'While I've spent considerable time there, my home is in New York. We have a residence not far from New York Harbour, where my father owns a shipyard, but we also own a home further north in Tarrytown, along the Hudson River, away from the hustle and bustle of town.'

It appeared as if he wanted to say something, but he wasn't sure how to put it into words.

Katrina tilted her head and studied his uncomfortable expression. 'Is there something you want to ask me?'

'I understand he is a widower. I was wondering... That is to say...'

'Do you wish to know about my mother?'

He nodded. 'Forgive me, I am certain it is a subject you do not wish to discuss.'

'There is no need to apologise for your interest. My mother died long ago.'

An unsettled expression crossed his face as he turned away. 'You have my condolences.'

'Thank you.'

She had never known her mother. From what she could tell from her father, her parents had loved each other deeply. That was what she wanted in a marriage.

She studied Julian's chiselled profile. He was an honourable man. He was easy to speak with and he made her laugh. Would she find a man like him when she returned to America? Her heart grew heavy, and she reached for more wine.

'You mentioned you have known Lord Hartwick since you were children. I cannot imagine you so young. What were you like?'

He appeared to consider her question thoroughly. Then his lips curved and his eyes sparkled. 'I wanted to be a pirate.'

That was an unexpected revelation. 'If I promise to keep your secret, will you tell me if you were successful?'

He smiled. 'I did have a swordfight in a boat. Do you suppose that counts?'

'I suppose. Did it have a crew?'

'I presided over a crew of one. My first mate attempted a mutiny, hence the swordfight. Apparently he was tired of rowing.'

'Your first mate didn't happen to be Lord Hartwick?'

Julian laughed and shook his head. 'Actually, it was my brother, Edward.'

That was a new revelation. Why had she never seen his brother at any of the social engagements she had attended?

'I was unaware you had a brother.'

'I did. He was killed in a riding accident nine years ago—a month before my father died.' Pain and loss were reflected in his eyes.

She held out her hand to offer some comfort. He threaded his fingers through hers and then stared at their intertwined hands as if he had never seen his hand placed with another.

'Were you very close?'

A sad smile crossed his lips. 'We were born only ten months apart and were inseparable.'

'You are very fortunate to have had him in your life, even for a short while. I always wanted a brother or a sister to share in my amusements. And I have a sneaking suspicion the two of you might have enjoyed a bit of mischief together.'

His eyes crinkled at the corners as a full smile brightened his previously melancholy demeanour and he let go of her hand. 'We might have found ourselves in trouble a time or two. I recall one autumn we decided to hide in piles of leaves and startle the gardeners as they worked on tidying up the gardens around our estate. I don't believe they found it as amusing as we did.'

'Did you receive a scolding or did news of your antics never reach your parents?'

'My parents were unaware. However, my grandmother informed us that if the gardeners refused to clean up the leaves Edward and I would be forced to do it ourselves.' He rubbed his hands on his thighs, as if he was eager to recount another amusing tale. 'There was also one summer when a vast number of frogs were mysteriously finding their way into my mother's bedchamber.' He let out an uncharacteristically loud bark of laughter. 'To this day I can still recall the sound of her screeches each time she discovered one.'

How was it possible that this reputable duke was more mischievous as a child than she had ever been? The very thought of his very dour mother jumping around her bedchamber made Katrina laugh.

It surprised Julian that there wasn't any hollowness in his chest as he discussed Edward. In fact, in an odd way, he felt closer to his brother now than he had in a long time.

A dragonfly landed on his sleeve and fluttered its wings for a few moments before it flew away.

His brow furrowed. 'Are you eager to head back to America?'

'It's not easy to be away so long from what is comfortable and familiar.'

'I suppose it isn't,' he agreed, out of politeness. All his life everything around Julian had been familiar— everything except the way he felt being with this woman. Being around Katrina made him feel somehow different, somehow more alive.

'I say, Miss Forrester, may I open that bottle of wine for you?' Hart asked as he and Miss Forrester joined them on the blanket.

Julian dragged his gaze away from Katrina. 'Did you enjoy the scenery?'

'Miss Forrester and I took note of every building we were able to see from here—twice.' Hart poured some wine and handed the glass to Katrina's friend. 'I say, Miss Vandenberg, is that pigeon pie?'

'It is, my lord. Would you care for some?'

'Yes, please,' Hart said, sending her one of his charming smiles. 'And you do not have to "my lord" me, Miss Vandenberg. Hartwick will suffice.'

Julian was uncertain if he liked them being on familiar terms. But it was not as if he thought Hart would seduce her. He knew his friend would never betray him. And it most certainly was not that he thought Katrina might prefer gregarious Hart to him.

After the four of them had finished eating most of the delicious food that had been packed into the basket, Hart took off his coat and reclined on the blanket, placing his hands behind his head. 'That was the finest picnic fare I have ever eaten.'

Had his friend forgotten entirely how to act around proper unmarried women?

'Hart, ladies are present. Put your coat back on,' chided Julian.

Hart tilted his head back. 'I am comfortable this way. We are on a picnic, far from prying eyes. Ladies, are you offended by my shirtsleeves? Honestly, it isn't as if I were attempting a seduction.'

In exasperation, Julian threw a strawberry at Hart's head.

'Hey, what was…? Oh, I love strawberries.' He bit into it.

'You will apologise for that last remark.'

'About strawberries? But I really do like them.'

'Not *that* comment, dolt!'

Miss Forrester snorted.

Hart jerked his head around. 'Did that sound come out of such a delicate lady?'

'Apologise,' scolded Julian, losing his patience.

'Fine!' Hart spun around and stood. 'Ladies, I am terribly sorry I have offended you with my shirtsleeves and my glib tongue. It is not often that I find myself in such estimable company, and I will try my best to refrain from offending you in the future. However, I feel I must state that chances are great that I will offend in some way.' He bowed down low with great flourish.

The women exchanged a glance and laughed. 'You are forgiven, Hartwick,' said Miss Forrester with a wave of her hand. 'Keep your coat off if you wish. I assure you Katrina and I will not be offended. It is not such an unusual sight back home.'

Hart turned to Julian. 'America sounds like a place I would enjoy immensely.' He reclined back on the blanket and crossed his hands behind his head.

It was difficult for Julian not to kick him.

Katrina bit into a strawberry and studied Hart's relaxed pose. 'Why do you suppose it isn't proper for a lady to see a man in his shirtsleeves?'

Hart flipped onto his stomach and rested his chin in his hand. 'I was wondering that very thing myself.'

Miss Forrester, who was sitting next to him, raised her wine glass. 'It isn't as if we would swoon at the sight of a man's arms. At least *I* would not.'

'You need to take a closer look at my arms,' Hart stated.

'I see your arms now, Hartwick, and I find myself amazingly upright,' she replied.

Katrina turned to Julian. 'Do you suppose someone

thinks a woman might lose control of her actions if she sees a man's broad shoulders and muscular arms?'

'Not *all* arms are muscular,' commented Miss Forrester.

Julian shrugged, tying not to think of spending time with Katrina in a state of undress. His blood pounded through his veins. 'We could test your theory.'

Bloody hell! When had he lost the ability to think before he spoke?

Hart choked on his Madeira. 'Capital idea, Julian. Why don't you take your coat off as well?'

Miss Forrester smiled brightly. 'Yes, do, Lyonsdale. Apparently Hartwick, while finely made, simply is not causing Katrina and I to question our moral fibre.'

Hart narrowed his eyes at her.

'Well, I did acknowledge that you were finely made,' she amended. 'However, to test the theory properly we need more than one subject.'

Both Miss Forrester and Hart stared at him.

'You want me to remove my coat?'

'It was your idea,' Miss Forrester pointed out.

'His Grace never does anything improper,' Hart muttered, refilling Miss Forrester's glass.

Katrina thought that Julian had done nothing *but* act improperly with her since the moment they'd met. However, she was not about to voice that thought. She had seen men in their shirtsleeves before. Why was the mere thought of Julian in his making her feel different? Suddenly she was very eager to see him remove his coat.

He looked over at her. 'What is your opinion on the matter, Miss Vandenberg? It is your question we are addressing.'

She rubbed her lips. 'Hartwick in his shirtsleeves is

having no effect on me. I suppose if we are to be scientific on the matter we need you to remove your coat as well.'

He smiled at her and her stomach flipped. 'I am glad to hear he has no effect on you.'

'Yes, yes…we know. I have no effect on the ladies,' Hart said impatiently, with a wave of his hand. 'Just take your damn coat off.'

'Tut-tut, Hartwick. There is no need to resort to such language,' Sarah said in amusement.

'Very well,' Julian said.

Reluctantly, he stood and removed his coat.

The air left her lungs as she watched his brown coat fall away, revealing a broad chest behind his yellow waistcoat and a pair of strong, curved shoulders. Maybe the English were correct. Maybe women should not see men in their shirtsleeves.

'I am sorry,' Sarah said. 'It appears we still have no answer as to why men need to remain in their coat-tails.'

'Wait, Miss Forrester,' Hartwick said slowly. 'Miss Vandenberg hasn't given us her opinion.'

What could she say? *Could you remove your waistcoat and shirt as well?*

She scratched the back of her neck and bit her lip. 'You look very nice without your coat.'

He looked triumphantly at his friend.

'Just because she gave you a compliment it doesn't mean you look better than I do. Miss Vandenberg is being polite and doesn't want to hurt your feelings.'

'This is not a comparison of who looks better, Hartwick,' Sarah said. 'We are trying to determine if seeing a man in his shirtsleeves causes us to act irrationally.'

'Are you sure, Miss Forrester, that you have no desire to act the least bit irrationally?' Hartwick asked, wiggling his brows.

'No, Hartwick. I have no desire to do so at all.'

Katrina shifted her gaze to Julian's yellow silk waistcoat and bit her thumb. She had a longing to slide her hands over his firm chest to his broad shoulders. Her gaze edged to those inviting lips of his...

'I have already showed you the view of the river, have I not, Miss Forrester?' Hartwick called out.

'Yes, but I suppose one can never fully appreciate such a lovely view unless one sees it for a second time.'

Julian was staring at Katrina, making her feel incredibly warm.

'We *can* hear you,' he bit out.

Sarah laughed, and Hartwick cleared his throat. 'Would you like us to leave the two of you alone?' he asked.

'That would be highly improper, Hartwick,' Sarah said, 'since His Grace is in his shirtsleeves.'

'Sarah! Honestly...' chided Katrina, narrowing her eyes at her friend.

Julian turned to Hartwick. 'So when I finally do something improper *this* is how you react?'

Hartwick raised his hands in surrender. 'We are only trying to be accommodating. So, I think we have determined the reason why it's improper for men to be seen in their shirtsleeves by ladies.'

Katrina turned to Hartwick. 'No, we have not. Sarah and I are completely composed.'

'Well, *I* am anyway,' muttered her traitorous friend.

'What other rules can we test today?' asked Hartwick eagerly. 'Is there some article of clothing you are not supposed to remove in our presence? I am open to suggestions.'

'You rake!' replied Katrina, laughing. 'Are you trying to get us to show you our ankles?'

'Your hair,' Julian said suddenly.

All three turned to him, and he shrugged.

'A lady's hair is usually pinned up.'

Hartwick sat up. 'That's the spirit. We are in our shirt-sleeves and you owe us a boon. I think Julian has a fine idea. You ladies should take down your hair and Julian and I will see if we can resist you.'

Sarah eyed Hartwick. 'Suppose you lose your senses and your over-amorous nature overcomes you?'

'That's what Julian is here for. He is forever proper.'

'*He* is sitting here in his shirtsleeves,' Katrina pointed out sceptically as she eyed him up and down.

'Oh, please… He has so much restraint that even if his life depended on it he would never touch you. *He* is the epitome of the proper English aristocrat,' Hartwick said, with sarcasm in his voice.

Julian turned to his friend. 'You speak as if being responsible and acting honourably is a bad thing. Maybe you would find yourself in less trouble if you tried it.'

Katrina peered through the lowest hanging branches towards Sarah's barouche. 'What do you think the footmen will say if they see us like this?'

'Do not fret. No one can see us,' replied Hartwick as he chewed on a long piece of grass.

'Why do I believe you have said that before?' Katrina muttered.

'Why, Miss Vandenberg, I am offended,' Hartwick said, bringing his hand to his chest. 'I think there is a bit of fire in you.'

She turned to Julian. 'Was that a compliment?'

The enticing man with the broad shoulders shrugged. 'It's difficult to tell.'

'Of course it was a compliment. A lady with a bit of fire in her is much more enjoyable than a milksop.'

'You thought I was a milksop?'

'No. As I said, you have a bit of fire in you. Miss Forrester, on the other hand, is infinitely boring.'

Sarah shook her head. 'You are only saying that because I did not swoon when you removed your coat.'

'No. For that, I think you may need spectacles. But we are getting away from the point. I believe Julian challenged you ladies to take down your hair?'

'It was hardly a challenge. I was simply curious.'

'I am trying to help facilitate your request,' Hartwick replied impatiently. 'Perhaps you could persuade the ladies. They seem to trust you more than me.'

'I can't imagine why,' muttered Katrina.

Sarah cleared her throat, catching their attention. 'I believe we are testing theories today. Katrina, please remove the pins from your hair.' Sarah began to arrange her own hairpins on the skirt of her cinnamon-coloured gown. 'We can easily re-pin each other shortly.'

Hartwick laughed out loud. 'Well done, Miss Forrester.' He made a show of studying her. 'Now, what colour is that, exactly?' His eyes dropped to his mud-splattered boots and he smiled. 'Oh, I know. You hair is an earthy colour.'

'It is chestnut, Hartwick,' Sarah said, shaking out her hair. 'A gleaming, glossy chestnut. Which you would realise if you weren't so self-absorbed,' she teased.

'*I* am self-absorbed? How many times today have you admired your slippers?'

'What has that to do with anything? I like my new slippers.'

'Apparently so. Julian, have you seen anyone look at their feet...?'

The moment Katrina removed one pin from her hair Julian was transfixed. He watched as little by little ringlets of golden silk cascaded past her neck, down her back, and over the slope of her breasts.

Many nights he had pictured her in his bed with her

hair down, and he had wondered how long it was. Would it cover her breasts if she rode him? Would it bounce against the small of her back as he took her from behind? Now he knew that the ends of her hair curled against the lower curves of her breasts. His mouth began to water as he imagined the feel of her hair against his cheek as he slid his tongue along those breasts...

Before he was aware of what he was doing, he slid his fingers into the soft strands. Everything around them fell away, and the only thing that mattered was the woman next to him. He kissed her softly and she placed her hand on his chest. He deepened the kiss, certain she must feel his heart and soul pounding against her hand.

'I thought you said he was always proper?' Miss Forrester's voice broke the silence.

'He was until he met your friend,' Hart replied.

'Maybe it's your influence.'

'I've tried for years to get him to follow his desires. This is none of my doing.'

'I don't believe they should be doing that, even with us in attendance.'

'It is just a kiss.'

'That is *not* just a kiss, Hartwick.'

'No. I suppose you are correct, Miss Forrester. That definitely is not just a kiss.'

It was the last thing he wanted to do, but Julian managed to pull his head back. Katrina buried her face in his shoulder and he rubbed his cheek against her soft hair.

'We can hear you.' His voice sounded strained, even to his own ears.

'We know,' Hart said, taking a sip of wine.

It had taken all his restraint to leave his hand on Katrina's jaw and not move it to any other part of her body. He was finally able to position one of his legs to hide the strain in his breeches. How could he have kissed her in front of Hart and Miss Forrester? How could the simple act of her taking down her hair have made him so excited? When could he get her alone to continue what they'd started?

'Don't you think it would be a good idea to show Miss Forrester the view?' he suggested to Hart.

His friend smirked at him. 'I have already done so.'

'Perhaps she hasn't seen all that this hill has to offer.'

'I believe I have seen quite a bit of what this hill has to offer,' Miss Forrester said dryly, raising her glass to her lips.

'Do the two of you have something important to tell us?' Hart said, as he crossed his legs in front of him and rocked his boots from side to side. 'You have kissed each other in front of Miss Forrester and me. Should I be requesting pistols at dawn to defend Miss Vandenberg's honour?'

Julian was about to chastise Hart, but Katrina spoke up first. 'Don't be nonsensical, Hartwick. You of all people should understand. It was simply a kiss.'

What did she mean, it was simply a kiss? Had it not been her lips he was kissing? Had she not felt that…that… *thing*?

'So there is no impending announcement you wish to share with us?' Hart asked.

'Heavens, no,' exclaimed Katrina with a light laugh.

Julian studied the woman whose lips were still wet from his kiss. She had moved away, putting distance between them. Did she have to sound so relieved that she would never need to marry him?

To hell with being cautious—he needed to see her alone again.

Chapter Eighteen

Walking among the rose bushes planted along the back wall of her garden, Katrina glanced up at the late morning sky. Earlier in the day, dark clouds had hung low. Now the sun's rays were peeking through, and the air was heavy with the scent of fragrant blooms.

Reaching out with her cutting shears towards a red velvet bud, Katrina winced as she pricked herself on a thorn. How could something so beautiful be so dangerous?

Drawing her hand back, she sucked on her finger. That was the third time she'd pricked herself today. A wise person would know when to stop. There was no sense in risking further injury.

As she stepped onto the gravel path that led to the house a dragonfly flew past, reminding her of the one that had landed on Julian's sleeve during their picnic. All too soon he would be a distant memory. He would marry a woman born to be a duchess—someone who had the family name and connections she did not. And she would return to America, hopefully to find a man who made her feel all the things Julian did. She had to believe that was possible, otherwise when their secret arrangement came to an end it would devastate her.

Wilkins met Katrina as she reached the steps of the terrace. He extended a polite bow. 'You have a caller, miss.'

When she read Madame de Lieven's name on the card she resisted the urge to hide back among the roses. But, after directing Wilkins to show her guest into the drawing room, Katrina removed her apron and went to make herself presentable.

When she entered the drawing room a short while later she found Madame de Lieven seated on the settee by the unlit fireplace, examining the blue Sèvres porcelain urn on the small table next to her. She looked up as Katrina took a seat across from her. They exchanged the usual pleasantries, and it wasn't until the ladies were in the middle of tea that Madame de Lieven broached the expected subject of Mr Armstrong.

'I understand he has sent you flowers?' she said, eyeing a very elaborate floral display of white lilies and pink roses.

'Yes, he has.'

'Why have I not heard that you have been seen together?'

Katrina gave a noncommittal shrug, not sure how to respond to end the questioning.

Madame de Lieven took a long sip of tea and then placed the cup down slowly onto the saucer in her lap. 'He is a man of means, with impressive connections. He will make you a fine husband. When will you see him again?'

'I couldn't say.'

'I will arrange something.'

Was this what it would be like to have Lady Morley for a mother?

Katrina placed her own cup and saucer down on the table. 'That is very kind of you, but as I have already mentioned I have no wish to find a husband here in England.'

'Nonsense. I think you are not as averse to the idea

as you might like me to believe.' She stood and adjusted her gloves. 'It was a pleasure to see you again, Miss Vandenberg.'

'Thank you for your kind visit.' The words were brittle on her tongue, but they came out smoothly.

She walked her guest down to the front door, but before she was free of Madame de Lieven for the day the woman turned with one final question.

'Will you be attending the Hipswitch garden party?'

Having an inkling of what was to come, Katrina took a resigned breath. 'I am. My father will likely be in meetings. I plan to attend with Mrs Forrester and her daughter.'

Madame de Lieven tied her bonnet. 'I'm certain Mr Armstrong will be pleased to hear it.'

Katrina watched her walk down the steps and into her awaiting carriage. It wasn't until the carriage had begun to roll down the street that Katrina closed the door and banged her head gently against the wood. Why hadn't Madame de Lieven focused her attention on Sarah? She would be remaining in London much longer than Katrina, and therefore her potential ties to what was happening in the United States were greater. Unless the woman believed she had more time to forge a friendship of sorts with Sarah and would be hunting her down next.

Hopefully, arranging the flowers she had managed to collect would pull her thoughts from speculating on how bad the Hipswitch garden party was sure to be.

A rustling sound from inside the nearby dining room caught her attention, and she walked to the doorway to see what it was. As she crossed the threshold she was startled by Julian's presence inside the room. He was wearing a navy tailcoat, a white silk embroidered waistcoat, and buckskin breeches tucked into a pair of shiny top boots.

She blinked a few times, trying to make certain that

he was real and not a figment of her wishful imagination. 'What are you doing here?'

'That is a fine way to greet your guest,' he said with an impish grin.

She stepped closer to him and closed the door behind her. 'You are skulking in my dining room. What did you expect me to say?'

He took her hands and pulled her even closer with little resistance. 'I'm not skulking. I came to read with you and was told Madame de Lieven was here. I informed your butler that I would wait for you in here.'

'You asked to wait in my dining room?'

'It is the closest room to your front door. I did not feel it wise to proceed further into your home.'

'You cannot stay. My father is working in his study. If he were to see you, how would we explain your presence?'

'I have an ideal solution. Come for a drive with me. We can read in the carriage.'

He nuzzled her neck and her legs grew weak.

She tilted her head, exposing more of her skin for his kisses. 'Someone will see.'

'We will be in a closed carriage with the drapes drawn.' His soft kisses were turning into nips. 'I promise no one will see us.'

'They'll see me entering it with you. That will never do. You should return another day.'

Turning him away was not what she wanted, but they had no choice. They were sure to get caught.

'I have Hart's unmarked carriage parked in the mews. I'll leave now and have the driver stop in front of your house. No one will know I am inside.'

'I don't know—'

His warm hands cupped her face and he kissed her deeply. Would there ever be a time when his kisses did not affect her so? He pulled back and studied her closely, as if he were looking for a reaction. What that reaction was, she couldn't imagine. A wisp of hair had come loose by her left temple, and she blew at the strand with a puff of air.

'Come for a drive with me before I have to leave for Westminster.' That devilish smile of his was not helping her resolve. 'You know you want to.'

'You are not as charming as you think,' she replied through a reluctant smile.

'Yes, I am.' He laughed low and cradled her neck in his hands. 'The longer we remain here, the greater chance there is for discovery. Now, go and retrieve the book and meet me in the carriage.'

There were times when anticipation and excitement could cloud one's judgement. For Katrina, this was one of those times. 'Very well. I will go with you.'

He held her gaze as he kissed the inside of her wrist. A tingle spread up her arm and down her side. If he continued in this fashion she would be tempted to suggest they lock the door and remain in the dining room all afternoon.

It appeared he had read her thoughts, and he straightened in an overly confident manner. 'I will show myself out. And Katrina…' he adjusted his cuffs '…do hurry.'

She stepped away from the door and his sleeve brushed against her arm as he walked past. Moments later she heard the door to her house open and close. Her heart raced. She tried to catch her breath. Low in her abdomen her muscles flipped as she imagined kissing him again…

It didn't take her long to gather her favourite bonnet and change into a celestial blue satin carriage dress. Grabbing her copy of *Frankenstein*, she dashed down the stairs and out through the door. An unmarked coach of shiny black lacquer was waiting with its curtains closed. Ignoring her uneasy feeling, she accepted help from the footman, stepped inside, and settled on the bench across from Julian.

His surprised expression was visible in the muted light. 'You have changed.'

'It seemed prudent.'

'There was no need. You look lovely in either dress.'

Warmth spread through her at this compliment. Then the carriage jerked and she was rocked back and forth as the horses began their journey. She wished she could peer outside, to see in what direction they were headed.

'Where are we off to?'

'Nowhere in particular. I have instructed the driver to return us to your home in an hour. However, it may prove a challenge to read the book together if you are not seated next to me.'

The carriage, while spacious, was not overly wide. If she sat next to him their bodies would be sure to touch.

She vaulted across the carriage.

His muscular thigh pressed against hers as she nestled her arm next to his and opened the book.

When Julian had arrived at Katrina's home and had been informed Madame de Lieven was already there he should have walked away. Hiding in the dining room with both the Russian Ambassador's wife and Katrina's father on the premises had been dangerous. However, sitting this close to her now, Julian was glad he had listened to the voice that had told him to stay.

Her warm, soft thigh was pressed against his, and that warmth was travelling over to him. It would not take much for him to harden. His body was begging to lay her down under him and explore every inch of her. Had she not been a virgin, that book she was holding would have been tossed somewhere on the floor by now.

He motioned towards the book. 'Shall we begin?'

She nodded and opened the book to a page marked with a worn strip of deep pink silk. With her permission, he took it out and rubbed it lightly between the fingers of his ungloved hand.

'This is true proof that you are a great reader.'

Her soft laugh made him smile. 'It is a remnant from a gown that once belonged to my mother. My Great-Aunt Augusta gave it to me when I was a child. I've kept it ever since.'

'That was very thoughtful of her.'

'She was all that is kindness. The Dowager reminds me of her.'

Had her aunt smuggled gin into assemblies, faked a malady when she wanted her way, and entertained herself in her later years by inserting herself into situations that weren't any of her business? He wasn't inclined to believe so.

Handing the strip back to her, he looked down at the open book. In the low light he would need to squint to read the words. 'Perhaps this isn't the ideal location for reading.'

'*Now* you decide this isn't wise?'

He took her hand and kissed it. 'I still believe being alone with you in this carriage is the finest idea I've had today.'

'You do realise that if this continues I will find myself finishing this book during my journey home to New York.'

The idea of her travelling home burned his gut. When she left England she would not be returning. Ever. A chasm opened in his chest, and he tried to rub it away.

'You once told me you had no interest in marrying anyone in England, and yet Madame de Lieven appeared eager to inform Greely's whelp that you will be at the Hip-switch garden party. Perhaps you've changed your mind?'

She sighed and shook her head. 'I have not. However, Madame de Lieven can be most insistent in her opinions.'

'Do you truly have no wish to live here?'

'On the contrary—I adore London and the sense of the past that surrounds me. I feel as if I could spend years here and I would still find something new to see. It is the men here who hold no appeal.'

As a man residing in London, to him that was rather insulting—no, it was highly insulting. He raised his chin and pulled his shoulders back. 'All men?'

'Yes,' she admitted without hesitation. 'Rather, not *all* but most—you appeal to me.'

'I'm relieved to hear it.'

'Somewhat,' she amended with a mischievous smile. 'However, I believe we were discussing my marrying an Englishman and not simply liking one.'

'Are you this charming with American men as well? It is a wonder you are still unmarried.'

Instead of offending her, his comment made her laugh.

He eyed her sideways. 'What is it that you find so distasteful about Englishmen?'

She was not destined to be his duchess. This was not a conversation he should be having with her. And yet a part of him wondered why she found him an unsuitable choice for a husband.

'We have different views on fidelity,' she blurted out rather abruptly.

Julian jerked his head back, not having expected that to be her reasoning. 'I wasn't aware we had had a discussion on such a subject. I must make a note to pay closer attention to what you say.'

'Don't be glib. I am well aware of what men of your station do, and I do not wish that for my marriage,' she said with a casual lift of her shoulder.

He leaned closer. 'Really? What is it we do?'

'Men of the *ton* marry women for their impressive ancestry or significant fortunes. When they grow bored with their wives they go about with other women.'

Julian's brows drew together. 'Is this about your earlier notion that I have a mistress? I assure you I still haven't taken one.'

'No. It's about you being an English nobleman,' she stated firmly, looking him in the eye in the dim light.

'And because of that you believe I would conduct myself in such a manner?'

'I have no reason to assume otherwise. You once told me that you do not expect a happy marriage, and you found my ideas on love provincial.'

'Opinions can change.'

She crossed her arms and tilted her head, sceptically. 'So now you will tell me you plan to be a faithful husband?'

He didn't want to think about being married to Lady Mary—not when he was sitting with his body pressed against Katrina. He took a deep breath and held in her lemon scent. Deep down he knew he would think of her every time he took Mary to bed. It was not an honourable notion, nor something he would ever admit to anyone—especially the woman sitting beside him waiting for a response.

Why the hell had he started this conversation with her?

'Well?' She was not letting the matter rest.

He needed her to know what kind of man he was. He needed her to see that he was a man who honoured his vows. 'I've already been married and, although the union was arranged by my father, I was faithful.'

It came out in a rush, and he turned his head away from her. He rarely spoke of Emma. It was difficult to take a steady breath.

Katrina fell back against the plush upholstery, her properly erect posture forgotten. 'You were married?' It came out as a whisper. 'We spent all that time together and you never told me.'

'I assumed you knew. Everyone in London is aware that I was married.'

'Well, no one told *me*.' She appeared to wait for him to continue.

He never intentionally discussed Emma. The subject of her death was too personal and much too painful. He tried to scrub the image of her lying dead out of his mind. It had haunted him most nights—at least until he'd met Katrina. That hadn't occurred to him until now.

He looked into her expectant eyes. An unwelcome lump was forming in his throat. 'My wife's name was Emma. She was the youngest daughter of the Duke of Beaumont. Our fathers arranged our marriage while I was away at Cambridge. She died while giving birth to our stillborn son.'

He leaned forward and rested his elbows on his knees. It was easier to move away from Katrina than to continue to look into her eyes.

'To this day I am sorry for her loss and the loss of my child.' *But his regret would never bring them back.*

She brushed the hair by his temple in a comforting gesture. 'I am sorry for your loss too.'

Not knowing what else to say, Julian gave a quick nod.

Katrina continued to stroke his temple. 'My mother died shortly after giving birth to me. My father feels her loss even to this day.'

Julian squeezed his eyes shut and scrubbed his hand across his face. There was comfort in the closed confines of the gently rocking carriage and muted light. It felt…safe.

'I never held him.' The statement left his lips before the thought had fully formed in his head.

The soft pressure of her hand on his back was an unexpected gesture. 'Did anyone ask if you wanted to?'

He shook his head and bit his lip. The lump in his throat was making it difficult to swallow. 'They only asked if I wanted to see him.'

'Did you?'

He nodded as tears that had never been shed rimmed his eyes. The physician and Emma's maid had been so focused on tending to her, they hadn't had time to clean his son. He'd been so small—and so still.

'I should have held him. No one held him.'

She rested her head lightly against his shoulder and a hot tear began to trickle down his face.

'A father should hold his son,' he choked out, 'even if just once. I named him John, after Emma's brother. They had been close, and it seemed only right. I had them buried together. My mother tried to insist John should have his own coffin in the family crypt, but I thought it best for them to be together. She said it was unseemly and that she was certain my father would have felt the same.' He finally looked over at Katrina and saw the shimmer of unshed tears in her eyes. 'What would you have done?'

She slid her fingers through his. 'I think Emma would have wanted to be with John.'

He'd thought so too. The crushing weight of indecision that had plagued him since her burial eased for the first time. He had needed to know he had made the right decision in honouring their memories. He'd needed someone he respected to say it to him. It had eaten away at his conscience for too long. And he knew Katrina would always be honest with him.

She rested her head on his shoulder again. 'I believe deep down we know what the right course of action is. We just need to listen to what our heart tells us. I'm sorry to have caused you to relive such painful memories. I should have realised.'

He kissed the top of her head and took a deep breath. The lump in his throat was dissolving. 'Do not apologise. I needed to hear that you believe they were laid to rest in a proper fashion.'

A comforting silence stretched between them as the carriage rocked them gently through the streets of London. The distant sound of voices and the rolling of the carriage wheels on cobblestones felt oddly comforting.

'I'm certain you're grateful you accepted my invitation today,' he said dryly after some time.

She lifted her head up and offered him a reassuring smile. 'There is no place I would rather be.' She tugged off a white kidskin glove and wiped the wetness from his cheek with the pad of her thumb.

His heart gave an odd flip.

'It's never easy to lose someone we love,' she said, running her thumb along his forehead.

It took him a few moments before he realised she was referring to Emma. 'I did not love her,' he said. 'I liked her enough, but I didn't love her.'

Love was something he knew nothing of. He had not been born to fall in love. He wasn't even certain he would know what love felt like. And yet… How would he define his feelings for the woman next to him? It wasn't love, but what was it?

'I believe I have taken you on a melancholy journey away from our original conversation.'

'I've forgotten what we were discussing,' she said, sitting up.

'We were discussing fidelity. And I think for all your notions about people prejudging you because you are American you are no better.'

'How so?' she asked indignantly.

'You've tarred and feathered the entire male population of the *ton*, accusing us all of infidelity. You believe my title leaves me incapable of devoting myself to one woman. I am informing you that you are wrong in your assessment of me.'

She crossed her arms over those enticing breasts.

'Do not look chastised.' He sat back and rested his head on the cushion behind them. Their conversation today had been far too grim. 'Have I told you how much I have come to appreciate the smell of lemons?' he commented casually.

Even in the muted light of the carriage he could see her faint smile. 'You might have mentioned it a time or two.'

The smile fell from his lips. 'I fear one day I will miss that smell.'

Silence stretched between them, and his heart sank in his chest.

Chapter Nineteen

Katrina was in excellent spirits when Sarah and Mrs Forrester asked her to join them on their shopping excursion along Bond Street two days later. The sun was out and the temperature pleasant, making it an ideal day to meander through the shops. Turning a corner, they noticed a small crowd gathered around the large mullioned window of one particular building. Ever the curious one, Sarah tugged Katrina along to see what was so interesting.

'Oh, it's a print shop,' Sarah said, eyeing the cartoons in each pane of the large window.

'Perhaps we will see someone we know,' Katrina mused as she studied a caricature of the Prince Regent attempting to squeeze his rather large body into a very small corset.

Next to her, an amused Sarah methodically studied each print one by one, letting out a giggle at a few in particular. Suddenly she gave a quick gasp and pulled Katrina out through the crowd. Dragging Katrina to the milliner next door, Sarah pulled Katrina to a stop next to where Mrs Forrester was waiting for them.

'We have a problem,' she announced rather breathlessly.

Mrs Forrester turned a questioning eye to her daughter. 'The two of you have been away from me for only a few moments. What could possibly have happened in such a brief time?'

Katrina caught the look of pity in Sarah's eyes.

Taking Katrina's gloved hand in her own, Sarah leaned closer. 'There is a caricature of you and Lyonsdale in a carriage,' she whispered.

Ice crept up Katrina's spine. *Their secret was out.* It felt as if all the people around them were whispering about her, even though their eyes were still on the prints in the window.

At Mrs Forrester's suggestion they made their way directly to Katrina's home with a stack of the scandalous prints. They had tried to acquire the printing plate, but had been told someone else had purchased it a few hours earlier.

It wasn't until they had entered Katrina's drawing room that she was finally able to study the image.

The illustration showed a carriage with the Lyonsdale crest emblazoned on the door and an American flag flying above, driving through London. Visible through the window was the head of a blonde woman wearing an Indian headdress. Her head was back and her eyes were closed. On top of her was a brown-haired man in his shirtsleeves with his hand on her bare leg, pushing up her skirt. The caption below read *Minding the Savages*.

For the first time in her life Katrina truly thought she might cast up her accounts in front of other people. She dropped down on the settee and let her head fall into her hands. 'How can I show my face in Town after this?'

Crouching down beside her, Mrs Forrester stroked Katrina's back. 'Do not worry, my dear. Anyone who has encountered you thus far has seen you comport yourself as a lady. I am certain this will be forgotten when some new bit of gossip has the tongues wagging.'

The woman was trying to reassure her, but Katrina did not miss the concern in her voice.

'Katrina, I do have to ask—*did* you go for a carriage ride with a titled Englishman?'

She looked into the gentle eyes of the woman who had kindly offered to chaperon her. How could she say she had been secretly seeing Lyonsdale? The woman would never look at her the same way again.

Needing to put distance between them, Katrina jumped up and headed towards the window. It was time to confess everything.

'Mother, it was all my fault,' Sarah blurted out. She looked regretfully at Katrina. 'Please forgive me. I never thought this would happen.'

What was Sarah saying?

Mrs Forrester stared at her daughter with trepidation. 'What did you do?'

'Do you recall when Katrina and I went on that picnic? Well, two gentlemen we are acquainted with happened upon us, and I asked them if they would care for refreshment. They sat with us for a time and then went on their way. It was all very innocent, but our footman or coachman must have told a tale.'

Mrs Forrester rubbed her eyes, as if she could wipe the image of the caricature from her mind. Katrina had already tried that. It didn't work.

The woman took both of Sarah's hands and looked her in the eye. 'Who were the gentlemen?'

'The Duke of Lyonsdale and the Earl of Hartwick.'

Mrs Forrester's loud groan filled the room. 'Sarah, you *didn't*?'

Sarah's hands fisted at her sides as she tried to defend her action. 'The hour was very early. I was certain no one would see.'

But this image clearly showed an exaggerated version

of what had occurred as Katrina drove through Mayfair with Julian. This was not a depiction of the picnic.

She began to tremble, and drops of cold sweat dusted her skin. 'What will I tell my father?'

Mrs Forrester quickly took her by the arm and gently lowered her to the settee. 'Have no fear. I will talk with him first. There might be a way we can avoid a scandal. I doubt the Duke of Lyonsdale has any desire to enter into one.'

Julian's reputation meant everything to him. If his family name suffered because of the implications of the caricature he would hate her for ever.

Her stomach dipped and flipped. Running to the potted palm in the corner of the room, Katrina reached it just in time.

Later that afternoon, in the Palace of Westminster, Julian was taken aback when he entered the Chamber of the House of Lords and a hush fell over the stately room. Appraising faces turned his way, and for the first time in his life he was confronted with critical stares from many of his peers. He had been up late last night and home all morning, finalising the speech he was about to give. What could he have possibly done to warrant such a reaction?

The white-haired Duke of Skeffington toddled up to him. His bloodshot eyes studied Julian over his wire-framed glasses. He was the oldest duke in the chamber, and liked to remind everyone of the deferential treatment he should be given because of it.

He rapped his cane on the floor, narrowly missing Julian's foot. 'Well, boy? Explain yourself.'

They were frequently on opposing sides in this room. His eagerness to hear what Julian had to say was unusual, but it could perhaps be attributed to the man's recent bouts of narcolepsy.

'I will explain myself when it's my turn to address the chamber,' Julian said, ready to push past him.

'I don't give a fig about your speech. I am speaking of you and the American.'

Julian's blood ran cold and every muscle in his body locked. He could not possibly have heard the man correctly. 'I beg your pardon?'

'You have ancestors who were killed by their hands in their war for independence, and now you engage in behaviour such as this? It's disgraceful,' he spat out. 'Your father would have been appalled by your actions.'

He tapped the handle of his cane into Julian's chest before he walked away, unconcerned with a reply.

Julian broke out into a cold sweat. How did Skeffington know about Katrina? He had been so careful. His thoughts turned to their drive through Town. They had been in an unmarked carriage with the curtains drawn. Surely no one had seen them?

More eyes were upon him, and heat crept up his neck. The Duke of Winterbourne came to stand beside him, carrying himself with his usual commanding air. It was a relief to see a friendly face.

'That was quite an entrance you made,' said Winter, casually adjusting his cuff under his robe. 'I imagine Skeffington was gracious enough to offer his opinion on the matter?'

'He was his usual charming self,' Julian managed to say through his bewilderment.

'You surely must have realised that when word got out it would be remarked upon. Both Ardsley and Brendel lost their youngest in our last skirmish with the Americans. Lockwood's two brothers died in America's war for independence. And those are just the men around us. Many men in this room lost family members there, and they place the blame on the colonials. But I do not need to remind you of that.'

He motioned for them to make their way through the crowd and take their seats.

'I do not understand why I am garnering such a reaction now, after dancing with the woman weeks ago,' Julian said.

A look of amused confusion crossed Winter's face. 'You do not know what this is about?'

'Know what?'

'There was a caricature published about you today, my friend. A rather suggestive one about you and an American. The question is, how accurate is it?'

Their secret was out. He needed to see this print. Unfortunately, the session was about to begin.

Bloody hell! How could he answer for something when he wasn't quite certain what he was being accused of?

As the room began to settle down Lord Allyn approached them and nodded a greeting. Julian was expecting his friend to wish him luck today—instead Allyn had a request.

'I'm aware you're scheduled to present your speech today, Lyonsdale. However, with recent events being what they are, I think it best if you refrain from giving it.'

Confused, Julian tried to grasp what Allyn was saying. He had worked on his speech for weeks. He had been asked to deliver it because he was an influential peer, and his speeches were known to sway voters. Now, because of one print, he had become a liability.

'Perhaps Allyn is right,' Winter said in a low voice as he leaned forward.

'Et tu?'

'Listen to him.' Winter pointed towards Allyn. 'This is not an attack on you.'

'Of course it is,' Julian said with quiet emphasis.

'No. It's about certain men who won't listen to you because they will be focusing on the possible scandal surrounding you—a man renowned for your moral character—and an unmarried American.'

Scandal.

Bile rose up in his throat. His family had been untouched by scandal for generations. Would he be the one to let their good name fall? He thought of the Fifth Duke—the one who wasn't fit to have his portrait hung in the gallery. Was that to be his fate?

Clenching his jaw so tightly it might have shattered, Julian shifted his gaze to the row of peers next to him. His pride was crushed. The last thing he needed to see was pity in his friends' eyes.

'Fine. You drafted this speech with me—you give it.' His composure started slipping as he thrust his notes at Winter.

An indecipherable expression passed between his friends, and Allyn gave a brief tip of his head before returning to his seat.

Winter leaned sideways and lowered his voice to a whisper. 'I suggest you find a way to calm yourself before you draw even more attention your way. You are passionate about your work here. You always have been. But you are not the only one of us who can reach these men and change their minds. You are not a party of one man.'

Julian knew that to be true. But he also knew that the career and reputation he had built for himself was the most important thing in his life. It was the legacy he would leave to future generations. How could he have risked all of it for a few stolen hours with a woman? The problem was, it wasn't just any woman—it was Katrina. And, although he was chiding himself for being so incredibly foolish, he knew he would recall every minute of those hours they spent together for the rest of his days.

Oh, God, what had he done? He had promised Katrina he wouldn't do anything to risk her reputation. If only he had been honourable enough to make that so.

His stomach pitched. There was no telling if her reputation was beyond repair until he saw the print.

Katrina rolled off her wet pillow and stared up at what she knew were blue flowers stitched onto the cream silk that hung from the top of her tester bed. But the image was blurred from the teardrops clinging to her lashes and she rubbed her palms over her eyes. That was better. Now, if she could only concentrate on the details of the flowers and not on the image that had been haunting her for the past four hours…

It was no use. Once more she could see the scandalous caricature of her and Julian—a caricature that announced to all of England that she was a lightskirt. How could she show her face in London Society again?

Agreeing to go for a ride with Julian was probably the most foolish thing she had ever done. Now their time together was surely over, and scandal would follow her.

Her heart ached and she wasn't sure it would ever be the same. She was such a fool! How could she have thought her feelings would not become engaged? It had happened so gradually there had not been one particular instance. Had there been, she might have had a chance to resist him.

She smothered her face with her pillow and let out a scream. The problem was she cared too much. She cared that right at that very moment he was probably telling himself he was better off without her. He would never want this kind of attention cast his way.

She thought she heard a knock, but she wasn't certain since she was still squashing the pillow over her head. Tossing it aside, she sat up and looked at her door. There was another knock, and Katrina groaned at the intrusion. It was probably Meg, trying to get her to have some tea. What she really needed was something a bit more fortifying. This would be an excellent time to try the brandy her father kept in his study. Perhaps if she drank enough of it she would forget this day had ever happened.

The knocking grew louder. She slid off the bed and trudged to her door. Opening it slightly, she jumped when a foot encased in gold silk damask pushed its way inside.

'If you close this door on my new slipper I shall be vexed.'

Katrina closed her eyes and took a deep breath, preparing herself for Sarah. Opening the door wider, she invited her friend inside and locked the door behind them.

Sarah tugged off her white kid gloves and tossed them carelessly onto the rumpled bed. Spinning around, she ran her gaze over Katrina.

Brushing the wetness away from her face, Katrina avoided Sarah's piercing stare. The last thing she wanted was to see pity in her friend's eyes.

'You look as if a bear has sat on your head.'

'Forgive me. Had I known you were planning on calling I would have been sure to have Meg arrange an elaborate coiffure.'

Sarah made her way over to the window and sat at Katrina's dressing table. Picking up a brush, she appeared to study the monogram engraved into the silver. 'If anyone enquires if I have been here this evening, please inform them that you have not seen me.'

'Why?'

'Because I was told quite firmly not to disturb you.'

'By whom?'

Sarah tapped the brush in her palm. 'My mother. Luckily your very proper English butler has taken a shine to me, otherwise I don't know when I would have seen you next.'

Katrina trudged back to her bed and sat on the edge across from Sarah. 'I am not very good company right now.'

'So I can see. I knew you'd take this to heart. But it might not be as horrid as you think.'

'Of course it is. That caricature has announced to all of London that I am a woman of loose morals who let herself be compromised in a carriage!'

'Katrina, those caricatures are meant to be satires. They aren't meant to be viewed in a literal sense.'

'I am aware of that, but the implication is there. It's very humiliating.' She flopped onto her back and covered her eyes. 'And I have tried very hard to act in accordance with all the *ton's* ridiculous rules.'

The bed dipped as Sarah sat next to her. 'Anyone who has met you will know that the drawing is a gross exaggeration of your character.'

'I disagree—many will believe all American women conduct themselves as such.'

'Some people already had those notions before we even stepped ashore. In time, as more and more American women arrive in England, people here will have a better understanding of our true character.'

Katrina raised herself up on her elbows and her eyes met Sarah's soft amber gaze. 'Why is it that I am the one who has garnered all this attention? Madame de Lieven doesn't pester you. The papers do not write about the gentlemen you dance with, and you have never been the subject of a scandalous caricature.'

'You are more attractive than I am.'

'You are simply saying that to try to improve my disposition.'

Sarah's lip twitched. 'Yes, that is true. Everyone knows *I'm* the pretty one.'

Katrina managed to smile before her thoughts turned

back to Julian. 'Lyonsdale cannot be pleased by this. He prides himself on being above reproach.'

'Has he called on you today?'

Katrina shook her head, not wanting to consider the significance of his absence.

'Katrina, that man is taken with you. I doubt a bit of satire will give him cause to announce that he will marry Lady Mary Morley.'

'Lady Mary?'

'Yes. She is the only other woman I've seen him dance with, and I hear she has the approval of his mother.'

Oh, God! Katrina flopped down again. All this time she had been worried about his association with Lady Wentworth. What she should have been worried about was how she would feel when Julian announced that he would marry the very proper, very respectable Lady Mary Morley.

She started sobbing, convinced she wouldn't stop till morning.

Chapter Twenty

As Julian sat in his elegant coach he leaned his head back and took a deep breath. The rocking motion was contributing to the queasiness that had been plaguing him. He closed his eyes, grateful to be away from the prying eyes of Westminster.

Winter had given the speech he'd been supposed to give. Knowing that if he had delivered the same address some of those men would actually have cast their votes in opposition was humiliating. The words 'foolish' and 'disgraceful' were still knocking about in his head.

His stomach pitched again.

Two months ago he hadn't even known Katrina existed. He'd been respected, focused and content. As much as he hated to admit it, his mother had been correct. A man in his position was made for contentment—not some intangible emotion that made him feel as if he were standing on the edge of a cliff not certain if he was ready to jump off.

Katrina had turned his life upside down.

He wanted his orderly life back.

The only way he knew how to get that was to cut his ties with her and pursue Lady Mary Morley. Lady Mary was the ideal woman for a respectable duke.

His chest tightened. He squeezed his eyes shut and tried

to take a deep breath. But if Katrina's reputation was in question he would have no choice but to do the honourable thing. He was an honourable gentleman before all else.

Dammit, he needed to see this print!

His carriage slowed to a stop and he stormed into his home, prepared to contact his secretary and obtain a copy of the print. He stopped when he was informed that Hart was waiting for him in his study. Dealing with Hart was *not* what he needed at the moment.

'Finally!' Hart said from where he sat reclining at Julian's desk, with his ankles crossed, a brandy in his hand. 'I have been waiting here for hours.'

'I am in no mood. Finish your drink and go.' He knocked Hart's boots off his desk.

'That's a fine thank you for all my efforts today. Are you aware that there is a caricature of you and the lovely Miss V?'

'I am. However, I'm warning you. Do not toy with me. I will not be responsible for my actions.'

'Then you've seen it?'

Julian strode across the room and poured himself two fingers of brandy. 'No, I intend to acquire one tomorrow.'

'Luckily for you I've brought one with me to give to you.'

The pounding of Julian's heart echoed in his ears as his gaze was drawn to the paper resting on his desk. He took a long gulp of brandy and moved slowly to get a closer look. When he spotted his crest on the carriage door he saw red. Burning with rage, he let his eyes scan the print illustrated by Cruikshank. He crumpled the paper and threw it across the room.

'I will destroy him!'

'I must confess I never thought I'd see the day your likeness appeared in a print shop window.'

Julian was so enraged he barely heard his friend's words. 'Tell me you have the plate!'

Shaking his head, Hart narrowed his eyes. 'Odd, but when I enquired I was told the plate had already been sold. Perhaps Vandenberg bought it.'

Julian dropped down into a chair. *Dear God, Katrina will hate me when she sees this!* Her reputation was in tatters, and it was all because he had been selfish enough to risk her good name for a few extended hours with her before he committed his life to an unhappy marriage. What kind of man did that make him?

He was a man of honour, and he would fix this.

He turned to Hart. 'I need to borrow your coach.'

Julian sat across from Mr Vandenberg in the man's study and wondered if Katrina's father had poisoned the brandy he had just poured for him. The man was not pleased. That was plain to see from his stern expression and detached demeanour.

'I wondered if you would call here,' he said in a controlled tone. 'The hour is rather late.'

In all his life he had never been uncomfortable sitting across from a man. He was now. 'I was in session today. However, I felt it best to discuss matters before word travels further than it already has.'

Mr Vandenberg sat back in his wingback chair. The amber liquid in his glass held his attention. 'I see. Am I to assume you are here to discuss a certain caricature?'

'I am.' He had never asked for anyone's hand before. He probably should have thought about what to say before he'd entered Katrina's home.

'I have been assured it is not an accurate depiction of events. Is that true?'

His heart dropped at the realisation that Katrina had

been forced to explain her actions to her father. What exactly would she have told him? 'No, sir, it is not. I—'

Mr Vandenberg held up his hand. 'There is no need to continue, Your Grace. I imagine you are here to offer an honourable solution to this unfortunate matter. However, I assure you that won't be necessary. You have no wish to marry my daughter, and she has no wish to marry you. There is a way to address this without forcing you both into a trip to the altar.'

He should have felt relief at the words. Instead, hearing that Katrina didn't want to marry him was like a hard fist into his gut. 'I don't understand.'

Mr Vandenberg folded his hands on his desk and pierced Julian with his gaze. 'If you voice an interest in the upcoming negotiations between our two countries people will assume that the print is a satirical depiction of your interest in the United States and not a bit of gossip about a scandalous ride with my daughter.'

The suggestion ruffled Julian's principles. He sat up taller and pulled his shoulders back. 'That almost sounds like blackmail.'

'Not at all. I am not asking you to voice your support of my country—just to meet with me at the Chancery so we can discuss the issues. You are known to be a fair and honest man. You can make up your own mind if you think we are being unreasonable with the boundaries we are suggesting. Regardless of what you decide, you can express your opinions on the matter openly and present that print as a political satire attacking your involvement with us.'

It was not an unreasonable request. The logic behind it was sound. He hadn't admitted to anyone today that he had actually taken a drive with Katrina. They could each move forward with their own lives and there would be no scandal associated with their names. He could have his reputation back.

'There is one more thing, Your Grace.'

Julian cleared his vision and focused on the man across from him.

'Whatever fascination you have with my daughter, it needs to end now—for both your sakes.'

All Julian could do was nod his agreement. Blackness was swallowing him up as he realised that he would never again know what she was thinking, or receive one of her smiles, or make her laugh.

Their time together was over.

Katrina waited until the front door had closed before she stood up from where she had been perched on the top step of the staircase.

Her father did not even have to look up. 'He has agreed to my proposition. It is done.'

Those three little words sliced into her.

He wasn't going to marry her.

Tonight her father gave him an easy way to avoid scandal—and he had taken it.

'It is for the best, my dear.'

If it truly was, why did her heart feel as if it had been ripped into tiny pieces that would never be put back together? How could this be for the best when the man she loved had just walked away without even saying goodbye?

Chapter Twenty-One

'Men are dogs.'

Surveying a plate of sweet delicacies, while seated at a table on the terrace of Hipswitch House, Katrina wished she could openly agree with Sarah's declaration. Unfortunately she knew that if she did, it would instigate a discussion that would open the wound she was trying desperately to heal.

She had foolishly fallen in love with a man who was more concerned with what the world thought of him than he was with her. If Julian believed she was lacking, then he deserved a life devoid of the love she could give him. She only wished she could feel that way without wanting to dissolve into a puddle of tears each time she thought of him.

Sarah leaned closer from her seat beside Katrina. 'I said men are dogs.'

'I heard you.' Katrina finished her last bite of moist almond cake and eyed a small bowl of trifle.

'Am I to receive no reply?'

The trifle looked lovely. The creamy custard and vibrant red strawberries were calling out to her. One could not take a beautifully made creation such as this and not eat it. It would be an insult to her hosts.

'What would you have me say?' Katrina said, scooping up a large spoonful.

Sarah sipped her champagne and silently watched Katrina savour every last bit of trifle in the bowl. 'Surely you do not intend to eat those Shrewsbury cakes as well?'

Katrina's hand froze midway to the plate containing three biscuits. She did not miss the censure in Sarah's tone. 'I might have thought about it.' She shifted her hand to pick up her glass of champagne instead.

'I am aware that you would be content to sit here and assist Lady Hipswitch in trying all the delicacies she has provided, however, it is a garden party.' She gave the rolling lawns and hedgerows a marked glance. 'I believe it is customary to actually venture into the garden.'

It was safer on the terrace. This was where the desserts were. Katrina liked it here. Julian might be out there somewhere.

'Why would you want to risk the pristine condition of your slippers on grass and soil when you can sit on this lovely stone terrace and admire the view from up here?'

Sarah took another sip of champagne and sighed. 'Because for once I have found myself in a lovely garden during the day, and I am sitting up here when I could be exploring the rose garden or the maze. Haven't you always wanted to attempt to find your way out of a maze?'

Katrina took a Shrewsbury cake. 'I would rather eat biscuits.'

When she went to take another, Sarah grabbed her hand. 'This will not end well if you do not move from that chair. It is a wonder you are not complaining of stomach pains.'

She hadn't eaten that many desserts. Had she...?

Katrina licked her lips and wiped her mouth with a pristine white napkin that now held traces of custard. 'Oh, very well. However, should you ruin those slippers you have talked of endlessly it will not be my doing.'

Sarah stood and opened her white parasol, shading her eyes from the afternoon light. 'I will risk these stunning silk creations just so you do not become permanently affixed to that chair.'

Before Sarah turned back, Katrina grabbed the last Shrewsbury cake and took a big bite.

'I can hear you chewing,' Sarah commented from over her shoulder as she made her way to the terrace steps.

They passed a number of guests who nodded polite greetings while they walked down the stone staircase and scanned the gardens before them.

'Where shall we go first?' Sarah asked.

Katrina's new bonnet shielded her eyes from the sunlight as she looked to her right. An archery competition was taking place in the shade of a large tree, between six stylishly dressed gentlemen in tailcoats, breeches and boots. Ladies and gentlemen stood about in small groups, offering their encouragement. Her heart ached.

Afraid of seeing Julian, she looked to the left and allowed her gaze to roam around the rose garden, which was enclosed with a low boxwood border. It was there that she had spoken to Madame de Lieven earlier in the day. It seemed to be where she was still holding court. Speaking with the woman once today had been enough.

The safest destination was probably ahead of them, where an enormous thick privet hedgerow divided the vast lawn in half and directed the eye to the garden's maze off in the distance.

Katrina waved towards the hedgerow. 'There are paths on either side. Which one should we take?'

Sarah chose the one on the right, and they started down the gravel path as a soft breeze blew against Katrina's cheeks. She kept her attention on the maze instead of on the carefree people strolling around the lawn, afraid she would see Julian or Mr Armstrong.

'You cannot avoid Lyonsdale for ever,' Sarah said, adjusting her parasol.

Katrina ripped a leaf from the hedgerow and tossed it aside. 'I am not avoiding him.'

'You've hidden yourself away in your room for three days.'

'I was absorbed in some good books.' She plucked another leaf.

'Katrina, soon you will return to New York and meet a man who will become so captivated with you that you will consume his thoughts. He will not be afraid to do whatever is necessary to be with you. You will fall in love, and you will forget all about Lyonsdale.'

Just the sound of his name was like a foot crushing the pieces of Katrina's shattered heart.

'And you know this for a fact?' Katrina certainly did not.

Sarah gave her a reassuring smile. 'I do. You will find love, Katrina. Of that I have no doubt.'

She had found love, only her love wasn't returned.

She could not discuss this with Sarah. Not here. Not now. Possibly not ever. How she wished they had never left the safety of the terrace.

They walked side by side in silence as the gravel crunched under their feet. The maze was still a distance away. If she got lost inside it, could she remain in there for ever? Spending the rest of her life trying to find her way out might keep her from thinking about Julian and recalling every moment they'd spent together.

She needed to keep her thoughts from drifting to him. 'Madame de Lieven has been so kind as to inform me that Mr Armstrong is in attendance today.' She plucked another leaf. 'She even saw fit to say that he had accepted today's invitation with the express desire to see me.'

Sarah scanned the grassy lawn to their right. 'It would be easier to avoid him if we knew what colour he was wearing.'

'Men like him should wear garish shades to match their personalities.'

'If only it were proper to run away if we see him approaching.'

Katrina plucked yet another leaf and tore this one is two. 'Whoever drafted these English rules of conduct must certainly have been a man.'

'A very *boring* man,' Sarah amended, adjusting her parasol.

Katrina looked past Sarah and immediately wished she hadn't. Madame de Lieven was strolling with Mr Armstrong, and from the way she was examining the ladies around her, it was apparent she was searching for someone in particular. The woman was much too persistent. Katrina feared that in a moment of weakness she might agree to allow Madame de Lieven to chaperon her on an outing with that windsucker.

She needed to reach the maze—and she needed to do it quickly.

She grabbed the handle of Sarah's parasol and tilted it, obscuring their faces from the guests on the lawn.

As Julian walked down the gravel pathway on the back lawn of Hipswitch House with Hart, he tugged at the brim of his John Bull hat to shield his eyes from the sun. They walked in silence, each consumed with their own thoughts, and Julian stared at the garden's maze in the distance.

He had not attended any social engagements since the day he had been humiliated by Cruikshank's caricature.

He had tried to convince himself it was because he needed to spend time learning the issues surrounding Britain's North American territories. But he knew the real reason he had not ventured out was because it would have been agonising to see Katrina again.

Days had gone by since his agreement with her father—days when Julian had worried over whether he had made the right decision. They might have been married by now. Instead he had sat alone in his study, reading every word of Katrina's father's book and searching the text for anything that might have been a reference to her. He had even tried reading the remainder of *Frankenstein*, but it was too painful a reminder that now he was all alone. Never again would her lemon scent drift towards him as she leaned on his shoulder while they read together.

The nights were worse. He would toss and turn, and dream about losing her all over again. He hadn't had a decent night's sleep in days. If this continued he was certain to drift off in the middle of his next speech. That was why he had decided to come here today. Seeing her from a distance might somehow put his decision to rest.

'Do you have a destination in mind?' Hart asked, breaking into his thoughts. 'Or are we to continue to pace this path all day?'

'There is no need for you to remain in my company.'

Hart tipped his hat to some passing gentlemen they often saw at Tattersalls. 'Winter and Andrew suggested I join them for archery. However, Lady Morley has been enquiring about you for weeks. Fortunately for you, my reputation is not nearly as impeccable as yours. She will never approach you with Lady Mary while I'm near.'

The thought of conversing with Lady Morley made his head pound. 'Perhaps it's time I become accustomed to her company.' He ripped a leaf off the hedgerow of privets that ran along the pathway to his right.

'And perhaps I have a desire to have leeches suck my body dry.'

'I think it's time I offered for her.'

The silence between them was deafening.

'That is what you truly want?'

Julian continued to stare straight ahead of him. 'It's time.' The maze in the distance was getting closer.

From the corner of his eye, he saw Hart shake his head.

'That is not what I asked.'

'I need an heir.'

'And Lady Mary Morley is to be your choice to give you one?'

'She is the perfect choice to become Duchess of Lyonsdale.' A lump settled in Julian's throat, as if blocking the words.

Silence.

'The perfect choice for who? For your mother? For the Lyonsdale Dukes lying in your family's crypt? She certainly is not the perfect choice for *you*.'

Julian stopped and rounded on Hart. 'She is the perfect choice to bear the next Duke. She is the perfect choice to bear my son.' The words tasted false even as he spat them out.

'And what if you only have daughters? Will it still feel as if you made the perfect choice in choosing Lady Mary?'

He needed to speak of something else—anything else. He had regained his political clout. His opinions had weight once again. That was what mattered in life. That was the life his father had led.

'Morley approached me last night at White's. He wanted my views on the fate of the Hudson Bay Company when the Anglo-American Conference convenes. I'm assuming he holds substantial interest in the company and is concerned his investment may suffer.'

'So now you have become a respected voice on the

facts behind the upcoming negotiations between Britain and America? Interesting how you were able to achieve that.'

Julian refused to look at Hart, and instead ripped off another leaf from the hedgerow. 'I find I'm becoming more and more interested in the matters that need to be settled between our two countries. It is in our best interests to try to achieve amiable relations with them. We need the trade, and that last war with them cost us unnecessarily.'

'Perhaps you have found your purpose. Each of the Lyonsdale Dukes is known for something glorious. Improved Anglo-American relations might be your achievement. A bitter irony, it seems.'

Julian glanced over at his friend and caught the mocking glint in his eyes. This time Julian grabbed an entire stem from the hedge and pulled all the leaves off. They fluttered to the ground, unwanted. With each step the sound of crunching gravel was loud over the silence that stretched between them. He closed his eyes and reminded himself that he would forget her.

Hart adjusted his lazy lock of hair. 'She is here. I spotted her earlier today up at the house.'

Julian's dying heart stirred. 'I told you I have no wish to ever discuss her again.'

'I have not mentioned anyone by name.'

Julian glared at Hart, and he was wise enough not to make any further comment.

Hart's attention followed the new group of leaves that Julian was yanking from the hedgerow. 'Hipswitch's gardeners might take umbrage at your pruning techniques.'

Damn the gardeners!

Julian clasped his hands behind his back. Hart would never understand that Julian couldn't even say her name without causing a stabbing pain in his chest. He knew that eventually she would be a distant memory. There would even come a day when he'd wake up and not recall her face. His stomach churned at the notion.

'Well, this should improve that pained expression of yours,' Hart said. 'It's the woman you've been so eager to see.'

Julian closed his eyes. He prayed he would remain composed when he looked at the lovely woman he could not have. Taking a deep breath, he followed Hart's gaze— and froze when he spotted Lady Morley, walking towards them across the lawn with a determined stride.

The maze was not too far ahead. Hopefully he would reach it before Lady Morley caught up to them.

Helena settled onto a bench facing the entrance to the Hipswitch maze and opened her grey silk parasol, sharing the shade with the Duchess of Skeffington. The day had been fruitless so far. The only other eligible duke who wasn't decrepit was a recluse who never came to London. She had no chance of securing him, and the thought of sharing her marriage bed with a wrinkly old man, even if he was a duke, made her stomach turn.

Today she was focusing her quest on finding a marquess. It was possible Lord Boreham had enough funds to be the answer to her prayers. She was rapidly running out of money. She needed to work quickly, but she had yet to see him.

Her friend adjusted her gloves with a satisfied smile on her face. 'I believe Lord Andrew missed his target today because he was distracted by my presence.'

The only reason Lord Andrew had missed the target was because he'd sneezed at an unfortunate moment. When would Lizzy learn that this brother of the Duke of Winterbourne had no interest in her? *The poor, deluded woman.*

'I asked Olivia if she thought her brother-in-law would be attending the Finchleys' masquerade,' continued Lizzy, 'but she informed me she isn't privy to Lord Andrew's schedule and walked off rather abruptly. That was rather rude, was it not?'

'Olivia and Winterbourne barely speak to one another. What would make you believe she would know what his brother does? Lord Andrew has made no advance towards you in ten years. Do you truly believe the man is attracted to you in any way? He barely acknowledges you.'

Lizzy huffed and turned away. 'Have you chosen a costume for the Finchleys' masquerade?'

This was Lizzy's latest way of reminding Helena that she was the one married to a duke. She knew Helena had no association with the Finchleys.

She could go to the devil!

'No, I'm afraid I've not been invited.'

Lizzy's eyes grew wide with false innocence and she blinked. 'Oh, forgive me. I was certain you would have been. The Marchioness is usually so generous with her invitations. The Americans are even invited. I wouldn't have broached the subject if I'd thought an invitation had not been extended to you. That would have been most unkind of me.'

'And you are all that is good and kind,' Helena replied in an overly sweet manner.

'My, you are in a foul mood today. If you'd had a desire to attend all the most sought-after pleasures of the Season perhaps you should have married a man who had a better standing than the one you did.'

'It wasn't as if I had a choice.'

'Well, you should have selected a more discreet place for your romp with Wentworth, then.'

'How was I to know that that area of his father's estate

had a riding path not far away? I thought he would have had more sense.'

'I really did believe when we came out together you were going to be the one who made the best match. You were the most sought-after girl that Season. Well, there is no going back. You should try to improve your station now, at least.'

As if she hadn't been trying for the last five years!

She had done everything possible to marry a marquess or a duke. And all her efforts had exploded in her face.

Lord Blackwood had even had the nerve to laugh at her when she'd reminded him that he'd promised to wed her if she helped him remove Lady Caroline Shaw from his son's life. She'd never understood why he had wanted to separate her from Lord Hartwick, but if Helena had gained the title of marchioness and the wealth she deserved she really wouldn't have cared. And now Lyonsdale had left her. She was running out of available wealthy men with prominent titles.

Miss Vandenberg strolled past them, deep in conversation with her friend. As they entered the maze Helena wondered for the hundredth time what it was about her that Lyonsdale found attractive.

'I assume there is no opportunity to reconcile with Lyonsdale now that he is pursuing the American?'

Helena snapped her head towards Lizzy. 'What are you talking about? That caricature was merely a political satire. Everyone has heard how involved he has become in the details of the relations between our two countries. There is nothing between them.'

'That is not what Blackwood said when I spoke with him at Carlton House last night.'

If Lizzy mentioned dining at Carlton House one more time, Helena would be shoving her down a flight of stairs the next time the opportunity presented itself.

'And what *did* he say?'

Lizzy's mouth curved into a satisfied smile. 'He said he found it vastly entertaining that after spending time in *your* bed Lyonsdale preferred an American. He said that if there was any truth to the notion that Lyonsdale would make her his duchess, then every member of the *ton* would finally say what he has always known to be true…that, as pretty as you are, you do not have the character of a real lady.'

Helena's grip strangled her parasol handle. *Lord Blackwood should die a slow and painful death!*

She would not be made into a mockery by Lyonsdale's perverse interest in Vandenberg's daughter. She would rather die than be the subject of the derision of the *ton*. Who would want her then? As it was, she was much older than the girls most men sought for a bride. And Wentworth had left her with no children. To any titled gentleman needing an heir that made her a questionable choice.

She'd thought she had seduced Lyonsdale sufficiently that he would be willing to take the risk. She had been wrong.

Lyonsdale couldn't possibly choose an American over her. It would mean disaster for her marriage prospects. She knew Boreham valued his opinion more than any man should. If he thought Lyonsdale preferred an American over her, he never would consider her a suitable choice for his marchioness. She was running out of money. If she didn't marry soon, she didn't know what she would do. She couldn't appeal to her brother for help. The insolent nob would rather see her live in the streets than offer her assistance.

As fate would have it, at that very moment Lyonsdale appeared from the path that ran along the hedgerow and strolled into the maze with Hartwick. The very same maze Miss Vandenberg had entered a short time ago. Helena clenched her jaw to prevent herself from screaming. It couldn't possibly be true. He *couldn't* have left her for an American!

'Was that Lyonsdale who just walked into the maze? What an odd coincidence. I thought I saw Miss Vandenberg enter it earlier,' Lizzy said with a bemused expression.

It was taking all Helena's effort not to beat Lizzy with her parasol. 'I hadn't noticed.'

This was not to be her fate. She would *not* be taken to debtors' prison. She would find a way to end this association between Lyonsdale and the American for good—before it was too late.

Chapter Twenty-Two

As Katrina and Sarah strolled further into the maze the sound of rhythmic splashing grew louder. After making yet another right turn, they were rewarded with the sight of a marble fountain situated in the middle of a large gravel-covered square. The statue at the centre of the fountain was of a Greek or Roman woman, with water pouring from the urn in her hand and splashing into the pool below her. If Katrina had saved all the tears she'd cried over Julian they would have filled numerous urns.

She took off one of her white silk gloves embroidered with forget-me-nots and skimmed her fingers through the cold water in the fountain's base. 'It is lovely here.'

'I told you we would reach the centre. Now let's find a way out.' Sarah marched across the clearing towards another break in the hedgerow.

Katrina watched the water droplets slide from her fingers. 'There is no reason to leave. We are fortunate no one else is here. Can we not simply enjoy the solitude for a bit longer?'

Sarah took her time walking over to her, and sat next to Katrina on the rim of the fountain. 'You cannot hide here forever.'

'I have no intention of remaining here for the rest of the day. Just a few more minutes. Please?'

The noise of the garden party seemed far removed from where they were. Katrina closed her eyes and concentrated on the sound of the water splashing and the birds chirping. For a few minutes, at least, she could pretend she was far away, sitting on a rock alongside the babbling brook that meandered through her home in Tarrytown.

Only now she would be returning to a very different home. Her great-aunt would no longer be there. Her home would never be the same.

She took a deep, steadying breath. Miraculously, Sarah appeared content with the silence between them as well.

Then the sound of crunching gravel ruined everything. Their solitude would soon be interrupted. They agreed that it was time to leave and walked towards another opening in the hedgerow. Hopefully they would get lost for hours, trying to find their way out, and Katrina wouldn't have to pretend her heart wasn't shattered into countless pieces as they spoke to the other guests.

As they entered the hedgerow Katrina bumped into the large form of Lord Boreham. Sarah caught her by the elbow before she tumbled to the ground.

'Forgive me, Miss Vandenberg,' he mumbled, looking flustered after their accident. 'I was not aware you ladies were in here.'

Katrina rubbed the back of her neck. 'And we were not aware you were walking this pathway. I fear we are all to blame.'

He appeared to be grasping for something to say. She had no interest in prolonging an encounter with the man and thought it best to spare him the misery.

'Well, do enjoy your time here, my lord. The fountain is lovely.' She curtsied and edged around him, pulling Sarah with her.

He mumbled his goodbye just after they had turned the first corner on their journey out of the maze.

Julian stepped into what he assumed was the centre of the maze and was surprised to see Lord Boreham on the opposite side of a Grecian fountain, bent over with his bottom raised to the sky.

'You present an interesting sight, Boreham,' Hart called out over the splashing water.

Lord Boreham jerked his body into a standing position, his face flushed bright red. In his hand he held something white. As they strolled around the fountain and stepped closer to him Julian could see that the slip of white was a delicate silk glove with a line of blue flowers trailing down its length. Where had he seen it before?

His heart flipped over when he realised why it looked familiar, and he snatched it out of Lord Boreham's hand. 'Where did you get this?' he demanded.

Lord Boreham went to take it back. 'Miss Vandenberg must have dropped it.'

Her name felt like a kick to the chest. 'And how would you know this is Miss Vandenberg's?' he asked, holding the glove out of Lord Boreham's reach.

'Because she was just here.' He reached for it again.

'I shall return it to her.' Julian knew Hart was watching him. He didn't care. This was all he would have left of Katrina, and he was not letting anyone take it from him.

The next night when Julian arrived home from Parliament he took off his tail coat, grabbed a bottle of brandy, and entered the portrait gallery to find some reassurance from the men who had come before him. He walked from painting to painting, studying the men staring down at him, as he drank from the bottle. They were all very good at appearing to be intimidating and grand, but they did look like a miserable lot. Had any of them been happy?

If anyone had ever understood the heavy weight of being the Duke of Lyonsdale it had been these men. They had known that life entailed sacrifice. They had known that their wants and desires did not matter. Every decision they had made had been made with the consideration of how it would impact their legacy. His father had understood this.

Julian took a long drink. The brandy burned all the way down.

He knew nothing of the women these men had married. Portraits of the duchesses hung in his various estates. He had never had any interest in looking at them before. Now he wondered about the women who had spent their lives alongside these men. Had any of them had the fire and charm of Katrina?

He pulled the flimsy white glove from his waistcoat pocket and touched the raised stitching of the forget-me-nots. He laughed to himself over the irony. He would never forget her, but he wondered if she thought about him at all—even for a fleeting moment each day. Did she feel the heavy weight of their parting? Did she long to hear his voice as much as he longed to hear hers?

The glove held faint traces of her lemon scent. Some day soon he would no longer have even that small reminder of the woman who had come to mean so much to him. He raised the glove to his nose and took a deep breath—holding her scent in for as long as he could.

'I'm surprised to find you here at such a late hour,' his grandmother called from the doorway.

Julian shoved the glove back into its hiding place. *Couldn't a man find a bit of solitude in his own home!*

'I wasn't aware there were restrictions upon when one

might visit a room in one's own home.' He took another drink.

She walked slowly towards him, adjusting her shawl and glancing at the six candelabras that lined the room. 'I don't recall ever seeing this room lit with so many candles.'

'The better to see my illustrious ancestors,' he said, waving the bottle towards the portraits. 'I didn't think they would approve of me skulking around in the dark.'

She eyed the bottle in his hand. 'I see. And what have you noticed about them at one in the morning that you hadn't noticed before?'

'The Dukes of Lyonsdale are a bloody surly lot.'

'I can't speak for all of them, however, your grandfather was known to smile on occasion.' She gestured towards the bottle. 'What are you drinking?'

'Brandy.' He handed her the bottle.

She took a small sip.

Had any of the other duchesses drank brandy from a bottle?

Looking at these men, he doubted it. He walked over to the portrait of his grandfather and tilted his head. 'What was he like?'

She followed him and looked fondly upon the man she had married. 'He was a fine, just man who cared for the people who depended on him. He enjoyed country life more than coming to Town. And he loved his family deeply.'

'Did he love you when he married you?' He motioned for the bottle and she handed it to him.

'No. We came to love each other in time.'

That was what he would do. He would fall in love with Lady Mary. Why hadn't he thought of that before?

He took a long drink and wiped his mouth with his sleeve.

'I hear you have been here for quite some time.'

He had almost forgotten his grandmother was standing next to him. She had been unusually quiet. Perhaps she was feeling poorly.

'I've been here since I returned from session.'

'Have you eaten anything at all? I've noticed you seem to have little appetite of late.'

Had he eaten? He must have, although he couldn't recall. 'I suppose I have.'

She threaded her arm through his. 'Why don't we call and have something brought up to my sitting room?'

They walked towards the doorway, past the blank wooden panel that should have housed the portrait of the Fifth Duke. Julian dragged his grandmother back to stop in front of it. He cocked his head and stared at the grains in the wood.

'He wasn't fit to hang with the others,' he mused out loud.

'That is what we have been told.'

'Why?'

'I do not know.'

He looked down at her and squinted till her image came into view. 'But haven't you ever wondered?'

He took another swig from the bottle. *This brandy was exceptional!*

'I'd wager it was something dreadful,' he said. 'Or, worse yet…scandalous! That was it, wasn't it? He did something scandalous.'

The floor dipped. He should mention that to Reynolds in the morning. They might need to fetch a carpenter.

He looked back at the empty panel. 'Poor cove. I'd wager he fell in love with an unsuitable woman and married her. Worst thing you could ever do, you know. There is no redeeming yourself from that.' He tilted his head to his grandmother and pointed the bottle at himself. 'No one will take *my* portrait and shove it in some dusty attic. *I* will not be marrying the woman I love. Some American lob will get that privilege. I will have the honour of marrying a seventeen-year-old chit who, as far as I can tell, has never had an opinion of her own.'

The floor dipped again, and Julian stamped with his booted foot to get it to stop.

His grandmother reached up and patted his cheek. 'You look very tired, my boy. Perhaps we should walk to your bedchamber.'

'That is very far. I think I'll just sleep here.' He went to sit down on the floor, but the annoying woman wouldn't let him.

'Your rooms are not that far, and on the way you can tell me about the new curricle you have purchased.'

'It's beautiful…very shiny. But I'll not drive Lady Mary around in it. She can have her own carriage.'

He trudged down the hall and went to take another swig of brandy, but the bottle was empty. They should make these bottles bigger.

'I'm marrying her, don't you know? Plan to ask Morley soon. Maybe tomorrow. Best to do it quickly. No need to wait. It's inevitable.'

Chapter Twenty-Three

*W*here *was he?*

Katrina worried at her lip as she stood in the ballroom of Finchley House, studying the guests who meandered around the elaborately decorated room in various costumes. The columns had been dressed to resemble trees and there was greenery tied with flowers that hung from the crystal chandeliers. Even though each guest wore a mask, she was certain she would be able to recognise Mr Armstrong in this imitation woodland forest. At least she hoped she would. Perhaps she should have asked which costume he would be wearing when they had spoken briefly at the Hipswitch garden party.

'May I help you find someone, my dear?'

Katrina jumped at the sound of the Dowager Duchess of Lyonsdale's voice. 'Your Grace, you startled me.' She turned to find the sweet, diminutive woman dressed like a man, with a ruffled collar, jacket, doublet and hose. For the first time in days Katrina had the urge to smile.

The Dowager turned in a circle and bowed. 'What do you say, Miss Vandenberg? Don't I cut a dashing figure?'

A soft laugh bubbled up in Katrina's throat. It sounded scratchy from lack of use. 'That you do, indeed. Are you a particular gentleman?'

'Why, Shakespeare, of course.' The Dowager stood a bit taller—or at least as tall as a woman of her height could. 'That is a beautiful costume,' she said, admiring Katrina's gold armbands.

The warmth of the Dowager's smile tugged at the scattered pieces of Katrina's heart. She missed this woman who had kindly offered her friendship and had taken her under her wing. How she wished she could reach out and hug her.

'Thank you. I must confess I wasn't certain what I wanted to be.'

'I'd say a Greek goddess was the perfect choice.'

It definitely was an improvement over the three hundred shepherdesses she had seen milling about the house since her arrival with the Forresters.

The Dowager scanned the area around them. 'You appeared to be searching for someone. May I offer some assistance?' She raised herself up on her booted toes to improve her view.

Katrina crossed her arms and fingered her armband, fighting the urge to be honest with the Dowager. 'I was just admiring the dancers.'

The Dowager lowered her heels and turned an assessing eye on Katrina. 'From over here?' She leaned closer and lowered her voice. 'You cannot fool me. Now, tell me, am I acquainted with this person?' Her eyes sparkled with anticipation.

Katrina bit her lip again. 'I'm trying to determine what Mr Armstrong is wearing this evening. Do you know the gentleman?'

The smile on the Dowager's face dropped to a frown. 'Yes. I know the man. I was not aware you were well acquainted.'

There was no sense in holding back her sigh from the

Dowager. 'We have been brought together on a number of occasions. I only wish this not to be another.'

'You are trying to avoid him.' The smile was back, brightening the Dowager's face.

'I am. However, if you share that with anyone I will deny it.'

The Dowager placed her finger to her lips. 'I am the soul of discretion.'

As Katrina scanned the room once more she finally spotted him. He was dressed as an ancient emperor with a crown of gold. It was no coincidence. How had Madame de Lieven found out what Katrina was going to wear?

'I have found him,' she said, and groaned.

The Dowager was back on her toes, scanning the crowd. Then she turned sharply and covered her smile with a gloved hand. 'Oh, heavens. He does look very pleased with himself.'

'I've yet to observe him *not* looking pleased with himself.' Katrina stepped behind the Dowager. Unfortunately the woman's height would do nothing to block Armstrong's view of her. 'He is bound to find me. I'm certain he knows what I am wearing. There aren't many women draped in gold gowns walking around this evening.'

'You are only the third I have seen as yet.'

Coming here had been a mistake. While Katrina loved spending time with the Dowager, it brought back memories of the time she had called on the woman at Lyonsdale House—the day Julian had almost kissed her in his library.

How long would the pain last? Perhaps when Sarah's dance ended she would be able to keep Katrina's mind off her broken heart.

Julian stood in the ballroom of the Finchleys' masquerade between Winter and Lord Andrew Pearce, trying to concentrate on what the brothers were talking about and not on the skull-crushing pain pounding in his head. Did the Finchleys *really* need this many candles in one ballroom? Didn't they realise that a darkened ballroom was preferable to one that appeared to be lit with the brightness of seven suns?

He looked down into his untouched glass of champagne and wished it were coffee. *Could one actually hear the sound of champagne bubbles?*

One of his friends might have just asked him a question. He wasn't certain. 'They are a valuable trading partner, and our borders in North America will be expensive and difficult to defend should another war break out. It is in our best interests to improve our relations with them.'

Could he go and lie down now?

'Thank you for clarifying that for us, Lyonsdale,' Andrew said with a smirk over the rim of his glass. 'Should I have any interest in Anglo-American relations in the future, I will be sure to inform you.'

That reply had seemed to work with everyone else this evening. Why were his friends so difficult?

'Pardon me—I thought you had asked me a question.'

'I did,' Andrew replied. 'I asked you what it was you drank this morning?'

'Last night. It was last night. From what I can recall it was brandy. I am not completely certain of that, however.'

Both men shook their heads in pity.

Winter removed the glass from Julian's hand. 'This will not help.'

'I need something to do with my hands that does not include squeezing my forehead so tightly that my brains pop out.'

His friends laughed—which was a very cruel thing to do since the sound bounced around in his head.

'Why did you even bother attending this evening?'

Andrew asked. 'You've been avoiding all forms of entertainment recently anyway. Two days ago you attended Hipswitch's garden party. That alone should have left you free to avoid any other outings for at least another two weeks.'

'I need to see Morley and arrange a time to call on him.'

There was no mistaking the look that passed between Winter and Andrew. 'And what would you have to discuss with him?' Winter asked.

He was a tall man, of intimidating size. If Julian hadn't know him so well, he might have taken his question as a demand.

'I've decided to ask for Lady Mary's hand.'

Andrew began to choke on his champagne, and Winter's sharp eyes bored into him through his black mask.

'She is a logical choice,' Winter commented evenly. He understood the personal sacrifices one must make as a duke.

Julian rolled his shoulders and glanced around the room until he spied his grandmother. Whatever had possessed her to choose the costume she had? Then his attention shifted and every muscle in his body locked at the sight of Katrina standing next to her. He needed a deep breath, but his lungs refused to cooperate.

As if some cruel force in nature had called to her she suddenly looked up, and their eyes met through their respective masks. His dying heart gave one weak effort to stir.

He couldn't look away even if he wanted to. Which he should—but he didn't.

She was breathtaking, in a sleeveless gown threaded with gold that sparkled in the candlelight. Her hair fell past her shoulders in ringlets, and bands of gold encircled her upper arms. She was Andromeda—and he was no Perseus.

Everything he had ever wanted was across the room from him. And he could not have it.

'Lady Mary will come into her own some day,' Winter said.

A sharp pain stabbed at his chest. Julian blinked and Katrina turned away. The connection was gone, as if it had never existed. Two people who had known each other once—now were strangers.

He needed to go somewhere—somewhere dark—where he could be alone and lick his wounds. The Finchleys had a library. No one would go to the library in the middle of a masquerade ball. It would be his refuge.

Julian locked the door behind him after he entered the unoccupied room and untied his mask. It was dark enough that the moonlight streaming in from the terrace doors cast a bluish white light into the room. He dropped into a plump wingback chair near the fireplace and closed his eyes. There was an advantage to dressing like a pirate. They did not wear restrictive tail coats.

The rattling of the library doorknob broke the peacefulness of the room. Thank God he had had the forethought to lock the door. Let whomever it was find another room to carry on an assignation. This room was his, and he needed to be alone.

After some time he realised he must have dozed off. He stood and stretched, but it did nothing to alleviate the tension coiled tight in his body. He couldn't put the inevitable off any longer. It was time to approach Morley.

He rubbed the ache in his chest, finding it was becoming hard to breathe. With luck the cool night air might help.

As he turned towards the French doors leading to the terrace he stumbled at the sight of Katrina's familiar silhouette in the moonlight.

He recalled standing with her on the Russian Ambassador's terrace the night his life had changed. No woman had ever affected him the way she did. And deep down he knew no one else ever would. Would there come a day when he stopped caring about her? *Caring?* It was much more than that. It was more than anything he had ever felt for anyone.

Julian gripped the back of a nearby chair. Suddenly it all made sense. He loved her—he had from the moment he'd spoken with her under the stars. That was why he had such a burning need for her. That was why no other woman could compare to her—and that was why, now they were apart, all he wanted to do was hold her in his arms and never let her go.

The terrace appeared to be deserted except for her lovely form. The need to know if she felt the same was consuming.

But before he could take another step towards the door, a man dressed in a black domino costume with a half mask and tricorn hat approached Katrina's side. Julian would wager one hundred pounds it was Armstrong. His heart sank. It was too late.

His vision clouded over with images of Armstrong dancing with her at the Whitfields' ball. It cleared just in time for him to see the man covering Katrina's nose with something white, shortly before her body fell limply into the man's arms.

Julian's brow furrowed. Katrina never swooned.

Before he was able to react, the man had hoisted her into his arms and carried her off into the darkened garden.

What the bloody hell was going on?

Julian ran for the French doors, raced down the terrace steps and through the garden. Just as he charged through the gate onto South Bruton Mews a carriage pulled away. Julian was certain Katrina was inside it. His almost dead heart now pounded furiously in his chest. He ran after it, but wasn't fast enough, and the carriage made its way over the cobblestones towards Bruton Street.

Julian slammed his fist into the garden wall, not even feeling the pain. There *had* to be a way to reach them.

Finchley House was one of only two houses on Grafton Street whose gardens backed directly onto the mews. All the other houses had stables separating the mews from their gardens. Julian scanned the long narrow lane, searching desperately for a horse. What he found was Hart's driver, sitting idly on his bench in an unmarked carriage a few doors down. Thank God his friend was always prepared for a hasty departure.

Julian whistled for Jonas just as Hart ran up beside him.

'I saw you hurry past. What has happened?'

'Someone has taken Katrina. I'm taking your carriage.' Julian climbed onto the driver's box, next to Jonas, and looked down at Hart. 'Find Miss Forrester and let her know. You both must keep this a secret. Watch for my return.'

Hart nodded, and stepped back as Julian and Jonas sped away.

The carriage rocked as it travelled over the bumpy cobblestones. There was a bend in the lane ahead. Hopefully the other carriage would be visible once they had made the turn.

'There was a carriage here just now, Jonas. Did you see it?'

'Aye, Your Grace. The one with the unmatched pair?'

'That's the one. We need to follow it.'

Jonas nodded as if chasing down another carriage was a common occurrence and then called out to the horses. 'Come on, boys, on with you.'

The carriage picked up speed.

'We won't know which way they went once they

reached Bruton Street,' he pointed out to Julian over the sound of turning wheels and clattering hoofbeats.

'I'm aware of that. Let us pray they are not that far ahead of us and we see them.'

Julian had no idea what he would do if they did not. He clenched his right hand into a fist.

Thankfully when they reached the end of the mews, they spotted the driver's green coat and the mismatched pair of horses as they turned right onto New Bond Street. Julian knew that once they were away from the street lights of Mayfair it would be harder to track them.

'Whatever you do, do not lose sight of them,' he ground out.

They followed the carriage out of Mayfair towards Cheapside. He thought of trying to overtake it, but was afraid it might cause an accident and Katrina might not survive. He would follow this carriage to the far corners of the land to get her back, and when he did he was going to beat Armstrong senseless.

If it *was* Armstrong, could it be possible that he was taking her to Gretna Green? Was he that desperate? Certainly by the way he had rendered her unconscious, this elopement was not by choice.

If they were headed there they would have to change horses in two hours. Julian needed to force himself to remain calm until then. He would do Katrina no good if he could not think clearly. In two hours he would have her back. And Armstrong would regret the day he had planned this.

When Jonas lost sight of the carriage near St. Paul's it was nearly impossible for Julian not to lash out at the coachman. They could not have disappeared. They had to be somewhere close by.

He gripped the rail in front of him until his knuckles were white. *Dear God, please let me find her.*

The streets in this part of London were not very familiar to him. Thank God Jonas appeared to know his way around. After circling the streets for what felt like hours, but had probably been less than fifteen minutes, they spotted the carriage parked on Newgate Street. He had Jonas stop far enough back that their presence would not be easily noticed.

Looking closely at his surroundings, Julian realised he knew this place. The carriage was parked in front of the Crypt of St Martin's le Grand. He, like other people in London, had ventured out here to inspect the crypt when it had been uncovered not long ago.

The implication of where they were made his palms sweat and the hair on the back of his neck stand on end. This was not a forced elopement. What was Armstrong up to?

Before Julian had a chance to determine the best way to approach the situation the cloaked figure hurried out of the crypt empty-handed, and re-entered the carriage. Julian's blood ran cold. His gut told him Katrina was in the crypt.

As the carriage pulled away Jonas spoke up. 'Shall I follow it?'

He shook his head. He knew where to find Armstrong—and he *would* find him. But first he needed to reach Katrina. He only prayed he wasn't too late.

Chapter Twenty-Four

Katrina's head felt as if it was being squeezed between two bricks. She tried opening her eyes and found her lids exceedingly heavy. Raising her chin from her chest was also proving difficult. The air had the earthy scent of a root cellar, and the smell made her nose twitch. She should leave this place. If only she wasn't too tired to move from this chair.

'Oh, you're waking up,' a female voice drawled. 'That should make this a bit more interesting. I suppose the ropes were necessary, after all.'

That velvety voice was familiar, but Katrina couldn't recall who it belonged to. With much effort she forced herself to blink, and when her vision cleared Lady Wentworth slowly came into view a few feet in front of her. She was wearing a dark cape over a jonquil gown.

Katrina had no recollection of leaving the Finchleys' with this woman. In fact she couldn't even remember leaving the ball at all.

Lady Wentworth cocked her head, and Katrina felt like a butterfly pinned in a case.

'I've tried,' the woman mused, 'but I still cannot fathom what he finds attractive about you.'

Katrina tried to place where in Finchley House they

might be. This was not any of the beautifully decorated rooms she had seen. The floor and walls were made of crumbling stone and dirt. Aside from the chair she sat on, the only other furniture was a little table near Lady Wentworth. There were items on it, but she couldn't make out what they were in the shadows. No windows were evident, and the only light came from a lantern on the floor.

Not far away was a deep stone box, large enough to house most of Katrina's gowns. She tipped her head back and squinted at the arched vaulted ceiling divided by stone pillars.

Katrina swallowed hard. It did little to relieve the scraping at the back of her throat. 'Where are we?'

'In a crypt. A very convenient choice on my part.'

A cold chill ran up her spine. Why couldn't she remember coming here? Her chest tightened as her muddled head started to clear, and she tried to suppress the panic that was taking hold. Why, of all places, were they in a crypt? Dead people belonged in crypts. She needed to leave.

Her arms felt numb. When she tried to lift them up she couldn't, and realised her hands were tied behind her back. She tugged on the rope, but it wouldn't budge. When she tried to raise her body, she saw her ankles were tied to the spindly chair.

'You have tied me up?' Katrina let out an incredulous breath. 'Why would you do that?'

'My associate did it before he left. It seemed prudent at the time.' There was an odd, satisfied glint in Lady Wentworth's eyes. 'The ropes are very secure. Struggling will not help. Your waking has forced me to adjust my plan,' she said, picking up a small bottle from the table, 'but rest assured you won't be leaving. The man I hired will make certain of that.'

She glanced pointedly at the large stone box in the centre of the room and Katrina realised it was a tomb.

Muscles and veins strained against Katrina's skin as she pushed with all her might to break the ropes that bound her. Warm rivulets trailed down her hands but she barely felt the pain.

Julian had followed the darkened steps that led down into the Crypt at St Martin's le Grand, holding the carriage lamp Jonas had handed him. The rapid pounding of his heart echoed in his ears as he navigated the underground stone passageways. Rounding the second corner, he spied the faint glow of light far up ahead and hoped it meant he had found Katrina.

Not knowing what or who he would be facing, he turned down the flame in the lantern. He crept slowly along, trying for the hundredth time to imagine why someone would take Katrina. As he made his way closer to the entrance of a chamber he could hear the sound of muffled voices and listened closely for hers. When he heard it, he almost stumbled to his knees in relief. *She was alive.*

He placed the lantern down outside the entrance, and when he looked inside was dumbstruck to see Katrina with Helena. None of this made any sense.

The domino wasn't Armstrong?

'What the bloody hell is going on?' he bellowed, advancing into the earthen chamber and avoiding the stone coffin in the centre.

Both women let out a gasp. Helena jumped and something fell from her hand, shattering on the floor. She backed away, moving closer to the wall.

Katrina was sitting in a chair about twenty feet to his left. Her eyes were closed, probably out of relief. When she opened them she glared at him.

'You have horrid taste in women!' she yelled at him. 'That's what is going on. Now untie my hands and feet so I can beat her to a pulp!'

He took a step towards Katrina, uncertain how he would handle her when she was this furious.

'Stay where you are,' Helena ordered.

She was aiming a pistol at his head and looking him directly in the eye. The sound of her rapid breathing could be heard across the chamber.

This could not be happening.

He was about to extend his hand and demand she give him the gun when he noticed the dead calm in her eyes. An unsettling shiver ran up his spine and he recalled her violent temper when he had ended their affair. He had seen how unpredictable she could be. The question was, would she use that gun?

He glanced over at Katrina, who sat frozen in place. It almost looked as if she had stopped breathing. Thank heavens she had stopped talking. Her eyes darted to his and he gave her a restrained nod. Her eyes seemed to say she was willing to stay quiet and allow him to determine how best to disarm Helena.

Now, if only he knew what the best way was...

She liked expensive things—he would start there. He looked back at the woman who had a gun pointed at his head.

'What is it you want, Helena?' he asked, hesitant even to move his hands.

She laughed and shifted on her feet—the gun didn't waver. '*Now* you ask...now that I have your life in my hands. That is rich,' she spat. 'I want the life I was destined to have. The life I deserve to have.'

'No one is saying you cannot have it.'

She shook her head. 'I cannot have it now. I might have before you arrived, but not now.'

'Why did you do this? Why did you take Miss Vandenberg?'

'You chose an American over me,' she ground out.

'An *American*!' She licked her lips nervously. 'It was bad enough when I thought you were going to listen to that harpy of a mother of yours and marry Morley's brat. But then the *ton* would have assumed you had finally given in to your mother's pestering. That chit ranks higher than me. It would not be seen as an insult to my person. But this...' she waved the pistol towards Katrina '...this is an *American*.' The final statement was said through her clenched teeth.

He needed to direct her attention away from Katrina. He took a step closer to Helena. The pistol was back, pointing at his head.

'Don't. Move.' She cocked it. 'No one of worth will want me if they think an American is above me. You don't understand. You're a *man*! You live in your lofty world, with all your money and power. You are free to choose the life you want. You. Have. *Everything!*'

At the moment it felt as if he had nothing. He raised his hands in an attempt to steady her.

'You have built a fine life for yourself since Wentworth's death.'

'I have *nothing*! I have taken to selling my possessions to pay off my debts. The money is gone and there is no way for me to get more unless I marry well.'

How could he not have realised she was in such dire straits? 'But the gambling... I have sat in card rooms with you,' he muttered out loud.

'I was there to attract men like *you*! *You* have reduced me to spreading my legs in search of the money and prestige that already should be mine. Every time I had one of you inside me I earned that title! Every time I waited for you and turned down other invitations I earned it! And every time someone asked if a proposal was imminent, and I had to smile and say nothing, I earned it!

That chatterbox Lizzy Skeffington should not be a duchess! *I* should!'

All her screaming had made her voice hoarse.

'Surely you could find a husband with a lesser title? There are many wealthy men who would beg to marry you.'

Her body began trembling with rage. 'You expect me to marry a viscount or a baron?' she shrieked.

He put his palms back up. It was like trying to settle a skittish horse. His brief moment of sympathy at her situation had clouded his knowledge of her pride and her sense of entitlement. Knowing he had once felt affection for her was making him physically ill.

'How will taking Miss Vandenberg help? I still do not understand?'

She let out a mean laugh. 'You stupid man—this isn't about taking her. It's about *killing* her. If she is dead you can't marry her, and my reputation as a desirable woman will be secure.'

Every bone in Julian's body seemed to disintegrate, and it was taking great effort for him to remain standing tall and firm. Katrina wasn't going to die tonight. Somehow he would make certain of it.

'You have it wrong about Miss Vandenberg and myself. We barely speak.'

Helena's eyes darted between the two of them and for the first time he could see her confidence waver. 'You're lying. I saw her enter the maze at the Finchleys' shortly before you did.'

This was all for nothing. Katrina wasn't even his. And if Julian hadn't witnessed her being kidnapped he would have been asking Morley for his daughter's hand about now.

He shook his head sadly. 'It was simply a coincidence. I never saw her.'

He looked over at Katrina, bound in the chair. He could tell she was frightened. So was he. But she was remaining quietly composed, allowing him to try to defuse the situation. He prayed he knew how.

'His Grace is telling the truth,' Katrina called out, keeping her eyes on Helena. 'We barely know one another.'

Helena licked her lips and shifted her feet slightly, staring at Julian. 'I've seen the way you look at her. There is something between you.'

He shook his head. 'I find her to be attractive.' *Beyond compare.* 'She is American, so her mannerisms are different.' *And charming.* 'But, as I said, we barely speak.' *But she will have my heart forever.*

Helena's eyes darted between them again. Her bravado was weakening. But if he grabbed for the pistol it could go off, and the shot might hit Katrina.

Slowly he held out his hand. 'Give me the pistol, Helena. No one needs to die tonight.'

She steadied her hand. 'I know I will swing for what I've done.'

'It does not have to come to that,' he said reassuringly. 'Now, hand it to me.'

Her knuckles whitened around the gun and her face set with determination.

He motioned for the weapon. 'As angry as you are with me, you will not shoot me. You are not that evil.'

Dear God, he hoped it was true!

Her breathing had become erratic, and in the glow of the lantern he saw tears rim her eyes.

'If I hand you my pistol, what will happen then?'

He took a step closer. 'I will untie Miss Vandenberg and the two of us will leave. That is all.'

From the corner of his eye he saw Katrina look his way. *Keep silent, Katrina. Do not say a word.*

He knew he needed to take her back to the ball. If the *ton* found out she had been kidnapped, her reputation would be beyond repair. He would find a way to deal with Helena later. Debtors' prison would be enough of a punishment. If he involved Bow Street in this, the kidnapping would be all over the newspapers by morning.

'Give me the pistol.'

She took two deep, uneven breaths and uncocked the gun.

He stepped closer and motioned again with his fingers. This time she handed him the pistol.

Relief flooded through Julian, and it was a wonder he had the strength to hold the gun in his hand.

He rushed to Katrina's side and began untying her hands. She rubbed her wrists as he worked on the bloody knot near her ankles. He needed to get her outside before Helena did something else irrational. When the knot was finally free and he had unbound her legs, he stood, ready to take her in his arms. But she lunged for Helena instead.

Julian grabbed her by the waist before she was able to get close to Helena and pulled her back. 'We need to leave. *Now.*'

She tore herself free from his grip, her eyes drilling holes into Helena. His former lover was sitting on the floor, staring sightlessly at the ground. It appeared the realisation of what had transpired had hit her.

He needed to get Katrina out of there quickly. Helena was too unstable. He would deal with her tomorrow. They needed to return to the ball.

Julian tugged Katrina's arm and together they escaped out into the passageway and to freedom.

'There is a carriage waiting for us above ground,' he said, taking her hand. 'I will return you to the masquerade. All will be well.'

* * *

In the darkness of the rocking carriage Katrina wrapped her arms around herself, attempting to alleviate the chills that had begun racking her body the moment they left the crypt. All she wanted was to crawl into bed and tuck herself into mountains of blankets. With any luck she could remain there for days, and avoid telling her father about any of this for as long as possible.

'You're shivering,' Julian said from his seat across from her. His body jerked in hesitation before he crossed the carriage. 'Forgive me—in this costume I have no coat to give you. I can only offer you my warmth.' He shifted closer to her on the bench and drew her to his side.

Her body should have melted into his. Instead it stiffened into stone. Although she would be forever grateful to him for coming for her, he was still the man who didn't want her. She was afraid that if she let herself find comfort in his embrace she wouldn't be able to let go of him when they arrived at Finchley House.

'She told me she had hired someone who would dispose of me later tonight. We were fortunate he did not return.' She rubbed her forehead. 'What do you think will happen to her?' she asked into the darkness.

Julian shrugged. 'She will not say anything about tonight. She would be sealing her fate at the gallows. I will make certain her debts are called in tomorrow. If she cannot pay them, as I suspect she can't, she will be taken to debtors' prison.'

She turned to him and met his gaze for the first time in the dim light of the carriage lantern. 'Won't her family help her?'

'I do not believe so. I do not know the particulars, but I am aware that she does not speak to her brother.' He cleared his throat. 'Are you in need of a physician? Were you harmed?'

The sound of his true concern was evident. It was breaking her heart all over again.

Katrina shook her head. 'There is no need. I have come to no harm.'

It occurred to her that the last time they had spoken it had been in a carriage such as this. As far as she knew, this might even be the same carriage they had travelled in.

She hugged herself tighter as the shards of her heart crashed around her chest. 'How did you find me?'

'I saw you taken from the terrace. I followed you out to the mews and was lucky to find Hart's driver parked nearby. We tracked you to the crypt.'

Silence stretched between them. After some time Julian cleared his throat. 'We will be arriving at the Finchleys' soon. As much as it unnerves me to leave you alone, I will enter the ball and send Miss Forrester out to bring you back in through the garden. Although it's a masquerade, and everyone is in disguise, it would be best to have her with you to ensure your reputation.' He appeared to realise his commanding nature. 'With your permission, of course.'

Katrina nodded. This night could not end soon enough for her liking.

They travelled the remainder of the way to the house in silence. It didn't take long before the carriage slowed, made a number of sharp turns, and eventually came to a stop. They were back at Finchley House.

She felt the hesitation when Julian withdrew his arm from around her shoulder. 'Thank you, Julian, for coming after me.'

He gave her a solemn nod. 'I am truly sorry,' he replied before he opened the door. Looking at her one last time, he turned and left her.

Katrina didn't have the physical or emotional energy to try to determine what he was sorry for, and she rested her head back on the squab while she waited for Sarah. It wasn't long before the door opened and Sarah jumped inside.

'Oh, thank God you are back,' Sarah said, throwing her arms around Katrina and hugging her.

Katrina knew she would have to walk through the ball-room as if nothing harrowing had happened. In order to do that, she could not allow herself to sob in Sarah's arms. It was taking all her effort to remain composed.

'I was so very worried,' Sarah continued. 'Hartwick told me you had been taken. I made an excuse to my mother about you being sick. I told her you must have eaten something disagreeable and that when your stomach was better it probably would be wise for us to leave.' She hugged her again. 'Dear God, you're shaking.'

Sarah took off her highwayman's black cape and draped it around Katrina's shoulders.

'How long have I been gone?'

'A little over two hours.' She ran her hands up and down Katrina's arms. 'Are you well? Did they harm you? Who was it that took you?'

Although Katrina was relieved to see her friend, Sarah's chattering was making her head pound. She quietly relayed all the details of what had happened as she donned the mask Sarah had handed her and they re-entered the garden to find Sarah's mother.

Hopefully, it would be easy to get her to agree to leave the ball. Katrina just wanted to be safe—in her home. She should have learned that standing alone on a terrace during a ball was never a good idea.

Katrina entered her home an hour later. The familiar smell of lemon oil in the entrance hall made her muscles soften. She was home. She was safe. If only she could sleep for days.

She was well on her way to bed when her foot landed on the fifth tread of the staircase and it creaked.

'Katrina, is that you?' Her father's voice called to her from the direction of his study.

She was about to call out her answer when he entered the hall in his dressing gown. It took all her effort not to run into his arms. 'You are up rather late,' she said.

'I could not sleep. Did you enjoy yourself at the ball?'

She had never been able to lie to him. So she simply pasted on a smile.

'Come with me to my study and you can tell me all about it while I put my papers in order.'

Reluctantly, Katrina walked down the stairs and followed him. He moved behind his massive desk, closed his inkwell, and shuffled through his papers.

'Was the music to your liking?'

She nodded.

'And the costumes? I imagine some were rather elaborate?'

Again, she nodded.

This time he looked at her over the rim of his glasses and tilted his head. When he narrowed his gaze on her, she shifted on her feet. He grabbed at her right hand from across his desk.

'What has happened? Why do your wrists look as if you have been bleeding?'

She tugged her hand out of his. 'It is nothing.'

'Nothing!' He stepped out from behind his desk to stand in front of her. 'You have been injured. Was there an accident? Why was I not informed?'

His concern was too much. She could no longer continue the pretence that she was unaffected by what had happened. She threw her arms around her stunned father and held him tight.

Thankfully, he didn't say anything when she began

to cry. He just hugged her and patted her back as he had done when she was a little girl.

He waited patiently until she had finished crying before he spoke. 'Tell me what happened.'

She took a deep breath and stepped back from him. 'I am fine. Know that. The only harm that has come to me are these bruises on my wrists.'

He nodded, but there was wariness in his eyes. He guided her to a chair and she curled up on it. She told him what had happened and he listened without interrupting.

It wasn't until she had finished that he finally spoke. 'I knew any association you had with Lyonsdale would not end well.'

'It is not his fault. You cannot blame him for what that woman did.'

Her father stood and paced the room. 'That woman would not have done what she did if it weren't for his interest in you.'

'It is not as if he intended for this to happen.'

'Why are you defending him?' he demanded.

'I'm not. However, I do find it grossly unfair to blame the man when the fault lies elsewhere.'

He stopped pacing and came to her. 'We will agree to disagree on this subject.'

Chapter Twenty-Five

'You need to move it more to the left.'

The footmen rehanging the massive painting shifted it according to Julian's direction. He leaned against the wall opposite where they were hanging the portrait of the Fifth Duke and sipped his coffee. He had been having breakfast in his bedchamber when Reynolds had arrived to inform him the portrait had been located. Eager to see his mysterious ancestor, Julian had left his untouched plate and met him in the gallery.

This painting stood out from the others. It showed a man standing tall in a country setting, with a hooded falcon perched on his gloved hand. He looked out at the viewer with the expression of a man who enjoyed life. Julian almost smiled at the notion that Katrina probably wouldn't have minded having him at her dinner table.

One of the hardest things he had ever done was leaving her in Hart's carriage last night to go and find Miss Forrester. If he could have had his way, he would have spirited her off to his home and tucked her into his bed, where he would have been able to hold her in his arms for days. But it had not escaped his notice that she had not wanted his comfort. His heart ached unbearably.

During his ride home from the ball, Helena's words played over in his head.

'You are free to choose the life you want. You have everything.'

He didn't have everything. He didn't have Katrina. And she was more important to him than anything else. One day he would close his eyes for the last time, and deep down he knew he would still be thinking about her. Was that the life he wanted? A life of sadness and regret?

It was time for him to live his own life and not an imitation of his father's. His mother was wrong. He deserved more than contentment. He deserved to be happy. It was time he wrote his own story of what made a man an honourable duke.

'Reynolds told me I would find you here,' his mother said, marching into the gallery and eyeing the footmen with a perplexed expression.

He dismissed the servants as she approached his side, dressed for an outing.

'You're venturing out early today, I see,' he remarked.

'The renovations are complete. I want to inspect my home before I have my things moved back tomorrow,' she said, adjusting her gloves. 'I assume you have heard the news about your old friend?'

Julian closed his eyes and let out a resigned breath. 'What has Hart done now?'

Her forehead creased before she caught herself and relaxed her features. 'Not him. Lady Wentworth.' The crease in her forehead was back. 'Did you not read the papers this morning?'

He shook his head. It was the first day in ages he had not. He had been too busy resurrecting the Fifth Duke. His stomach bottomed out. He had planned to speak with someone about pushing for her debts to be called in today.

'She was found in her home late last night. She poisoned herself. The papers are saying she could barely pay her bills. The servants confirmed it.'

His blood ran cold. So this was how things would end between them. 'Was there a note?'

His mother shook her head. 'The papers didn't mention one.'

Part of him knew he should feel some sympathy for her, but after having a gun pointed at his head and knowing what she had planned to do with Katrina, he felt nothing but relief.

Next to him, his mother turned and studied the portrait of the Fifth Duke, now hanging where it belonged. 'Where did that come from?'

He welcomed the change in subject. 'The attic.'

'Is that the Fifth Duke?'

'It is.'

She turned to Julian and eyed him up and down. 'There is a striking resemblance between the two of you.'

Was there? The shape and colour of the eyes were similar, as was the shade and wave of the man's hair. He had a square jaw, and his aquiline nose seemed to possess the same small bump in the middle that Julian knew his had. Now that she mentioned it, he could see the resemblance.

'Why is he here? He is not fit to hang with the others.'

Julian took a slow sip of his coffee. 'I think he is.'

The Fifth Duke had been on Julian's mind since Katrina had asked about him. He wasn't sure what the man had done, since there was no reference to him in the family history. Perhaps he had simply lived a good life in the country, taking care of his estates and the people who lived on them. A man could be a good duke without needing the world to tell him he was.

Winter was right. He was not a party of one man. Others shared his political and ethical beliefs. Together they were stronger than one man alone. If he could share his knowledge and write impassioned speeches, did it really matter who said the words to get the votes they needed? And it truly was in Britain's best interest to improve its relationship with America. There were others who believed that as well. He recalled Hart telling him that Julian's great achievement might be to aid in improving relations between the countries.

He wasn't certain if he was simply convincing himself of this to justify marrying Katrina, or because it was true. What he *did* know, without a doubt, was that he would place his need to be with her above everything else. He was a duke of England, but life was fleeting—it was time he took what he wanted!

'There is something you should know,' he said to his mother, who was staring at him with trepidation.

'Why do I believe I will not approve of what it is you have to say?'

'I will be asking for Miss Vandenberg's hand today. God willing, she will accept.'

His mother blanched. 'You can't mean that. She is an American. She has no understanding of what it means to be a duchess.'

'You told me you would defer to me on who I choose to marry.'

His normally aloof mother shook with anger. 'Yes, but that was when I was certain you would be choosing Lady Mary! You assured me that caricature was a political satire and nothing more.'

'Miss Vandenberg is an intelligent, charming woman who is the daughter of a diplomat. She would make an excellent choice for my duchess.'

'Have you gone mad? Your father would never have approved of her. He understood what was expected of your title. That was why he chose Emma for you. You are

Lyonsdale. Miss Vandenberg's family isn't even English! Your ancestors fought alongside Kings and served in the courts of many of our monarchs. *She* comes from a family of shipyard owners, and her father writes novels. What honour is there in that?'

Julian placed his cup down on the nearby window ledge and tried to steady his anger. 'She will bear my heir if *I* decide that is what I wish. I suggest, madam, that you remember I am the head of this family. I will no longer tolerate your interference with my life.'

'You will lose the respect of influential men, and people will mock you behind your back,' seethed his mother.

Not everyone would feel that way—although he knew there were men who *would* be angry with him for choosing to marry an American over their very suitable daughters. 'I can manage the *ton*.'

She placed her hand on her stomach and seemed to labour for breath. 'If you do this there will be no turning back.'

He didn't want to turn back. Behind him were the choices he had made about Katrina that he wasn't proud of. He prayed she would find it in her heart to forgive him.

Hours later, Julian stood on the steps of Katrina's home, staring at the round brass knocker and wondering for the tenth time if he would be received. He was a duke from one of the most respected families in the realm. However, he wasn't certain that would make much of a difference this morning to Katrina's father. The man had forbidden him from calling on his daughter. Common decency dictated that he respect the man's wishes. Perhaps he would blame this transgression on lack of sleep.

Before he could lift his hand to knock, the door opened smoothly and he was met with the sight of her butler. The man was English, and therefore well versed in the respect a duke should be given. However, this man also knew of the times when Julian had called on Katrina in secret, and there was something in his eyes that told Julian he would bar him entrance into the home if he could.

'Good day, Your Grace. May I help you?'

'I am here to see Miss Vandenberg. Is she at home?'

There was a hesitation before the door was opened further and Julian was ushered inside. This time when Wilkins went to present his card to Katrina, he left Julian waiting in the entrance hall. It was a silent statement that Julian did not miss. He was not welcome here.

The sound of footfalls caught his attention, and he wasn't entirely surprised when Mr Vandenberg walked into the hall. The man did not extend his hand in greeting. 'Good morning, Your Grace. Would you care to join me in my study?'

The coolness of his tone could have chilled a steaming cup of tea.

What exactly did Katrina's father know about last night?

Julian followed him into the study and took the seat by the desk that was offered.

Mr Vandenberg walked around his desk and sat down. 'What can I do for you today?' His voice was professional and not the least bit friendly.

Julian pushed his shoulders back and raised his chin. 'Actually, sir, I am here to see your daughter.'

'I thought we had agreed you would not have any contact with her. Yet here you are.' Julian opened his mouth to reply but the man held up his hand to stop him. 'Let's not speak in pretence. I am well aware of what occurred last night, and I have read the papers this morning.' He arched a knowing brow. 'While I am in your debt for bringing her home safely to me, it does not change the fact that the two of you have no reason to see one another. Twice you have almost damaged her reputation. That is reason enough. Rumour has it you are a man of high moral standards. If that is true, why are you here? What do you want?'

All last night Julian had tossed and turned, worrying about how she was faring, both physically and emotionally. He had wanted to hold her in his arms until she fell asleep and assure her all would be well. But he hadn't been able to—and it had burned in his gut. He needed to apologise and he needed to do it now.

'I am sorry for all the pain I have caused her. It was not done intentionally, I assure you. I have the highest regard for your daughter.'

'And yet you do not regard her highly enough.'

The last time Julian had walked out of this house he had been devastated by the loss he'd felt. Now he knew what his grandmother had meant about finding that spark in life. Katrina was his. She had helped him realise he did not need to carry the weight of the world on his shoulders and that he was entitled to have some happiness.

'You do not understand the depth of my feelings for her.'

'I understand that, given a choice, you chose to end your association with her instead of offering for her hand.'

'To save her reputation.'

'To save your own.'

'And my heart has suffered for it every day since! I am here to speak with your daughter because of just how highly I regard her. If you would be so kind as to inform her I am here, I would be grateful.'

Her father's forehead wrinkled. 'With wealth and privilege comes sacrifice. However, certain things should never be sacrificed.'

'And if I agreed with you, how would you feel?'

'I suppose we will know after you speak with my daughter. Katrina is out on the terrace.' He stood and rang for a servant. 'I would ask you to make your visit brief. We wouldn't want the neighbours to talk,' he said with a pointed look.

Julian pressed his lips firmly together to hold in his sigh of relief. Every nerve in his body hummed as he accompanied the Vandenbergs' butler onto the terrace while the man delivered Katrina a cup of tea. She sat with her back to them on a long wooden bench with her watercolours in her hand. She appeared intent on an oak tree that was growing just on the other side of the balustrade.

'Thank you for the tea, Wilkins,' she called out, keeping her gaze on her subject.

Julian took the Wedgwood cup from Wilkins and silently dismissed the man. He placed the tea beside Katrina. She continued to look at the tree as she reached for the cup. He cleared his throat and she looked at him.

The tea in her hand sloshed from the cup into the saucer. 'How long have you been standing there?'

'Not very long.' He nodded towards the paper on her small easel. 'I wasn't aware that you paint.'

'I find it calms me.'

She calmed him. He felt worlds better, simply being in her presence.

'May I?' he asked, gesturing to the space on the bench beside her.

She hesitated, but shifted closer to the end, making room for him. Once he was seated she returned her attention to the tree.

'The weather is fine today,' he said.

Katrina kept her eyes on the tree while she continued to outline the branches with her brush. It was easier to focus on the tree than to look at Julian. 'I doubt you're calling to discuss the state of the clouds.'

From the corner of her eye she saw him rest his elbows on his knees and look down at his clasped hands. 'This is true. It could be raining. I would hardly notice.'

It had been raining in her heart for over a week, thanks to him. She placed the brush into her glass of water and faced him. If they finished their conversation quickly, it might not hurt as much when he left.

'Is there something you've come to tell me?'

His attention dropped to the bandages around her wrists, which were peeking out from the long sleeves of her pale blue muslin dress, and his brow wrinkled. 'Last night you assured me you were well.'

The sound of his tender concern tugged at her. 'I tried to pull my hands out of the ropes. These are simply abrasions. By tomorrow the bandages will not be necessary.'

'Did you suffer other injuries? Tell me truthfully.' He looked into her eyes.

'No, just my hands.' She lowered her voice even more. 'Did you read the papers this morning?'

Relief had washed over her when she had read about Lady Wentworth. She knew it was uncharitable to feel that way, but she couldn't help it.

'I have. It is now truly over.'

Silence stretched between them and then he let out an audible breath. 'There is something I need to tell you.'

Her palms began to sweat at the seriousness of his tone. Had word of her kidnapping begun to spread?

'I'm listening.'

'It is difficult for me to know where to begin.' He appeared to choose his words carefully. 'I am sorry for everything that happened last night. Had I known Lady Wentworth was capable of doing such a thing, I would have somehow stopped her before you were ever put in danger.'

'There is nothing you could have done to stop her unless you had remained in her company every hour of every day.'

'Still, I accept full responsibility.'

She shook her head slowly. 'It is not necessary. I do not blame you for it.'

He smelled of leather and...Julian. Did every man have a unique scent? He certainly did. She hoped she would soon forget it.

'If that is all, Your Grace, you may leave. Rest assured I do not blame you for what has occurred.'

She reached over to pick up her paintbrush and her eyes widened when he took her hand. Warmth spread up her arm.

'There is something else you should know.' His voice faded in the hushed stillness of the terrace.

'Go on.'

He swallowed hard, and his green eyes searched hers. 'I've come to realise something of late. It should have occurred to me earlier, however, I have had no experience with it until now.'

The intensity in his gaze held her, making it impossible to look away.

'I love you with every fibre of my being. I have from the first moment I saw you.'

A lump settled in Katrina's throat. His words were just pretty sentiment. He didn't mean them.

She was ready to pull her hand from his when he knelt before her.

The world stopped.

'Katrina, I never want to live another day without you and I pray that in your heart you love me, even just a little.

All I want to do is cherish you and call you my wife—if you will have me.'

She blinked. 'Did you just ask me to marry you?'

'I did.'

She shifted uncomfortably under his piercing gaze. 'I know you are a man of honour, and that you think offering for my hand is the proper thing to do because of what occurred last night, but there is no need. I'll return to America and you can live the life you are destined to lead, uncomplicated by our association.'

Katrina was amazed she said all that without her voice cracking.

'Did you not hear what I said? I do not want to marry you out of a sense of obligation. I want to marry you because I love you.'

His lovely green eyes looked at her earnestly.

'I will not marry a man who will cast me aside after we are wed.'

'Do you truly believe I will?'

'You suffered derision because of a carriage ride and cut ties with me. Do you believe marrying me will be easier?'

'I had everything I thought I wanted after we parted. I regained the respect of most men in Westminster. My counsel was sought on affairs of state. I was asked to give speeches again. But none of that mattered. What mattered was what *you* thought of me. Other people's opinions and esteem do not define me. My actions define me. I am finished with living the life Society tells me I should.'

Butterflies danced in her chest. 'You truly love me?'

His kissed her hand slowly. 'With all my heart.'

'Always?'

'Always. Do you love me? Even just a little?'

The lump in her throat was back. 'I do love you, Julian, with all of my being.'

He released a deep breath and closed his eyes. 'Do you love me enough to marry me?'

'I do,' she said in a rush.

He leaned over and kissed her—deeply and passionately. When he finally pulled his head away they both were breathing hard.

Chapter Twenty-Six

Three weeks later

Wedding breakfasts could be so tedious.

Julian took a sip of champagne and wondered how long he and Katrina were obligated to stay at their own celebration. Surely they did not have to remain until the last guest departed? That could be hours from now—hours that would be better spent by him exploring the enticing curves of his new wife's body.

Fortunately for Julian, the Russian Ambassador could carry on a conversation with a potted palm. Julian nodded periodically, to keep up the pretence of interest, but his attention was fixed on Katrina, who was visible to the left of the Russian Ambassador's shoulder.

Once she had agreed to marry him, he had found himself constantly preoccupied with thoughts of bedding her. He wondered how tight she would feel when he entered her for the first time. Would she cry out her release or remain silent? Would she allow him to explore every bit of her?

His thoughts were interrupted when Hart nudged his shoulder. 'I was hoping this fixation you have with your wife would end once you were married. But I suppose you will need a few days alone with her before you are cured.'

Julian glanced around, wondering what had happened to the Ambassador. And how long had Hart been standing by his side?

'He walked off about five minutes ago,' Hart explained. 'I thought I would come to your rescue. If you'd been standing alone much longer I fear Madame de Lieven would have approached you. She has been regaling everyone with tales of how she was responsible for bringing you and your bride together. I'm certain she would enjoy sharing them with you.'

'Madam de Lieven? I had assumed my grandmother would have already made certain everyone thought it was *her* doing.'

The look of surprise on Hart's face made Julian laugh.

'In truth, the only reason you and Katrina are together is due to some careful planning by Miss Forrester and myself. If we'd left it to the two of you, you would still be sending her weeds.'

Julian glanced at his beautiful wife and recalled the first time he had called on her at her home. 'Do not discount those weeds. I think they may have helped win her love.'

'Love!' Hart spluttered into his glass of champagne.

'Yes, love. We are in love. She is all I will ever need.'

'You say that now. It is your wedding day. It would be poor form to say otherwise. But no woman can hold a man's attention forever.'

Julian studied his friend, wondering if he truly believed that. 'Some day, Hart, you will meet a woman and find that you cannot stop thinking about her. You will try, but to no avail. She will frustrate you, and excite you, and make you feel as if you are losing your mind. Then one day you will wake up and realise you never want to stop thinking about her, because if you did your life would be empty. There will never be anyone else for me.'

Hart was about to reply when Julian's grandmother

approached his side. 'Lord Hartwick,' she said, 'you surprised me this morning. I had a wager with my maid that we would need a search party to find you. Well done—you arrived before the ceremony began.'

'Had a search party been required, I can promise you, ma'am, that I would not have been found.'

She narrowed her eyes at him and Julian was grateful he was not on the receiving end of her assessing gaze.

'Why don't you see what is keeping Miss Forrester? I believe I saw her step onto the terrace some time ago.'

Hart rocked back on his heels and gave her a cocky grin. 'I'm certain Miss Forrester is clever enough to find her own way back inside.'

'Then fetch me a glass of champagne. I don't want you spoiling my fun.'

'It would be my honour.' He bowed flamboyantly and walked away.

Julian wasn't certain if he was relieved that the odd exchange had ended or wary because his grandmother felt the need to speak to him with no one else about.

'That was hardly subtle,' he said.

'That man needs a woman to take him to task.'

'Do I dare ask what fun you were referring to?'

She smiled up at him, clearly pleased about something. 'He did not tell you? Capital! I was certain he would not be able to resist exposing my secret.'

The idea that Hartwick and his grandmother shared any sort of secret was making Julian's head ache. 'Is this a secret you'd care to share with me?'

'Of course. That's why I came over here. Your wedding gift from me has been placed in the study. You may do with it as you wish.'

'Would you like me to ask what it is?'

'I would.' She tugged his arm and Julian brought his head down so she could whisper in his ear. 'Do you recall that caricature printed of you and Katrina together in your carriage? You are now in possession of the printing plate.'

Julian jerked his head back and stared at her. 'How did you acquire it?'

'When I had someone I trust inform Cruikshank about your carriage ride, I specified that I wanted the plate in return for the information.'

He could not have heard correctly. '*You* gave Cruikshank the information that fuelled that caricature? Why? Why would you do that?'

It was a struggle to keep his voice down.

'He was not aware I was the one providing him with the information. I am careful about such things.'

'You never answered me. Why did you do that? Katrina could have been ruined,' Julian said through his teeth.

'Nonsense. I needed to force your hand. You did not see that you loved her, but I did. I expected you to do the honourable thing. Instead you took a different approach, you frustrating boy.'

Julian closed his eyes and began to count to ten. Hopefully by eight he would no longer have the desire to pack his grandmother's bags and send her off to his mother's house—right now.

'How did you come by this information?'

'I live in this house with you. I notice things. While I wasn't certain you would actually go on a carriage ride with her, I suspected you were spending time with her. You were much too cheery. I was correct in my assumption, was I not? Hartwick would not confirm or deny anything to me. However, that boy does not hide his amusement well.'

Julian was back to counting. He took a deep breath. 'So you have been in possession of that plate all this time?'

'I have—and now it is yours. You may thank me by producing a number of great-grandchildren for me.'

'You might want to consider remaining far away from me until Katrina and I return from Devonshire.'

She laughed and looked past his shoulder. 'Very well. However, remember I don't have many more good years left. A house filled with children would have me dying with a smile on my lips.' She tapped her fan on his shoulder and walked away.

He scrubbed his hand across his brow and shook his head. How he wished he could leave for Devonshire now. Once more he eyed his wife. How many days of bedding her would it take until she was with child? *His* child.

Katrina was deep in conversation with Winter's wife, and her tempting lips were raised in a warm smile. His gaze skimmed down her long neck to the swell of her breasts, searching for that beauty mark he knew was barely visible over the silver edging of her gown. Would her skin taste salty when he slid his tongue along that edging? Would her nipples grow hard?

This. Was. Torture.

As if sensing his gaze, Katrina raised her head and caught his eye. Slowly she sank her teeth into her plump lower lip. His control snapped. There were advantages to being a duke. Leaving his own wedding breakfast early with his beautiful duchess was one of them.

When he finally reached his wife's side, he took her hand, and brought it to his lips. It was all he could do without raising too many eyebrows and embarrassing her. 'You ladies seem to be enjoying yourselves.'

The Duchess of Winterbourne smiled congenially. 'We were discussing a new portrait painter I've recently become acquainted with. I believe you would find his work most pleasing, Lyonsdale.'

Julian looked back at Katrina. 'Of course—we will need a portrait of you for the gallery.'

The women shared an indecipherable look and Julian's eyes narrowed as he caught the exchange.

'I will leave the choice of artist up to you, although I assumed you would use Lawrence,' he said.

'Mr Lawrence is going abroad with a commission from the Prince Regent,' Katrina said. 'Olivia has been kind enough to offer me other suggestions. Although I do not know if this one particular painter's work is suitable for the gallery.'

The Duchess of Winterbourne tried to hide her smile, but was unsuccessful. 'Please excuse me, I believe I am needed across the room.'

Once she was far enough away, Katrina leaned towards Julian. 'Perhaps you should stop looking at me as if you plan on having me for dinner,' she said into her champagne glass.

'But I *do* plan on having you—as soon as I can manage it,' he said, brushing his lips against her ear. 'Now that you are finally my wife, we can be alone for longer than a few brief moments at a time. And, Katrina, I plan on being alone with you for a very long time.'

There was a catch in her breath. 'Are you trying to frighten me?'

She tried to nudge him away, but Julian tugged her back. 'I don't believe you frighten easily.'

'Then what are you trying to do?'

'I am attempting to make you want me as much as I want you at this very moment.'

She took another sip of her champagne as she glanced at the people around them. 'I don't believe any effort on your part is necessary.'

Julian could see the rise and fall of her breasts. Knowing what they looked like under her gown had Julian imagining all the different things he wanted to do with them.

He cleared his throat, trying to summon his voice. 'One

of the advantages of being a duke is that I can escort my wife upstairs right now and no one will question me.'

His voice sounded low and hoarse, even to his own ears. Moving his head away from Katrina's, he drained the rest of his glass and tried to regain some of his composure.

'What are some of the other advantages?'

Katrina's voice had acquired a husky quality. The minx knew exactly what she was doing.

Bending his head back down towards her ear, he let out a low, warm breath. 'Another is that I can taste every inch of my beautiful duchess's body for hours.'

To his satisfaction, Katrina wobbled ever so slightly against him.

'Have you been thinking up ways to scandalise me?'

'No…not exactly…possibly…'

Chuckling against her ear, he heard her *harrumph*.

'Then you're going to have to do better than that.'

Ah, a challenge! What would she do if he told her what he had wanted to do from the moment he'd first seen her?

'At this moment all I can think about is sinking into you and filling you. Do you understand my meaning?'

This time there was a more distinct wobble. It was probably visible from across the room. Before he even had time to gloat about what his words had done to his bride she had placed her glass down on the tray of a passing footman and tugged on Julian's arm, propelling them to the doorway.

As they passed her father's questioning gaze she gave the worst performance of a woman with a headache. In less than two minutes she was dragging him up the stairs towards their suite of rooms.

When they reached the landing Katrina let go of his arm and slid her gaze boldly down his body. 'Now, what was it that you were saying about all the things a duke can do?'

He imagined taking her right there, on the floor at the

top of the stairs—or, better yet, bent over the banister. She must have realised his sense of urgency, because her sweet lips parted and she began to step backwards.

There was nowhere for her to go. The hallway led directly to the end of the house, and if she wanted to escape him her only choice was to enter one of the rooms that were connected to the hall. If she did, he would lock the door behind them and take her on or against the nearest possible surface.

It didn't matter to Julian which room it was. He was finally going to make love to Katrina. And he was going to do it now!

Stalking her slowly, like a tiger after its prey, Julian began to unbutton his jacket. The faster his clothes were off, the faster he could get her out of her gown. What would she look like in just her chemise? Was her chemise plain or did it have frills? Was it thin enough that he would be able to make out the shade of her nipples through the cloth?

Katrina made a sound resembling a squeak. 'What are you doing?'

Looking down, Julian noticed his navy tail coat was open and his fingers were already unbuttoning his waistcoat. 'Undressing.' Flashing her a devilish grin, he arched his brow. 'I suggest you do the same.'

'In the hallway?'

Yes, her voice had definitely squeaked. She was still backing away from him, although her pace had slowed considerably.

'What if someone should see us?'

'News of our early departure will have reached the servants by now. I'm sure they know enough to stay away. Take your hair down.'

She hesitated.

'Take it down,' he repeated, undoing the knot of his neckcloth.

He froze as silken strands fell to her shoulders and down her back. Just like that day in Richmond, urgency drove Julian. In two strides his body was pressed against her. His hands were in her hair and he was kissing her—claiming her—exploring her mouth. She tasted like champagne and…Katrina.

She tasted like heaven.

He might have groaned, or maybe it was Katrina.

Pins fell from her hands, scattering silently on the rug. Her fingers twisted in the linen of his cravat, which now hung around his neck like a scarf. She was pulling the cloth towards her, and Julian could not have moved his head away from her even if he'd wanted to. She kissed him back hungrily, her lips dancing with his.

Julian pushed her up against the closest door. If he didn't turn the knob soon he might very well be lifting Katrina's skirts at any moment to taste her. Soft, warm hands found their way under the collar of his shirt, and she ran her palms against the hot skin near his collarbone. He cupped her breasts. They were a little less than a handful, and they were perfect. Her smooth skin tasted salty against his tongue. She moaned, and his breeches grew even tighter.

He kissed her again, needing to sink himself into her warmth. He turned the door handle and they stumbled into the room. There was just enough common sense left in him that he remembered to kick the door shut behind them.

Almost immediately Katrina pushed off his tail coat and her fingers fumbled to unbutton his waistcoat. 'I want to be closer to you,' she murmured between kisses.

He was painfully hard. He needed to slow things down or it would be over much too quickly.

Breaking the kiss, Julian tugged his shirt over his head.

Katrina's eyes widened. Her graceful fingers skimmed across his chest. His heartbeat quickened..

Leaving their wedding breakfast early had been a brilliant idea!

They might have been in a closet for all Katrina knew. Her entire focus was on the man making her tremble all over. His rounded shoulders were broad, and his chest had a light dusting of hair. Wondering at the feel of him, Katrina trailed her fingers across his chest to the thin line that led to the band of his breeches. There was a distinct bulge in the fabric. She traced her fingers over it and discovered it was thick and very hard.

His body shivered. She met his intense gaze and Julian gave a hard swallow.

'Need to see you,' he rasped, and he motioned for her to turn around.

It felt so good to finally be able to touch him that Katrina just continued exploring the contours of that bulge.

Throwing his head back, he groaned, and then grabbed her wrist. 'Turn around.'

This time she turned her back to him. Within no time he had unbuttoned her dress and helped her step out of the delicate creation. He pulled slowly on the ribbon of her corset. The confining fabric loosened, and then it too was on the floor, followed by her petticoat.

His gaze travelled over her body and settled on her breasts. The longer he looked at them, the tighter her breasts felt. It was as if her skin was too small for her body. Julian's raised his right hand and his fingers grazed over the swell of her breast. Then he rubbed his thumb back and forth over her nipple. It strained against his finger and began to ache. It was becoming difficult to breathe, and Katrina tried to pull air into her lungs.

His fingers slipped under the silk ribbons at her shoulder. 'You look lovely.'

The idea that he liked her in such a flimsy garment made Katrina smile. Slowly he untied the ribbons at each shoulder and it slid down her body. He ran his tongue across his teeth and then dropped his head, rubbing his brow.

Her smile faltered. 'Is something wrong?'

Shaking his head, Julian met her gaze. 'I'm trying to convince myself that I should lay you down before I taste you.'

She hesitated as she tried to understand why they couldn't continue to kiss while standing up. But before she came to any conclusions he'd lifted her into his arms. The next thing she knew, she was lying naked on a bed in her stockings. Julian slid her shoes off and tossed them over his shoulder. Kneeling at her feet, he let his gaze burn a trail over her body. When their eyes met, Katrina's stomach flipped and her body tingled with restless energy.

'Do you trust me?' he asked, running his fingers along the inside of her calf.

She nodded, uncertain as to why he was asking. When he parted her legs and crawled between them she almost asked him. But before she could, Julian had lowered his head and slowly slid his tongue between her thighs.

Katrina almost jumped off the bed. He was still watching her while he tasted her again. There was no way to describe what he was doing. She had licked honey off her fingers in the same way he was licking her now. Katrina didn't want to think about what he was doing, she just knew that what he was doing felt so very good.

When he slowly slid his finger inside her she tried to scamper up the bed. With his free hand he held her down. He moved his hand faster, and her legs trembled uncontrollably.

'Don't be frightened, Kat, just relax.'

That was easy for him to say. Every nerve in *his* body wasn't being pulled into a tight mess. He lowered his lips to join his finger and she shattered into a million pieces.

When she could think clearly, she realised that Julian's lips were brushing against her neck. The weight of his warm body was comforting, and his heavy breathing was blowing warm air against her hot skin.

'What happened?' she managed to ask, confident he would be able to offer an explanation.

Julian brushed his nose against her neck. 'Your body let me know that it liked what I was doing to you very much.'

After kissing her several times, he pulled himself up and sat at the edge of the bed, taking off his shoes and stockings. Needing to watch his every movement, Katrina rolled to her side and propped her head in her hand.

When he stood, Julian turned, and appeared surprised to find her watching him. 'Would you like to do the honours?' he asked, gesturing to the buttons on the placket of his breeches.

Feeling as if she was about to unwrap a highly anticipated present, she rose to her knees and crawled towards him. Kneeling before him on the bed, she stroked the pads of her fingers over his warm chest. She didn't think she would ever grow tired of feeling his skin against hers.

He caressed her arms and kissed the sensitive area where her neck met her shoulder. Dropping her hands lower, she ran her hand over his hard length. He was breathing more deeply into her neck, and when Katrina had opened the last button on his breeches she took him into her hand.

Wanting to see all of him, she moved back a bit. Their foreheads touched. They both watched Julian cover her hand with his and show her how to give him pleasure. *Was this part of him always this hard?*

The tip of his length grew slick. Lifting her hand, she marvelled at her wet finger. She wasn't the only one growing wet from all this touching and kissing. Wondering what it tasted like, Katrina licked her thumb.

'Oh, God...' Julian groaned.

She looked up at him, worried she had done something wrong. 'Should I not have done that?'

He answered by pushing her back onto the bed and stretching his body over hers. 'Please tell me you know what occurs in the marriage bed.' His chest was rising and falling as if he had run a far distance.

She nodded. Julian closed his eyes, and Katrina held her breath. Then he thrust himself inside her.

Her body stiffened at the invasion and she clutched his shoulder. His motionless body felt like marble above her. She wished he would go back to doing what he had been doing to her earlier. It had felt much nicer.

She shifted a little, to adjust her position. Julian lifted his eyelids slightly and looked down at her. 'Please, Kat, don't move.' He let out a breath and closed his eyes again.

Was this painful for him? Having him inside her was very uncomfortable. She was certain she was going to be sore afterwards. But Katrina refused even to twitch.

'How long do we have to stay like this?'

Julian opened his eyes, a questioning look on his face.

'For there to be a child,' she explained.

He started to laugh, and it reverberated throughout her entire body. Grinning, he kissed her forehead. 'We need to do a little more than this.'

Well, *that* wasn't an answer. Would they stay like this for a few minutes? Surely he couldn't mean an hour?

He must have noticed her confusion, because he lowered his head and kissed her slowly. Then he pulled his hips back. Katrina thought they were finished—until he thrust into her again. This time she grabbed his hips to hold him in place. That had felt good—very, *very* good! Her eyes dropped to where their bodies were joined and her lips parted.

When she looked back up at him, Julian arched his brow. 'You like that, do you?'

Unable to form words, she nodded and wrapped her legs around him, trying to bring him closer. What had started off as gentle soon became urgent.

He seemed to grow even larger inside her.

Katrina's muscles tightened again.

The veins in his neck became more pronounced and he let out a loud groan.

She might have made a noise. She wasn't certain.

Suddenly his body dropped down, pressing her into the bed. They were each struggling to catch their breath and the sound was loud in her ears.

He eventually propped himself up above her on his forearms and she wrapped her arms around his waist. She felt safe and secure.

His gaze was laced with concern. 'Did I hurt you?'

Shaking her head, she traced his lips with her finger. He caught it between his teeth and drew it into his mouth. His warm, wet tongue twirled around it before he began to suck on it the way he had sucked on her nipples—pulling and drawing. There was a ripple from her finger down to where they had been joined.

'Oh, you're very good at this, aren't you?' she said.

He grinned and released her finger.

'I'm glad you convinced me to leave our wedding breakfast early,' she said, drawing circles with her nail on the small of his back. 'I find I am very content with you here.'

He lifted his head from where he was nuzzling her neck. 'Did you just say you were content with me?'

'Yes, I believe I did.'

'Content. *Content?* That seems a bit…insulting,' he said with a twitch of his lips.

'Forgive me. I did not intend to injure your pride. Perhaps I should say I'm pleased with you.'

'*Pleased?* Yesterday you said you were "pleased" with the book you were reading.'

She grinned. 'Very well. Perhaps you should tell me what you think of me. It may serve as inspiration.'

'Somehow I believe you are simply looking for pretty compliments.'

'And you are not?'

His eyes sparkled with amusement. 'Had I only known I would be facing discourse such as this across the breakfast table each morning, I might have reconsidered speaking with you on the de Lievens' terrace.'

She recalled that night, and how they had bumped into one another in the drawing room. What if her father had never been asked to come to London? And what if Julian had stood somewhere else? If it had been raining, would they even have spoken? They certainly would not have done so on the terrace.

He kissed her temple. 'I love you, Katrina.'

'And I love you, Julian.'

Life could be strange that way. Moments you thought were mundane could be the moments that change your life forever.

* * * * *

AN UNCOMMON DUKE

Many thanks to my editor Kathryn Cheshire for your insightful input and encouraging words. And to Linda Fildew, Nic Caws, Krista Oliver and the rest of the Mills & Boon Historical team, thanks for all you've done to help bring Gabriel and Olivia's story into the world.

To my agent, Courtney Miller-Callihan with Handspun Literary Agency, your generous spirit is a gift. Some day both of us will sleep past six in the morning. In the meantime, I toast you with my coffee.

Jen, Mia, Lori, and Lisa, thank you for being such wonderful critique partners, beta readers, and friends. For Marnee, Terry and Gareth, thanks for being there on those days when chocolate and coffee were of no help.

To my family, I'm sorry to say there are no unicorns, aliens or vampires in this book. Some day I'll write a story about an alien vampire unicorn just for the three of you. In the meantime, know that your love and support mean the world to me.

For the kind people who helped me with my research, thanks for taking the time to answer my questions. And to those of you who shared unusual Regency era titbits and antiques with me, because you thought I'd find them interesting, thank you. I hope you have fun seeing how I used those items in this story.

Chapter One

London, England—1818

Being shot at always left Gabriel Pearce, Duke of Winterbourne, in a foul mood. It didn't matter that this time he wasn't the intended target. It didn't matter that he had saved the Prince Regent by tackling him to the floor of his coach. And, it didn't matter that the shot had narrowly missed Gabriel. Being shot at was a nuisance that meant his orderly life would be thrown into chaos for the unforeseeable future.

Three hours after his coach had sped down the rutted country road, whisking the Prince Regent to the safety of Carlton House, Gabriel stood in his dressing room attempting to tie his cravat into a perfect *Trône d'Amour*. He had performed the task countless times. One would think he could do it in his sleep. Apparently, with the events of today playing out in his mind, one would be wrong.

Peering closer at his reflection in the mirror, he tore the linen from his neck. *Bloody hell! There should be no ripples in the knot, only one dent!* Hodges, his valet, immediately handed him another freshly starched neckcloth.

'Just tie it into a waterfall and be done with it,' his brother Andrew called out, walking into the room and dropping into the wingback chair beside the mirror.

'Too plebeian,' Gabriel bit out, his attention fixed on the task at hand.

'That's how I tie my cravats.'

Raking a critical gaze over Andrew's brown tailcoat and the unimpressive shine to his shoes, Gabriel arched a brow.

'Ho, I see now,' Andrew said with a smirk. 'Some day I will shock you and wear something you deem acceptable.'

'If you would finally allow me to find you an acceptable valet, that might happen sooner rather than later.'

'I'm quite content with the one I have, thank you. How many neckcloths have you handed my brother, Hodges?'

'Six, my lord.'

Andrew sighed and studied the coffered ceiling. 'Shall I wait in your study? If you continue on this path to perfection it might take some time and I could be enjoying your fine brandy while I wait.'

'I'll be but a moment. There is brandy by the window.' Gabriel closed his eyes and managed to push all thoughts of gunshots, shattered glass and a frightened Prince Regent from his mind. Concentrating on each specific turn of the cloth, he finally tied a perfect knot.

Now he could attend to more important matters.

He nodded to Hodges, and the elderly man quietly left the brothers alone behind closed doors.

'Please tell me we caught the blackguard,' Gabriel said, accepting a glass of brandy.

Andrew dropped back into the chair and stretched out his long legs. 'Spence jumped from his tiger's perch the moment the shots were fired and caught the man. He was taken to the Tower—however, he refuses to talk.'

Gabriel took his first sip of brandy since returning home. The heat sliding down his throat did nothing to relieve the tight tension in his muscles. 'We need to know if he was working alone. I don't care what it takes. Make him talk.'

Andrew pulled a scrap of paper from his pocket and held it out. 'My thought is he had assistance. We found this on him. I don't believe our gunman had access to Prinny's plans. Someone had to have given him this information.'

Scrawled in pencil were the date, the name of the road and town they had travelled to, as well as a sketch of Gabriel's coat of arms. Apparently whoever had supplied the information to the gunman knew Prinny would be travelling with Gabriel today and knew where they'd be going. But how was that possible when Prinny had only approached Gabriel last evening about taking him to purchase the painting?

Bringing the paper to his nose, Gabriel sniffed the unfamiliar pungent oily scent mixed with tobacco. The letter 'm' had an interesting swirl to it, but other than that there was no way to identify the author. 'There's no cipher, so it appears we are dealing with an inexperienced lot.'

As he took another sip, he organised the information before him. He was the man ultimately responsible for protecting the Crown. Unrest was rampant throughout the country. If his people failed to protect King George and the Prince Regent, there was no telling what anarchy might occur.

'How is Prinny faring?' Andrew asked, interrupting his thoughts.

'He is shaken but unharmed.'

'And you?'

'I have this scratch on my forehead from shattering glass and my right shoulder is a bit bruised. As you know, I've survived worse.' He handed the paper back to Andrew. 'Show this to Hart. He may be able to identify the smell. Then remain at the Tower and notify me when the gunman is broken. I need to know who else wants Prinny dead.'

Andrew stood and placed his glass on a nearby table. 'Please give my regrets to Olivia and Nicholas. I'm sure you'll devise a plausible excuse as to why I had to miss his breeching ceremony.'

Demmit! Nicholas would be devastated his favourite uncle wasn't there for such a momentous occasion, but Andrew was the only person Gabriel trusted completely. He needed answers and Andrew would make certain he got them. He shook off the guilt trying to settle in his gut. 'Make an appearance, but slip away shortly after the ceremony begins.'

'Very well, I will send word when we know more.'

'And watch your back.'

'I always do.'

Glancing at the ormolu clock on the mantel, Gabriel let out a curse. He was late. Now he would have to endure the customary icy demeanour of his wife. Tonight they might even be forced to actually hold a conversation. He took another sip of brandy, bracing himself for an encounter with the woman he had married.

Olivia, Duchess of Winterbourne, bounced her nephew on her knee and stole another glance at the longcase clock beside the drawing room door. The breeching ceremony should have begun twenty minutes ago. Her son was eager to take this first step towards manhood. How much longer would Gabriel keep them waiting?

She shifted her attention to her mother-in-law, who sat nearby talking with Olivia's mother. When their eyes met, the Dowager gave her a slight sympathetic smile.

The sofa Olivia was sitting on dipped as her sister, Victoria, leaned closer. 'Do you think he forgot?'

'What man forgets his own son's breeching?' Olivia rubbed her forehead and prayed her husband was not such a man. 'Mr James is a reliable secretary. I'm certain he reminded Gabriel of the occasion.'

'Perhaps Mr James was unclear of the time.'

Olivia had reminded him of the time during their daily meeting that morning. This delay fell directly on Gabriel's shoulders. She would give him five more minutes. Then she would ring for Bennett to locate him. It should be of no surprise to her that he was late. She had learned long ago Gabriel only thought of himself. 'I'm certain Mr James relayed the correct time.'

'Do you truly not speak at all now?'

'Being in his presence is still a constant reminder of what he did. It's best if I avoid him.'

'Mother taught us to expect nothing from the men we marry. She always said that to them we are simply means to an heir. You should have listened to her,' Victoria said gently.

Their mother knew first-hand how true those statements were and Olivia had never expected more. Their father married their mother to create a political alliance with Olivia's grandfather, the Duke of Strathmore. He had never shown any interest in his wife as a person and their brother had followed suit with his wife. When he'd sought the Marquess of Haverstraw for Victoria, it was because the man had lands bordering their family's Wiltshire estate. And he could not have been more pleased when the Duke of Winterbourne, a favourite of the Prince Regent, had shown an interest in Olivia. His pleasure had nothing to do with his daughter's feelings on the matter. Not once had he discussed Gabriel with her before or after he consented to the marriage.

But Gabriel had taken her by surprise. This was a man who listened to her—really listened to her opinions and interests. To have the complete attention of a man who was that handsome and powerful had been intoxicating.

After having courted her for a month, he gave her the consideration of asking her for her hand before approaching her father. Foolishly she fell in love with him and believed some day he would grow to love her in return. But he never did.

'You cannot direct your heart's actions,' she said to Victoria. If she could, Olivia would have saved herself many tearful nights.

'I never understood why your heart became so engaged. The two of you fought quite regularly.'

'We did not. When did you ever witness such behaviour?'

'Usually during dinner.'

'A discussion of contrasting opinions is not an argument.'

'I would find such interaction with Haverstraw tiresome.' She held her arms out towards her son. 'I can take Michael from you. I fear he has become rather heavy.'

Olivia bounced Michael higher, pleased she was able to make him giggle. 'Nonsense, he is a feather. I remember when I could pick Nicholas up this easily. Now he will have his ringlets cut and leave behind his gowns to don skeleton suits.'

As she rubbed her nose against Michael's fuzzy blond

head, he grasped a tendril of hair resting along her neck. 'How I miss the smell of a baby.'

'Should you hold him after he's eaten, you might change your opinion.'

Olivia grinned in understanding.

Then, she felt it.

Even though she had tried to ignore the sensation, somehow she always knew when Gabriel entered a room. It was as if a ribbon was tied from one end of him directly to her.

His tall, broad frame obstructed the view beyond the doorway and his unruffled demeanour told her he was unaware he delayed the ceremony—or, perhaps, he didn't care.

As if he felt the invisible connection as well, his unreadable hazel eyes found her and he nodded politely. He surveyed the room, his square jaw and carved features remaining impassive, until he spied Nicholas looking out the window with Gabriel's brother, Monty. Only then did his lips curve into a smile that made the corners of his eyes crinkle.

She forced herself to look away. Years ago, that smile was given only to her, and it would always make her heart swell. Now, whenever she witnessed it, her heart would squeeze painfully.

Gabriel paid his respects to their mothers before advancing across the room to where Olivia sat. His eyes softened briefly when they settled on Michael, who was shoving his entire chubby fist into his own small mouth.

'Duchess, Lady Haverstraw, I hope you're both well.'

The brandy on his breath told Olivia how he had been occupying himself while their families waited patiently for his arrival. 'Thank you, we are. I dare say I thought you might have been feeling poorly since you arrived so

late, but I see you were relaxing with some brandy while
we were debating on how long we could occupy the children before they began climbing the curtains,' she said
in the sweetest tone she could muster.

'Forgive me. Urgent business kept me occupied until
now. Had I been able to disengage myself and join you
here, I would have.'

As he turned his head and watched Andrew approach
Nicholas, Olivia noticed a thin red line over his left brow.

'Did you injure yourself getting dressed today?'

He began spinning the gold intaglio ring on his
pinkie. 'I rode into a low-hanging branch in the park
this morning.'

The only other time she'd witnessed him fidget with
that ring was when he'd stood at the side of her bed after
Nicholas was born—before she threw him out of her
room. 'I imagine you would like to say a few words before the ceremony begins.'

He stared blankly at her for a fleeting moment. 'Of
course.'

'Very well, while you collect your thoughts, I'll inform Nicholas we are finally able to begin.' She placed
her nephew in Victoria's arms. As she stood, another
whiff of brandy filled her nose. He was making it very
difficult for her to resist the urge to step on his foot as
she sauntered past him.

Once the carriages of her last few guests had departed
down the drive, Olivia returned to the Green Drawing
Room to find her mother-in-law seated on a sofa watching Gabriel and Nicholas build a house of cards across the
room. Gabriel's muscular form was stretched out across
the Aubusson rug, while he supported himself on his
elbow. She recalled the last time she had seen him re-

clining in such a casual pose. It was six years ago on a rug in her bedchamber. Squeezing her eyelids shut, she tried to force the image from her mind.

She needed wine. Unfortunately there was only tea. Heading to the table with the cups, Olivia looked at Gabriel's mother. 'Would you care for more tea, Catherine?'

'If you are having another cup...I recall how trying it was to prepare for this occasion. Tea will be just the thing.'

Olivia handed Catherine a cup and poured another for herself, resisting the urge to steal another glance at Gabriel. It would be close to impossible to endure his presence much longer. Resentment rippled through her and tea would never relieve it.

'Your sister's youngest is beautiful,' Catherine said, shifting so Olivia could sit next to her. 'Watching you with him reminded me of how you would play with Nicholas when he was an infant. Now look at him. In those clothes and with his hair cut, he looks like a small version of his father and his uncles.' She studied Olivia over the rim of her cup. 'Soon he will be able to attend Eton.'

Olivia's heart stopped. Gabriel wouldn't do that to her. Would he? 'Has your son mentioned something to you about sending him away to school?'

'You're the mother of his heir. Haven't the two of you discussed plans for his education yet?'

Olivia shook her head. 'I assumed he would continue to be tutored at home like his father until he was ready to attend Cambridge.' Glancing at Gabriel, she wondered if he had other plans.

'Perhaps. However, you'll not know for certain unless the two of you discuss it.' Catherine gave an appraising stare before turning her attention to her son and grandson. 'My husband would build houses out of cards with the boys when they were children. Oh, how he would dote on them.'

She envied the woman. While the memories of the first year of her own marriage were quite lovely, there were none since Nicholas was born. Glancing back at the rug, she watched the playful interaction between father and son. Olivia knew Gabriel loved Nicholas. She just didn't want to witness it.

'Nicholas needs a brother.'

The sip of tea she had taken almost left by way of Olivia's nose. Her coughing was so fitful that the occupants on the rug looked her way.

'Are you all right, Mama?' Nicholas asked with a wrinkled brow that indeed made him look like a small version of the man next to him.

Nodding her head, Olivia tried to stop the spasms in her throat. When the coughing had subsided and the burning in her nose had lessened, she delicately wiped her eyes.

'Gabriel needs another son,' Catherine reiterated.

Well, Olivia knew that was not about to happen—unless she had an immaculate conception. She would never allow Gabriel in her bed again. 'Nicholas is a healthy boy. We already have our heir.'

'Life holds no guarantees. It is wise to plan for unfortunate occurrences. This family is known for its unbroken line of boys. It should not be difficult for you to have another.'

Olivia refused to look at her mother-in-law. A sharp pain sliced her heart at the thought of the death of her precious boy.

'Certainly you and Gabriel have discussed having more children.'

'Oh, we've discussed it,' muttered Olivia, taking a fortifying sip.

'Then it's simply a matter of nature taking its course?'

'You could say that.'

The realisation that she would have no more children felt like someone had carved out a chunk of her heart. If Gabriel did intend to send Nicholas away to school, there would be another tremendous void in her life that nothing would fill. And then she would be alone with no one to love.

The flames of the candles flickered as Olivia walked towards Nicholas and Gabriel. 'It is time for bed, my love,' she said, approaching Nicholas's side.

Gabriel recalled hearing those words before. It was the last night he had found release inside a woman— the last time he had bedded his wife. He bit the inside of his cheek to stop himself from dwelling on the image of Olivia lying under him, with her soft legs squeezing his sides. All these years of frustration had done nothing to quell his desire for her.

'Look at our fierce fortress, Mama. It's almost as tall as me.'

'Very impressive indeed. I commend your steady hand.'

Nicholas turned his large hazel eyes to Gabriel. 'Do I truly have to go to bed, Papa? I want to stay awake as long as you do. I am almost a man, you know.'

Gabriel glanced at Olivia to gauge her reaction. Her head was angled down towards Nicholas, obscuring her features. Instinctively, his attention was drawn to the swell of her lovely breasts, hidden in the lemon-coloured satin folds of her gown. How he wished he could trace the curve of one breast over to the next. He curled his fingers into a fist to stop the aching. Being this close to her was always torture. 'If your mother says it's time for bed, you must obey. However, we cannot leave our fortress unattended. Why don't you knock it down before the enemy attacks it while we slumber?'

'Oh, that is an excellent notion.'

Gabriel imagined the sound emanating from his son was something close to the war cry issued by the Indians across the Atlantic when they rode into battle. 'Well done, Nicholas. Now give us a hug.'

His son threw his arms around Gabriel's neck and squeezed tight. When Nicholas relaxed his grip, his wide grin highlighted his two missing front teeth. 'Goodnight, Papa. Thank you again for my prime bit of blood.'

Olivia smothered a laugh behind her hand at the exact moment Gabriel bit his lip to stop his. Their eyes met for an instant before she looked away.

'Who taught you that?' Gabriel asked, before holding up his hand. 'Never mind, I think I know which uncle it was. That is not the way a future duke refers to his horse.'

'Uncle Andrew told me my horse is a real sweet goer. He says for a gentleman to be a bang-up cove he needs to have a prime bit of blood the other gents would want to ride. He said I shouldn't name him something a chit would, nothin' flowery and such. Did you know some day I'll be able to ride him in a foxhunt? A real hunt! Uncle Andrew says he will take me. I will skip my lessons for the day and he will take me on a foxhunt! Will *you* take me riding, Papa? Can I ride my horse tomorrow?'

It was a miracle his son was not out of breath. 'Perhaps we could go riding in Hyde Park before breakfast.'

His son's eyes widened with anticipation.

'But you must rise early,' Gabriel continued. 'I have many things that require my attention and a gentleman always fulfils his responsibilities. Will you be able to rise with the sun?'

Nicholas threw his arms around Gabriel again. 'Oh, yes! Oh, yes! I promise, I will be awake before you.'

Gabriel hugged his son tightly. It was always difficult to disengage his arms from the one person who meant more to him than anyone.

His son jumped back and turned to Olivia. 'Oh, Mama, did you hear that? Papa is taking me riding tomorrow.'

'Yes, I heard. I dare say you and Buttercup will make such a sight.' Her lip twitched, giving away the mischief behind the serious tone of her voice.

Nicholas's features hardened, making him look older than his five years. 'I cannot be calling my prime bit o' blood Buttercup. Uncle Andrew said I need to name him somethin' fierce.'

Olivia chewed her lower lip and appeared to give his comment great consideration. 'Oh, you mean like Rosebush.'

He scrunched up his round face. 'Rosebush? That's not fierce.'

'Have you ever been pricked by a thorn? I assure you, rosebushes are quite fierce.'

Nicholas shifted his gaze between his parents. 'Is she sincere?'

Gabriel stood and caught Olivia's eye before giving Nicholas a slight shrug. 'Your mama is a girl. Girls do not understand manly ideas,' he teased. 'We shall find a very noble name for your steed.'

'Uncle Andrew said I should name him Cazznoah. I told him that was a silly name and he just laughed. Cazznoah is a silly name, isn't it, Papa?'

Gabriel closed his eyes and took a breath. 'Yes, Nicholas, Casanova is a silly name for a horse.'

Olivia cleared her throat and caught his eye. Her disapproving glare at his brother's suggestion spoke volumes. Andrew always did like to have a bit of fun at Gabriel's expense, but telling their son he should name his horse after a man who was known for seducing women crossed the line. Obviously Olivia agreed. It didn't take words for him to see she disapproved.

'Please bid your grandmama goodnight, Nicholas,' she said, turning him away from Gabriel. 'She would be disappointed if she did not get to wish you sweet dreams.'

Following the intimate picture of Olivia and Nicholas as they left the room, Gabriel stared at the doorway. How much longer would he have to wait for news of the interrogation?

His thoughts drifted to a stormy night long ago, when his body was chilled from the drenching rain that did nothing to wash away the sickening smell of blood from the air. He swore to himself that would never happen again. Andrew could be trusted and, God willing, he would be coming back.

Adjusting his cuffs, he walked towards his mother. 'Are you certain Andrew was not given to you by gypsies as an infant?'

She laughed and handed him a cup of tea. 'I do suppose that would explain many things, but I assure you he was not. What a pity he couldn't stay because he was feeling poorly. I believe I'll call on him tomorrow to see if he's improved.'

He sat down beside her. The idea of their mother fussing over Andrew, when his brother detested the attention, made it difficult to hold back his grin. Unfortunately he knew circumstances forced him to dissuade her. 'I happen to know the bounder is suffering from the ill effects of a questionably spent afternoon.' Now, at least, he could amuse himself imagining the lecture that would be given the next time his brother encountered their mother.

Taking a slow sip of tea, Gabriel closed his eyes and savoured the delicate flavour. He must remember to have James inform Olivia it was an exceptional blend.

'I spoke with Olivia about your need for another child.'

The coughing began in the back of his throat and rapidly moved to his nose. Was there a full moon, or was some other natural occurrence causing illogical things to happen today?

'What possessed you to do that?' he asked when he finally stopped choking.

'Well, it is about time you had another child.' His mother arched a regal eyebrow, which still had the ability to make him squirm. 'Come now, you can't believe that having only one son is a wise decision with the responsibility your title holds.'

'More than anyone I understand the responsibility entrusted to me. I also know I have brothers who may have sons should it come to that.'

Narrowing her eyes, she placed her cup down. 'It is not the same and you know it. You need more sons and you need to do something about it.'

He shook his head at the unusually demanding nature of his mother. 'What possessed you to bring this to my attention?'

'You are thirty-two. Your wife is twenty-six. Soon you both will run out of time. I do not understand this hesitation you both have.'

Gabriel took a deep breath. His mother had told the one woman on earth Gabriel was certain would never let him touch her that they needed to have sex. It's a wonder his mother wasn't wearing her tea. But then again Olivia was always perfectly composed when other people were present. Alone, he discovered, she could be a hellcat.

'You made your opinions known to Olivia?'

'I simply stated there was a need for the required second son.'

'And what was her reaction to your subtle suggestion?'

His mother hesitated before she took a small sip from her cup. 'I do not recall,' she mumbled.

The strip of linen tightened around his throat and he wished it were possible to begin his day all over again. Of course he wanted another child. The memories of his childhood were filled with times he had spent with his brothers. He wanted Nicholas to have that, too, but it was no longer possible. Years ago he'd resigned himself to that fact. 'I know you have the best intentions, but please do not interfere.'

Even though he wanted another child, Gabriel knew Olivia would never want him to get close enough to her to accomplish it. That part of his life had passed.

Chapter Two

From the doorway to the Blue Drawing Room in Carlton House, Gabriel could see the round table in the centre of the room was set for Prinny's breakfast. And for one man eating alone, there was enough food and drink to easily satisfy four people.

As Gabriel crossed the threshold he was taken aback when the burly Prince Regent pulled him into a hug. The man squeezed Gabriel's rib cage, making it difficult to breathe. Disengaging himself from Prinny, Gabriel placed him at a distance, only to be grabbed again into another firm hug.

When Prinny finally released him, he slapped Gabriel on the right shoulder—the very one bruised from being slammed against the carriage wall the day before. Gabriel held back a groan.

'Leave us,' Prinny instructed the four footmen, dressed in blue livery with gold lace, who were posted around the table.

The men filed out quietly, the last one closing the door behind him.

'I owe you my life, Winter. You protected me with

your own person. Bravery and loyalty such as yours is uncommon. You do your father proud.'

Another tight embrace followed and this time Prinny's large meaty hand clamped down on Gabriel's sore shoulder. Bloody hell! He didn't know how much more appreciation he could take.

'I am simply relieved you were unharmed. Please know I'm aware restricting your movements to Carlton House will not be easy for you, but I firmly believe, for now, it's the safest place for you.'

Prinny returned to his breakfast and unceremoniously dropped into a blue-velvet chair. With a wave of his hand he motioned for Gabriel to join him. 'Would you care for anything? If none of this food is to your liking, I will have my kitchen make whatever you desire.'

'Thank you, but I've already eaten.'

'Then a drink, perhaps?'

There were numerous bottles scattered across the table containing wine, champagne and brandy. Prinny appeared to be imbibing all of them. Gabriel shook his head, knowing he needed to keep his mind sharp.

Prinny resumed cutting into his pie. 'I don't understand why you want me to remain here. There no longer is a threat to my life. Your note said the scoundrel had been apprehended.'

'He was. However I believe he had assistance orchestrating your demise. I've come from the Tower and they have not yet been able to get the gunman to admit to anything.'

Prinny dropped his fork with a clatter and reached for his glass of champagne. His hand shook as he brought it to his lips. 'So you truly believe there is someone walking around England who still intends to murder me?' He drained the entire glass.

'I do and that is why it is imperative you remain here where you are under guard at all times.'

'Very well,' Prinny replied on a sigh, 'but you must find this person without delay. Devonshire is hosting a ball soon, it's reported Mrs Siddons will return to the stage to perform in *Douglas* at Drury Lane and I hear the new exhibition at the Royal Academy will be stunning. If I remain here too long, I shall miss all the fun.'

'I will do my best to ensure this is handled as quickly as possible. Since the threat could have come from anywhere, I think it prudent if you limit your visitors to an approved list of people.'

'Nonsense, no one visiting here would wish me harm.'

If only life were that predictable. 'Tell me about the gentleman you purchased the painting from. He appeared surprised to see you.'

'I imagine he was. He expected one of my agents to purchase it for me.'

'It would help if you could recall mentioning our outing to anyone. The gunman was carrying a drawing of my coat of arms.'

Pouring himself more champagne, Prinny appeared to give the question serious consideration. But after a few moments, he shook his head. 'I might have mentioned it in passing to a few people during Skeffington's musical. Capital evening. Selections from *The Marriage of Figaro*. You should have been there.'

'Opera does not appeal to me,' Gabriel said off-handedly. 'Who did you tell?'

Prinny shrugged and took another drink. 'Don't recall, don't you know. Talked with so many people and the champagne was flowing. Astonishingly I didn't have the devil of a headache the next day. But that was before I asked you to join me.'

To steady his exasperation, Gabriel looked up at the massive crystal chandelier and concentrated on the red and blue coloured flecks dancing in the sunlight. If only Prinny didn't like to brag so. 'And your household…who knew I'd be taking you in my carriage?'

'I informed Bloomfield that morning, but he is trustworthy.'

Gabriel knew Prinny's equerry. He appeared as loyal to Prinny as Gabriel was. Nevertheless, he would assign someone to watch the man. 'Very well, I shall let you know the minute you are safe to leave this building.'

'You don't expect me to remain inside on a rare day such as this? The sun is shining. Surely I can enjoy the gardens.'

There was a tightness forming between Gabriel's eyebrows and he pinched the bridge of his nose to transfer his attention to a new discomfort. Why did it feel like dealing with Prinny was the same as handling his young son? He leaned forward and folded his hands on the table. 'Your gardens share a wall with St James's Park. It would be very simple for someone to reach you, if you were out there.'

Prinny let out a snort before pouring the remaining contents of the champagne bottle into his glass.

Gabriel rubbed his eyes. He needed to return home where he didn't have to deal with anyone who was irrational. At least at home his life was predictable.

When Olivia entered the nursery that morning, she found Nicholas restless in his lessons with his new tutor. All he wanted to talk about was his ride through Hyde Park on his new pony. He told her how his father had taken them onto Rotten Row where he saw numerous well-dressed gentlemen out for their morning rides. He wanted to know when he would be old enough to wear a beaver hat of his own.

He was growing up.

For the first time, she noticed the little dimples that kissed the knuckles of his hands were disappearing. And Gabriel might be considering sending him away to school—or, worse yet, Nicholas would ask to go.

Olivia's heart sank with the weight of how much she would miss him.

For the remainder of the morning she thought about how wonderful it felt to hold her nephew. By the afternoon she desperately wanted another child to cuddle and love.

But in order to have that child, she would have to ask her husband to come to her bed.

And she would be forced to endure his company.

Five years ago she told him she could never bear to feel his touch again. If she wanted this, she would have to lower herself to go back on her word to him.

This wasn't something she could tell his secretary to pass on to him when he next saw Gabriel. Mr James would have an apoplexy on the spot. It also wasn't something she could pass along to her maid. Colette would be setting out Olivia's thinnest nightrail and placing rose petals on her bed before he would have even agreed to her request.

Perhaps she should write him a note.

After many drafts, some ridiculous and some obscene, Olivia decided to simply request a meeting. If she could focus her appeal on the need for another child they could avoid discussing how the child would get there.

And maybe that would help scrape the image of naked bodies and intimate conversations from her brain.

* * *

It was four in the afternoon when Olivia received word from Colette that Gabriel was available to see her. Standing outside the massive door to his private study, she pressed her hand against her stomach. What if Gabriel did not want another child? Or, suppose he no longer found her desirable enough to bed? She would never be able to face him again.

The answers she needed would not be found in the hall. She raised her chin, knowing she would regret it for the rest of her days if she didn't ask him for this. Her courageous side rallied, her knock echoed off the oak panel.

The deep rumble of his voice was audible from within as he bid her to enter. Her heart began to pound and she glanced down, praying it wasn't visible through the gauzy fichu tucked into her dress. She rubbed her sweaty palms down her skirt and turned the handle. Upon entering the impressive room, she spotted Mr James standing before Gabriel's desk awaiting a document her husband was sealing. Once the paper was in his hand, Mr James turned to face her and bowed. He appeared nervous, but she found that whenever Mr James was in the same room with Olivia and Gabriel, he always seemed as if he couldn't wait to leave.

'Good day, Mr James,' she said, smiling congenially.

He greeted her with a pleasant reply before excusing himself. The click when the door closed reverberated around Gabriel's private sanctuary. There was no turning back.

For the first time in years, they were alone. Suddenly the generously sized room felt much too small and she was certain he could hear her uneven breathing from across the room.

They stood there staring at each other for what felt

like an eternity. Then Gabriel moved out from behind his desk. Her heart hiccupped. He painted a handsome picture with his perfect posture and his fit frame impeccably encased in an expertly fitted Delft-blue tailcoat with a champagne-coloured embroidered waistcoat underneath. Buff trousers and highly polished top boots covered his muscular legs and his light brown hair looked slightly tousled, as if he had been running his hand through it as he worked at his desk.

At his suggestion, they took a seat in the two chairs placed in front of one of the long windows that over-looked the street. As he fixed an expectant gaze on her, she silently debated how to begin.

'I suppose you're wondering what it is I wish to discuss with you?'

He sat completely still, the picture of civility and physical perfection. 'I have some idea.'

'You do?' she asked, unable to hide her surprise. Had his mother spoken to him as well? From his sober expression it did not appear he was going to be amiable to her request.

'This is regarding last evening, is it not?'

Olivia's heart was jumping in her chest. 'It is. I have thought about this quite a bit and believe it is our duty.'

Gabriel nodded thoughtfully. 'The duty lies with me. I will see to it. I expect it to be an exasperating task, but I agree it must be done.'

Did he really say making love to her would be exasperating?

'I assure you, I will find absolutely no pleasure in the task,' she replied drily.

'That is why it's best done quickly.' At the clopping sound of horses riding by, Gabriel shifted his attention out the window. 'It's a logical request to make. I suppose it was inevitable.'

Inevitable and exasperating—this is how he described bedding her! It took enormous restraint not to rail at him. The point was to have another child. If she had to endure this insufferable man to do so, she needed to disguise her anger. She refused to let him see that his words had any effect on her. In that, she could be in complete control.

She stood rather abruptly, needing to get away before she did something rash—such as kick him in the only area of his that she needed.

'The sooner we attend to this, the better. I will see to it this evening.' He stood and walked her to the door, unaware how perilously close he was to having his head knocked into it.

The moment Olivia left his study Gabriel was able to breathe normally. Being close to her always left him restless, as if his body were fighting the knowledge that he was better off without her.

After pouring himself a glass of brandy, he returned to his desk and put his feet up. Their meeting had gone better than he'd anticipated. He knew only something of great importance would compel her to request an audience.

He considered various scenarios before recalling last night. It was no surprise she wanted to address it. He was impressed she thought they should do it together. However talking with Andrew about what was improper to say to Nicholas fell solely on his shoulders. He would be the one to explain to his brother that it was not appropriate for a boy of five to call his horse Casanova. Nicholas would be Winterbourne some day. He needed to begin learning now what it meant to embody the respectable title.

Yes, a talk with his brother was in order. It also gave him the opportunity to hear how the interrogation was progressing.

Chapter Three

As the melodic sounds of the orchestra filled the crowded ballroom of Devonshire House, Olivia stepped through the movements of the quadrille without hearing a single note. Since her conversation with Gabriel, she wondered if she had made the right decision in approaching him about having another child. Oh, she still desperately wanted another child, but after his reaction to her request, she wasn't certain she could bear to be in his company long enough to conceive one.

He had been horrid—and his comments continued to pierce her heart.

I expect it to be an exasperating task, but it must be done.

The sooner we attend to this, the better.

If she had any hope of having another child, she needed to lock away her contempt for him. Maybe then the thought of Gabriel touching her wouldn't make her want to injure his manhood—permanently. She would never conceive a child if she did that.

'I hope it is not my company that has caused that expression to darken your lovely face,' commented Comte Antoine Janvier.

Pulling her attention back to her dance partner, Olivia smiled apologetically. 'Of course not, I fear I am not very good company this evening.'

With a few final steps the quadrille ended.

'Perhaps a glass of champagne shall lift your spirits,' he said, escorting her off the crowded dance floor towards one of the many drawing rooms.

As they crossed the threshold, he took two glasses from a passing footman and handed one to Olivia. She took a long drink and he arched a dark brow.

'Shall I fetch another, or would you care for mine?' he asked, tilting his glass towards her.

The warmth of a blush rose up Olivia's neck and she turned away. Her gaze settled on the portrait of the previous Duchess of Devonshire. 'Forgive me,' she said, returning her attention to her friend. 'You are being very kind, considering I have not been an ideal companion.'

He gave a careless wave of his hand. 'It would be tiresome if you were always *plein de vie*.'

Olivia grinned. 'I wasn't aware you thought I was full of life.'

'There is a sense you find enjoyment in your surroundings, but I suppose you can be as selective as you wish with the entertainments you attend since you are the Duchess of Winterbourne.'

'Yes, there are advantages to the title.' Being married to her husband was not one of them.

'I notice you and His Grace rarely accept the same invitations.'

Their friendship was still new. If he wanted to know how wide the rift was between her and Gabriel, Olivia was certain any of the gossips in attendance would be happy to recount the tale of what had driven them apart. It was something she never discussed with anyone, except

Victoria. 'His Parliamentary affairs keep him busy into the evening. Oh, look, more champagne.' Olivia didn't wait for Janvier to procure her another glass. She took one off the tray of a passing footman and replaced it with her empty one.

A low chuckle escaped Janvier's lips before he took a sip from his glass. 'Not something you wish to discuss. I understand. Let us change the subject. Tell me, have you heard Mrs Siddons may return to the stage soon?'

'I have.'

'Do you suppose you will attend one of her performances?'

'It would be a shame to leave my box at the theatre empty for such an anticipated return. I don't suppose you are an admirer of hers?' she asked with an amused smile.

'What kind of man would I be if I were not?'

'Would you care to join me on opening night?'

Janvier leaned forward, placing his lips close to her ear. 'I would like nothing better.'

His warm breath fanned her neck and an uncomfortable shiver travelled down her spine. Pretending she had an itch, Olivia stepped back and scratched her left shoulder.

He studied her over the rim of his glass. 'But the royal box would probably be occupied opening night. That would mean there would be such a crush. You would not mind?'

She gave a slight shrug. 'A crush is no bother, if the entertainment is worthy.'

Janvier's dark eyes twinkled mischievously. 'Then I would be honoured to join you.' He scanned the salmon-coloured room. 'I am surprised your Regent is not here this evening.'

'Georgiana told me the poor man is suffering from

the gout again. If it is as severe as last time, it would not surprise me if he missed Mrs Siddons's performances altogether.'

By the time she arrived home, Olivia was certain she had drunk enough champagne that she could endure Gabriel's presence in order to have another child. He said he would come to her tonight. Now, she was ready for him.

After sending Colette away, she stretched out on her bed in an excessively large, white-linen nightrail. Her bare feet were cold on top of the blankets, but she reasoned it would be over quickly, and there would be no chance of Gabriel's scent remaining on her sheets.

What was taking him so long? He was home. She'd heard his muffled voice along with that of Hodges through the door that connected their rooms over an hour ago. His strong knock made Olivia jump. Bringing her hands to her chest to steady the pounding of her heart, she called for him to enter.

The door opened slowly and it was difficult to see his expression in the shadows of the room. 'Why is it so dark in here?'

'I thought you would prefer it this way,' she replied, relieved her voice did not give away her nervousness.

Gabriel closed the door behind him and walked further into the room. He was still dressed impeccably for an evening out. Turning this way, then that, he spun in a circle. Finally, he spotted her. 'Are you well?'

'Of course.'

'Are you not cold?'

'No,' she lied.

There was a hesitation, then he cleared his throat. 'It's late. Perhaps we should discuss this in the morning.'

He was leaving? After all this time agonising and

waiting for him, he was leaving? How much was she expected to endure? She jumped off the bed and ran to the door, blocking his way. 'I thought we had an agreement.'

'We do…I mean we did.'

'You've changed your mind?'

Gabriel held up his hands, appearing as if he couldn't bear to touch her. 'I simply thought we could do this tomorrow.'

'Oh, no, we will do this now or not at all.' Olivia closed her eyes and prayed he would agree to stay.

'Very well,' he said, sounding as if he was trying to calm a skittish colt.

Olivia nodded and walked back to the bed. When she laid back down, she noticed he hadn't moved from where he stood by the door.

'It will not work with you all the way over there,' she bit out sarcastically.

'I am fine over here,' he said with a raspy voice. 'I can hear you just fine.'

'Well, I do not expect to do any talking so that really should not matter.'

Gabriel cleared his throat. 'You are certain you would like me come closer?'

If he made her explain exactly how this would work, she was bound to strangle him with her sheets. 'I believe that is how this is done—if memory serves me correctly.'

He approached the side of her bed. She waited for him to do something, but all he seemed capable of doing was staring at the landscape by Constable that hung behind her.

Now it was her turn to clear her throat, but this was to get his attention. Once she had it, she motioned to his tailcoat with her finger.

He nodded and plucked a string off his sleeve. 'Yes,

it's new. Mr Weston continues to prove himself the finest tailor in London.'

Resisting the urge to smother him with one of her pillows, Olivia took a deep breath and looked at the idiot she married. 'Fine, leave it on. Just open your trousers.'

An odd sound emerged from Gabriel. 'My what?'

'Trousers.' Olivia began to slide the hem of her nightrail up her legs. 'Fear not, I will not look.'

With her eyes squeezed firmly shut, Olivia missed her husband's shocked expression that quickly turned to a heated gaze. Abruptly he grabbed her wrist, preventing her from raising the material any higher than the middle of her thighs.

Refusing to open her eyes, she let out a sigh. 'Very well, you take the lead.'

'Olivia, what exactly are you doing?' he asked in a husky voice.

She threw her forearm over her eyes. 'I thought you said you wanted to get this over with quickly?'

He let out a soft laugh and she peered out from behind her arm.

His face was cast in the shadow of the crackling fire behind him. 'I thought we were discussing Andrew this afternoon. However, I now believe you were talking about something else entirely.'

'Andrew? Why would you think I was talking about having a child with Andrew?' She yanked the yards of material over her knees and sat up, tucking her legs under her. Reaching over for one of her numerous pillows, she hit him with it.

He grabbed it. 'I thought you wanted me to speak with Andrew regarding his behaviour around Nicholas. What did you think we were discussing?' He tossed the pillow next to her on the bed.

Relieved that the room was cast in such low light, Olivia was certain her face was crimson. 'How could you possibly mistake me wanting to have another child with me wanting you to reprimand your brother?' she asked with annoyance.

'A child?' he choked out. 'Is that what you wanted to discuss? Why didn't you simply say so?'

'I did!'

She hit him with another pillow and he caught this one as well.

'No, you did not,' he said as if he were speaking to someone Nicholas's age. He tossed this pillow next to the other one. 'Not once did the word "child" leave your lips.' He cleared his throat again. 'You want another one?'

Olivia was too emotionally spent to say another word, so she simply nodded and closed her eyes.

'You are certain?'

Again she nodded and this time she met his shadowed gaze.

He tossed his head back and closed his eyes. She waited. Any dealings they had with one another from now on hinged on this very moment. Her palms began to sweat.

'Slide over,' he commanded softly.

She shifted towards the centre of the bed and closed her eyes when he began undressing. Was he as smooth and muscular as he had been years ago? Opening one eye, she peeked. He stood there shirtless, tugging off his trousers. She closed her eye quickly before he caught her. Blast it! He looked as good as he had the day she'd married him.

The bed dipped next to her and she felt a tug on the ribbon at the neckline of her nightrail. 'You have too many clothes on.'

She swatted his hand away. 'We can do it like this. I'll just raise my hem.'

He steadied her hand as she began to move the fabric up her legs. 'Is that what you were planning to do? Lay here with your eyes closed and lift your voluminous skirt for me?'

'I won't complain. Just do what needs to be done.'

Gabriel's body jerked back as if she slapped him and he combed his hand through his hair, making the ends stand up in all directions. 'Bloody hell, Olivia, what kind of man do you think I am?'

'Oh, I know very well what kind of man you are,' she spat.

'What does that mean?'

'It means I know you are only interested in your own needs.'

He glared down at her. 'Like hell I am. And how am I to attend to your needs, when you are trussed up like a Christmas goose? It's a wonder you aren't suffocating.'

'I'll have you know this fabric is the finest French linen,' she said through her teeth.

'Then you should have had three gowns made from it instead of one.'

She hit him with another pillow. This time he threw it on the floor.

'Just take me!' she shouted, surprising herself, as well as Gabriel.

They didn't move. They simply stared at one another as their chests rose and fell in unison. The only sound was the occasional pop from the logs in the fireplace.

Abruptly he jumped out of bed and began tugging on his trousers. 'I cannot do this,' he repeated.

'Wait! Where are you going?' she asked, rising to her knees, stunned by his rejection.

He jerked his shirt over his head and began gathering the rest of his discarded clothing. When he had them all in his arms, he stalked over to the bed. 'Regardless of what you think, Duchess, this is not going to work,' he ground out.

'All the world thinks you are a man of honour, but it's a lie. You only ever think of yourself.'

Gabriel gathered up his boots and stormed to the door leading to his room. When his hand clutched the handle, he paused. 'You are lucky you are not a man,' he said through his teeth before he slammed the door behind him.

A pillow, book and hairbrush hit the door in rapid succession. Just when she thought she was finished crying over him, Gabriel pushed her to the emotional edge— again. The tears were falling and she couldn't make them stop. She would not give him the satisfaction of hearing her cry, so she pressed her lips firmly together as her body lurched with her silent sobs.

He didn't want her. He couldn't even bring himself to bed her to get a spare. What was wrong with her? Why couldn't she hold the attention of the one man who had once meant the world to her?

Olivia still wanted that child, now more than ever, but now she would never conceive one.

She hated him for that!

She hated him for what he had done to her five years ago!

And she hated him for reducing her to tears by taking away her only chance at experiencing unconditional love again.

Chapter Four

The next morning before the sun had even begun to rise Gabriel rode his horse around the Serpentine as if the demons of hell were chasing him. He continued to circle the lake in Hyde Park, hoping the pounding of Homer's hooves would knock his brain back together.

His wife had wanted him in her bed after five years, four months and eleven days. That alone should have been cause for celebration. The fact that she wanted another child with him should have made him the happiest of men. But at the moment, he wanted to drown her in the lake he rode around.

If she had been a man, she would have paid for the insults she threw at him as he left her room. Did she really think that little of him? Had she ever understood what kind of man he prided himself in being? His wife was as much a stranger to him as the girl who sold flowers at the entrance of the park.

The idea that she thought he would bed her by throwing up her nightrail and thrusting inside her, while she would have been in obvious discomfort or planning the week's menus, was just too much to bear. Did she really believe he was such a beast? Oh, he knew she did not like him. She had made that very clear, but to think that poorly of him was infuriating. From the day he had entered his cradle, honour and duty were drilled into him. Whether she believed it or not, he was a man bound by honour. And that honour had cost him more than she knew.

Up ahead, three men on horseback cleared the trees. The sun had begun to paint the sky in pinks and yellows, and the rumble of his stomach told him a good breakfast might settle some of his anger. It was time to head home.

Gabriel was sitting in his breakfast room, tucking into his meal and reading *The Times*, when Bennett informed him the Earl of Hartwick was calling. Hopefully his friend was here to tell him something about the smell of the note belonging to the gunman. Glancing up, Gabriel followed Hart's progress as he strolled into the room, his black frock coat fluttering behind him. If he had not handed over his coat to Bennett, Gabriel knew this wasn't a social call.

Hart dropped into the chair next to him and tipped his head towards Bennett. The butler looked at Gabriel for approval before fetching a glass of his best brandy for the Earl. After taking a small sip, Hart ran his hand through his black hair, attempting to move a lock that had fallen over his bright blue eyes. 'It's a good thing you're so predicable that I knew I'd find you here at this hour. I want you to know I had plans last night that I altered especially for you.'

Gabriel cut into his ham and studied Hart. 'A bit early for brandy, wouldn't you say?'

'I've not gone to bed yet. Well, that is not exactly true...'

'So I take it you have something to tell me.'

'I do.' Hart reclined back, a sly smile peaking over the rim of his glass. 'I know who the gunman is.'

Gabriel put his fork down and leaned forward. 'How?'

'Do you not want to know how I reasoned it out?'

'I fear I don't have much of a choice, now do I?'

'Not if you want that name. What has ruffled your feathers this morning?'

'I'm unruffled, now talk.'

Hart studied him and took another sip of brandy. 'It was a good thing Andrew mentioned the man's accent when he showed me that note.'

'His accent?'

'Yes, he said he recognised it from his time near Manchester. Using that bit of information, I took a trip by the river to the Black Swan. Many of its patrons hail from up north. I simply asked a lively lass of my acquaintance who is a barmaid there if she would take a look at him for me. I was pleased to discover that she did indeed know the man.' He took another slow sip, savouring his drink. 'She also found identifying a prisoner quite exciting. So for that, I thank you.'

'You took someone to the Tower without my consent?' Gabriel tried to relax his fist.

Hart waved his hand casually in the air, which was all the more infuriating. 'Apologies…deep regret…whatever it is you need to hear. But be aware I did not exactly have the opportunity to contact you at the time.'

'And how did you explain your need to identify the man, and why he was being held in the Tower?'

'I told her he attempted to rob me. She believed it, saying he was an unsavoury fellow who was known to annoy the patrons with talk of his disgust of the monarchy and those that serve it. And we played a game of sorts. She was blindfolded for our journey. I never told her we were in the Tower.' Hart removed a folded piece of paper from the pocket of his black waistcoat and slid it towards Gabriel. 'Here. That is his name, an area of town *and* information about the man's family, because I am that good at what I do.'

Maybe now they would finally get some answers. Without opening it, Gabriel tapped his finger on the folded paper. 'So maybe you are as good as you think you are.'

'I will attempt to ignore the surprise in your voice.'

'Had anyone at the Tower overheard the information your barmaid gave you?'

Hart shook his head and surveyed Gabriel's breakfast. 'I thought it best to gather all the details while she and I were alone.'

'Hopefully there is useful information about his family to finally force him to talk. Andrew has been observing the interrogations. He informs me the man has a high threshold for pain.'

'He will break sooner or later. How is our illustrious friend faring?'

Knowing how restless Prinny could be, Gabriel assumed he wasn't handling his confinement well. 'I am sure he can use a good card game or two to lift his spirits.'

'I imagine I can spare some time. Unless you have something else you need me to do. Shine your boots?'

'From the state of those Hessians, I believe I will continue to have Hodges tend to my boots.'

'Some day you'll have to remind me how I became involved with the lot of you and why I continue to remain.'

'My father had said he asked for your assistance because you were cunning and had a greatness inside of you that you weren't aware of. If you decided to end this association of ours, I assure you that you would be quite bored.'

'You're probably right, but I have a feeling I am not the only one who lives for excitement.'

When Gabriel returned home that evening, having more excitement in his life was the last thing on his mind. As he handed over his hat, gloves and walking stick, he noted the sound of laughter drifting into the entrance hall from somewhere else in the house. He raised a questioning brow to his butler.

Bennett cleared his throat. 'It is Wednesday,' he said as a way of explanation.

How could he have forgotten? It was the one day of the week that he and Olivia had agreed she could entertain at home and he would stay out. It had been a long time since he had been in his London residence this early on a Wednesday evening. All this pressure of finding out who was behind the assassination attempt must have caused the normal function of his brain to shut down.

He would go to his study and have a dinner tray sent there. But as he stepped down the hall, a distinct deep male laugh could be heard coming from the private dining room a few doors away. Gabriel moved to the open doorway and peered inside.

His wife was seated at the head of the table, with Andrew to her right. They were leaning close to one another, deep in what appeared to be congenial conversation. It was the very picture of a warm family moment, something Gabriel had not experienced with his wife in many years.

He had never looked to marry for love. Love was a bunch of sentimental drivel some of his classmates at Cambridge would drone on about, usually referring to a local girl who could lead them around by their passions. Thank goodness he and Olivia had been sensible enough not to seek that in a marriage. They'd had a comfortable friendship based on a mutual respect for each other's opinions and interests. That, and the fact that he'd wanted to sink deep inside of her from the moment he saw her, told him this was the woman he needed to marry. She had been the ideal wife for him, until his responsibilities got in the way.

Leaning against the doorframe, he watched her smile widen at something Andrew said. That dimple that he hadn't seen in ages graced her cheek and the urge to interrupt the quaint domestic scene overtook him.

'I was unaware you would be dining here tonight,' he called out, crossing his arms.

Olivia's startled expression was a contrast to Andrew's friendly greeting. Approaching her side, Gabriel raised an inquisitive brow at his brother while he snatched a grape off his wife's plate.

She watched him bring it to his lips. 'I didn't expect you to be home.'

It was the first thing she had said to him since he'd stormed out of her room the night before. He was surprised by her attempt at civility, but then again, they were not alone.

'It is my house,' he replied, taking another grape. There were so many emotions running through him that it was difficult to grab on to one. His only thought was to wonder for the first time what exactly happened in his house on Wednesday evenings.

'Would you care to join us?' she asked, sounding as if she was chewing on glass.

Gabriel took a seat to her left instead of his customary chair, which was down the table across from hers. She ran her gaze over him with a wrinkled brow and Gabriel refused to consider why he felt an odd desire to stay near the warm sense of companionship. He motioned for a glass of claret from his footman. 'So, what had you both so entertained when I walked in?'

Andrew shrugged and looked to Olivia. Gabriel raised his brows, waiting for her response, plucking yet another grape from her plate.

Her nostrils flared. 'Frederick, please bring another place setting for His Grace,' she said, glaring at Gabriel throughout her entire request.

After the words she'd spat at him last night, he found perverse pleasure in annoying her today. The footman was about to turn to enter the butler's pantry when Gabriel stopped him with a raise of his hand. 'No need, Frederick.'

Frederick turned back to resume his place by the door.

'Nonsense. Frederick, the setting.'

The footman turned again towards the pantry.

'Frederick, I said that will not be necessary. The Duchess's plate holds just what I desire.'

The footman once again turned back to face the table, but this time instead of keeping his eyes fixed straight ahead, he watched Olivia.

'Perhaps you are mistaken,' she said, taking the last three grapes and popping them into her mouth in rapid succession. She narrowed her eyes at Gabriel, challenging him to take anything else from her plate.

He reached across and broke off a small wedge of cheese. It was a childish thing to do, but he could not resist the impulse. 'I do believe you never did say what the two of you were discussing when I walked in,' he said to her.

'No, I do not believe we did.' She lifted her plate and

Frederick jumped to take it. 'I know you are a very busy man. We do not wish to keep you from your business.'

Gabriel took a long drink and looked between his wife and Andrew. 'My business can wait.' He didn't like the feeling of being pushed to the side—of not being privy to something that was going on under his roof.

He felt like an outsider.

He caught his brother's eye. 'I'm surprised to find you here.'

'I don't see why. I enjoy Olivia's company.'

'Andrew came here looking for you. I invited him to join me for dinner and he kindly accepted,' Olivia broke in, glaring at Gabriel like she wanted to throttle him.

The gilded candelabra resting on the table a few feet away appeared to be very heavy and Gabriel wondered if he should have one of the footmen remove it.

'I take it your presence here means your health has improved,' Gabriel said to Andrew, wishing he could grab his brother and drag him out of the dining room without causing suspicion. If he had searched Gabriel out, there was a reason.

Andrew narrowed his gaze at Gabriel and leaned forward. 'It has. Even though our mother is under the assumption I was suffering from the effects of too much ale. Now where do you suppose she acquired that notion?'

It took great effort for Gabriel not to sputter his wine back into his glass. He could not, however, hold back his smile. 'I have absolutely no idea.'

Andrew nodded and fell back into his chair. 'Just as I thought.'

'I still cannot believe you were set upon by thieves on your way here,' Olivia broke in. 'I find it astonishing they would consider attacking you with your intimidating size. Hopefully, the bruises on your hand will heal quickly.'

Andrew shot a quick glance at Gabriel before looking at the knuckles of his right hand and flexing his fingers into a fist. 'I'm sure the bruises will be gone in a day or two.' He smiled warmly at Olivia. 'You are very kind to be so concerned.'

'Nonsense,' she replied in earnest. 'I wish you would let me send you home with some healing salve.'

'I will be fine. Stop fussing so. Save your mothering for Nicholas,' he said reassuringly.

The colour drained from Olivia's face. The topic of mothering brought back all the horrid events of last night and Gabriel knew she was remembering them as well. He should be angry with her—hell, he had been. She had insulted his honour. But he couldn't ignore the fact that he was to blame for what she thought of him.

The sight of her in that ridiculously large nightrail had set his blood on fire and made him instantly hard. He knew he would have embarrassed himself if he had managed to get all that fabric off her. It had been so long since they were together. Olivia had the most amazing bottom he had ever seen and over the last five years, four months and eleven days he'd found himself sneaking a glimpse of it whenever her back was to him.

His thoughts were on her curves when he heard his brother call his name. Shaking his head, he looked at Andrew.

'I asked you how Nicholas liked his ride through Hyde Park. Olivia told me you took him.'

'He liked it very much.' He took another sip of claret, needing to redirect his thoughts away from Olivia's soft skin and enticing curves. As he motioned for more wine, he caught Andrew's amused expression.

'What name has he settled on?'

'To my knowledge he is still undecided.'

Olivia looked as if she was about to say something, then took a sip from her glass instead. He stared at her expectantly, but she turned away. There was an uncomfortable silence. Gabriel knew she wanted him to leave. He was not welcome at his own dinner table. She already thought he would take her with no consideration for her comfort. Did he really want her to believe he was a bore as well?

Rising from his seat, Gabriel took his glass and strode to the door. 'Come to my study on your way out, Andrew,' he said, not waiting for a reply.

An hour later, his brother strolled into his study without even knocking. 'Why do I feel as if you do not like me spending time alone with Olivia?'

'Don't be absurd. She considers you her brother.' Gabriel sat back at his desk chair and watched Andrew walk to the table set with crystal bottles and pour two glasses of brandy. 'How often do you dine here?'

'You mean since Nicholas has been born?'

Gabriel nodded and Andrew sighed, sliding the stopper back in the bottle.

'I don't know. I've never counted. You should try it some time. She is vastly entertaining.' He placed a glass of brandy in front of Gabriel and sank into the chair across from him.

Gabriel leaned forward and narrowed his gaze. 'What do the two of you talk about? I was never under the impression you had anything in common. Dear God…has she developed a love of gambling?'

Andrew shook his head, laughing. 'Our discussions are quite varied. Were you aware she recently began acquiring a repertoire of bawdy tales? They're quite good.'

Gabriel's brain almost exploded. 'You're joking.'

'I'm quite serious. Probably from that painter she has been spending time with.'

'What painter?'

'The one she is sitting for.'

Gabriel wondered which painter Andrew was referring to. She knew so many and had been patron to a few over the years.

'You do know she is sitting for a portrait, don't you?'

Did Andrew have to look so smug? Gabriel rubbed his lower lip and looked away. The idea his brother knew more about his wife than he did was beginning to bother him. 'Of course I do.'

'I should hope so, considering the man has quite the reputation.' Andrew sank back further into his chair.

'Reputation for what?'

'You really don't know anything about her or her friends, do you?'

'I do,' he lied. 'We live in the same house.'

Andrew nodded slowly. 'Well, in any event, I'm glad you came home when you did. I wanted to tell you in person our gunman has finally begun to talk. We were able to use the information Hart gathered to convince our Mr Clarke that if he cared at all for his family, he would tell us what we needed to know. It appears thoughts of his sickly mother helped him find his voice. He says he was contacted by a note left for him at the post about assassinating Prinny and he was told that he would find information on Prinny's whereabouts in a book he was to check in each day at Hatchard's bookshop on Piccadilly. He has no idea who leaves the information, just that when he completed his job, he would receive a thousand pounds. Since he has no love for our monarchy, he didn't see a problem with profiting from Prinny's death.'

'I assume we have men at Hatchard's?'

'We do.'

'Let's hope that whoever was providing this information is not aware Mr Clarke is no longer in circulation. That is the only way we will find out who wants Prinny dead.' Gabriel sat back in his chair and took a long draw of brandy, grateful they were one step closer to ensuring Prinny's safety.

There was a long, comfortable silence between the brothers before Andrew had to ruin it. 'Five years is a long time to be apart from your wife.'

'Your point?'

'You still want Olivia.'

'No, I don't.'

'So while you were in the dining room with us, not once did your mind turn to taking her?'

No, he was thinking about running his hands over her sweet round bottom. However now, thanks to Andrew, he was thinking about much more. 'It did not cross my mind.'

'Liar.'

Gabriel narrowed his gaze. 'You are lucky we are family, or I might call you out at such an insult.'

'Fine. Tell yourself you are not calling me out because I am your brother and not because I am a better shot than you.'

'You are not. I bet I could shoot that taper by the window in half and you could not.'

Andrew sat up straighter in his chair, the excitement of besting his brother evident in his expression. 'What if I shoot the taper in half?'

Gabriel removed a pistol from his desk drawer. 'You won't. But if you do and I don't, I'll buy you a new pair of Hessians.'

'Hoby's?'

'Do you truly believe I would even consider purchasing anything else? And if I win, you tell me about your entire conversation with Olivia.' *What? What an idiotic thing to win!*

'That's what you want?' Andrew asked, as if he too couldn't believe Gabriel's stupidity.

'Just go first.' Exasperation was in his voice as Gabriel handed his brother the pistol.

'That taper is much too close to make this interesting. I propose we try this in your ballroom.'

Once they were settled in the cavernous room, Andrew loaded the pistol and took aim at the gilded candelabra in front of an open set of French windows. The shot rang out, and the top half of one of the tapers fell to the floor, splattering wax on the wood. With a satisfied smile, he handed the gun over.

Gabriel reloaded it and took aim. Hoby's would not be receiving an order for new boots from this house. He also cut a taper in two, but the top of his fell out onto the terrace. The sound of racing footsteps caused both men to turn towards the door.

Bennett skidded to a halt just inside the threshold. 'Sir, is everything all right?' he asked through laboured breath.

'Yes, Bennett, my brother and I were just settling a bet.'

'Very good, sir,' Bennett said still breathing heavily. 'I will inform madam of it, in the event she questions if you are still alive.'

Gabriel wondered if it would even matter to her.

Andrew strolled to the windows and peered out into the darkened garden. 'We should have checked to see if anyone was out there.'

'If anyone is skulking about in my garden at night,

they deserve to be shot,' replied Gabriel, shooing his butler away.

Perhaps if he plied Andrew with enough brandy, he could still manage to get his brother to tell him what made Olivia laugh.

Chapter Five

Morning sunlight streamed through the large windows of Mr John Manning's portrait studio directly into Olivia's eyes, forcing her to keep them closed.

'Are you certain no one will recognise me?' she asked from her reclined position on the crimson divan.

The artist took a long tendril of her dark unbound hair and adjusted it over her gown on the swell of her breast. 'I assure you, with your head turned this deep in profile, no one will know it's you unless you tell them.'

She felt a pull near her hip at the grey satin gown he had given her to wear. 'It is to your credit that I trust you as I do. I feel quite foolish lying here like this.'

The pressure from his warm hand moved her left leg. 'You look sinful.'

She wished she could swat his hand. 'That is not helping.'

He laughed. 'But it's true. Any man would kill to have you in his bed.'

Now it was Olivia's turn to laugh, knowing just how false his statement was. 'How often do you suppose you have said those words to the women who sit for you in this very room?'

'Not as nearly as often as I'd like.' He retreated back towards his easel. 'Many women require thought to discover what is beautiful about them, but you will make my canvas sing without much effort on my part. Thereby, your allure will help me create a masterpiece all of London is sure to talk about.'

'I already agreed to sit for you for this experiment of yours. You have no need to work your charms on me.'

'I only speak the truth.' He was back by her side again, his warm fingers tilting her neck up just a bit more. When she squinted up at him, his dark brown eyes were smiling down at her and his unfashionably long black hair had begun to come loose from the leather tie that held it back from his face. His unpolished appearance was a sharp contrast to her husband's fastidious grooming habits.

'I am relieved you do not expect me to remember this exact pose each day,' she said, taking note of the position of her arms.

His grin widened, and he moved a strand of hair away from her face. 'My sketch guides me. You are always quite accommodating with all my poking and prodding. Once we are finished for the day, you may jerk my body into any complex tangle of your choosing.'

That created an amusing image and she closed her eyes again. 'What a capital notion! Now if you don't grant me the breaks I require, I will devise painful retribution.'

'My, what a bloodthirsty duchess you are.'

The sound of his chalk scratching as he drew eased some of her tension. 'Are you certain I do not appear large to you?' she asked, trying to imagine what the sketch looked like.

Chuckling, he continued to draw. 'You are far from large. Although even if you were, it would be of no concern. Men enjoy curves on a woman. It gives us something to hold onto when we are in the throes of passion.'

'Then I believe I have so many places for a man to hold onto, he would be at a quandary where to begin.'

He laughed again. 'I know where I would begin.'

How she wished she could turn her head and peak at his expression. 'Where?'

'I am sketching it right now.'

'Well, that was not very forthcoming.'

'No, it was not.'

Olivia began to laugh.

'Do not move,' he commanded.

He adjusted the folds of the silk by her thigh. She bit her lip and prayed he didn't notice the catch in her breath at the unexpected contact.

'You have the kind of body that tempts men to steal a touch.' He moved her left arm a fraction of an inch.

Olivia opened one eye to study him. They had known each other for more than a year. Not once, in all that time, had he exhibited any form of inappropriate behaviour with her. Even now, she knew he saw her only as an object in his painting. He must be attempting to make her feel at ease, since she was sprawled out over his divan in a most unrefined pose. She was well aware what her body looked like and, as she had discovered from her recent encounter with Gabriel in her bedchamber, tempting was not how she would describe it.

'So what exactly is one to interpret from this pose?' she asked, fighting the urge to scratch her nose.

'It is the pose of a woman who has just reached complete fulfilment,' he replied as if discussing the weather.

Olivia raised her head and stared at him aghast, unable to voice a response.

'You must stop moving,' he yelled. 'This will be a

masterpiece of movement and light. But each time you shift, you force me to readjust the folds of your gown. I cannot sketch you in a timely manner if I have to continually walk over there.'

She rested her head back down and tried to move her head into the exact position he had placed it. Manning readjusted it a fraction of an inch and then adjusted the hair cascading over her breasts.

He raised his eyebrow at her and pointed his chalk at her in warning. 'Do. Not. Move.'

'Fine, but I honestly do not believe anyone would be interested in seeing how I look after…well, after…' Olivia was certain she could not blush any deeper than she was. 'I am not the best subject for this. You should have asked someone younger. Men would find that much more enjoyable to look at.'

'You believe you know us that well?' The sketching resumed.

'There are many beautiful girls you could have chosen.'

'True—however, I am not interested in girls. Their innocence colours their sensuality. A woman with experience in the activities of the bedchamber has an innate sensuality that is apparent to any man over the age of sixteen.'

'I am not sensual.'

'Of course you are. It's in the way your body moves and the way your eyes acquire a wicked glint, as if you know the secret of bringing a man to his knees.' His voice was so calm and nonchalant.

'So you really prefer women of my age?'

'And older, but if you tell that to any of the young women that sit for me, I will deny it.'

Managing to laugh without moving a muscle, Olivia

considered what he said. She had spent years after their estrangement wondering what Gabriel found attractive. The notion of what other men preferred never entered her mind.

When he finally broke the long stretch of silence, it felt as if hours had passed. 'I am almost finished with my preliminary sketch. Have any parts of you lost all sensation?'

'My right arm is beginning to grow numb. This really is an indulgent pose. I believe I may have dozed for a few moments.'

'I believe you did. Your breathing became quite rhythmic.'

He approached her side, then rubbed her right arm. The warmth and pressure felt heavenly.

'What the bloody hell is going on here?' bellowed a deep, angry voice from the other end of the room.

Olivia jerked her head towards the doorway and closed her eyes, pretending her husband was not standing there looking as if he wanted to toss them both out the window.

Manning groaned at her movement and stared daggers at the imposing man who had interrupted their sitting. 'Who are you to intrude in my studio, sir?' he asked.

'I am her husband. Now take your damn hands off her.' Gabriel's voice was commanding with no room for negotiation.

Manning backed away, raising his hand in surrender. 'I am simply adjusting her body for the portrait.'

'I know of no respectable portrait that requires such a pose.'

She would not move her body to inconvenience her friend. 'What are you doing here?'

Gabriel's fiery gaze shifted to her. 'I had an appointment not far away. I thought I would escort you home.'

How could he possibly have known where she was? And, why in the world would he want to escort her home?

'I believe your sitting is over for the day, Duchess,' Gabriel commanded.

'Nonsense, there is still more to do. Isn't that correct?' She turned her head towards her friend, who appeared pale.

He shifted nervously. 'There isn't much more to do. You are welcome to stay until I am finished for today.'

She was not about to allow that to happen, but before she could voice her opinion Gabriel walked to the easel, crossed his arms and studied the sketch.

'Continue,' he said with a nod.

'I will have to touch her to adjust her form.'

'He does not care,' Olivia murmured.

But the artist's eyes were fixed on Gabriel, who nodded his consent and watched as Manning went back to the easel to study Olivia's pose. He approached her and hesitantly moved her neck and arm. Very carefully he adjusted the folds of her gown.

The sketching resumed and Olivia could hear Gabriel move towards the chair near the door. Suddenly the pose she was in was not as relaxing as it had been a short time before. Why had she ever agreed to sit in this ridiculous position?

Although it probably only took fifteen more minutes of sketching in silence, to Olivia it felt like hours. Finally she heard him toss his chalk onto the table and she picked up her head to gauge his reaction. His grin was infectious.

'You're pleased?' she asked, smiling back at him.

'Exceedingly so. I'll need you to come back to begin

painting.' He walked to the divan and held out his hand to help her up.

Gabriel rose abruptly. Both Olivia and Manning turned his way.

Immediately, her friend dropped her hand. 'Will you be able to arrive before eight? I would love to capture the early morning light on the folds of the satin.'

She rolled her shoulders to relieve some of the stiffness. 'Yes, I believe I can.'

Manning walked to a cabinet and began removing bottles of pigment. She was about to enter the dressing room when she paused at the sight of Gabriel approaching his side.

Her husband picked up a dish with something brown resting in it and held it out. 'You smoke while my wife sits for you?' Gabriel asked, arching an intimidating brow.

'No, I would never.'

'See that you do not.'

Olivia shook her head as she walked into the dressing room, wondering why it should even matter to him. A short while later, she emerged wearing her very proper bonnet and cinnamon-coloured walking dress with Colette at her side. As her maid walked towards the door, Olivia approached the easel, curious about the composition. What she saw surprised her.

Her face was turned away from the viewer so only her neck and the outline of her left cheek were visible. Her hair was fanned out around her with one dark curl sloping down her neck and gliding over her breast. The fingers of her left hand appeared relaxed as if they had no strength left in them. True to his word, no one would know who the subject was.

'Well?' Manning asked, approaching her side.

'I do not even recognise myself.'

'I told you to trust me. It will be breathtaking when I am finished. Mr West will be begging me to exhibit it.'

She hoped for his sake that would be true. The man was a highly skilled artist. The more people exposed to his work, the more commissions he would receive.

There was a distinct clearing of a throat from the doorway where Gabriel stood, looking down at his watch. If he was so impatient to leave, he could do so without her. For years he had completely avoided her and last night he interrupted her dinner with Andrew. Now he wanted to escort her home. What was he about?

As they walked out onto the pavement, Gabriel had to squint to adjust to the bright sunlight. After last night's discussion with Andrew, he was curious about this artist Olivia had taken an interest in. Luckily it did not take James long to find where the man's studio was located.

'Where is your carriage?' he asked, scanning the busy road.

'Colette and I walked. One of the wheels of my carriage required some work this morning and I saw no reason to wait on such a lovely day.'

'My carriage is always at your disposal should there be a need.'

He took her by the elbow and steered her around some young boisterous bucks. The moment they passed them, she shifted her arm out from his grasp.

'Where are you planning on hanging the portrait?' he asked, clasping his hands behind his back and redirecting his thoughts away from the idea that she could not bear for him to touch her.

'We hope to have Mr West agree to exhibit it at the Royal Academy.'

Gabriel froze and Colette almost collided with his

back. He could not have possibly heard her correctly. That portrait of his wife—looking as though she had just been thoroughly and completely satisfied—was to be on display for all of London to see? Like hell it was!

'No,' he stated firmly and resumed walking. At least that was taken care of.

Olivia caught up to him and did her best to keep pace with his long strides. 'What did you say?' she asked.

He glanced down at her. She was not pleased.

'I said no. That portrait is not leaving our house.'

'The decision is not yours to make. I did not commission it. I am sitting for him as a favour.'

Again Gabriel stopped abruptly, and again Colette pulled herself back from knocking into him.

He must have misunderstood. 'Pardon me?'

'I said that portrait is being painted with the intention for exhibition to show the breadth of his skills as an artist.'

'And you agreed to be his model? Why would you agree to such a thing? That portrait is indecent.'

She snorted. His refined wife actually snorted at his statement. 'You are one to say what is indecent?'

They were turning onto Bond Street, bustling with servants and members of the *ton*. He was aware they were garnering attention simply by walking together. The last thing he needed was gossip about this argument—and this was going to be an argument. She was much too stubborn for it not to be.

He directed his attention ahead of him. 'We will discuss this at home.'

'I'm not going home.'

'Yes, you are. We are going home to finish this discussion.'

'Then I suggest we finish it now because I. Am. Not. Going. Home.'

His nostrils flared when he looked down at her. 'When did you become so defiant?'

'When you showed your true colours,' she replied with clipped movements.

She didn't know him at all. If she believed he was going to allow that portrait to hang in the Royal Academy, or anywhere else outside one of their homes for that matter, she was sorely mistaken. 'Very well, you want to discuss this now, we will.'

Guiding her by the elbow, they walked past Gentleman Jackson's Boxing Salon and into William Gray's Jewellery Shop. The moment the bespectacled proprietor spotted the impeccably dressed couple, he came hurrying over.

'Leave us,' Gabriel commanded.

The mouse-faced little man retreated behind the curtain to the back of the store.

Next he turned his attention to her maid. 'You are to wait outside.'

It was of no surprise that Colette glanced at Olivia for her approval before she walked out the door. He was surrounded by women who seemed to have forgotten he was the Duke of Winterbourne.

Now he would settle this matter with Olivia once and for all. He tugged her into a corner of the shop away from the windows overlooking the street. 'You are the Duchess of Winterbourne, a respected member of the *ton* and my wife. You cannot display yourself for all of London in such a fashion.'

'No one will know it is me.' Her voice was low but strong.

'*I* will know.' He kept his voice down as well, but it wasn't easy.

When he had walked in on the roguishly dressed man standing over his reclining wife and touching her, Gabriel wanted to carve out the man's bollocks with a butter knife. 'You are not to go back there.' There! Now there would be no question where the painting would be hung since it would not be finished.

'You are mad and have lost all sense of reason,' she whispered sharply.

He wasn't foolish enough to deny what this was. He was feeling proprietary over a woman he hadn't taken to bed in years. And maybe he was just a little bit mad. 'No one should see you that way. I am the only one who should see you that way,' he bit out.

Yes, mad. He was definitely mad.

'But you don't. You cannot even bear to take me to bed.'

'Now who is mad?'

She fisted her hands at her sides and leaned closer so their foreheads were almost touching. 'It's true. So what if he thinks his study of movement and light is also a testament to female sensuality? So what if he believes I am striking? You do not.'

Now, *she* definitely was the one who was mad. He grabbed her by the back of her neck and crushed his lips against hers in a claiming kiss.

Olivia intended to push him away, but she had forgotten the feel of the curve of the muscles in his arms. A slow glide of his tongue against her closed lips had her weakening. And when he pressed his body into hers, all rational thought left her brain and her body took over.

She had missed him—missed the time they'd spent together early in their marriage.

Reluctantly she slid her hands over his shoulders and threaded her fingers through his thick hair. It was shorter now than it had been years ago. She deepened the kiss.

He groaned low into her mouth and slid his hands over the curve of her bottom. And then, just as quickly as it began, he let her go.

'Let that put to rest your false assumption,' he said, breathing deeply. He stepped away from her, spun on his heels and stormed out the door.

Olivia peered at him through the large shop window as he walked down Bond Street as if he owned the world. She rested her hand on the display case beside her, trying to steady her wobbly legs.

What had just happened? One minute he was being the most insufferable man and the next he was kissing her senseless.

And she'd kissed him back.

She pressed her hand against her forehead, silently berating herself for her foolishness. It must have been her discussion about sensuality with Manning that had caused her to give in to his unusual behaviour. It definitely was not the taste and feel of her husband. Those feelings of wanting him were long dead.

Weren't they?

Chapter Six

That evening, Gabriel sat at his desk and reread Andrew's letter. It was just three lines, informing him they had no new information at this time. At least that was what Gabriel thought the letter said. He would have to reread it yet again since his mind was preoccupied with reliving a kiss—a kiss with his wife of all people. And he could not stop smiling.

What the hell was wrong with him?

He should not be smiling. He should be furious that she would even consider having that painting hung in the Royal Academy. But instead of being blindingly angry, he was smiling simply because for the first time in ages he'd kissed his wife—and she'd kissed him back.

He *was* mad!

There was something about Olivia that always stirred such strong desire in him. It might be that she was beautiful, but many women were and he had no interest in bedding any of them. It was something else—some irresistible combination of beauty and a sharp mind. But for a man with secrets, her cleverness was more of a curse than a blessing. It was best he remember that.

Gabriel pressed his thumb against the bridge of his

nose. He needed to reconfirm his priorities. Someone had threatened Prinny. His duty was to find out who it was and to prevent them from making another attempt on the man's life. The weight of keeping Prinny safe and the safety of his people were heavy on his shoulders. He refused to allow anyone else to be killed on his watch. The last thing he should be thinking about was the taste of his wife's lips and the feel of her bottom as he held her against him.

At least there had been one benefit to her sitting for Manning. Their subsequent argument had led to that kiss—the kiss that he'd initiated and she'd participated in.

Gabriel closed his eyes. The taste of her lips had opened a floodgate of memories of what it felt like to be inside her. It had been so long since he'd had a woman—since he'd had Olivia. His thoughts drifted to one of his favourite memories, which included a warm bath and firelight. All of his attention now was firmly fixed on the image in his head. The letter in his hands fell to his desk.

Olivia was enjoying a 'ladies' dinner', as her hostess liked to call them. Periodically Katrina, the Duchess of Lyonsdale, would invite a few female friends to dine at her home in London while her husband would make himself scarce for the evening. This evening she'd invited Olivia, Victoria and Sarah Forrester, the daughter of the American Minister. Olivia found she looked forward to these ladies-only dinner parties where the conversations were often boisterous and they did not have to wait for the men to finish their port after the meal was over.

Tonight, Olivia stood next to her sister, staring up at the enormous portrait of Katrina, which hung above the fireplace in the library of Lyonsdale House. In the painting, Katrina sat in an elegant bergère chair with a book dangling gracefully from her long fingers and staring directly at the viewer. Manning had perfectly captured the hint of amusement that often crossed her face, and he had done a spectacular job with the shining folds of her ice-blue silk gown. Off to the side of Katrina's chair, an old globe sat on a small table, a silent nod to the fact the Duchess of Lyonsdale came from the United States.

'It arrived this morning,' Katrina said, looking up at the portrait. 'I did not anticipate it being so grand.'

The serious expression on Katrina's face while she studied the painting made Olivia smile. 'You are an English Duchess now. It should be grand to reflect your station.'

'I know, but it's just so…so…'

'Enormous,' Sarah added helpfully, placing her fingertips over her lips to stop from laughing. 'You're fortunate there was enough room to hold a life-size portrait of you.'

'Sarah, I've only just begun carrying this child.'

'I was simply referring to the size of the wall, not your size. Even you admitted it's rather large. It's as if there are two of you,' Sarah continued, looking between the portrait and Katrina. 'Although it is a beautiful likeness of you, I think I'm relieved I will not be immortalised as such.'

'I'm relieved as well,' came the voice of the Earl of Hartwick as he swaggered into the room alongside Lyonsdale and tossed a lock of his shiny black hair out of his eyes. 'One of you is more than sufficient in this world,' he drawled.

He was sinfully handsome, with a strong athletic build and the finest blue eyes God had ever placed in a man. Olivia had heard his name spoken quite often by women of her age. Delicious and virile were words that were frequently used in those conversations.

'It truly does amaze me that the women of this town find you so alluring, Hartwick,' Sarah said. 'I believe it will remain one of life's mysteries.'

'Perhaps it's because you are rarely in my company.'

'No, I am certain familiarity would not clear the reasoning.'

Lyonsdale came to stand beside his wife and kissed her hand. Witnessing the love they shared always filled Olivia with regret—regret that she had not found a man who loved her even just a little.

'We are off to White's,' Lyonsdale said, looking up at the painting. 'However, I wanted to show Hart your portrait.' The pride was evident in his voice. 'I told you that gown was the best choice.'

'You said you wanted me to wear the gown I was wearing the night we met. Fortunately for you, it is one of my favourites.'

'I envisioned you in it for so long, it will always be my favourite.'

Sarah and Hartwick rolled their eyes in unison while standing next to each other. Then the Earl walked closer to the portrait and took in the work with his hands fixed on his hips. He tilted his head a number of times before turning around and nodding to Katrina.

'He is right,' Hartwick said. 'The artist has captured you perfectly. Now be a good duchess and bear a child that looks more like you than it does my friend.'

Olivia thought the child would do well resembling either parent and wondered if she would ever conceive another. Gabriel's kiss today confused her. Instinctively her hand went to her stomach.

'You looked a bit pale, Sister. Some fresh air might do you wonders,' Victoria said, taking Olivia's arm. 'Would you mind if we went outside for just a bit?' she asked Katrina.

'By all means, there is a door to the terrace just down the hall,' Katrina replied with a sympathetic smile. 'We shall be returning to the Crimson Drawing Room shortly. Why don't you take your time and meet us there.'

Victoria guided Olivia into the portrait gallery outside the library and Olivia pulled her to a stop. 'What are you about?' Olivia demanded quietly. 'Now Katrina will think I couldn't bear to witness the affection she shares with Lyonsdale and you were trying to spare me the pain.'

'Nonsense,' Victoria said, tugging Olivia to begin walking. She lowered her voice to a whisper. 'I have wanted to get you alone and couldn't wait another minute. How is it that I hear of surprising actions of yours from Lyonsdale's grandmother and not from you, my own sister? Don't look at me like that. You had to know there would be talk of your unusual stroll down Bond Street with Winter. She mentioned it before we went in for dinner.'

Olivia's stomach dipped uncomfortably, recalling the last time she and Gabriel were the topic of *ton* gossip. 'If that mundane fact has people talking, they aren't paying close enough attention to the scandals around them. I cannot believe a simple walk between a husband and wife is cause for discussion.'

'When those two people act as polite strangers for years, I'd say that is cause for gossip. And how is it you did not see fit to tell me?'

'I did not think it noteworthy.'

Victoria looked about ready to stamp her foot on the parquet floor. 'How could you say that? A few days ago you wanted your cook to roast him for the inconsiderate way he delayed Nicholas's breeching. Now you are walking with him down a main thoroughfare and he is buying you jewels. Something is going on and I demand you tell me what it is.'

'Jewels? He did not buy me any jewels.' Olivia opened the door to the unoccupied terrace and stepped outside. The scent of rain was heavy in the air and thick clouds moved swiftly in the moonlight. 'I was sitting for Manning in his studio when Gabriel arrived quite unexpectedly. He said he was attending to matters close by and decided to accompany me home.'

'Why would he care to escort you home? You barely speak with one another.'

Olivia shrugged and rolled her eyes. 'The man is a mystery and always has been. As to be expected, on our way home we had a disagreement. The only reason he dragged me into a jewellery shop was so people would not witness our row.'

Victoria's eyes narrowed. 'Nevertheless people did witness you together and are speculating on a reconciliation.'

'That is absurd. You of all people should understand our marriage could never go back to being what I thought it was, not after what he did.'

'Well, something has changed and I believe you have some notion what has altered his behaviour.'

Olivia rubbed her forehead. Victoria had always been her deepest confidant. Hopefully she would not make her feel worse. She took a deep breath and let the words spill out. 'I told him I wanted another child.'

Victoria's eyes widened considerably.

'But, he has rejected me,' Olivia amended. 'At least I think he rejected me…please do not tell Mother. I could not bear to hear her prattle on about how relieved she is that I've cast aside my pride and started comporting myself like the Duchess I am. I believe my estrangement from him has been a cause of embarrassment for her.'

'I will not say a word to her—however, how could you not know if you were rejected? I would think it would be fairly obvious.'

'Well, I thought he had rejected me. We did not…that is to say he could not…'

'When did this happen?'

'A few nights past. Oh, it was so humiliating. I cannot believe I even considered it, but now I am so confused.'

Her sister placed a comforting hand over Olivia's. 'Like all men, he is a selfish beast who has no notion of how fortunate he is to have a lovely wife. What is confusing about that? We've known that for years.'

'He kissed me today. Do not groan.' Olivia closed her eyes and dropped her forehead into her palms, not wishing to see Victoria's next reaction. 'And what is worse, I kissed him back.' She was such a fool.

'Oh, no, Olivia, you didn't,' moaned Victoria. 'What in the world possessed you to do such a thing? You know he cares nothing for you. How could you be so foolish?'

'I know. I know,' she whispered back harshly. 'You do not have to remind me. I was the one lying in bed, weak and in pain, when he came to me from another woman's bed.' Why had she been foolish enough to believe he would remain faithful when most of the men in their circle, including all the men in her family, were not? Because she had been foolish enough to believe he might have been falling in love with her. He'd never said as much, but his actions spoke of a man who cared for her deeply.

'Why don't you tell me exactly what happened? Leave no detail out.'

'I do not know what happened. One minute we were

arguing, the next we were kissing. And it changed everything. Now I have no idea if he rejected me or not.'

'You love children. You are a wonderful mother to Nicholas and a doting aunt to my three. I understand why you would want another child, but you know what will happen. Men cannot remain faithful. It is not in their nature. I know that for certain. However, I never fell in love with Haverstraw and care not about his indiscretions. You were foolish enough to fall in love with Winter and the moment he turned to another, you could barely speak to him. It pained me to witness how much he hurt you. I beg of you, do not let him do that to you again. I am telling you, he will never be satisfied with just your bed.'

'But do you not see? I'm not the same naïve girl I was. This time I have no false illusions. I know he does not love me. I have thought this through. During my confinement, I will leave for the country. Gabriel will remain in London and I will be spared hearing about his liaisons. It's the ideal solution.'

'It would be if you had not kissed him back. I know you, better than anyone. If you try and have another child together you will not be able to repress your feelings for him. I saw how much he meant to you. I told you when you married him not to expect him to remain faithful. I told you it is a rare man that can be satisfied with only one woman. You should have heeded my warning, but you seemed to expect more.'

Olivia had never expected more, until she met Gabriel. And she'd never felt more alone than the day she realised she meant nothing to him.

'I have you to turn to for comfort. Who will Nicholas have? He should have someone dear to him if his world should fall apart.'

Victoria squeezed her hand. 'He will have his cousins. I am begging you. Be content with the way things are. You do not need another child.'

Olivia released Victoria's hand and walked a few feet to the balustrade overlooking the garden. Thunder rumbled in the distance. She rubbed the goose pimples on her arms. Was Victoria right? Maybe she did not need another child. But why then did the thought of not having another one leave her with an ache in her chest? And why had Gabriel kissed her?

Chapter Seven

The next morning Gabriel leaned silently against the doorway of Mr Manning's studio and watched Olivia recline along the divan, appearing to be a woman completely at ease in her surrounds. She was back here again, and he knew he had only himself to blame. If only he had been less interested in her when they were first married, he wouldn't be standing here with his arms crossed to prevent himself from dragging her out.

When they had first met, it was evident Olivia had too great a mind for it to remain idle. That was why when he saw how much she enjoyed going to the Royal Academy and admiring the artwork, he'd encouraged her to pursue her interest. It was why he'd introduced her to Mr West and spoke with the man about having Olivia study art under his tutelage. She'd had no desire to create art, but she had a burning need to understand why certain pieces were revered. With her enthusiasm and intelligence, it was no surprise she became a well-respected expert of the Italian masters. His reward came from the luminous joy that shone from her each time she would talk about what she was learning. It didn't occur to him until now that seeing her happy had meant that much to him.

And all these years later, she'd thanked him by posing for an indecent portrait that she intended to share with all of London. He should have encouraged her to pursue horticulture.

His thoughts were interrupted by Manning, who continued speaking with Olivia while mixing more paint. 'Were there any scandals of note at the musical?'

'None that I heard of,' she said on a sigh. 'Although, I try not to pay attention to such speculation.'

'No one was compromised? No one was challenged?' He approached her with a smile and adjusted her arm slightly.

'Not that I witnessed,' she replied grinning.

'How about the Prince Regent? Any interesting tales of his exploits?'

'None. In fact, he was not in attendance. I understand he is suffering terribly from the gout.'

'That must make getting around rather difficult.'

'I would think so.'

'Has he been about?'

'If he has, I've not seen him.'

Gabriel pushed away from the doorframe. 'That is probably because you are devoting too much of your time to charitable causes such as this.'

There was a soft gasp from his unmoving wife.

'Your Grace,' the artist said in an uneven voice, bowing deferentially. 'What a surprise.'

'I decided to show myself in…again.' He walked to the easel and crossed his arms. Today the canvas had paint on it. 'Do you always begin your portraits there?' Gabriel asked, looking at how Manning had captured the creamy skin of his wife's neck and shoulders.

Manning tilted his head and studied the canvas. 'No, it depends where my mood takes me.'

Gabriel's attention was drawn to the top swell of his wife's breasts, painted much too accurately. His fingers dug into his biceps. 'My wife has sat long enough. She needs some refreshment.'

'We have been stopping as often as she requires.'

'You have painted quite a bit. I am certain she needs another.'

'You may continue. I can assure you, I am well.' Olivia's voice rang out from across the room.

Manning shifted his gaze from his subject to Gabriel. Then his brown eyes widen momentarily. At least the man was not a complete nodcock. 'The light has shifted. I believe we are finished for the day,' he said, turning away from the canvas.

Olivia picked her head up and looked from the painter to Gabriel. 'It was fine a few moments ago.'

'It was shifting even then. I was only trying to finish the last few strokes.'

'There will be no more strokes today,' Gabriel said drily, strolling towards Olivia.

She glared at him but allowed him to help her to stand. 'What are you doing here?' she whispered sharply, adjusting the skirt of that enticing gown.

'I told you,' he whispered back, handing her a glass of wine that had been placed on a table near her, 'I have come to see you have some refreshment. Now go and change. I am taking you to Gunter's for ice.'

He expected her to argue, but she took a sip of wine and narrowed her eyes at him. He could tell she was up for a good row. He was starting to learn the signs.

A short while later, they sent Colette home in Olivia's carriage, and Gabriel helped his hesitant wife into his high-perch phaeton. When he climbed into the box from the other side, he looked over to find her eyeing his new equipage. It was an exceptional piece of craftsmanship, with its highly glossed black finish that reflected the London streets like a mirror.

'Is your artist always such a washer-woman?'

'If you are asking if he enjoys gossip, I suppose he does. Talking, as you are well aware, helps to make portrait sessions bearable.'

'I would not think a man like that would be interested in the social life of someone like Prinny.'

'Come now, are you truly that jaded? Most everyone is interested in what he does. Manning is like most aspiring portrait artists. He would love to have the cache to say the Prince Regent sat for him. To have his work displayed in a royal residence would be quite the accomplishment.'

'You have introduced them?'

'Not yet.'

'But you plan to?'

'If the opportunity should present itself, I do not see why I would not. Manning is extremely talented. Surely you can see that from the pieces displayed in his studio? He has even painted Nicholas for me.'

'I will agree the man possesses talent, however did I not tell you that you were not to sit for him again?'

'You did.'

A scruffy dog darted out into the road, and Gabriel expertly manoeuvred the phaeton around it. The carriage rocked back and forth on its wheels. 'If you heard my command, why were you in his studio today?' He glanced over at Olivia, who was sitting with her hands gripped tightly together.

'I never agreed to your request.'

'It was not a request, and you knew that.' Now he pulled abruptly to a stop as a newsboy ran across the road.

Olivia made an odd sound. 'I honour my commitments, and I told him I would sit for him.'

'Now you must tell him you've changed your mind.'

'I cannot do that.'

'You mean you will not.' He snapped the reins, making the phaeton go faster.

Her hands moved to grip the seat.

'Tell him I forbid it,' he continued.

'You forbid it?' she ground out.

Gabriel nodded, glanced down at her hands, and focused his attention back on the road. If she was not wearing gloves, he was certain her knuckles would be white. 'Why are you so nervous?'

'I find I do not like sitting this far above the ground.'

He took the reins in one hand and pulled her closer to him. 'Do you feel safer away from the edge?'

Olivia nodded a fraction of an inch.

'I will not let any harm come to you.'

Her eyes searched his and everything fell away around them. Then she quickly turned away and watched the people strolling in and out of the shops. 'You should be looking at the road,' she advised him.

'But the view next to me is infinitely more appealing.' How he wished he could see her face past the rim of her bonnet.

'The road please,' she reminded him with a crack in her voice.

It was a good thing they were close to Gunter's. If he continued to be tempted to stare at her, he was sure to crash into something. They turned onto Berkeley Street, and the trees of the square came into view. 'We have not settled our discussion,' he reminded her, searching for a place to park.

'Yes we have. You do not want me to have my portrait done, and I do.'

'Just to clarify, I do not want you to have *that* portrait done for an exhibition.'

'I realise it is rather bold. However, you've seen the preliminary sketch. No one will know it's me.'

'Rather bold? It is much too provocative.' How could she not understand that?

'If I did not know you better, I would think you were jealous.'

He parked the phaeton along the garden across from the confectioner's shop. There was nothing he could say to her comment, so he chose not to acknowledge it. 'What flavour of ice would you care for?' he asked, purposely changing the subject.

She gave a slight shake of her head. 'I have no preference. You choose.'

Gabriel studied her passive features. If he selected a flavour she hated, would she turn that into an argument? He addressed the waiter that approached his side of the phaeton. 'I shall have bergamot ice and Her Grace will have pineapple.'

Olivia's eyes widened momentarily. He was certain he guessed incorrectly, until she granted him a small smile. 'How did you know that is my favourite?'

'You would order it when I would take you here years ago.'

'I'm surprised you remembered.'

So was he. They sat in silence, Gabriel recalling the times they'd sat under this very tree before their marriage fell apart. When the waiter arrived with their order, Gabriel relaxed and began to enjoy his ice.

'I never knew you liked bergamot,' she commented, sliding a delicate spoonful of ice into her mouth.

Gabriel shrugged. 'I have recently become partial to the taste. Have you ever tried it?'

'Yes, I found it rather good.'

'Well, this is mine. Enjoy your pineapple, and next time I will order you bergamot.' The thought of taking her here again made him grin.

Her forehead wrinkled before she turned away. Now what had he done wrong? He was only teasing her.

For the remainder of their time at Gunter's neither spoke. They were almost home when Olivia broke the heavy silence that hung over them. 'Why does it really matter to you if I sit for that portrait? For years you have made it quite clear you have no interest in me. I could have walked through the house in animal skins, and you would not have noticed. Now, you are concerned about a portrait and buying me ice. Why?'

Gabriel turned the phaeton into their drive and with the lift of his hand he dismissed the footman coming down the steps towards them. He faced her, staring into her brown eyes that were flecked with gold. 'You were the one who told me you never wanted me to touch you again. For five years I have had no notion if you still feel that way, or if you spoke those words in haste and have since regretted them. You would not speak to me, so I had no way of finding out. But the other night when you assumed I would take you with no regard to your comfort... I had no idea your opinion of me was that low.'

She looked at him as if he had sprouted a second head. 'The day I suffered through hours of birthing pains to have our son, you were with a harlot in her brothel. They searched for you for hours and could not find you. When you finally arrived home, no one had to tell me you were with a woman. I knew. Her scent was all over you. God, I can still smell that cloying perfume. What kind of man do you think that makes you? I believed you when you told me you cared for me.'

'I did care for you. I still do—'

'Apparently, not enough. I know what kind of man you are. The entire *ton* knows what kind of man you are. The very first ball I attended after giving birth to Nicholas I was plagued with pitying looks and whispers behind fans. I was the woman whose husband was bedding another while she was bearing his heir. And that name swarmed around me for weeks. *Madame LaGrange.* Everyone knew—everyone,' she said vehemently. 'Occasionally her name will still drift into conversations around me. Now you buy me ice and fuss over a portrait?'

Hearing Madame LaGrange's name on her lips made him want to vomit. No one should know of their connection—not even Olivia. And somehow, someone saw him leave her room that day and word spread among the *ton* like fire through a wheat field in autumn. Even the servants knew. He would not allow anyone to find out that Madame LaGrange worked for him. He had made that mistake once before with Matthew, and it had cost the man his life.

For a moment it was years earlier and Gabriel was back in the garden in Richmond, flashes of lightning were slashing the inky blackness around him, rain poured onto Matthew's bloodied body that was seeping his life out in Gabriel's arms, and the last person on earth he thought would betray him was standing over him, pointing a gun at his chest. It had become his reoccurring nightmare ever since.

How could he possibly explain to Olivia that he'd never bedded Madame LaGrange without divulging the woman's secret? A secret he would take to his grave. No one was ever going to die again because he placed his trust in the wrong person.

The pain dulling her eyes sliced through him. 'I never meant to hurt you.'

It was all he could say.

She lowered her head, her face now obscured by her bonnet. Although they were married just a few months before Nicholas was born, in that time he had come to care deeply for her. His lies of omission had cost them both.

When she raised her head, he caught the determination in her eyes. 'If you ever had any kind regard for me at all, you will grant me one thing.'

'What is it that you want, Olivia?'

'I want another child.'

That was not what he expected her to say. His thoughts had been on the portrait. 'Olivia, I've always wanted more children with you.' Now hopefully Nicholas would know what it was like to grow up with a brother or sister.

Chapter Eight

Olivia stared sightlessly at her reflection in the mirror on her dressing table while Colette brushed her hair. Her thoughts kept returning to her conversation with Gabriel earlier in the day. Confessing how she felt about him had been liberating. For years she wanted to tell him what a scoundrel she thought he was. Instead she'd stood silently by pretending she was indifferent to him when deep down she despised him for his betrayal.

She despised him for making her believe he might have had tender feelings for her. She despised him for making her feel as if she were not good enough for him. And she despised him the most for being the man she had fallen in love with.

Now that she'd told him what she truly thought of him, some of her hatred had lifted. She understood what place she had in his life, and now he knew what place he had in hers. She could not allow her feelings for him to return. It would be too painful.

'There's no need to plait it, Colette,' Gabriel's deep voice rumbled from the doorway connecting their rooms.

The hairbrush Colette was using fell to the floor. Perhaps she should have warned her maid that Gabriel would be coming to her room tonight.

'That will be all, Colette,' she said, finding it hard to stop staring at him. He was lounging in the doorway with casual elegance, wearing a navy silk-brocade banyan and holding two glasses in one hand. In the other, he held a bottle. It had been years since she had seen him out of his impeccable attire and it took her a moment to remember to breathe.

'I did not hear you open the door,' she said.

'Perhaps you were too wrapped up in your thoughts,' he replied, pushing off from the doorframe and advancing towards her. He poured out the ruby-red liquid into each glass and handed her one. 'It is the ninety-eight Château Lafite. As I recall, it was your favourite.'

'How is that possible? Bennett has been searching for that vintage for years.'

'That's because Bennett does not know about the bottles I have hidden away.'

'From me?'

'No, I simply have a few bottles left locked in my study.'

'And you have not drunk them?'

'The Lafite was your favourite. I had no desire to indulge until now.'

'I thought that might have been port. I remember thinking I was quite bold when we would drink it together in our rooms,' she replied. The wine tasted just as rich and smooth as she remembered.

'You always enjoyed trying new things.' His eyes dropped to her mouth as she licked the taste of the wine from her lower lip.

'You never made me feel self-conscious.'

'I enjoyed your enthusiasm for things I long took for

granted.' He stepped closer and poured more wine into her glass.

'Are you attempting to get me tipsy?'

'I thought both of us could use something to relax us.' He took a slow drink from his glass, his eyes not leaving hers.

'You expect me to believe you are nervous?'

Gabriel shook his head. 'I did not say I was nervous. Apprehensive might be a better word.'

'Because?' Oh, she really needed this wine. He was much too close and smelled wonderful.

'Because I want to depart from your bedchamber without having a piece of porcelain flung at my head.'

So he wanted to lay the cards on the table. That was fine with her. 'Continue to be your delightful self and we should have no problems. I do have two requests, though.'

'Of course, how may I be of service?'

'Since this is a temporary reconciliation of sorts, there is no need to pretend otherwise to the *ton*.'

'You wish for our accord to remain a secret.'

'I wish to avoid the questions that will arise when our behaviour towards one another returns to its usual state.'

He studied her as if she were a complex puzzle he was attempting to decipher. 'It may not.'

Her heart couldn't bear for it to be otherwise. Getting closer to him would only open the wounds that were just now starting to heal. 'I have no doubt it will.'

'And your other request?'

She swallowed the remainder of her wine to gather the courage. 'While we are here—' she motioned between them '—I would like your word as a gentleman that you will not have any intimate encounters with other women.'

'Here?' he asked, purposely pretending ignorance.

Dealing with him could be so exasperating at times.

'While we are trying to conceive a child, I would like you to refrain from bedding anyone else.'

'I see no problem with your request. Very well.'

She searched his eyes for a clue he was being sincere. 'Consider my request carefully. Make certain you can comply.'

He took a sip and nodded over his glass. 'I have no doubt I can comply.'

Was he telling the truth? He had a strong sexual appetite. Olivia knew this first hand. Did that mean he planned to bed her—a lot? She poured more wine into her glass. 'So then you will be monogamous.'

'I will expect the same from you,' he said, narrowing his gaze.

She had not strayed from their wedding vows—he had. Could she throw her wine in his face and still expect him to bed her? Probably not. 'I assure you I have honoured my marriage vows.'

Gabriel looked as if he were about to say something, but instead downed the rest of his wine. He lifted Olivia's glass out of her hand and placed it on the dressing table beside his. 'We need to get you out of that,' he said, looking down at her dressing gown.

This was it then. Now she would know if she could give him her body without opening up her heart. She turned away from him to avoid his gaze and prayed this would not be a mistake. Slowly she slid off her dressing gown. The warmth from his fingers as they brushed her hair forward over her shoulder made her skin tingle. Her body had changed since she'd had Nicholas. It was softer and rounder. Would he still find it pleasing?

'At least you are not wearing enough fabric to supply all the upstairs maids with aprons.'

'Your seductive skills are as impressive as ever,' she muttered and could not help but grin at his laugh.

'And yet I have only begun exercising them. Take care, you may swoon when you hear what I will say when I finally spring you from that bewitching garment.'

This time she did laugh. Maybe it was the wine. Maybe it was the realisation that they were going to have to do this a number of times before she actually conceived—perhaps for months. The very notion made intimate parts of her flutter.

'I am certain you will have me shaking with need,' she teased. But when she slipped her nightrail over her head and turned around, the smile fell from her lips.

His heated gaze left her practically without breath. He took one finger and trailed a line of warmth from her ear, down her neck, across her collarbone and finally between the curves of her breasts. His eyes traced every movement of his finger. It would be impossible for him not to feel her heartbeat quicken with each area he touched.

'You are even more beautiful than I remembered,' he murmured, cupping a breast.

It was all coming back to her. Every touch. Every kiss. Every time she'd cried out his name. When he lowered his lips to hers and coaxed her with gentle nips to open her mouth, memories of the times they'd spent together flooded her mind. She squeezed her eyes shut, trying to push images from the past out of her head. Part of her wanted to remind herself that he could not be trusted, but another part of her wanted to believe he truly wanted only her as much as she wanted only him. During this time together she would take her pleasure, but she would not allow herself to fall in love with him again.

The kiss deepened and a sense of urgency replaced the initial gentleness.

'We both want this, Olivia.' His words filled her mouth with his breath. 'I do not wish to fight with you any more.'

She tasted his familiar lips, sweetened with the delicious wine. She missed this—missed him. He groaned into her mouth and she could not resist unbuttoning his banyan to feel the heat of his hard smooth skin.

While they were together, she would take as much pleasure as she could stand. Then she would lock these memories away when their time together was over. She could resist the spell of his body.

When she slid her hands up his chest, the banyan fell to the floor. He stepped closer. Their bodies fit together like pieces of a puzzle. It had been so long. She traced the bumps of his ribs. How had a man who sat behind a desk all day remained this muscular?

As he caressed her bottom, he groaned again. Lifting her into his arms, he released her gently on the bed and his body followed hers.

'Are you comfortable?' he asked, trailing hot kisses along her neck.

Trying to breathe somewhat normally, she skimmed her hands along his spine and rested them at the curve of his lower back. 'I am quite well,' she managed to reply.

He bit gently into her neck and slid his thumb around her nipple. It was growing painfully hard and she didn't want him to stop.

'You feel very well,' he rasped.

'So do you,' she said with a moan.

He smiled against her neck and she lowered her hand even more. His weight shifted slightly, pressing her into the mattress. Sliding his tongue along the upper swell of her breast, he groaned loudly as he sucked her nipple into his mouth. She had forgotten how good that felt and gripped his head with both her hands. After giving her right breast exquisite attention, he kissed his way over to the left. She could feel the heat pooling between her legs and ground her pelvis into him. Then he kissed a path down to her stomach…

It was becoming difficult to remember how much she disliked this man.

He nipped at her thigh. 'I want you ready for me.'

'I am ready,' she managed to say through strangled breath.

He shook his head and his soft hair tickled the inside of her thighs. Fluttering her eyes open, she met his gaze.

She struggled for air as their eyes locked and he lowered his mouth between her legs. His eyes closed momentarily, as if he were savouring his favourite dessert. He placed long, slow licks while his gaze bore into her.

The air in the room disappeared as her body responded to the amazing things his mouth was doing to her. She did not want him to stop. He continued to torture her with his mouth until she began to tremble, then she let out a loud cry as she came. His strong arms held her down, as he continued to lick and suck her. She had to push his head away to make him stop.

Her eyes would not open. Struggling to catch her breath, she felt him rise above her.

'I believe you're ready now,' he whispered against her neck.

Before she could think of a response, he was sliding inside her. Her back bowed. How she had loved feeling this filled. Within moments she was meeting him thrust for thrust. He was bringing her to the edge all over again, watching her as sweat formed on his chest.

'You feel even better than I remembered,' he said,

brushing the hair out of her eyes as he continued to thrust inside her.

She did not want to remember, did not want to be reminded of everything that happened between them up to this moment. 'Don't. Stop.'

His movements became more urgent.

She dug her nails into his back.

'Hurry,' he ground out.

He was waiting for her and that lovely gesture set her over the edge again. As he let out a loud groan, he came and soon afterwards collapsed on top of her.

Gabriel's heavy weight was nearly crushing her. As if somehow he knew he rolled, taking her with him so her head rested against his chest. The rapid staccato of his heartbeat matched her own.

She could not move. Moreover, she did not want to.

'Livy, you still turn me inside out.'

Oh, no, not that! Why did he have to ruin it and call her that?

She opened her eyes. He was smiling down at her—smiling that smile that made the corner of his eyes crinkle and lit up her world.

That smile that he had given only to her, all those years ago.

She stumbled out of bed and reached for her nightrail. Throwing it over her head, she caught his bewildered expression. She needed to get him out of this room as fast as possible. If she did not, she did not know if her heart could stand it. She pressed her hand against her lips to prevent herself from saying anything foolish.

'Livy, what is the matter?'

Why did he have to keep calling her that? It was what he had called her when he was being all sweet years ago.

'You need to go.'

He closed his eyes and draped his arm over his face, showing her the curve of his biceps. 'I am tired, Olivia, and it is late. I just want to sleep.'

'Here?' she squeaked.

Picking up his head, he peered at her through one eye. 'Yes, here, I have done it before. Now come back to bed.' He closed his eye and settled into the blankets.

Now what was she to do? He was much too big to drag out of bed. She picked up his banyan and held it out to him. 'We never agreed you would sleep here.'

He lifted his head again and eyed her. His hair was tousled and there was a slight shadow on his face from his evening whiskers, giving him a roguish quality. 'I was not aware everything we do would be up for nego-tiation.' He rolled to his side, propping his head in his hand and exposing his hard muscular chest. 'We just had a brilliant time together, and to be truthful my legs are not quite steady at the moment. Let us not ruin tonight by arguing. Please, come back to bed.'

Olivia felt herself weakening, but if he slept here she feared it would be harder to keep him out of her heart. Especially when he was all sweet and rumpled. He eyed her expectantly.

Pushing back her shoulders, she took a deep breath. She could do this. She could sleep with him without it affecting her in the least. Many women slept with their husbands without even liking them. It was just sex, two bodies responding to one another. That was all it was. It had nothing to do with feelings of any kind.

She folded his banyan carefully and placed it at the foot of her bed. Reluctantly, she slid under the covers. If she laid on her back with distance between them, she would be fine.

Gabriel slid beside her and pulled her close. This

would never work. Squeezing her eyes shut, she turned on her side to get away from him, but his arm tightened as he spooned his body against her.

'Go to sleep, Livy,' he mumbled into her hair.

The ice around her heart melted a little bit more. Oh, good heavens! There had to be a way to resist him.

Chapter Nine

'Mama, Mama, you won't believe—'

There was a little voice in his dream. What was a little voice doing in his dream about Olivia? Gabriel shifted his weight and breathed in her honeysuckle scent.

'Papa, is that you? What are you doing in Mama's bed?'

The warm softness below him began to shift and then poke him. Gabriel tightened his arm around it to get it to stop.

'Wake up,' Olivia whispered sharply.

Why was she telling him to wake up? She should be telling him that she wanted to feel him deep inside her. Gabriel groaned, rubbed his whiskers against the soft linen draped over her enticing breast and cracked one eye open to the faint morning light.

And was met with his son's curious expression an inch from his nose.

Startled, Gabriel jerked away from Olivia.

'Hello, Papa. Good morning, Mama,' said Nicholas from where he was standing beside the bed, playing with Olivia's sleeve.

She turned and kissed their son. In an attempt to wake

up his muddled brain, Gabriel rubbed the back of his head and stretched.

'Your hair looks silly, Papa, and why aren't you wearing a shirt?'

Olivia arched her brow at Gabriel, leaving the explanation to him.

'It was very warm last night,' he replied, rubbing his eyes.

'No, it wasn't. There was a fire in my room all night.' Nicholas crawled up on the bed and sat cross-legged next to Olivia. His doe-like eyes widened with excitement. 'Did you hear the rain? There was a mighty storm. Why are you here? Did the thunder scare you?'

She gave a small snort and glanced at Gabriel. At least she believed he was manly enough to withstand a thunderstorm without retreating to the inside of his wardrobe.

'Your papa came to enquire after me and was too tired to return to his rooms so I let him fall asleep here.'

'That was nice of you, Mama. What's that?' Nicholas asked, poking Gabriel below his ribcage.

With bleary eyes Gabriel looked down to the puckered scar from his old gunshot wound, his constant reminder of his costly mistake. 'It's an old fencing injury.' One more lie in that chain of many he was forced to tell.

'Uncle Andrew says chits like men with scars.'

'You have spent entirely too much time with your Uncle Andrew,' he mumbled.

Olivia traced the outline of his round scar with her delicate finger and caught his eye with a curious expression.

'Do you like Papa's scar, Mama?'

She turned to Nicholas. 'Would you like to see *my* scar?'

'You have a scar?' Nicholas asked with eager anticipation.

'I was thrown from a horse.' She rolled her sleeve up over her elbow.

Gabriel peered over and saw a jagged white line about two inches across. He had never noticed it before. When was she thrown from a horse? James should have informed him of any injury she had sustained.

Nicholas gave a low whistle. 'Did it hurt? Did you cry, Mama?'

She ran her fingers through their son's hair. 'For just a bit, my love. Now up you go so your father and I can begin our day.'

'Will you have breakfast with us too, Papa?' Nicholas asked with a wide smile. 'You never do and I would like that very much. I am rarely with you and Mama together. I rather like this.'

And lying there in bed with his wife and child, Gabriel realised he liked it too. They were shut away from the problems and whispers of the outside world. It felt like they were a true family and it was awfully intimate. Suddenly going back to sleep in his room and having breakfast alone held no appeal.

Olivia shook her head and began to say something when he interrupted her. 'Of course we will take breakfast together,' he replied, noticing his wife's surprised expression. Was she at all happy about his announcement? 'Run off and tell Bennett we will dine together in the breakfast room.'

Nicholas's smile brightened his face. 'That's a capital idea,' he said, before jumping off the bed and running out the door.

'Is this part of your ritual each morning?' He rubbed his eyes and looked at the clock on the mantel. 'My word, it is barely six o'clock!'

She laughed. 'From what I recall you also rose with

the early streaks of dawn. He does not come in every morning, but a fair amount.'

He had forgotten how sinful she looked when she had just woken up. The lids of her eyes were a bit lower and those loose tresses of her dark hair reminded him of how she looked after a rather vigorous bout of lovemaking—like they'd had last night.

'Why are you looking at me like that?' she asked, moving her head away from him.

He climbed on top of her and propped himself up by his elbows. 'Like what?' he countered, rubbing his nose on the side of hers, needing to touch her in even the smallest of ways.

'Please move. We must get dressed.'

'But I like the way you look without your dress.'

'Gabriel.'

He placed coaxing kisses along her mouth. If he could only get her to kiss him back, he was certain he could easily convince her to let him enter her again. When her lips parted to accept his kisses, he hardened in anticipation. She was heaven and sin wrapped all in one. Mornings such as this came flooding back to him. 'I love being inside you when we are both half-asleep.'

The loud crash startled them both and they swung their heads to the doorway in unison.

Colette stood frozen, the remains of Olivia's chocolate and a broken cup at her feet. Gabriel let out a low curse and jerked the sheet up to his waist. This day was not starting out as he planned.

'I…I…knocked but…I saw his lordship leave and thought you'd be needing my assistance getting dressed.'

'I will ring for you shortly, Colette,' Olivia murmured while covering her eyes. 'You may tend to the mess later.'

The maid dashed from the room and thankfully closed the door behind her.

Gabriel sighed and dropped onto his back. Hopefully the remainder of his day would not hold any more unexpected interruptions.

When Gabriel entered his breakfast room at the unusually early hour to the smells of chocolate, coffee, eggs, ham, warm bread and strawberry jam, he found it hard not to smile. Olivia had shooed him from her room without one more taste of her tempting lips. If he was not able to make love to her this morning, at least he would eat well. He went directly to the sideboard, filled his plate with his favourite morning fare, then took his seat at the head of the table between his wife and son.

As Bennett poured him coffee, Gabriel could have sworn he heard the man humming. 'Can I get you anything else, sir?' he asked with an unusually cheerful lilt to his voice.

'No, that will be all, Bennett.' Gabriel scanned the freshly ironed copy of *The Times*. Thankfully there still was no mention of the assassination attempt. The fewer people who know about it, the safer Prinny would be.

'This just came for you, madam,' Bennett said, handing Olivia a missive sealed with red wax.

Who would send his wife a note so early in the day? Was that common as well? How was it that he knew the exact time Prinny rose each morning, but he did not know the most mundane things about his own house? Gabriel surreptitiously looked at the handwriting and tried to identify the imprint on the seal. Without tilting his head to the side, he would not be able to distinguish the mark.

'You do eat a lot of food in the morning, Papa.'

Olivia placed the note down and pursed her lips. His opportunity was lost.

'Nicholas, it is not polite to comment on what other people place on their plates,' she corrected him.

Their son turned to her in amazement. 'But do you see his plate?'

Olivia picked up her cup of chocolate. 'I see it. Grown men have rather large appetites.' Her fine dark eyes met Gabriel's over the gold rim of her blue Sèvres cup and she took a slow sip.

If he didn't know any better, he'd think she was being flirtatious. The very idea of it made him smile.

'Lord Andrew is here to see you, sir,' Bennett announced from the doorway. His previous cheerful demeanour seemed to have got lost on his way to escorting Andrew to the breakfast room. Apparently, this morning, when he wanted his family all to himself the outside world seemed determined to disrupt their private moments.

It was just after seven o'clock. Gabriel hoped the urgent news that brought his brother to his doorstep would be good.

'I realise I am calling early, but—' Andrew froze in the doorway and his wide-eyed gaze travelled from Gabriel to Olivia and finally to Nicholas.

'Uncle Andrew,' Nicholas screamed. Jumping out of his chair, he hurled himself at his uncle. Andrew easily caught him and spun Nicholas around so that the boy rested around his neck like a scarf.

There was no indication from Andrew's demeanour the direction this visit would take. From the playful attention Andrew was paying to Nicholas, it was impossible to tell the urgency of his call.

'Is everything all right, Andrew?' Olivia asked with concern.

He stopped trying to drop Nicholas to the floor. 'Yes. Forgive me for the early hour.' His gaze darted to Gabriel and back to Olivia. 'I found I could not sleep and I know that Gabriel is an early riser. I thought a good ride through the park would clear the cobwebs from my head.'

Patience was a virtue. As much as he wanted to ask the reason for Andrew's visit, Gabriel would bide his time so as not to draw undue attention from Olivia. 'Would you care for breakfast, or have you eaten already?'

'I would never refuse to dine at your table.' Andrew dropped his nephew into the seat Nicholas had vacated and strolled to the sideboard as if the domestic scene was commonplace and he was in no hurry to speak with Gabriel.

While Gabriel watched Andrew sit next to Nicholas with a plate full of food and accept coffee from Bennett, he fought the urge to lean past his son and swat his brother on the head. He had offered food to Andrew to appear polite. The arse wasn't supposed to accept it.

Andrew was halfway through eating an enormous serving of ham and eggs when he finally noticed Nicholas, watching him with an open-mouthed stare. The acknowledgement pulled Nicholas out of his stupor, and he studied his bowl of porridge.

'Mama, may I have eggs and ham instead of porridge?'

Olivia shifted a glance between Andrew and their son. 'If you'd like.' She signalled for a footman to bring another plate to Nicholas and opened the note that had been taunting Gabriel since it arrived. Her brow wrinkled as she scanned the paper.

'Have you received distressing news?' Gabriel asked.

The footman re-entered the room with a plate for Nicholas as she turned to Gabriel. 'It's a note from—'

'Papa never eats breakfast with us, Uncle Andrew, but since he slept in Mama's bed last night we asked him.'

The plate slipped out of the footman's hand, landing on the table with a thud as Gabriel choked on his coffee and Olivia turned crimson.

Andrew leaned closer to Nicholas and arched a brow. 'You don't say,' he said through a devilish grin.

Nicholas opened his mouth to continue when Olivia quickly chimed in.

'Your bruises have not improved. Perhaps now you will agree to take some healing salve home with you.' Bless his wife's polite diversionary tactics.

Andrew shot Gabriel a meaningful look and removed his hand from her inspection. 'It is nothing.'

'Papa has a scar. Mama and I saw it this morning since he wasn't wearing a nightshirt.'

Andrew was quite familiar with that scar. It was thanks to his brother's quick actions that Gabriel's body hadn't received another wound—a fatal one. Still, he needed to speak with his son about the importance of keeping certain aspects of their family life a secret. The sooner he learned that lesson, the better.

Meanwhile Andrew seemed to be thoroughly enjoying Nicholas's loquaciousness and propped his head in his hand. 'It seemed rather cool last night to be sleeping without a nightshirt.'

'I said the same thing,' Nicholas said in astonishment as his stomach rumbled loudly. Excusing himself, he hopped off his chair to fill his plate at the sideboard. It seemed discussing his parents' private activities was not as interesting as selecting the perfect slice of ham. Thank heavens for small miracles.

Andrew went back to eating his breakfast and Olivia returned to that mysterious note.

'I hope the news you've received is not too distressing,' Gabriel said. 'I gather from your expression that you have not received happy tidings.'

She eyed him intently. 'I suppose it depends on who you ask. Mr West is not well and has asked me to go to the Royal Academy this morning to settle the arrangement of the paintings for the upcoming exhibition in his place. I will have to cancel my sitting for today.'

'That is unfortunate. Did he say what is troubling him?' He took a sip of his coffee to hide the smile that was about to spread across his face at the very notion his wife would not be continuing that bloody portrait session.

Shaking her head, Olivia leaned close enough that he could smell her honeysuckle perfume. 'I am certain this pleases you immensely,' she said for only his ears.

'I would not wish ill on Mr West. You should know that.'

Olivia leaned back in her chair and rolled her eyes. She took a sip of her chocolate and her soft pink tongue slipped out to lick her lip. It was almost impossible for Gabriel to hold back a sigh of yearning.

Andrew shifted in his seat, taking Gabriel's attention away from Olivia's lips. Prinny's safety was his priority. Why was he having difficulty remembering that? 'I have appointments today, Andrew. What say you we go for that ride now?'

Andrew gulped down the remainder of his coffee before he tossed his napkin on the table. 'Excellent. Thank you for breakfast, Olivia.'

Nicholas stuck out his lower lip. 'You're leaving already, Uncle Andrew?'

'I'm afraid so. However, I'd venture to say you will

see me again.' He ruffled Nicholas's hair as he walked past him.

Gabriel crouched next to his son and Nicholas gave him a tight hug. 'I rather like having breakfast with you, Papa,' he said, releasing his hold.

And Gabriel realised how much he rather liked having breakfast with his wife and son. It was an improvement from eating alone, reviewing paperwork. Without thinking, he kissed Olivia on the forehead on his way to the door.

Chapter Ten

Why was everyone riding so slowly down Piccadilly at this hour? Even Gabriel's horse was pitching forward, trying to poke his nose past all the slow goers. If they did not arrive at the park soon Gabriel feared he would no longer possess any patience at all. In the meantime he continued to scowl at every driver, rider, merchant and pedestrian he saw.

When they finally turned into the park, they steered their horses sedately onto Rotten Row. At this hour, the only people on the bridle path were a few servants exercising horses some distance ahead. Finally, he would get some answers.

'Tell me what brought you to my door.'

Andrew guided his horse closer to Gabriel's. 'You will not be pleased.'

'Is that meant to soften the blow?'

'Mr Clarke is dead.'

Gabriel's blood ran cold as he jerked the reins to hold his ground. 'Care to explain?'

'Dead. I think that just about explains it.'

'I beg to differ. How in the bloody hell is the man dead when he is being hidden away in the Tower under lock and key? No one was to be informed he was there.'

Andrew rubbed his lips together. 'We were all shocked by the news. He was alive last night when they brought him his food. Hours later they found him dead on the floor.'

'Poison?'

'It appears so. We have questioned everyone involved and have no leads. It's as if some spectre appeared and disappeared just as mysteriously.'

'Then no one involved in holding him and the interrogations can be trusted. Perhaps this is why they have been unable to uncover any tangible leads. Say nothing of what we suspect and keep me apprised of anything suspicious.'

'Of course.'

'From this moment forward, finding out who wants Prinny dead falls solely on our shoulders. We must make certain he is not harmed. I do not know how much longer I can keep him safe inside Carlton House. Each day he becomes more and more restless. He is like a child and I cannot force him to follow my directions. I only wish he were not so trusting.'

Gabriel went to turn Homer around when his brother stopped him.

'We are not finished,' Andrew said. 'I believe there is one more thing that requires discussion.'

What more could they have to discuss?

'You are honestly not about to acknowledge that ideal family portrait I just witnessed? I believe an explanation is in order.'

Gabriel did not agree. Pulling the brim of his beaver hat low over his forehead, he shaded his eyes from the sunlight filtering through the branches above them. 'Olivia and I are attempting a reconciliation of sorts.'

'Of sorts?'

'Yes.'

When Andrew raised an expectant brow, Gabriel let out a sigh.

'You did not arrive at my doorstep so early to discuss the state of my marriage.'

'No, I did not, but after that unusual display, I find myself too intrigued not to. Now why is it normally you barely speak to her, the other night at dinner she was throwing daggers at you with her eyes and today you are kissing her goodbye? And please note, I am not even mentioning the entertaining information which Nicholas kindly provided.'

'It's complicated.'

'Women always are.'

Andrew had no idea. 'Olivia and I would like to have another child.'

'Well, it's about time.'

'Pardon me?'

'You know it is best for you to have more boys for the ducal line. Don't count on any of us to help you fulfil your obligation. Michael broods too much. No woman would ever want to marry him. And by the time Monty is old enough and finds a woman who can ignore his exasperating nature, you will be long dead.'

Gabriel narrowed his eyes at Andrew. 'Skeffington is in his dotage. When he gives up the ghost, I am certain his Duchess would be more than happy to lower herself to marry you. In fact, it would not surprise me if she attempted to pull you behind a tree while he was being lowered into his grave.'

Andrew visibly shuddered. 'Do not even jest. That woman is becoming more and more difficult to avoid. But we are getting away from our discussion of you and Olivia.'

'No, that discussion is over. I told you why this morning's events were a bit unusual.'

'A bit? I would say the events I witnessed were monumentally unusual.'

Gabriel could feel Andrew studying him and he kept his gaze fixed firmly ahead of them. He'd had a remarkable night with his wife. He did not need Andrew poking him with a stick to make him analyse what it meant.

'Have you told her that you have always been faithful?'

He knew this would happen. 'Of course I have not told her.'

'She is your Duchess.'

'It is not that simple. I would need to reveal everything to her. Our father never disclosed anything to Mother. To this day she does not know what we do and what responsibility he had. I put my trust in the wrong person once. I will not let it happen again.'

'Olivia is not Uncle Peter and the situation is vastly different.'

'Is it? Is it truly different? Tell me how?'

'She is your wife.'

'And he was our beloved uncle. A man I looked up to all my life, much as my son does you. *I* went to him for advice after Father died. *I* told him what we do, foolishly believing he already knew. When Father said to suspect everyone and trust no one, he was right. My mistake cost Matthew his life. I was the one who felt his life slip away in my arms that night. No amount of rain could have washed his blood from my hands. Every day it eats away at me that I continue to allow his family to believe he was the victim of a robbery that night. Lord Scarbury should have known his youngest was a man of heroic actions who gave his life protecting the Crown. Matthew deserved at least that.'

'You had me give his widow a substantial amount of your money and say I was settling a gambling debt to help support her and their son. You did all you could do considering the circumstances.'

'I couldn't bring him back!' It was the first time he allowed Andrew to see how deeply he had been affected by the events of that night. If he could help it, it would be the last.

'You are not the only one to feel the sting of one's actions where that night is concerned.'

And now he felt even worse. 'Forgive me. I didn't mean to imply it had been easy on you.'

The muscle in Andrew's jaw twitched. 'I'm glad you realise that.'

They rode in silence towards the path out of the park. Eventually, Andrew cleared his throat. 'If you explained you never tupped that woman, she would not think you're a bounder.'

'And tell her what exactly? She knows I was with Madame LaGrange. Shall I tell her that I was, in fact, with the woman in her brothel while Olivia's life was in danger bearing our child, but I did not bed her? Then the question becomes what was I doing there? Olivia is an intelligent woman. You cannot give her half-truths. I will not reveal Madame's secrets. Not now. Not ever.'

All this talk of Olivia had distracted him. He needed to readjust his priorities—quickly. Prinny was in danger and he had no idea from whom.

Olivia dangled a small basket from her hand as she stood in the Blue Drawing Room of Carlton House and smiled at the man seated before her.

'You are truly an angel, my dear. Have I mentioned

that to you?' the Prince Regent said, his eyes fixed on her basket.

At times he could be so easy to please. 'You are only saying that because I brought you marzipan.'

'That is simply not true. I would have said it if you brought me macarons instead.' He motioned for her to sit near him as he took the basket she held out and began to sample the sweet confections.

'I called on you to enquire about your health—however, you appear quite well. Much better than the last time the gout struck,' she remarked, noticing neither of his feet was bandaged. 'I am surprised you are not in bed.'

Prinny's mouth was full and he mumbled something, but it was impossible to distinguish what it was. He shifted on the sofa and studied his next morsel. 'My physician says I am to stay off my feet. He didn't say where.' He gestured with his head towards the tea tray on the table next to them. 'Why don't you pour yourself some tea and we can have a nice chat.'

The deep red liquid in the glass that rested on the table caught her attention. Certainly he wouldn't be drinking port. Not if he had the gout.

She gripped the ebonised wooden handle of the silver teapot and poured the aromatic liquid into a Sèvres cup. She had seen the white Sèvres tea set before with its gilding and its bucolic scene of a young man gazing adoringly at his lover. What she hadn't seen before was the oval straight-sided silver teapot with the swan-head spout that was engraved with Napoleon's imperial coat of arms.

'This is a new acquisition. I've lost count of how many items of his you own. Are you determined to collect all of his possessions?' she asked, placing the teapot back on the tray.

'That little man thought he could conquer the world—that he could best me. Well, I showed him. I defeated him and now I get to enjoy the things he held dear.' He popped a piece of marzipan into his mouth.

She narrowed her eyes. 'You never sent word about the painting. Did you go to purchase it? I hope you did not encounter any trouble.'

There was a hesitation to his movements. 'It went well. I am deciding where to hang it. I still do not understand why he would not loan it to you so you could show it to me while I decided if I wanted to purchase it.'

'I imagine he was concerned he would not receive payment and the artwork would remain here.'

He gave a careless snort. 'Why don't you tell me what I have been missing?'

'There is not much to tell. I've come from the Royal Academy where Mr West has asked me to assist him in determining the placement of works for the latest exhibition. I hope you will be feeling better by the time it opens. The works are quite moving. And, if you were planning on attending the Nettlefords' ball, I understand they will be serving lobster cakes. That alone should tempt you enough to leave this house.'

Prinny's hand stilled over the treats, and he cleared his throat. 'I hope to be…feeling right as rain by then,' he mumbled.

Evidently the prince was feeling better, since he was eating the marzipan as if it were his last meal. Perhaps she should have brought him a smaller selection. Eating that many pieces in rapid succession could not be good for one's digestion.

'I'm glad you're enjoying the marzipan.'

Prinny looked down as if he hadn't realised he had

eaten nearly the entire basket and held it out to her. 'Would you care for one?'

She selected the smallest piece. 'I assume you will be well enough to attend the opening of *Douglas* at Drury Lane. They say Mrs Siddons will be returning to the stage.'

Prinny's smile dropped. 'I hope so.'

'Then I look forward to seeing you there. I assume you will not bar me from your box,' she teased.

He smiled affectionately at her. 'I would never do such a thing to you.'

'I have the notion that a small stroll would serve you well, since you did finish that entire basket of marzipan. What say you we take some air in your gardens?'

Prinny's eyes darted from Olivia, to the guard by the door, and back to Olivia again. 'I suppose one short stroll outside could do no harm.'

Chapter Eleven

Gabriel had arrived home from Parliament and been sitting at his desk, staring at his only clue for what felt like hours. Something about the handwriting on the note found on the gunman tickled his brain, but he could not for the life of him determine what it was. Hopefully a quiet evening at home would lift his spirits.

By the time he emerged from his rooms dressed for dinner, he was looking forward to a pleasant meal and another night in his wife's bed. From the staircase landing, his gaze travelled down and settled on Olivia, who was speaking with Bennett in the entrance hall.

Her shiny dark hair was swept up, exposing the creamy skin of her neck and graceful shoulders. Her gown was the colour of irises and her arms were visible through the long semi-opaque sleeves. As she turned towards the staircase, the diamonds around her neck sparkled in the candlelight and Gabriel was blessed with a delicious view of the upper curves of her breasts. His lips rose, knowing he would have her all to himself for the entire evening.

Then he spied the wrap Bennett was holding out for her. As he dashed down the stairs, she spotted him.

'Where are you off to?' he asked without even offering her a greeting.

She dismissed Bennett with a slight nod and their butler disappeared down the hall. 'I am going to Vauxhall to meet friends for dinner and to see a performance of Madame Saqui.'

Was he acquainted with these friends? Deciding she looked much too enticing to be strolling about Vauxhall without him, he pulled the sides of her wrap together over her breasts. The fabric was warm and soft, and reminded him of her skin. To stop himself from touching her, he held onto the edges of her wrap.

'What are you doing?' she asked, looking down at his hands.

'Making certain you do not catch a chill.'

She narrowed her eyes, but did not push his hands away. 'That is very considerate of you. I suppose this concern has nothing to do with any late-night activities you are anticipating.'

'I have no notion of which activities you are speaking of,' he replied with what he hoped was an innocent expression. 'You look quite beautiful this evening.'

Her body stiffened. 'Thank you,' she replied, backing away from him so he was forced to release her wrap.

Had he offended her? He had not intended to. 'It is a cool evening. I shall inform your coachman to place a warm brick in your carriage.'

'Comte Janvier has kindly offer to take me in his carriage, so there is no need to concern yourself.'

Every nerve in Gabriel's body snapped to attention. Her phrasing could not have been worse. 'He is to be your escort for the evening?' he asked, raising his chin.

'Yes, he was invited as well and offered to accompany me weeks ago.'

'Well, I believe I shall wait with you and greet the Comte when he arrives.'

'There is no need. You should go about your affairs.' She walked away from him to the gilded mirror next to the door and adjusted her hair.

'Dinner and a good book await me this evening. I am in no hurry.' Not wanting her to witness his jealousy, he turned away and met the condescending gaze of his great-grandfather, staring down at him from a life-sized portrait of the man on horseback. Gabriel wanted to tell him to mind his own business. It was quite evident he was behaving like an overly protective bore, but she was his wife. His. He simply needed to be certain that Comte Janvier understood that.

A knock echoed through the marble hall and drew Gabriel's attention to the front door. As he adjusted his cuffs, soft footsteps filled the hall, announcing Bennett's arrival before he appeared.

'You can leave now, Gabriel. I am certain that is Janvier and Bennett can manage the door.' She addressed his reflection in the mirror and raised her brows expectantly.

'I believe I will remain right where I am.'

She looked as if she was about to speak, but there was no time since Bennett had opened the door. Gabriel was standing out of Janvier's line of vision when the man walked inside. Not that it would have mattered anyway since the Frenchman's eyes were firmly fixed on Olivia. He couldn't blame him. She was stunning. It was apparent to Gabriel that Janvier was considering the different ways he would like to take her. The man was perilously close to losing consciousness.

Gabriel cleared his throat. Janvier turned and his head snapped back as he realised Olivia's husband was standing a few feet away.

'Ah, Your Grace, what an unexpected surprise.' He held out his hand.

Gabriel took his gloved hand and squeezed the man's long, slender fingers tightly, wishing he could break a bone or two. When he released his grip, he was pleased to see Janvier wiggle his fingers around before placing them at his side.

'It's kind of you to accompany my wife this evening, since I will not be available to attend to her until she arrives home.'

He was staking his claim and Gabriel was satisfied to catch the understanding that crossed Janvier's face.

'I shall make every effort to ensure Her Grace's every need is met.'

French bastard. 'I shall have to recommend my tailor to you. Mr Weston cuts a very fine coat.'

A forced smile rose on Janvier's lips. 'That is very kind of you. However, I believe my tailor does an exceptional job.'

From the corner of his eye, Gabriel could see Olivia cross her arms. So they weren't exactly being subtle. They were men. He turned to her and held out his hand. 'I will see you into the carriage.'

He knew she was fighting a desire to turn around from both of them and stomp back up to her rooms. She placed her white-gloved hand onto his arm and, for the briefest instant, the pressure of her fingers dug through the sleeve of his tailcoat. He bit back a smile at her subtle silent statement.

They stopped a few feet from the carriage and waited for the footman to open the door. Gabriel leaned down and let a small puff of breath float over his wife's ear and neck. 'Hold on to some of that fire till you return, Livy. It will make for a most enjoyable night in bed.'

She glanced at her friend, but he was busy speaking with his coachman.

'You are presuming I will allow you in my bed after that display,' she scolded him in a low voice.

'In order to have another child, I believe I need to be in your bed—frequently—if we are truly intent about this. One time probably was not sufficient.'

'Perhaps it was sufficient. Perhaps I am already carrying a child.'

Our child. The child would be ours. Gabriel looked over at Janvier and wanted to plant a facer for all new reasons. 'I believe it is best to keep trying until we are certain,' he whispered back, taking her gloved hand to his lips, searching her eyes for even the slightest reaction.

Immediately, she pulled her hand away and readjusted her wrap. 'You believe I can be so easily charmed after that display of male dominance? I am not a bone to be fought over by two dogs.'

'No, you are not a possession. You are the woman I chose above all others to marry and would do so again without hesitation. I was simply reminding him that you are my Duchess and should he offend your honour in any way, he will answer to me.'

Janvier approached Olivia's side and she shifted her attention to adjusting her gloves.

'Shall we?' Janvier asked, moving his gaze between Olivia and Gabriel.

'Yes, let's not keep our friends waiting.'

She allowed Gabriel to help her into the carriage. His eyes were still on her when Janvier edged past him.

'I shall have her home before sun up,' the Frenchman said as he entered the carriage and took his seat across from Olivia.

Gabriel gave a curt nod before he stepped back, allowing the footman to raise the step and close the door with a click. Within minutes, Comte Janvier's carriage pulled away with his wife inside.

Striding into their house, Gabriel went directly to the dining room, needing to focus on the food and drink set before him and not on the fact that his wife, who might already be carrying his child, was out with another man. As Gabriel settled into his chair, Bennett nodded to one of the footmen to begin serving the first course.

'Bennett, has Comte Janvier been a frequent guest of the Duchess?'

'He has attended a few of her dinner parties.'

'And has he escorted her anywhere else in his carriage.'

'No, sir. This is the first time.'

Gabriel sat back on the red-velvet cushion of his chair and watched one of his footmen ladle turtle soup into his bowl. He knew that he and Olivia had lived separate lives under the same roof. In regards to his responsibility to the Crown that situation had made things infinitely easy for him. Yet seeing a man drive off in his carriage with Olivia had set the pulse in his temples pounding.

He knew they'd agreed to be monogamous with each other while they were trying to conceive another child. He trusted Olivia to hold to their agreement. What he did not trust was that slippery Frenchman.

Gabriel scraped his chair back suddenly, startling the footmen and Bennett. He walked to the window and looked out at the cobblestone street below. The sound of carriage wheels and men on horseback going to and fro could be heard through the glass. He had not lied to her. He would marry her all over again, even knowing it would lead to their estrangement. The time they had spent together during their courtship and before Nicholas was born was some of his happiest, before things went horribly wrong. Would it be possible to have that again?

He should have insisted on going with her. He should not have handed her into the care of that wolf. It was too late now.

Drawing in a deep breath, Gabriel turned and slowly walked to the table. Sitting back in his chair, he reminded himself that Olivia was very capable of handling men.

By the time Olivia and Janvier left Vauxhall a soft rain had begun to fall. In the dim light and the gentle sway of the comfortable carriage Olivia should have felt completely relaxed. She'd had a pleasant dinner with friends and enjoyed an entertaining performance. Unfortunately the spectre of her husband had hovered over her all evening.

When Gabriel had asked her about her plans, good breeding had almost prompted her to suggest he join their little party. She'd had to bite her lip to prevent the words from escaping. There was no reason to foster a friendship with him when their reconciliation was only temporary.

Then she heard his voice rattling around in her brain once more. *You are the woman I chose above all others to marry and would do so again without hesitation.*

She rubbed her brow and mentally berated herself. Giving in to thoughts of Gabriel could only lead to confusion and heartache. She couldn't trust him. Those were simply pretty words that fell from his lips to charm her. He was not sincere.

If only being around him hadn't felt so wonderful.

Her thoughts drifted to the kiss he'd placed on her hand. She could not deny that simple kiss on her gloved hand had left her body anticipating more of his touch. What was wrong with her? She hadn't even felt the warmth of his lips through the kidskin, just the pressure, and suddenly she felt eager to be home. She rubbed her knuckles, trying to erase the sensation.

'I shall venture to blame the hour on your silence and not my company,' Janvier said with a smile as he watched her from across the carriage.

Pulling her thoughts from Gabriel's lips, Olivia gazed at her friend. 'Forgive me, your carriage is quite comfortable and the hour is late. I fear the combination of the two has made me rather sleepy.'

'It pleases me that you are so relaxed in my presence. I could sit beside you and you could rest your head on my shoulder. I would gladly be your cushion.'

'That would not be proper though, would it?'

'No one will see. We are alone. My staff is trained to knock before they open the door. Do not concern yourself with what they would think if we are discovered together.'

Before she could object, Janvier moved across the carriage and settled himself next to her, pressing his thigh against hers. The scent of bay rum followed his movement. There was no denying he was an attractive and charming man who probably would make an ideal lover if she were so inclined. Wondering about how his kisses would compare to Gabriel's, Olivia let her gaze drop to his smooth, full lips.

A small devilish grin creased the corners of his mouth. 'My shoulder is at the ready.'

'I do not believe I am that tired.'

'Shall I return to my side of the carriage?'

She shook her head. 'I am no longer the young ingénue.'

'Were you ever naïve? Somehow I think you were born with an air of sophistication.'

'That is because we met when I am already at such an advanced age.'

Janvier's laughter improved her mood. Friends could do that. 'You are far from your dotage.'

'That is reassuring to hear. I simply meant you did not know me when I was a young girl. I suppose, like most, I harboured romantic fantasies.'

'And now?'

'And now I understand the realities of life.'

He shook his head. 'In life there is always room for romance.'

'Is there? I do believe I have long disregarded that notion.'

'Perhaps you need to be reminded.'

His lips were touching hers before she even realised he'd moved. The only sound was the raindrops pinging off the carriage roof and the turning of the carriage wheels over the cobblestones.

She was so stunned by the soft, coaxing seduction that it took her a few moments to react. Realising he was actually kissing her, Olivia pushed against his chest and pulled her head back.

Before she could issue him a set down, Janvier spoke. 'Forgive me. I misunderstood the direction of our conversation. I assure you, I meant no disrespect.'

The sly man had already stopped her from accusing him of being insolent and issuing a slap across his face. Years of wearing a polite mask made it easy for her to appear completely composed. 'Let us be clear, I have no intention of beginning a liaison with you. I enjoy your company, but if you are seeking something more we should part ways.'

Janvier slid across the carriage and resumed his seat.

'I understand. I hope you will continue to allow us to be friends.'

'As long as we understand one another.'

'We do. It will not happen again.'

The carriage came to an abrupt halt and as predicted there was a knock on the door. Once Janvier uttered his consent, the door to the carriage opened and the steps were lowered. 'Until I see you again,' he said, tipping his head respectfully.

Olivia nodded and allowed the footman to assist her onto the wet pavement as he held a large umbrella over her. Placing a hand on her stomach, she took a deep breath of the damp air and looked up at the vast expanse of her house. There were times when thoughts of retreating to the country with no men for miles appeared to be an excellent notion.

By this time of night, the fire in Gabriel's study had died to a low flame. Hours before, he'd discarded his coat and reclined in his most comfortable chair in casual elegance, resting his feet on an embroidered footstool. Tonight he had chosen to reread the *Iliad* while he sipped his favourite port. He should have been completely relaxed. Except every so often, his attention was drawn to the bracket clock on the mantel.

Eventually Bennett informed him that Comte Janvier's carriage had pulled up to the house. Glancing at the clock, Gabriel snapped his book shut and took note of the late hour. He walked into the entrance hall just as Olivia began to climb the stairs. She appeared lost in thought. He called her name softly, but she continued her ascent. He called to her again, this time a bit louder.

She jumped and turned towards him. This was not the way he would have preferred to begin seducing her.

She approached him slowly, her concentration fixed on unbuttoning her gloves.

He searched for something to ask instead of questioning why she had remained out till such a late hour, making him worry for her safety. 'Did you enjoy Madame Saqui?'

'She was exceptional as always.' The buttons on her right glove seemed to hold great interest and he realised she had yet to look him in the eye.

'Would you care for my assistance with those?'

Her eyes finally met his and she smiled politely. 'No, thank you. Were you on your way upstairs, or did my arrival disturb your work?'

He wondered if he was persistent in questioning her, if she would tell him what was occupying her thoughts. It was obvious something was troubling her.

'I was just reading and heard you come in. Would you care to join me?'

She hesitated before she nodded and walked past him towards his study. Once inside she dropped those troublesome gloves on the table beside the chair he had vacated and walked towards the fire to warm her hands. Her delicate profile was illuminated in the soft glow and Gabriel took advantage of the opportunity to study the slope of her nose and her enticing bow of her lips.

Realising Janvier must have done nothing to warm her during their ride home, Gabriel went to the table near his desk and removed the stopper from the crystal decanter housing his favourite port. His gaze continued to shift to her as he poured the wine into a glass. By the time he reached her side it appeared her attention was back to her surroundings.

He held the glass out to her. 'This should warm you.'

'Thank you, although I truly am not that cold.'

Could her quiet demeanour be a result of his actions with Janvier? If he wanted to regain her favour, he needed to extend an olive branch of sorts. He was not accustomed to apologising, but there were times it was necessary.

'Please forgive my behaviour with the Comte earlier this evening. I only wished to ensure that he would treat you with the utmost respect.'

She looked up from her glass. 'You had said as much before I left. I accept your apology.' Their eyes held as she slowly took a sip. Her small smile peeked out from the rim. 'Giving a woman port while entertaining her in your study, what would people say?'

'Some might say I am a man bent on seduction,' he said with a quirk of his lips.

'Only some?'

'The others would just be shocked.'

'For inviting a lady into your sacred domain or for plying her with port?'

'Could I ply you with port to seduce you?'

Olivia slowly shook her head, her eyes never leaving his. 'You forget that I am quite familiar with your methods.'

Their verbal sparring matches always made him smile. She looked away suddenly. He placed a finger on the side of her jaw and directed her gaze back to him.

'And what are my methods?'

'You will see that I drink just enough wine to lower my inhibitions sufficiently so that I agree to do things that, in the light of day, I would never consider.'

The air left Gabriel's lungs and he laughed. 'Well, Duchess, I am *very* familiar with you and know even without the assistance of drink you have done things no proper Duchess would ever consider doing in the light of day. You cannot blame wine for your actions.'

'I have no idea what you are referring to,' she said, raising her brows innocently. 'I believe you have reached an age that causes one's memory to falter.'

'Is that so? So you never swam naked with me in a pond in Kent and then ravaged me on the shoreline?'

'Ravaged is such a strong word.'

'And you never tied me to your bed with your stockings while I slept, so I would be late for my morning appointments?'

'As I recall you were late for all your appointments that day.'

'Because we never left your bed.'

'That was not entirely my fault.'

'And then there was the time you dismissed the staff from serving dinner in the dining room.'

'I simply wanted to converse with you without being overheard.'

'Because you wanted to discuss which dessert tasted better on your skin.'

'A discussion that should not be had in the presence of servants. Every Duchess is aware of that rule.'

'What about the time you crawled onto my lap in a moving carriage of your own volition and whispered sweet suggestions in my ear, leaving me no choice but to take you then and there?'

She stilled, then sauntered to the chair he had recently vacated. His gaze was drawn to her shapely bottom, the curve of which would appear as she moved.

'You appear to remember quite a bit of what I did years ago,' she said.

'You did some very memorable things. In fact, if memory serves, during one visit to see my parents did you not—'

'Yes. Yes. You made your point. You had your moments as well.'

The annoyance in her tone made Gabriel laugh. He stepped closer, and she pick up his leather-bound book and cocked her head to read the spine.

'How many times have you read this?'

'I have lost count. In any event, that is Cowper's version. It's closest to the original text,' he replied defensively.

She tossed the book on the table and reclined back in his chair. 'I had forgotten how comfortable this chair was. It almost begs one to curl up with a book and not be proper.' There was sadness in her eyes, as if she too had missed the happy times they had spent together.

'And how improper did you want to be?' he asked as his body was pulled by an invisible force to stand in front of her.

She rolled her eyes and shook her head. 'I was referring to my posture.'

'So was I,' he replied, flashing her a devilish grin.

She shifted her gaze back to the fireplace. If only he knew what was whirling through that mind of hers. Perhaps he could distract her enough to erase the sadness in her eyes.

Slowly he removed the glass from her hand and placed it on the table. This didn't seem to improve her mood, but he wasn't finished. Lifting her effortlessly into his arms, he resumed his seat and settled her on his lap with her legs draped over the armrest. Then he handed her back her glass.

'You were in my chair.' It was as much an explanation of his action as he was willing to admit to her. He guided her hand with the glass to his mouth and took a sip of port.

'I did not agree to share that with you,' she said with a furrowed brow.

'Would you care to have the wine back? I believe if you slip your tongue into my mouth you may taste some of the remnants.'

A smile tugged on the corner of her lips. 'I am in a generous mood. You may keep the wine you have stolen.'

'Unlike you, *I* do not mind sharing.'

She hid her smile with the rim of the glass and was forward enough to lick her lips slowly after taking a sip. It would be miraculous if she didn't feel his arousal underneath that beautiful bottom of hers.

He wanted her. He wanted to taste those lips. He wanted to feel the softness of her skin. He wanted to bury himself deep inside her and not pull out until they both were completely spent.

Taking his finger, he angled her face towards him and lowered his lips to hers. At first he had to coax her to open up to him, but it didn't take long before she was participating fully in the kiss—tasting like hot cherries from the port. Could he ever be this close to her without wanting to lose himself in her?

She pushed against his chest and he reluctantly pulled back.

'I have no desire to ruin my gown with wine.' She sat up and placed her glass on the table next to them. But instead of resuming their kiss she rested her head on his chest.

Did that kiss have no effect on her at all? Gabriel stared up at the ceiling debating if he should kiss her again. Then he felt Olivia's fingers work on the knot at his throat.

'Do not assume I am doing anything more than ensuring that I am not the only one who is slightly dishevelled,' she said.

'I would not dream of it.'

She wasn't dishevelled in the least, but he wasn't about to point that out.

As she sat up, she unwound the linen from his neck and carelessly dropped it over the side of his chair. 'You looked a bit uncomfortable,' she explained, placing her head back on his shoulder, her soft hair tickling his neck. 'You are not considering picking that up and folding it neatly, are you?'

Surprisingly he hadn't been, until she mentioned it, and then he sneaked a glance towards the rumpled linen on the floor and resisted the urge to pick it up. The graceful fingers of her left hand parted the opening of his shirt and she softly combed her nails around his neck.

He should not be the only one missing some attire. That hardly seemed fair. Knowing where he would begin, he trailed his hand over the curve of her hip, down her lovely leg to her dainty feet, where he removed one and then the other shoe.

'What are you doing?'

'I am simply returning the favour.'

'Your heart is beating rather quickly. Are you well?' she asked in an amused voice.

He skimmed his fingers up her leg to the back of her knee and was rewarded when she shivered. 'I am well. Although I could be very well.'

'Is there such a thing as being very well?' Her warm fingers slid along his collarbone and traced the veins of his neck.

Closing his eyes at the sensation, he knew for certain there was such a thing as being very well. She enjoyed playing the unaffected minx, but when his fingers slid between her thighs he was pleased to discover she was slick.

Her body stilled and she parted her legs further for him. As he slid one and then a second finger inside her she clenched his collar. He slowly pumped his fingers in and out, spreading her wetness.

'I believe this might constitute being very well,' he commented with a satisfied grin.

'It might,' she moaned, moving her hips to his rhythm.

'Now that hardly sounds promising. I think I need to try harder.'

'Harder, yes.'

He pumped his fingers more forcefully. Her legs began to tremble. She was rubbing her face on his shoulder like a kitten and he was uncertain who wanted her to come more. He loved knowing he could make her feel this way.

'Come for me, Livy.'

She crushed her lips to his. The kiss was urgent and demanding, and within seconds he swallowed her cry.

Gabriel kissed her softly. The small kisses she gave in return gave him hope that she still felt this burning attraction whenever they were together.

He cradled her in his arms. There were nights early in their marriage when he had held her in unguarded moments just like this. 'I want you, Livy. I want you now.'

Her eyes met his. 'Then let us go to bed.'

'I cannot wait.'

'Where would you like me?'

'Here, in this chair.'

She appeared amused by his statement—amused and intrigued. 'In this chair?'

'You did say it was comfortable. I believe you remember how it is done.'

She glared at him until the corner of her lips twitched. 'I do believe that would be highly improper for people of our station.'

Gabriel lowered his mouth so his lips were less than an inch from hers. 'Blame it on the wine.'

He kissed her again, savouring her sweet taste. As she shifted on his lap, the friction did wonders for what was inside his breeches. Her hands were in his hair and his hands held the sides of her face, not wanting her to pull away.

She shifted again. Now she was straddling him, with her gown tangled up between them. He always loved this position and slid his hands around her to cup her bottom. She undid the buttons of his waistcoat as he trailed slow kisses along her jaw on the way to her neck. His tongue licked her skin. Every inch of her tasted like heaven.

Olivia worked frantically on the last few buttons of his waistcoat before she cried out in frustration. A gentleman's duty was always to assist a lady in need. Pushing her hands aside, he pulled hard at the opening of his waistcoat. Buttons popped and flew to the floor.

Before long his waistcoat was off and all he could think about was losing himself inside her. She pulled his shirt over his head and it went sailing somewhere to his left.

They were kissing again and her warm hands slid over his chest. She had too many layers of clothing on. He reached for her breasts. Her stays had pushed them up so a good amount of them were already exposed. His hands were trying to lift them from their confines, but Olivia's bloody dressmaker had her body secured tightly in her gown.

Gabriel moved his hands and tried to unfasten all the tiny corded loops on her back. It felt like hours before he was able to slide the sleeves of her gown down her shoulders. She pushed against his chest, stood and shimmied out of her gown till it pooled at her feet.

If their heated kisses hadn't made his body burn, the outline of Olivia's curvaceous form through her chemise with the light from the fireplace behind her was incinerating him.

Jumping to his feet, he kissed her hard, trying to give his body time to calm down enough so he wasn't throwing her over the chair and pounding into her.

She moaned and it almost did him in.

He tugged on the silk ribbon of her stays and she broke the kiss to remove it. Their eyes locked. He took hold of the linen near her thigh, lifted her chemise over her head and threw it behind her. A faint *whoosh* sound came from the fireplace and the firelight flared. They looked in unison as the remnants of her chemise were swallowed up by the flames. She shifted her open-mouthed stare to him, then pressed her lips firmly together.

'I'll buy you twenty more,' he said and sucked on the tip of her breast until her back bowed.

She was so warm—and tasted so good. He practically tore off his trousers before he lavished attention on the other breast. He needed to be inside her and he was going to do it now in that chair. Olivia let out a soft gasp when he picked her up and tugged her down onto his lap.

Within minutes she shifted and straddled him again. The feel of her warmth as she slid down over him brought a groan from his lips. He didn't even need to move her. She was setting a rhythm on her own. He was in heaven. Nothing existed outside this room and the only thing he was aware of was the woman above him. He dropped his head back as she picked up the pace and rotated her hips. His hands fell away at his sides. She could do anything to him at that moment and he would let her. He would grant her any request.

It was impossible to steady his breathing when he watched himself enter Olivia—again and again. The delicious friction would soon be his undoing.

He needed to go deeper inside of her and coaxed her to shift positions so she was kneeling on the seat of the wingback chair facing away from him and he was standing behind her. The first time he entered her, he drove himself so deep he almost came with that first thrust. He tried to hold back his release as long as he could, entering her again and again. Eventually his mind shattered into a million pieces as he came. When she let out a raspy cry and her body collapsed against the chair, he knew she had found her pleasure again.

Dropping his head down on her back, he wrapped his arms tightly around her limp form. The erratic pounding of her heart matched his own. He had no notion how long they remained that way, just that he had the strongest desire not to let her go—ever. It was a notion that unsettled him.

Eventually he released her. Her cascading sable hair shone in the firelight, the pins were lost somewhere in and around his chair. She looked sinful. She looked like a woman thoroughly satisfied. She looked like a woman he would have an impossible time putting aside again.

He sat back in the chair, cradling her on his lap.

When her lips rose into a mischievous grin, that dimple he always adored appeared on her left cheek. 'This was entirely your idea.'

'I take full responsibility for the state you are in,' he replied, placing a kiss on her nose.

'Good. I am glad we agree I was the innocent party in this episode.'

'If I do not contradict that statement, will you agree to such episodes in the future?'

She ran her fingers through the strands of his hair. Gabriel was positive it was standing on ends, making him look rather ridiculous. 'You burned my chemise,' she stated simply.

'You made me ruin one of my favourite waistcoats and I have a neckcloth lying on the *floor*.'

'What will the servants think?' she teased.

He trailed a finger down her neck to the swell of her breasts and then the valley between. 'I'd venture to think the maids will be shocked to finds buttons and pins scattered around this rug come morning.'

She really had beautiful breasts. Just as he began circling the tip of one with his finger, it hardened to a delicious bud. He would never grow tired of eliciting a reaction from her.

'We should go upstairs,' she suggested. 'The staff will be up and about soon, and I would not want them finding us like this.'

She was just too tempting. He lowered his mouth and ran his tongue around her nipple. 'Like what?'

She pushed his shoulder playfully. 'Do stop, Gabriel, unless you can finish what you are attempting to start.'

He placed his hand over his heart. 'You wound me, madam.'

'Your sense of self-worth is quite large. You can easily withstand the small wounds I can inflict.'

But could he? And why did Gabriel get the sense that the wounds she could inflict on him were worse than those given by anyone else?

He helped her to stand. 'The rain has stopped.' Then he glanced down. 'I am still wearing my shoes and stockings.'

'It appears so. At least you will have an easier time dressing. What will I do without my chemise?'

'Here.' He picked up his shirt and lowered it over her body. The hem came down to her knees.

'I am not even remotely respectable in this.'

He looked up from buttoning his trousers. She was right. If anything she looked wanton—like a woman who knew how to coax a man into her bed and keep him there for days. Her breasts were visible through the linen of his shirt, and he instinctively licked his lips.

'See.'

'It's late. No one will see you. However if you truly are that concerned how you look…' He took his waistcoat with the missing buttons and helped her into it. Then he picked up his cravat and draped it loosely around her neck a few times. 'That's better.'

She eyed him sideways. 'Somehow I do not believe I would be admitted to Almack's dressed like this.'

'Dressed like that, it would be best if I never saw you anywhere near Almack's—or anywhere else for that matter.' Thoughts of her in Manning's studio flooded his brain and he unclenched his fist.

'Never fear, I can assure you this will be the last time I will be wearing your clothes.'

The statement, uttered so casually, left him disconcerted. Focusing his attention on his wife's bottom as she bent down to retrieve her slippers and gown, Gabriel ran his hand up the inside of her thigh, making her jump.

'Are you trying to seduce me, Gabriel? At your age, I would think you would not have the stamina.'

'I think we should find out.'

When he grabbed for her as she ran to the door, her laughter filled the room. He cursed his stupidity for not locking the door earlier when he invited her inside.

He was about to throw her over his shoulder to take her up to his bedchamber and prove to her that he had the stamina of a young buck, when he noticed she stood frozen in the open doorway. Stepping behind her, he looked over her head and saw a flustered Bennett with one of the upstairs maids. The young girl's eyes were wide as she looked at Olivia and they opened wider when she spotted Gabriel's bare chest.

Quickly he pushed Olivia behind him and motioned for them to enter the room as if nothing unusual had occurred. Turning slowly while keeping Olivia behind him, he backed her out into the darkened hall and closed the door.

'I wonder if Bennett will ever recover?' she mused.

'He has been exposed to our scandalous ways in the past.'

'Yes, but I do not recall him ever finding us in such a state.'

'Colette appears to have recovered nicely from her shock. The last time I saw her, she bobbed her curtsy to me with only a slight blush.'

'Well, she did see a rather different side of you.'

Gabriel shifted uncomfortably, recalling how much of his backside his wife's maid saw.

'What time do you suppose it is?' she asked.

From the window at the end of the hall, faint rays of light were casting bluish squares onto the floor. 'Four?'

'No, that cannot be possible.'

'You did arrive home rather late. It must be four. Bennett watches over the cleaning of my study every morning at four.'

Olivia stopped ahead of him on the stairs. 'Why?'

He gently prodded her to keep walking. 'Why what?'

'Why does Bennett oversee the maid?'

'There are times I leave my papers about. He makes certain they are left undisturbed.'

'But why not Mrs Mitchell? She is our housekeeper. I would think she would oversee the cleaning of your study.'

Why did she have to be so astute? 'Because Bennett has been seeing to the study of the Duke of Winterbourne ever since I can remember. It is simply his domain.'

When they reached her bedchamber there was a distinct hesitation before she looked up at him. 'Will you be coming inside?'

He reached around her and opened the door. As much as he wanted to, Gabriel knew he could not sleep for long. He had much to do. If he left her bed two hours from now, he might disturb her sleep. Or worse yet, sleeping next to Olivia might cause him to oversleep. He shook his head and kissed her cheek. 'I will only disturb you when I rise.'

Was that disappointment he saw cross her face? In the dim light it was difficult to tell.

'Very well, but I will be awake before seven for my portrait session.'

Muscles that had been wonderfully relaxed suddenly tightened up. He was just about to ask her why she was torturing him, when she placed a finger to his lips.

'I assure you. No one will know I sat for it when it is exhibited. There is even the slight chance Mr West will not agree to include it.'

One could only hope.

They entered her room and he closed the door behind them. 'Does Colette know she is to tell no one of your association with the painting?'

'Of course.'

He should forbid her from continuing to sit for the artist, but it was clearly something that brought her joy. How could he cause her any more sorrow?

He tasted her lips one last time before pulling away

and striding to the door to his bedchamber. As he placed his hand on the cool metal of the handle, he had the strongest urge to have one last look at her. She had not moved from where he had left her. 'I may allow for these sittings, Livy, but I do not have to like it.'

When the door closed, Olivia's slippers and clothes fell from her hands. Squeezing her eyes shut, she tried to erase the memory of him standing near her bed without his shirt. His scent was on the shirt he'd placed on her, and she rubbed her arms over the soft linen. Instead of tearing it off, she decided it would be comfortable to sleep in.

She lit one of the candles flanking the mirror on her dressing table and peered at her reflection. She looked like a woman who'd spent the night rolling around in bed with her lover—only they had not used a bed—and those memories would not be easy to forget.

Closing her eyes and rubbing her forehead didn't help. Breathing deeply made no difference either. Every nerve in her body was tingling because she couldn't stop thinking about having Gabriel deep inside of her. She groaned and lowered her head to her arms.

Going back to a celibate life after they conceived another child was supposed to be the easy part. Now Olivia wasn't sure that would be true. Her body felt alive again. Making love to him made her feel desirable. It made her feel powerful. It was addictive—or perhaps that was Gabriel.

Janvier had kissed her. Olivia knew if she showed the least bit of encouragement he would take her to his bed—or in his carriage. She did not believe he would be very particular.

But she felt nothing from his kiss; no spark of passion, no desire to straddle him and no fierce need to have him all to herself. Those feelings were reserved for her husband.

Gabriel had said some lovely things to her tonight. He'd even apologised for his behaviour—an act that was unprecedented. Why was he being so nice?

Olivia grabbed her hairbrush and pulled it through her hair with forceful strokes, attempting to rattle her brain enough that she would stop considering his feelings about her. She was a grown woman who understood how the world worked. It was rare to have a marriage based on love. There were only a few marriages she knew of that were. While it might be painful to witness the looks those men gave their wives, long ago she'd accepted her husband would never look at her that way. She had been dealt a different hand in life and now she accepted that.

She was giving herself a headache, not to mention her eyes were having trouble staying open. Blowing out the candles, she crawled under the blankets and arranged all the pillows snugly around her. Their weight and warmth made her feel secure. Closing her eyes, she wondered if she really would manage to wake before seven o'clock.

Chapter Twelve

It felt as if she had been asleep for only five minutes when Olivia heard Colette humming. Placing one of her many pillows over her head to muffle the noise, Olivia rolled onto her stomach. There was definite activity in her dressing room with the splashing sound of water being poured into her tub. She would never fall back to sleep now. Tossing the pillow aside, she opened her eyes.

She spied Colette shaking out the dress that she had worn last night and then retreat into her dressing room. Peering over the edge of her bed, she scanned the floor and saw no other evidence of how she had spent the evening.

Her maid re-entered the bedchamber and stopped when she saw Olivia was awake.

'Why are you humming?'

Bobbing a respectful curtsy, Colette had no luck suppressing her smile. 'Please forgive me if I woke you. It's a lovely morning.'

Olivia thought it would be better if she were able to sleep longer. 'What is the commotion in my dressing room?'

'His Grace ordered a bath to be ready for you at seven. He said you were not to be disturbed until then.'

Olivia rubbed her brow and stood, allowing Colette to help her into her dressing gown. 'What about Nicholas? Surely he did not bar Nicholas from entering my room.'

'I do not believe so. However, His Grace did have breakfast with his lordship in the nursery already. Perhaps that is why he did not wake you today.'

'The Duke ate in the nursery?'

'Yes, madam.'

Her world was becoming a very strange place. First her husband appeared to have suddenly grown attracted to her again and now he was eating breakfast with their son.

The heat from the bath water was a balm for the areas of her body that were a bit tender after the vigorous activities of last night. She was not going to think about the thoughtful gesture on Gabriel's part. She was not going to reminisce about the times after rather spirited nights of love making, when Gabriel had ordered a bath drawn for her in the morning. And she absolutely was not about to consider why he'd left William Cowper's translation of the *Iliad* on the table next to her bath.

Gabriel was in excellent spirits as he made his way to see Prinny at Carlton House. Although he checked on Nicholas each morning, today he'd decided to have breakfast with him. Spending time with his son in the nursery brought back fond memories of when his own father had sat in that very room playing with Gabriel and his three brothers.

Perhaps his house might once again be the very noisy place it had been when Gabriel was a child. The image of playing blind man's bluff with Olivia in her picture gallery with four or five children dashing about made him smile. There was no reason they needed to stop at two children.

His carriage rocked to a stop under the *porte-cochère* of Carlton House and he looked out at the immense Corinthian columns. He needed to shake her from his mind long enough to focus on his duty to protect Prinny. But as he made his way down the hall to Prinny's private apartment, Gabriel couldn't help wondering if Olivia was enjoying the bath he had arranged for her. He glanced at his watch and pictured her smooth skin glistening in the water at that very moment.

Once again he arrived as Prinny was sitting down to breakfast, this time in the Gothic Dining Room. The Regent painted a lonely picture, sitting by himself at the enormous table in the long panelled room normally used for dinner parties. As Gabriel crossed the threshold, Prinny motioned with his fork for Gabriel to sit.

'This marks a change for you,' Gabriel said, taking the seat to his right. 'I had not thought you ever took breakfast in this room.'

Prinny swallowed a mouthful of ham and reached for his glass of wine. 'I never do. But you have me held up in this fortress for a week and I am growing bored of my rooms.' A bored Prinny was not a good thing. 'Fill up a plate and join me, Winter.'

'Thank you, but I have already eaten this morning.' There was no mistaking the meaning behind the pursed lips of his host. 'However, I am sure I can find something to tempt me.'

That appeared to appease Prinny, because his mouth curved into a smile for the first time since Gabriel had entered the room. A plate and utensils were laid out before him and he accepted a cup of coffee to be polite rather than quench his thirst. Stirring sugar into his cup, Gabriel tried to find the perfect way to break the news that they were no closer to finding the person who wanted Prinny dead. He decided to be direct.

'You have said nothing about my new painting,' Prinny said, motioning with his fork to a painting that hung over the sideboard.

So they would make small talk first. Gabriel took a cursory glance at the painting of people. 'It's quite nice.'

Prinny snorted. 'Quite nice, he says. Quite nice is that cup in your hand. That, my friend, is a stunning example of an Italian master. Part of a collection owned by Boney's sister, Pauline.'

Gabriel looked back at the painting and then at Prinny, who had shifted his attention back to his breakfast. 'How in the world did you acquire that?'

'Olivia.'

'My Olivia?' Gabriel choked out, his eyes widening.

Prinny's hand paused with his glass halfway to his lips. 'What ho? *My Olivia?* Careful or you may catch yourself sounding like a man who actually cares for his wife.'

Not up for being baited, Gabriel knew enough to ignore the comment. For years Prinny had admonished him about the state of his marriage with Olivia while he went about ignoring both of his wives and taking a number of mistresses.

How was it that Olivia would know about a painting that belonged to Napoleon's sister? 'How did Olivia help you acquire that?'

'She was approached to authenticate the piece and told me about it. Capital gel, that wife of yours. This is the painting you took me to purchase. In fact, she was originally to accompany me to Mr Owen's that day, but she needed to be home to personally see to the last-minute arrangements for your boy's breeching ceremony.'

Olivia would have been in the carriage that day? Ice crept along Gabriel's veins as he thought how close she had been to lying dead in a pool of blood.

'I suppose,' Prinny continued, breaking into his thoughts, 'I could have postponed the purchase, but I was too eager to see it so I contacted you instead.'

'I am surprised you did not go on your own.'

'Olivia said Owen was skittish and the royal carriage would have attracted too much attention in that area.' He began cutting into his ham and eyed Gabriel's untouched plate. 'I imagine you ate something delicious for breakfast. I always enjoy a meal at Winterbourne House. Say… what if I stay with you until you catch the villain trying to do me in?' His expression held all the excitement of a little boy with a master plan.

'That's not an option. We want people to believe you are forgoing all your engagements because you have the gout. If it becomes known there was an attempt on your life, it could provoke others to try to do the same. Have you forgotten that eighteen years ago your father faced two assassination attempts in one day? That second attempt might have been driven by the first. I will not take that chance with you.'

Prinny sucked his teeth, determination shining in his eyes. 'Well, I could have the gout at your house. That would not be unheard of.'

'No, you cannot. Have you already forgotten you were shot at riding in my carriage? You are safest here with the Guards protecting you. You also do not even appear to be a man afflicted. I believe people would notice.'

'Oh, pish!' he said, waving a fork in the air. 'Olivia already knows I do not have the gout.'

Gabriel's heart stopped. 'How do you know that?'

'Because she came to call on me.'

'When? You are not supposed to have any visitors outside the few people we agreed upon. Who else have you seen?'

'Only Hart and Andrew, but they are on the list. Really, Winter, I realise you do not speak to her, but she is your wife. I assumed you would give your consent and it was safe. More importantly, the dear gel brought me marzipan.'

'Which you should not have eaten because you have the gout,' Gabriel said with more force than he should have.

Prinny looked down at his plate and cut into more of his ham while he mumbled something under his breath.

'You did not eat any of the marzipan in front of Olivia, did you?'

Prinny tossed his fork on his plate. 'Demmit, man, I rule this country and if I want to eat marzipan, I damn well will eat marzipan!'

Gabriel closed his eyes and pressed his thumb against his brow. He counted to ten. When he opened his eyes he caught Prinny's pointed stare. How was it possible that this man did not realise the danger he was in? He wanted to chastise him like a child. Instead he took a deep breath and composed his voice.

'You ate all the marzipan.'

Prinny looked away. 'I might have.' Digging into the butter with his knife, he looked back at Gabriel. 'It is only Olivia. And since she already knows I am not afflicted with the gout, what say you I stay at your house? You can protect me there.'

'No, and why do you believe she knows you do not have the gout?'

'Well I did eat all the marzipan, and she told me I appeared to be doing quite well when we went for our...'

'Your what?'

'Oh, bloody hell, this is ridiculous. I defeated Napoleon, for God's sake. I went for a walk. In my garden. With your wife. There, I said it.'

Gabriel pressed his thumb against the bridge of his nose, praying it would prevent his brain from exploding onto the table. 'Your gardens are adjacent to the park.'

'You do not have to tell me that. I'm the one who lives here!'

'And whose idea was it to go for a walk in the garden?'

'It was Olivia's. But in all fairness, the gel is unaware of the danger I am in.'

The hairs on the back of Gabriel's neck rose and he rubbed them through his collar.

'I cannot look at these walls for another day,' Prinny continued. 'You must find whoever is behind this and put their plans to rest. Olivia believes Nettleford will have lobster cakes at his ball next week. Lobster cakes! I have things to attend to and places I need to be. The world is moving and I am standing still.' He buttered a slice of toast. 'At least tell me you are closer to finding out who is behind the shooting.'

'The man who shot you is dead.'

Prinny's knife clattered to his plate. 'Dead? How is that possible? He was being held at the Tower. To my knowledge there was no hanging.'

'He did not face the gallows. Although there was no blood nor sign of a struggle, it appears he was murdered.'

The colour left Prinny's face and beads of sweat formed on his forehead. 'Poison.'

'We believe so.'

Prinny looked down at his food as one would a gutter rat and pushed his plate away.

'You are safe here,' Gabriel tried to reassure him. 'And if that were poisoned, I assure you, you would be dead by now.'

'Murdered? But how is that possible when he was being held at the Tower?'

'I am not entirely certain, but I assure you I will find out.'

Prinny drained his wine and motioned for more. 'You need to find him.'

'We will. But for the love of all that is holy, do not leave this house, do not see anyone else and trust no one.'

Gabriel entered his house frustrated they hadn't yet uncovered who was behind the assassination attempt. There was unrest up north and in the streets of London. Many people were unhappy with Prinny for the cost of his extravagant lifestyle. The threat could have come from anywhere.

He was about to walk into his study and write a note to Andrew when Bennett gave a discreet cough.

'Lord Hartwick is waiting for you in the Gold Drawing Room, sir.'

'The Gold Drawing Room?' Gabriel echoed, reconfirming the location.

'Yes, sir. I felt it was the safest place to keep his lordship while he waited for you.'

Striding into the room, he found Hart seated at one of the game tables with a row of cards laid out before him. He was just about to lower the Queen of Hearts onto one of the piles when he spied Gabriel.

'It's about time. I don't know how many more rounds

of patience I could play before I grew bored enough to begin searching for hidden passageways.'

This was why Bennett was so indispensable. 'There are no hidden passageways.' At least none that he wanted Hart to know about.

Hart lowered the card and picked up a glass of what Gabriel assumed was his finest brandy. 'Bennett would not allow me to wait in your study, which I believe would have been infinitely more interesting than poking about here. By the way, one of your gardeners enjoys taking a nip from the bottle as he prunes your shrubbery. If Her Grace has noticed a lack of blooms recently, it's because he is cutting them off and disposing of them along with the dead branches.'

'I take it this is not a social call?'

'At this hour? While I do enjoy our amusing conversations, you are correct. I have news. You may wish to lock the door.'

By the excited gleam in Hart's blue eyes, Gabriel knew the news he had uncovered was of no trivial matter. He took his friend's suggestion and locked the door before he took a seat at the table and waited for him to continue.

'Have you determined who was providing the information on Prinny's whereabouts to Mr Clarke?' Hart asked, tossing his head to the side to shift a lock of hair out of his eyes.

'I have not.'

'Well, I have,' he said through a smug smile.

Gabriel leaned forward and rested his arms on the table. 'Who is it?'

Hart sat back in the chair and stretched his legs out. 'I was at Lyonsdale House recently, when Julian mentioned the wedding portrait of his wife had been completed. Always the polite guest, I asked to see it.'

'I do not understand what this has to do with the gunman.'

Hart leaned forward, their knuckles almost touching, 'Because the signature on that portrait matched the handwriting on your note.' He reclined back again and arched an arrogant brow.

'You are certain?'

'I wasn't at first. Something about the signature looked familiar, but then today I realised where I had seen such handwriting before. Are you still in possession of the note?'

Gabriel nodded.

'Let me see it and I will prove to you I have found your match.'

When Gabriel returned from retrieving it from his study, Hart spread the paper out on the game table.

'See here the swirled loop of the "m" and the down stroke of the "j"? I tell you, I have found your match.'

Although Hart was known to have an uncanny memory, Gabriel was not completely convinced. However, this was as close to a lead as he had had since the attempt on Prinny's life. He had to pursue it.

'Whose signature is it?'

'A Mr John Manning of Hanover Square.'

Gabriel's heart dropped to his stomach and the hair on the back of his neck rose. That man spent time with his wife…with his child.

'You have grown quieter than usual,' Hart said. 'What are you not telling me?'

'The gunman is dead.'

Hart's previously casual pose was replaced by one of rapt attention. 'How is that possible? He was under guard.'

Pushing away from the table, Gabriel stood and

walked a few paces in agitation. Spinning back around, he ran his hand through his hair. 'I do not know. You are certain Manning might be involved?'

'I tell you, that is the man's hand. If only you had a painting of his, we could...' Hart's gaze bore into him as if he could read Gabriel's thoughts. 'Your wife is his patron. Surely there is a painting of his here?'

Dear God, this couldn't be happening, not again. *Never discount the obvious.* His father had pounded it into his head. The more he considered the facts, the harder it became to steady his breathing. Olivia had arranged the meeting between Prinny and Mr Owen. She told him not to take the royal coach and that she would take him in hers. Her carriage had the Lyonsdale crest on the side, just as his did. Just yesterday she'd persuaded Prinny to go for a walk outside in his garden where anyone in the park beyond would have had an easy shot at him. And he had heard her discuss Prinny with Manning.

He did not believe in coincidences. He knew first hand anything was possible. His past had taught him that—at a great cost. An icy chill ran through his veins.

If she were part of this, she would be tried for treason and swing from the gallows. He tried to scrub the image from his mind, but it would not go away.

'Winter, did you hear me?'

He could not do this with Hart present. 'I will search for one of his paintings. With the collection my wife is amassing, surely you can see it will take some time for me to locate his work.'

'I have solved the informant's identity before you did and yet you will not look me in the eye. If he is the person who hired Mr Clarke, you will be able to put the mystery of this assassination attempt to rest. The vile criminal will swing.'

And that was what Gabriel was beginning to fear.

Chapter Thirteen

Once Hart was on his way, Gabriel rang for Bennett. 'Is Her Grace home?'

'No, sir, I believe she is at Mr Manning's studio for her sitting.'

Gabriel closed his eyes and prayed he was wrong. 'Do you know when she is expected to return?'

'No, sir, I do not.'

'Is Colette with her?'

'No, she was granted the day to visit her mother. I believe Lady Haverstraw is with Her Grace today.'

Gabriel rubbed the ring that had belonged to his father, not at all comfortable with what he was about to do. 'If she arrives home in the next hour, I need you to keep her from our rooms.'

Bennett did not look pleased and he knew it was taking all of his butler's control not to say what was on his mind.

'Do I make myself clear, Bennett?'

'Yes, sir,' Bennett replied before Gabriel took the stairs, two steps at a time.

Olivia had mentioned Manning had painted something for her. He paused in the doorway of her bedchamber and knew once he entered, his life with his wife might be changed for ever.

Taking a deep breath, he turned the handle and was met with the faint scent of honeysuckle. He had not been in the room without her in years. The curtains were drawn back, letting the light stream in through the mullioned windows. There were miniature portraits on her dressing table.

That appeared to be as good a place as any to start. He picked up each frame and squinted at the signature on each one. If any of these were painted by Manning, it would be anyone's guess from the small size of the writing.

He ran his hand through his hair and turned about the room. There was a landscape over her bed and two smaller ones flanking the large one. Who did she say Manning painted?

His entire body froze and his gaze shifted to the fireplace. There it was. Over the mantel was a portrait of Nicholas. His son was sitting on a bench wearing a blue-velvet gown, his arms wrapped around Gabriel's mother's spaniel, Caesar. Walking slowly towards it, he found the signature of the artist in the lower-right corner. His stomach dropped when he took note of the distinct curve of the 'm'.

There was no denying it. Hart was correct. Olivia's friend was the man who'd supplied the gunman with Prinny's whereabouts. However, the scrap of paper he held in his hand would not prove a thing in court. They needed to monitor Manning's movements and hope he revealed his actions.

He knew he should not waste the opportunity to try to find something that might tie Olivia to Manning's crime. His stomach rolled at the idea.

On the table beside her bed was a stack of books. He went through each one, looking for hidden notes, but found none. Her dressing table held the usual items a woman kept on hand. He checked and found no hidden compartments. Where would a woman hide her secrets?

He entered her dressing room, where just that morning he knew she'd reclined bathing in the warm water he had arranged for her. Even in the early years of their marriage, he had never had a reason to look inside his wife's wardrobe. Seven shelves of pristinely folded silks, satins and muslins were available for his perusal. How many gowns did one woman need?

Rummaging around the bottom of the immense painted cabinet, his hands touched a wooden box approximately one foot by eight inches. It didn't take long before he picked the lock. Pausing for a moment, he prepared himself for what he would find. When he lifted the lid, he stopped breathing.

Perched atop a stack of letters that were tied with a red ribbon was the miniature portrait of himself that he had given Olivia shortly after he had asked for her hand. At one time it had resided on her bedside table. Untying the packet, he thumbed through the many letters he had written to her during their betrothal. At the time, he found himself writing to her simply to receive a letter from her in return—a letter he could read over and over again.

She'd kept them. The way she had looked at him these past five years had made him believe she had burned them long ago—probably in a bonfire on one of their estates—or while singing a merry tune, drinking bottles of wine with her friends.

But she had kept them, tied with red ribbon.

There also were pressed flowers and the elaborately designed diamond-and-sapphire brooch he had given to her as a wedding present. He recalled having the brooch reset three times before he was completely pleased with the way it looked. And now it sat in a locked box at the bottom of her wardrobe.

Gabriel placed the contents back inside their wooden tomb and made certain to relock it. Standing up, he surveyed the room again. Going back into her bedchamber, he walked over to her bed and looked underneath. There he found another box. This one was unlocked and held his correspondence with her since Nicholas was born.

There were letters granting permission to order new furniture for the drawing room, his enquiries on the state of Nicholas's health when he was sick and notices to when he would be leaving town. She'd kept them. But these letters held no love tokens, no gentle reminders of pleasant memories. She hadn't even tied them with ribbon.

There they sat, the remnants of the last five years of his life—efficient, impersonal and orderly. For five years he'd buried the memory of the morning Nicholas was born. Now he could see her lying in her bed, exhausted. He thought she'd never looked more beautiful. But as he'd kissed her, she'd pushed him away and began demanding he tell her where he had been. He was not about to confess that he had been in a brothel with Madame LaGrange, so he'd said nothing.

Then she began throwing things at him—anything she could get her hands on that was close to her bed. He was so taken aback by this unprecedented outburst that he was stunned into silence.

She told him she had no wish to speak to him or let him touch her ever again. Gabriel was not the type of man to demand conjugal rights of an unwilling wife. So for five years he'd left her alone, waiting for a sign that she had forgiven him. It had appeared in these last few days that she might have found a way to move past his supposed indiscretion. Now that was the least of his concerns.

There was nothing here. He'd looked everywhere and there was no evidence that Olivia had plotted anything with the artist. She considered Prinny a friend. But she had known where he would be the day the shots were fired. Part of him believed Olivia could never intentionally harm anyone. But another part of him knew anything was possible.

Andrew walked into Gabriel's study looking like a man who needed to spend a week in bed—and not in the company of a woman. His eyes were glassy and he blinked a few times from the opposite end of Gabriel's desk as if he was having a difficult time remaining awake.

'I hope this is important enough to have James drag me here when all I have is a desire to crawl back into bed,' Andrew said.

'I take it you had a late night?'

'Hart ran off and left me to play cards alone with Prinny until sunup. I believe I owe him a decent sum, but I could not tell you for certain since I think I fell asleep in the middle of the last hand.'

'I spoke with Prinny this morning. He appeared no worse for wear.'

'Yes, well, I imagine he went to sleep when I left. I, on the other hand, had a meeting with Mr Donaldson of Bow Street, apprising him of the investigation, followed by a meeting with Colonel Collingsworth. Yet again, he offered the services of the Guards should we have need.

I had finally fallen asleep, when James came knocking upon my door.'

'I believe I know who the man behind the assassination attempt is.'

That appeared to have woken Andrew up. 'How? Is it anyone I would have heard of?'

'The artist, Manning, supplied Prinny's whereabouts to Mr Clarke.' Gabriel's hands grew clammy as he said it out loud for the first time.

Andrew's eager expression fell. 'Are you certain? Olivia's Mr Manning?'

Gabriel curled his right hand into a tight fist. 'He is not Olivia's Mr Manning.' He took a deep breath. 'I want to believe she is not involved in any of this, but I never thought our uncle would do what he did. Olivia knew where Prinny would be the day of the shooting. She was the one who told him not to take the royal coach. Hell, she even arranged the meeting.' He rubbed the back of his neck.

'If what you are saying is true, she will be charged with high treason. You are her husband. She could possibly implicate you, saying it was done with your directive.'

'I am well aware of the law, Andrew. There is no need to remind me.'

'What will you do?'

'We need proof Manning is indeed the man we are looking for. I want to know his comings and goings. If he leaves, I want him followed.'

'I take it you would like my assistance in this?'

Gabriel nodded. 'Devise a schedule for the watch. Have the men report to you and come to me the minute you uncover anything. Should you have enough evidence to take him into custody, bring him to the house in Richmond. We will hold him there for his interrogation. I want him far from the Tower and the danger that is there.'

Andrew stood. 'Of course.'

'And, Andrew, do not breathe a word of Olivia's connection to the man to anyone.'

Olivia was convinced it had been hours since anyone had uttered a word in Manning's studio. Didn't they realise how boring it was to lie still for this long? She opened her eyes and focused on the chipped wooden frame of the large mullioned window. From this angle, she could see the tops of the trees in Hanover Square. Unless someone was planning on climbing any of them, nothing outside held her interest. Surely it had to be close to the time they'd agreed her sitting would end?

Her friend had been uncharacteristically quiet for most of the morning as he painted. She had no desire to interrupt his concentration. Her sister was another matter.

'What are you reading, Victoria?' Olivia called out to where she assumed Victoria was still sitting on the sofa near the door.

'*Nightmare Abbey* by Thomas Love Peacock.'

Olivia stifled a laugh. 'Truly? What possessed you to read such a thing?'

'Who could possibly pass by a book by someone named Love Peacock? It is rather satirically amusing. I'm rather enjoying it. You may borrow it when I am finished, if you like?'

Olivia's right arm began to grow numb and she wiggled her fingers. The sound of a page being turned broke the silence of the room. Was it possible to die of boredom?

'You might want to mention to Lady Nettleford the

next time you are together that I spoke to Prinny regarding her ball. I expect he will be attending.'

Victoria sighed and closed her book. 'You realise if I do mention it to her, she will talk of nothing else.'

'Yes, but she tends to become all befuddled around the man. Perhaps this will give her time to prepare herself.'

'I thought he was suffering with an unusually severe bout of the gout. Do you think he will be recovered in five days?'

He was completely recovered, as far as Olivia could tell. It was perplexing why he continued to maintain this ruse, but she had long given up trying to understand Prinny's motivation on most things.

'I believe he will be well enough by then. Please be sure to inform her that he is partial to lobster cakes.'

'I shall send a note off to her later today,' Victoria replied with amusement in her voice.

There was no feeling in her arm. She needed to move. 'Do you have much more to paint today?' she called out, hoping that Manning was paying enough attention to hear her.

A rustling sound came from behind the canvas, then a grunt. 'I am finished for the day. The light is changing.'

When Olivia lifted her head and turned towards him, she found him scratching his pencil upon a scrap of paper at one of the tables that held his pigments. She stood and arched her spine, relieving some of the stiffness. Finally she could go to Victoria's for luncheon and stimulating conversation.

With her sister's help, Olivia changed into her own dress before they walked out from his studio onto the pavement to look for her carriage. In its place, they found a black town coach, the lacquer dulled to a matt finish, drawn by grey horses. It was unmarked, with no crest.

She would have not given it further consideration except her driver was perched atop the coachman's box. She exchanged perplexed looks with Victoria before turning to her footman. 'Where is my carriage?'

He cleared his throat and shifted slightly on his feet. 'This one belongs to the household, madam. We were preparing to return for you when one of the stable hands noticed a wheel on your carriage was loose again. In order to arrive in a timely manner, we decided not to wait to have it adjusted. Unfortunately, this was the only carriage available for your use.'

She glanced at the coachman who had been recently hired. 'Why did you not bring His Grace's carriage?'

'His Grace left shortly before we did in it.'

Victoria backed away from the offending carriage and removed a handkerchief from her sleeve. 'Why do you even have such a thing? I cannot believe Winter would stand for something so decidedly worn. He probably changes his shirt at least five times a day. Why would he allow such a carriage to be kept in your stables?'

For the life of her, Olivia had no idea. She had never seen it before. She walked to the steps and climbed inside. Considering the outside of the coach looked unremarkable, the inside cushions were clean and rather plush, with black-velvet coverings. The windows, on the other hand, could use a bit of a cleaning.

Victoria sat next to her and wrinkled her nose. 'I shall send you home in my carriage.'

'Nonsense, I shall take this one. It is just for the day.'

The rain from the night before had left the roads in poor condition. Even though the cushions were plush, a number of times Olivia and Victoria had to hold on to the leather straps to keep from being jostled off the bench.

* * *

During Olivia's ride home from her sister's the road conditions had not improved and as the carriage turned a particularly sharp corner Olivia was thrown from her seat onto the rear-facing bench. She righted herself and began to adjust her skirts when she noticed a rectangular panel had opened near her feet. Assuming it was a storage area for firearms in the event of a robbery, she bent down to close it. Her attention was immediately drawn to a wooden box inside. Curious as to the contents, she lifted it out and placed it on her lap.

Expecting to see a pistol, she was confused when she looked inside. She had seen boxes like this before. Usually, the households who favoured entertaining their guests with theatricals used them. Inside she found a small mirror the size of her palm, tufts of grey, black, and red hair, pots of glue and facial paint, eye patches and glasses with plain glass lenses. Why in the world would it be in this carriage?

She had just enough time to return the box to its hiding place when the carriage slowed to a stop at her home. By the time her footman had lowered the step and opened the door, no one would've guessed Olivia was riddled with questions. Did Gabriel know about this? Surely he must since the carriage belonged to them.

Striding off towards his study, Olivia wanted answers. She raised her hand to knock and then thought better of it. She turned the handle and the door swung open. The ticking of the bracket clock was the only sound to break the silence. Her gaze skimmed over his desk to the long windows and, finally, to the chairs by the fireplace. Her husband and his secretary were nowhere to be found.

Walking further into the room, she dropped down into the chair behind his desk. Her eyes travelled to the portrait of her father-in-law, which presided over the room from his position above the fireplace. The distinguished-looking man sat regally, with his chin raised. On his pinkie he wore the ring he had given to Gabriel shortly after they were married on the night he died. A familiar pair of hazel eyes stared down at her. She could almost feel his disapproval that she was sitting in his son's chair. Well, she had a reason. His son was becoming quite an enigma.

The more she thought about that box, the more her brain filtered through the other odd things she had noticed about Gabriel over the years. The scar that Nicholas had pointed out was the most recent one. He had said it was from a fencing accident. Olivia was not convinced. There were also letters that she had seen arriving for him at strange hours of the day and night, their butler's presence during the cleaning of this room and the times he would not be in attendance at events she was sure he would have wanted to go to.

The more she thought about it, the more questions she had.

Her gaze travelled to the silver inkstand on his desk—the only object on the polished wooden surface aside from the silver Argand lamp. When she gave a pull on the brass handles of the drawer of his desk, it didn't budge.

Resting her forearms on the desk, she drummed the surface with her fingers. Something tugged at the back of her brain. It was as if she was staring at an unfinished portrait, unaware who the sitter was.

When she was a young girl, she had been adept at picking the lock of Victoria's letterbox. Did she remember how it was done? She pulled out a hairpin and lowered it to the small keyhole of the drawer.

'Olivia?'

She jerked her head up. There, in the doorway, stood Gabriel.

It was just her luck.

Chapter Fourteen

After closing the door, her husband advanced towards her. She was not about to show him that she was rattled by his presence. While holding his stare, Olivia dropped the hairpin. It landed silently on the rug under his desk. Thankfully, he didn't appear to notice.

'Hello,' she said, folding her hands on the desk's gleaming, wooden surface.

Her greeting was met with silence and she felt like a child caught taking sweets intended for guests. She was a grown woman. This was her home. And she should be able to wait for her husband in any room of her choosing.

As if nature disagreed, rain began to plink a steady rhythm on the windowpanes.

'Would you care to sit down?' she asked, rising from his chair.

From the opposite side of the desk, he held up his hand to stop her. 'No, by all means.' He took a seat in one of the two cabriole chairs across from her, crossed his legs and raised a speculative brow.

Slowly she sat back down. 'I came here looking for you.'

'And you thought I would be hiding in the drawer of my desk.'

Blast it, he did see her trying to pick the lock!

She attempted to appear composed while her heart beat wildly in her chest. 'Why do you keep the drawer locked?'

'Because I do not want anyone to see the contents,' the annoying man replied, crossing his arms over his chest.

'Why?' she asked, mimicking his movement.

'I value privacy.'

'Would I find the contents shocking?'

'That depends. Suppose you tell me what you were hoping to find and I can save you the trouble of attempting to pick the lock tonight while I'm asleep.'

'I have no idea how to pick a lock.'

'Forgive me if I say I do not believe you. If you do not intend to tell me what you were hoping to find, perhaps you can tell me why you are here?'

'I sat for my portrait today.'

'I see. And is there a reason you are telling me this?'

'Yes, because the oddest thing occurred when I left the studio.'

His entire body stilled and Olivia was almost certain he was holding his breath.

'Apparently my carriage was in need of repair,' she continued, 'and when my driver returned at the designated hour to collect me, he arrived in what could only be described as a hackney coach.'

It was refreshing to know she could still shake his composed demeanour.

'He collected you in a coach for hire?'

'No, I was told it was a spare carriage that we keep. They brought it out since you were using yours.'

He leaned forward. 'What did this carriage look like?'

'As I said, it resembled a hackney coach. It was a

dusty black with no coat of arms and the windows were decidedly dirty.'

'And John Coachman took you home in this?' he asked, fiddling with his ring. There was no mistaking he knew of this carriage. And he was not happy she was now aware of its existence, as well.

'He did. Why do we keep such as a conveyance?'

He shrugged nonchalantly. 'I imagine it to be one of the carriages the staff uses to move between town and the country.'

Olivia had seen those carriages before and this was not one of them. And there was also the matter of the box. She was certain there was more to it than her husband was letting on. 'There was something else odd about the carriage,' she said.

'What?'

The slightest reaction on his part might be the only clue she would gather. She leaned closer. 'I discovered a trapdoor at the bottom of one of the benches and inside I found a box.'

He broke their gaze for just a moment. If she wasn't looking so closely, she might have missed it.

'What kind of box was it?' he asked, appearing nonchalant.

'It was a box quite similar to the ones that are used for amateur theatrics.'

Not one bit of surprise crossed his features.

'Isn't that odd, Gabriel? Why do you suppose such a box as that is stored in one of our carriages? To my knowledge we do not even own a box for that purpose.'

He remained composed—too composed for her liking. 'I could not say. However, you are correct. There appears to be no reason we would own such a box.'

'So you have no explanation why it would be there?'

He shrugged again and picked an unseen string off the sleeve of his navy tailcoat. He knew something.

'Perhaps Bennett would know,' she said, as if she truly thought she would find out the answer from a man so loyal to Gabriel that he supervised the cleaning of this very room. Then it occurred to her. There was something in this room Gabriel wanted to make certain wasn't discovered by a maid while she cleaned away the dust and ashes.

Olivia glanced at the fireplace. It would be an ideal place to destroy letters he did not want other people to see.

She rose abruptly, knowing he would not give her any of the answers she needed. 'I will leave you now Gabriel. I am certain you have many matters that require your attention.'

He stood up and nodded at her—always striving to appear the perfect gentleman. 'Good day, Olivia,' he replied and she felt his gaze follow her until she crossed the threshold and closed the door.

Demmit! Gabriel shoved his chair back. Who in the hell thought it best to place her in that carriage? Very few members of his household even knew of its existence and those that did knew it was only to be used for surveillance.

Someone would be made to answer for this. Now, more than ever, they had to be operating with extreme caution. One small blunder could lead to Prinny's demise.

Olivia wasn't foolish. She knew there was significance behind the contents of that carriage and he was fairly certain she knew it led back to him.

He took a seat at his desk, scanned the room and took in her perspective. His gaze settled on the portrait of his father. He rubbed the Pearce coat of arms on his ring. His father knew enough not to trust anyone with what he did. He was even wise enough not to trust his closest brother. Gabriel had learned that lesson the hard way.

Olivia had been about to pick the lock to his desk drawer. Of that, he was certain. He just had no notion of what she would have been searching for.

Taking off his ring, he slid out the small shaft that was hidden within a well behind the stone and twisted it until it clicked securely in place, forming a small key. He used it to unlock his desk drawer. His gaze skirted past the loaded pistol and sheets of blank paper to the small red box tucked into the corner—the box that held the reason he always kept this drawer locked. He placed it on the centre of his desk and stared at the square that was smaller than the palm of his hand. It hadn't been opened in years.

Letting out a deep breath, he raised the lid and stared at the gold oval pin, outlined with seed pearls. His attention was drawn to the centre of the brooch, to the painting of his wife's fine brown eye. He removed the lover's eye from its silk nest and held it between his thumb and forefinger. It had been painted from her wedding portrait and delivered to him in this very room the day after their son was born—the day after Olivia told him she no longer wanted him in her life.

It was purely sentimental drivel that made Gabriel wear it on his waistcoat every day for a year. She had just delivered their son. It was his way of honouring her for that. Originally he believed Olivia would eventually forgive him for his supposed indiscretion, just like most women of the *ton* were apt to do. However, by the time Nicholas turned one year old, it became apparent she would not. The day he returned the trinket to its box and locked it away, he understood the level of sacrifice he would have to make in order to continue his work and protect his people. Now he was relieved he'd never wavered and told her about Madame LaGrange.

At the soft knock on the door, he returned the brooch to its hiding place and called for his intruder to enter. The door slowly opened, and Bennett hesitated before walking into the room. Good. The man should be nervous to approach him after that carriage had been used to fetch Olivia.

It wasn't until Bennett was a few feet away from the desk that Gabriel noticed the missive in his butler's hand. All thoughts of railing at the man left him when Gabriel spied the smooth, black seal used by Andrew for confidential communications. Surely Manning could not have tipped his hand this quickly. Then he remembered Olivia had been there to sit for the man that morning. His heart thundered in his chest. Dismissing Bennett with a nod of his head, Gabriel waited until he was alone once again before he slid his knife under the seal and unfolded the paper. It was only one line—but it said so much.

An urgent package has arrived for you in Richmond.

He crumpled the note as he walked to the fireplace. Knowing they were one step closer to finding out who was behind the assassination attempt should have filled him with relief. Instead he was filled with trepidation.

The watchful gaze of his father looked down at him as he tossed the note towards the fire. Then that familiar voice rang in his head one last time.

Trust no one and suspect everyone.

*　*　*

Gabriel approached the observation room in the small brick house in Richmond to find Andrew waiting for him outside the doorway. To expedite his journey, Gabriel had taken Homer and raced him through London. Even though it took him about an hour, it was the longest ride of his life.

'I assume this means my suspicions were correct,' he said, approaching his brother.

Andrew nodded. 'There is a bottle of your favourite claret on the other side of this door. Colonel Collingsworth has already arrived with members of the Guards should we require them. He is eager to help with the interrogation. I expect Mr Donaldson will arrive shortly.' He pulled Gabriel by his elbow to a nearby alcove behind the stairs. 'I still believe this could have been accomplished without anyone else present. You are placing yourself at great risk.'

'That is not the way of the law. In order to have a proper trial, we must proceed accordingly. If it appears we tampered in any way with the investigation, he will be released and all of this will be for naught. Prinny's life comes before all else.'

'But—'

'I appreciate your concern, little brother, but I am firm in my conviction. Now tell me about our guest.'

'You had the right of it about Manning. He was providing information to Mr Clarke regarding Prinny's whereabouts.'

Gabriel tried to steady the pounding of his heart. He should be relieved that they were one step closer to eliminating the threat to Prinny. Instead, he might be one step closer to condemning Olivia.

'What was observed?'

'I left your house earlier today with Spence in tow. I stationed him across from Manning's studio with a stack of newspapers to sell so no one would question his presence. Approximately an hour later, Olivia and Lady Haverstraw were seen leaving his studio in our carriage. Not her carriage, mind you, our carriage.'

'Yes, yes, I know, just tell me what the bloody hell happened.'

'Fifteen minutes after their departure Manning left and Spence trailed him to Hatchard's.'

'Who was inside Hatchard's?'

'I happened to be in Hatchard's to check on Williams when we saw Manning place a note into a copy of Dante's *Divine Comedy* tucked under a bookshelf on the second floor. Immediately after he placed the paper inside the book, Manning left the premises. Once I was secure in the knowledge we were alone, I removed it from the book and read it. It was evident it was penned by the same hand as the other note. I left Williams to see if anyone will retrieve it. Harris and Spence were able to subdue Manning in his studio and they brought him here. The note referenced Nettleford House on Park Lane.'

Nettleford? Gabriel tried to steady his heart, which he was certain was going to crash through his chest. This was the second time a letter intended for an assassin referenced a location Olivia knew Prinny would be.

His stomach turned. In his heart he didn't want to believe it was true.

'What is it?' Andrew asked, lowering his voice further. 'You know something.'

He needed to remove his emotions and think logically. First and foremost was his responsibility to the Crown. He ran his thumb over his ring. 'Olivia spoke of Nettleford's ball to Prinny. He told me she tried to persuade him to attend.'

Andrew looked as if he wanted to send his fist into the wall. 'Demmit, Gabriel! Do you see why inviting Bow Street to this inquisition was not in your best interest?'

'That is precisely why Donaldson needs to be present. If she is involved in this, she needs to face the consequences of her actions.'

'And as her husband, you might pay for her crimes as well.'

'Then I will face the hangman's noose if that is God's will.'

'But, Gabriel—'

'Not another word, Andrew. If this is to be my fate, so be it.' But he prayed to God it was not. And he prayed even harder that his wife wasn't a murderer.

Chapter Fifteen

Olivia had watched Gabriel ride off from behind the curtains of her bedchamber. His impatience to arrive at his destination was evident by the speed with which he mounted Homer. In the past she would not have cared in the least about any trip he took. But today, after discovering that mysterious box in the odd carriage, Olivia wondered what was so urgent that Gabriel needed to race away on horseback this late in the day. Her need for answers was driving her to distraction.

Convinced the answer to the riddle about him would be found in his study, she made her way downstairs. When she tried the handle to the door she found the blasted man had locked the room—probably because he knew she would be back. The only thing that prevented her from kicking the door in frustration was the knowledge she would do more injury to her foot than to his massive door.

Well, she was not about to let a mere lock stop her from finding answers. Removing one of her hairpins, she inserted it into the keyhole and after several attempts she managed to open the door.

The shutters were closed and the only light came from

the glow of the dying embers in his fireplace. As she bent down at the hearth to light a candle, a small scrap of burnt paper caught her eye. Dragging it out of the ashes with the poker, Olivia picked it up and blew off the soot. Returning the unlit candle, she walked to one of the tall windows, cracked open one of the shutters and read the words on the paper in her hand.

...package...in Richmond...

So whatever had caused him to speed away from their home, at least she had an idea of his general direction. The question was, what was inside this package that made his departure so urgent? And exactly where in Richmond had he gone?

The sparsely furnished, windowless observation room in the house in Richmond was lit by one small candle placed on a table in the corner. It took Gabriel a moment before he spotted Colonel Collingsworth and shook his hand.

'Well done, Your Grace. I understand from Lord Andrew that man, Manning, has much to answer for.'

'We believe so, Colonel. My brother tells me you brought men to guard him in the event we need him to remain here until a trial?'

'I have. If you have a secure room, my men will make certain no one has a chance to kill this one before he is brought before the court.'

Just then Mr Donaldson entered the room and Andrew slid a glance at Gabriel.

'I say, Winterbourne, what the devil is so important you took me away from Bow Street so urgently?' His eyes skidded to Colonel Collingsworth and then Andrew, before a look of comprehension settled on his face.

While Andrew relayed the events of Manning's capture, Gabriel peered through one of the small holes in the wall and took his first look at the prisoner. Although the long white shutters on the windows were closed, the candlelight from four large, silver candelabras illuminated the room in a bright glow.

Manning was sitting in a chair with a strip of white cloth covering his eyes and his hands were cuffed behind his back. Brennan, one of Gabriel's men, lounged against the wall behind the artist with his arms crossed over his massive chest, watching silently.

'Although he has questioned where he is, we have not said a word to him since we removed him from his studio,' Andrew offered, approaching Gabriel's side.

Manning repeatedly licked his lips and periodically turned his head, as if listening for even the slightest sound.

Gabriel stepped back from the wall. 'He appears rather skittish.' He turned to Colonel Collingsworth and Mr Donaldson. 'My man Brennan is inside with Mr Manning. Should you require his assistance, do not hesitate to let him know.'

Mr Donaldson nodded. 'Is there any further information about the prisoner that Lord Andrew has not told us that might assist us in interrogating him?'

Gabriel's hands began to sweat and he purposely avoided his brother's eyes. He should tell them about Olivia's association with the man. He should tell them she had been prompting Prinny to attend Nettleford's ball just a few days ago. And, he definitely should tell them Olivia had been to see Manning prior to the artist's departure for Hatchard's.

Instead he shook his head and firmly pressed his thumb into the stone of his ring, feeling more protective over her than he expected. 'As far as I know, my brother has given you all the relevant details.'

Mr Donaldson peered briefly into one of the holes in the wall. 'Very well.' He gestured towards the door. 'Colonel, I believe it is time to see what he knows.'

After the door closed, all the air in the room appeared to leave with them. Gabriel wanted to take a deep breath to steady his nerves, but found the tight pressure on his chest prevented him from drawing in much air. He caught Andrew's concerned expression before he sat down in the chair and focused his attention on the prisoner on the other side of the wall. Through the vent near his boots, he heard, rather than saw, when Mr Donaldson and Colonel Collingsworth entered the room. So much had come down to this very moment.

They took seats across from a very alert man, who shifted in his chair.

'I know there is someone there,' Manning said with a shaky voice.

Mr Donaldson nodded to Brennan to remove the man's blindfold. Manning blinked a number of times before narrowly studying the well-dressed men in front of him and then eyed Brennan from his scuffed boots to his sturdy legs, broad shoulders and black hair that fell past his collar. Once he had sufficiently taken his measure, he turned back to the men seated across from him.

Eyeing Colonel Collingsworth's scarlet uniform with gold trim, he addressed him first. 'You're a Guard to the King. What business do you have with me? Why was I brought here?'

Colonel Collingsworth leaned his tall, athletic frame

closer and folded his hands on the top of the table. 'Is your name John Manning?'

Manning's gaze shifted between his inquisitors and he blinked four times before he nodded. 'I am.'

'John Manning, you are charged with high treason, for conspiring to murder the Prince Regent of the kingdom of Great Britain.'

All the air missing from Gabriel's lungs appeared to push its way out of Manning's with a loud *whoosh* and the man fell back against the chair. 'I have done nothing of the sort. Surely, sirs, you are mistaken.'

'Do you deny visiting Hatchard's bookshop today and placing information about the Prince Regent's future whereabouts into a copy of Dante's *Inferno*?'

The colour drained from Manning's face and his chest visibly rose and fell as if he had been running instead of sitting for so long. 'I...I...'

'You should be aware before you attempt to deny it that you were seen doing so by noble men who protect the Crown,' the Colonel informed him.

Manning sat up tall and cleared his throat. 'Even if I did place a paper with the date and location of a ball, that does not mean I am conspiring murder.'

'And what if I told you that someone with your hand recently provided an assassin with the location of the Prince Regent the very day someone tried to kill him?'

The colour drained from Manning's face and his wide-eyed gaze moved from Colonel Collingsworth to Mr Donaldson and back again. 'Assassin?'

'That is the term for a person who attempts to kill someone.'

Under the table, the artist's right leg began to tremble. Pressing his lips firmly together, he lowered his head and stared at Colonel Collingsworth through his lashes. His chest rose and fell rapidly, matching time with Gabriel's.

From behind the large mural on Manning's right, Gabriel rubbed the stone of his ring, praying that Olivia was not part of this treachery. It would destroy him to find out the woman he had chosen to marry had the heart of a murderer. The image of Olivia being led to the gallows was making him feel sick.

Gabriel focused his attention on the scene before him.

'Do you know the penalty for treason, sir?' This time it was Mr Donaldson who spoke. 'You will be sentenced to death. You will swing within a fortnight.'

Manning's head jerked in his direction, but he remained silent—except for the sound of the rapid tapping of his boot.

'Tell us about Hatchard's. Tell us why you placed a note into that book. Who were you attempting to contact?'

The tapping sound was now replaced by the sound of heavy breathing, as Manning appeared to struggle with his decision to talk. Finally, he let out a shaky breath. 'I have no notion of who takes the information I leave. I was told to place the information in that book each time I learned of somewhere the Prince Regent would be. I swear to you I had no idea what they would do with the information.'

They? Dear God, there was someone else involved.

'Who told you to do this?'

'I do not know. I am innocent of any treachery against the Crown. I had no notion what they would use my information for.'

'Why should we believe you?'

'I am telling you the truth. I have no idea who has been retrieving my notes. They never told me their names.'

'Who told you where to place this information of yours?' Colonel Collingsworth asked.

'I do not know. You have to believe me. I never met them. A note was delivered to my studio one afternoon, early in the month. This person knew of a child of mine— a child that is far from London with his mother. If I did not provide them with the information they wanted, they threatened to harm my child. They told me they would mutilate him so badly that his life would be a living hell.'

'Were you contacted by one person or were there others?'

'I only received the one note.'

'How long were you to supply them with information?'

'I do not know. They said they would notify me when they no longer required my services.'

'Do you still have the letter?' Mr Donaldson asked.

'No, I destroyed it as they directed.'

'How many notes have you deposited at Hatchard's?'

'Four...I think.'

'And the information on the Prince Regent's plans, where did you get it?'

Manning looked away.

The pounding of Gabriel's heart was so loud, it almost blocked out the noise from the other room. From of the corner of his eye he saw Andrew turn his way. He sucked in a deep breath and squeezed his eyes shut, forcing a sense of calm to steady his frantic heart.

Manning shifted in his seat. 'Are these handcuffs necessary? I have answered your questions and they are chafing my wrists. Surely with that mountain of a man behind me and the two of you between me and the door, you don't believe I could actually escape. Do you?'

Colonel Collingsworth nodded to Brennan and the cuffs were unlocked. Immediately, Manning began rubbing his wrists. The men sitting with him might have missed his tactic for avoiding the last question, but Gabriel had not. Why did he not want to reveal where he had gathered his information? Was he protecting someone or fearful of them?

'The information on the Prince Regent's whereabouts. How did you acquire it?' Mr Donaldson asked again, and Gabriel almost wished he had forgotten that he hadn't received an answer the first time.

'They will know you have me and that I have told you things. They will want retribution. Please, sirs, I beg of you. Please do not let any harm come to my child and his mother. They have had no part in this. They should not be made to suffer because of me.'

'You are in no position to make any requests,' Colonel Collingsworth said, clearly disgusted.

'Then I have nothing else to say.' Manning leaned back in his chair and closed his eyes.

'Cooperate with us fully, Mr Manning, and should you be found guilty, transportation might be an option.'

Manning said nothing as he stared at his captors.

'Then I believe this interrogation is over,' Mr Donaldson said, rising to his feet. 'Colonel, you may take the prisoner now.'

He walked to the door and it wasn't until he touched the handle that Manning called to him.

'Sir, I shall tell you everything, if you promise to safeguard my family.' He chewed his lower lip and fixed his gaze on Mr Donaldson's back.

Gabriel was fighting the urge to shut his eyes. Olivia was too young to die now.

Turning slowly, Mr Donaldson walked back to the table and sat down. 'I will do what I can to keep your family safe.'

'I need your word as a gentleman.'

Mr Donaldson visibly bristled, but after pursing his lips together, he gave a curt nod. 'You have it.'

'Very well, I've gathered the information on the Regent's whereabouts from my acquaintances.'

'Tell us the names of those acquaintances.'

Manning shifted once more in his seat and he looked about the room before his gaze returned to Mr Donaldson. He took a deep breath. 'Lady Abernathy and the Duchess of Winterbourne.'

The silence in the room was deafening.

Gabriel broke out in a cold sweat and his heart twisted in pain. If only he could pretend this day had never happened. But it had—and Olivia's name was now linked to an assassination attempt on Prinny.

His right hand clenched into a tight fist. He glanced at his brother and the expression on Andrew's face told him, in no uncertain terms, that he thought Gabriel was a fool for allowing other men to conduct this interview. Now, he wished he had listened. But strangely enough it was to protect Olivia more than he worried about saving himself.

He focused his attention back to the interrogation room. It appeared some of the candles had gone out and he squinted to adjust to the lower light. Colonel Collingsworth and Mr Donaldson were staring at one another in silent communication and Manning's eyes shifted between the two men while he chewed his lip.

Finally, Mr Donaldson cleared his throat. 'What information did Lady Abernathy give you?'

Manning's right leg bounced rapidly. 'She told me of the Prince Regent's trip to Brighton on the fourth.'

'I see. And did you forward this by a note left at Hatchard's?'

'I did.'

'And the Duchess of Winterbourne, what information has she provided you with?'

Both of Manning's legs were bouncing now as he rubbed the back of his neck. 'She told me of a trip she was taking with him to visit a Mr Owen to purchase a painting by Titian, and today I heard about his plans to attend Lord and Lady Nettleford's ball.'

Both Donaldson and the Colonel turned to the wall hiding Gabriel and Andrew. If Gabriel didn't know any better, he would have thought they could see him rubbing his hands on his thighs. The smooth buckskin helped dry his sweaty palms.

Mr Donaldson leaned forward. 'And this information the Duchess of Winterbourne provided you with, what did you do with it?'

'I wrote the information down and placed it in the book at Hatchard's.'

'Did these women who provided you with information know you would be forwarding it to someone else?'

'No. No. Of course not.'

'You are certain they were not part of this?'

'Yes. I'm certain.'

'Did you ever discuss harming the Prince Regent in any way with Lady Abernathy or the Duchess of Winterbourne?'

Manning's eyes widened. 'No. Lady Abernathy is the gentlest of souls and Lady Winterbourne looks upon the Prince Regent like a father. Neither could ever consciously hurt him. And I have no desire to see him harmed. I told you I had no knowledge what was to be done with the information. I just wanted to protect my son.'

'Who takes this information you leave?'

'I do not know. I was told to place the information on page eighty-nine in the book and leave.'

'And you never remained, out of sight, to see who comes to collect it?'

'No, I just wanted to leave as quickly as possible.'

Mr Donaldson turned to Colonel Collingsworth. 'I have no further questions. Do you?'

Colonel Collingsworth shook his head.

'Very well, then. You will remain in Colonel Collingsworth's custody until we determine if you will stand trial.'

Manning squeaked. 'But I told you I had no knowledge of a plan to murder the Prince Regent.'

Mr Donaldson stood and turned towards the door. 'Then you should have no problem convincing a jury of that should that be your fate.'

Falling back in his chair, Gabriel rubbed his eyes. He could breathe again.

'You're one lucky devil,' Andrew said, standing up and stretching. 'That could have ended very differently. Do you think he was telling the truth? About Olivia?'

'I do.' He felt it in his bones. And Manning was right, Prinny was like a father to Olivia. Guilt ate away at him that he had even considered she would want to see the man dead. It was disturbing to know the man on the other side of the wall understood his wife better than he did.

Andrew opened his mouth to speak, as Mr Donaldson stormed into the room, pointing an accusing finger at Gabriel. 'Dem you. You knew she would be named.'

Gabriel stood, preferring to face Mr Donaldson at eye level. 'She had nothing to do with the attempt on Prince George's life.'

'She bloody well did! Your wife's information was

used to determine where he would be the day he was shot at.'

'My wife gossiped to an artist while he was painting her portrait to pass the time. She had no notion he would take that information and give it to someone intending to harm our sovereign. You heard him.'

'And how can you be so sure? Surely you do not expect me to believe that she discussed this with you over the breakfast table? The two of you barely speak to one another.'

The state of his marriage was common knowledge. While veiled comments in the past had annoyed Gabriel, more because he considered his private life his business and no one else's, this time he battled with himself to keep his right fist from crashing into Donaldson's jaw.

Just as he was about to inform the man that he could go to hell, Andrew stepped up to his side. 'I am certain he was telling the truth. In fact, the Duchess of Winterbourne told me about her conversation with the artist,' he said, not even glancing at Gabriel.

'Why would she have told you?'

'Because I asked her.'

'You expect me to believe this?'

Andrew raised his chin and moved his hands behind his back. 'You have my word as a gentleman.'

Gabriel glanced up, expecting lighting to strike Andrew through the roof of the house.

'You have had no time to question her since he was apprehended,' Mr Donaldson said, eyeing Andrew sceptically.

'We discussed her portrait session recently over dinner. I enquired how she could sit for someone for days and not grow bored. She said their conversations helped to pass the time and she gave me examples of what they discuss.'

'She still may have been aware this information would be passed on.'

As far as Gabriel knew, Mr Donaldson had never spoken to Olivia. He knew nothing of who she was and yet he thought nothing of questioning her character. His stomach turned as he realised he'd had the same thoughts about her less than an hour ago.

Gabriel never used his height and muscular form to intimidate men. He had never needed to. His title had been enough—until now. Now, he would use whatever means to deter Mr Donaldson from pursuing any suspicions about Olivia. 'My wife is the embodiment of all that is good. I will not have you besmirch her character. If I thought she was involved in any of this, do you honestly believe I would have you here to question that man?'

It appeared Mr Donaldson was suddenly at a loss for words.

Gabriel needed to return home and sort out his jumbled thoughts. He knew he had been right to pay attention to the facts that pointed to Olivia. However, he now began to realise she was probably the last person in London who would want to harm the King or Regent. And it hadn't escaped his notice he had been more worried for her facing the gallows than himself. He had much to consider—but there was one thing he needed to do first.

Chapter Sixteen

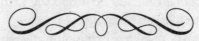

Hanover Square was nearly deserted at this late hour of the evening—or rather early morning if one was to be exact. However, one building stood like a beacon with the glow of candlelight in one of the upper windows. Thankfully for Gabriel it was not the building he needed to break into.

As Andrew stood guard, Gabriel crouched before the front door. Squinting in the dim light, he pressed two metal pins into the lock and jiggled them.

'Are you certain you do not wish to have me give it a go?' Andrew asked over his shoulder.

'I almost have it.'

'Do you even recall how it's done? I cannot imagine you've had a need to do that for quite some time.'

How he wished he could go back to a time when he was not the kind of man who would pick the locks of his wife's possessions—to a time when he had no idea of the horrors of betrayal. What would his life be like now if he had never gone to his uncle for advice?

A satisfying click broke the silence. Slowly he turned the handle of the door to the building that housed Manning's studio. Hopefully the man's landlord was a heavy sleeper. The last thing he needed was to have to explain his presence in the house.

He pulled Andrew inside the darkened hallway by the sleeve. Faint streaks of moonlight from the transom over the door lit their way to the staircase. They took the steps gingerly, hoping to avoid potential squeaks. When they finally reached the third floor, both Gabriel and Andrew took a deep breath.

With all the practice he'd had recently, this time it only took Gabriel two tries to pick the lock. Moonlight flooded into the studio from the large windows, making it easy to navigate the large room.

'What exactly is it you believe we will find?' Andrew whispered.

Gabriel's gaze landed on the easel, draped with a white cloth. That was what he had been hoping to find. 'We are looking for anything that might prove he was black-mailed.'

'But we agreed he was telling the truth. Why are you questioning it now?'

'It's prudent to be certain.'

Andrew studied him carefully. 'How do you propose we divide and conquer?'

'I'll search out here. There is another room behind that screen. See what you can find.'

Gabriel waited until Andrew was in the next room before he removed the knife from his boot and uncovered the painting of Olivia. Most people would never know it was the Duchess of Winterbourne reclining on the divan—but he would. He would not leave it here unattended. Should Manning be executed or transported, who knew what would become of this painting? He needed to bring it home. He needed to protect her reputation. It was the least he could do after today.

With a resolved breath he sliced the canvas from the frame, rolled it up and secured it with a strip of black ribbon.

'What are you doing?' Andrew asked from the doorway.

'It's of no concern of yours. Did you find anything?'

'Amazingly, I did not. Have you even begun your search or have you spent all this time taking Olivia's portrait?'

'What do you know of her portrait?'

Andrew walked closer to him. 'I know she was sitting for the man. Was he able to complete it?'

Gabriel shook his head.

'Pity. I'm sure it would have made a nice addition to the gallery.'

Thank God this painting would never see the light of day in any gallery, but Andrew did not need to know that.

'Yes, a shame. Well, if you are finished in there, perhaps you can help me look out here.'

With the portrait secure, Gabriel was eager to finish searching the studio and put this day behind him.

Throughout his ride home, guilt over his suspicions about Olivia continued to plague him. She didn't deserve his suspicions and had never done anything to indicate she could not be trusted, or that she hated the monarchy. She wasn't Peter.

For over five years Gabriel had had to live with the fact that Matthew's death was all his fault. He was the one who had confided his responsibilities to his uncle. When Peter asked to accompany Matthew up north to gather intelligence on the rumblings of a plot against the Crown, he should have said no. He knew Peter was a zealous supporter of Catholic emancipation. And that year Prinny was very vocal he was not. But in his wildest dreams Gabriel never thought Peter would try to prevent them from stopping an assassination attempt over it.

He would never know if Peter had intentionally killed Matthew to stop the intelligence they uncovered from reaching Gabriel. It might have been an accident. Peter took that knowledge to his grave. What Gabriel did know was that night when his uncle stood over him with cold rain pelting them both, Peter had every intention of killing him.

After that night, Gabriel vowed he would never again be responsible for anyone else's death. He would never again share what he did or the names of those that worked for him with anyone else. But his feelings for Olivia were running deep. During Manning's interrogation it became apparent he cared more for her life than his own. He wanted to trust her. He wanted a real marriage. Perhaps there was a way to have one.

When Olivia awoke the next morning, her suspicions about Gabriel and the mysterious package in Richmond continued to plague her. Luckily she would be spending her morning in Manning's studio. He would be a welcome diversion and today she would make him hold an extended conversation with her, whether he wanted to or not.

When she knocked on his door after breakfast no one was home, which did nothing to improve her mood. At least he could have sent a note cancelling her sitting for the day.

There was no sense in returning home where she would be tempted to enter Gabriel's study and probably get caught trying to pick the lock to his desk again. So she took Colette with her to Madame Devy's to lose herself in a morning of shopping.

When she walked out of the dressmaker's shop an hour later, she spotted Janvier standing in front of the milliner next door, deep in conversation with a willowy, dark-haired woman with fine features and a prominent brow. Olivia couldn't recall seeing the woman before, and from the simple appearance of her dress one could assume she did not move within Olivia's elevated circle.

Having no desire to interrupt their conversation or stand on the pavement on such a windy day, Olivia was about to walk towards her carriage when Janvier appeared startled to see her. She gave him a friendly smile and he whispered something in his companion's ear before he left her and approached Olivia.

'What a pleasant surprise,' he said with a tip of his hat.

'This is a surprise. I was just seeing about a dress for the theatre.'

'For the opening night of *Douglas*?'

'Perhaps.'

'Will you tell me the colour or will you keep me in suspense?'

'A bit of suspense keeps life exciting.'

He flashed her a grin. 'I agree. Well, I am certain whatever colour you have chosen, you will look lovely in it.'

It was just like Janvier to try to charm her after being seen with another woman. She held on to her bonnet as a particularly strong gust of wind blew down the street. 'I must be off before the wind takes me. Good day, Janvier.'

He tipped his hat and helped her into the carriage, where Colette was waiting to accompany her to more shops. It would take quite of bit of funds to distract her from thinking about the enigma she had married.

Hours later the man himself emerged from his study as she stood in the entrance hall, removing her bonnet. Crossing his arms over his broad chest, he leaned against the doorframe of his private sanctuary. 'You've been busy,' he remarked casually as he watched two footmen carry in boxes and wrapped packages from her carriage.

She handed her bonnet and gloves to Colette, then dismissed her with a nod. 'I realised I was in need of new slippers and gloves, and I saw a lovely fan for the theatre.'

'How many slippers does one woman need, I wonder?' he asked, with a slight smile.

'As many as she can afford.'

He nodded slowly, holding her gaze across the empty hallway. 'There is something I need to discuss with you… when you have the time.'

'I have a few things to attend to. Perhaps we can speak before your family arrives for dinner this evening?'

He tipped his head. 'I shall look forward to it. Shall we say six in my study?'

She nodded her agreement, even though having a conversation with him, knowing he was hiding something from her, was the last thing she wanted to do. What if he discovered she had been in his study and taken the cryptic note he'd tried to burn? Well, so be it! She needed answers and she was not afraid to press him to get them.

The idea of sharing his secret life with Olivia terrified Gabriel. There was no other word to describe it. But after weighing his options all morning on how he could have a real marriage with Olivia while also keeping his people safe, he knew it was the only solution.

She had sat in that carriage. She had found that box. And just yesterday he'd caught her trying to pick the lock to his desk.

He'd always known she was a smart, inquisitive woman. A person like that would not stop until they had answers. If she decided to poke into his affairs she might uncover the truth anyway—along with the identity of any number of the people who worked for him. He might be able to trust her with his involvement protecting the Crown, but he could not trust her with the identity of his operatives. The scar below his ribs was a daily reminder why. He would tell her the truth—at least the part he thought she needed to know.

At precisely six o'clock Olivia arrived at the door to his study. From the determined expression on her face, it appeared she had come with a purpose. It wouldn't surprise him if she wanted to discuss that carriage again.

'I gather from your earlier comment about the fan you purchased, you're planning on attending the theatre,' he said, closing the door behind him and leaning against it. That wasn't exactly a polite way to begin a conversation, but it was something.

She walked to the fireplace, where the ashes appeared to be more interesting than he was. 'Yes, *Douglas* will be opening, and Mrs Siddons is to return to the stage. Prinny and I were recently discussing how we've missed her performances.'

'He told me you brought marzipan. That's an interesting gift to give someone with the gout.'

'While you and I both know he suffers from terrible bouts of it, we also know he's not plagued with it now.' She finally looked at him. 'Was there a particular reason you wanted to see me? I cannot imagine it was to discuss Prinny.'

All of this had to do with Prinny.

Gabriel pushed away from the door and walked towards her. 'I have something I would like to discuss with you.'

'You said as much.'

He waited politely for Olivia to sit before taking the chair next to her. For the last hour he'd thought about what he would say—now he wished he'd considered how to begin. He spun his ring, searching for the right words.

When Olivia raised an expectant brow, he knew he needed to forge ahead. 'I believe we have spoken to each other more now than we have in the last five years. We are behaving as a family, in every sense of the word, and I was wondering if it would be possible for this reconciliation between you and I to continue, even after you are with child?'

Her eyes widened momentarily before her forehead wrinkled. He waited for her response. The awkward moment stretched between them and Gabriel began to wonder if she understood what he was asking.

'Why now?' She only said two words, but her scepticism spoke volumes.

'I told you—'

'No, not really.' She stood and took a few steps away before spinning on her heels to face him. 'I know what you're about. I am not naïve. You believe I was trying to pick the lock to your desk. That carriage and odd box I asked you about, they have significance even though you claim to know nothing about them. You are hiding something and think that by flattering me I'll run into your arms and brush my questions aside.'

He stood so she was no longer looking down at him.

'I'm not asking for a true reconciliation to trick you. I'm asking because I have genuine affection for you and I'd like to try to start over again with you if that is possible.'

'Interesting timing.'

'Is it? We have just begun this temporary reconciliation. I've just started to realise how much I've missed you. Is that truly questionable timing? I couldn't possibly have realised I missed you, a year ago. You weren't speaking to me. You weren't giving me the opportunity to remember how much I enjoyed your company.'

Gabriel spun his ring, uncomfortable with admitting he cared for her and missed her when she had yet to tell him she felt anything close to that about him. Early in their marriage he could see she had genuine affection for him. He thought he'd sensed those feels returning. Perhaps he was wrong.

'Yes,' he continued, 'I do believe you were attempting to pick the lock to my desk and, yes, we did discuss that carriage and the box, but my wanting to be with you has nothing to do with that.'

It now appeared it was her turn to search for the right words to express herself. 'I like you, Gabriel, I do, but I do not trust you.'

The absurdity of her not trusting him when all along he had never trusted her almost made him laugh. If neither of them trusted the other they had no chance of being happy together. Prinny was her dear friend. She would never want to see him harmed. It was time she knew the truth. 'There is something I need to tell you, Olivia, but before I do, I need you to swear you will not reveal what I am about to say to anyone.'

'That's a bit dramatic, wouldn't you say?' But when he remained silent, waiting for her agreement, she must have realised his earnestness. Her eyes searched his. 'Very well, I swear.'

He gestured to the chairs beside them and they both sat down.

'Do you remember the day my father died? No, wait, it began before that. It started when I was a child.'

Confusion crossed her brow.

'My father had very strong opinions about the French Revolution. He had a deep-seated fear that what had happened in France would cross the channel and cause a revolt here. He believed strongly that King George needed protection and Prinny as well. Believing if they were safe, there would be little chance of members of the *ton* facing the same fate as the French aristocracy. You see, he worried for the safety of this family. He created a secret organisation made up of men and women whose sole purpose was to ferret out any threats against the Crown and to protect the royal house with their lives, if necessary. On the day he died, he made me promise him that I would do everything in my power to ensure King George and Prinny remained safe before I assumed his role in overseeing that select group of individuals.'

The look of confusion was still in her eyes, along with some disbelief. 'Surely you are joking.'

He shook his head. 'It is all true.'

She pointed to the portrait of his father above the mantel. 'You expect me to believe that man organised a secret society to protect the Crown? *That* man?'

'He did.'

She studied the image of his father through narrow eyes, as if she would find a clue to his father's secret dealings within the portrait. Then she turned back to him and gave him the same appraisal. 'I do not know why you find it necessary to tell me such a fantastical tale, but I do not find it amusing and it does not improve my trust in you.' She looked away and brushed out non-existent wrinkles from her lap.

'Olivia, what I am telling you is the truth. I am responsible for protecting the Crown.'

'And I am a Grand Duchess of Russia, simply raised in England as a girl,' she bit out with sarcasm.

'You yourself admitted you have suspicions about me. That is why I am telling this to you. Why did you feel it necessary to try to open a locked drawer to my desk? You know deep down what I have told you is possible.'

Her hand stilled from where she had been about to pick an invisible thread from her sleeve and she stared at the hearth. Her eyes were moving as if she was reading a message in the ashes and he could see she was considering what he said.

'You are too clever to discount what I am telling you, Olivia. You know what I am saying is possible—that it is the truth.'

She looked back at him and he could see she was struggling to believe him. 'How long have you been involved in this?'

'I took a vow to give my life for the Crown when I was at Cambridge.'

'So when we were introduced you were already working for your father?'

He nodded and saw the moment she realised what he told her was possible.

'You've been deceiving me from the moment we met!'

'We are sworn to tell no one. One of the reasons we have been successful in stopping plots against Prinny and King George is because we operate in secret. My own mother and most of my closest friends do not even know. Lyonsdale doesn't know.'

'Lyonsdale is not your wife. I am,' she spat with fire in her eyes.

'I swore an oath.'

'Then why tell me now? What has changed?'

'Everything has changed,' he replied forcefully. 'I misjudged you and did not know you well enough to trust you with something like this years ago. I see now how much you have come to care for Prinny and know you would never do anything to cause him harm. If I continued to keep this secret from you, it would pull us further apart. I do not want that.' He placed his hand over hers. They remained cold under his touch through her embroidered silk gloves. 'I do not want to go back to the way things were between us. I like waking up to you. I like being together with you and Nicholas even if at times it is at an absurdly early hour of the morning. And I like knowing that when I want to see you, I will not be turned away. I have missed your intelligence and your wit. And there is no place I would rather be than in your bed. There is no other woman I want more than you, Livy.'

She slid her hands out from under his. 'Explain the carriage I was brought home in yesterday.'

'It's used when we have a need to observe people who we suspect have plans against the Crown.'

'And the box?'

'There are times disguises are necessary.'

'Tell me about the package in Richmond.'

Bloody hell, she was even craftier than he thought! 'What do you know of Richmond?'

She reached inside her glove and withdrew a charred piece of paper. 'Tell me about the package you received in Richmond,' she repeated, holding it out to him.

'An attempt has been made on Prinny's life—'

'He is hurt? Is—'

'He's fine. I have him in Carlton House to keep him safe until we are certain we have in custody all those involved in this plot. The package this refers to is a person. It's the man who has been supplying information on Prinny's whereabouts.'

'You saw this person last night?'

'I did.'

'Well, I hope someone beat him to a bloody mess.' From the anger rolling off her, he'd wager she would volunteer if given the chance.

'You may not feel that way when I tell you his name.'

'Why should I show concern for such a person?'

He had an urge to beat Manning himself for the hurt this was sure to cause his wife. Instead he walked to the fireplace to take his anger out of the logs. As he jammed the poker into the flames, sparks flew up the chimney.

'Gabriel, do I know this man?' she asked, walking over to him.

From her expression he thought it best to place distance between Olivia and the heavy metal object in his hand, so he hung the poker back on the rack. 'Mr Manning was informing the assassin of Prinny's plans.'

She backed away from him. 'That's not amusing.'

'It was not meant to be.'

'John Manning would never do such a thing.'

Gabriel took a step closer to comfort her, but she took another step back.

'You are just saying that because you do not like me sitting for him. You will find any excuse to prevent him from painting that portrait.'

'That is not true. He was gathering information about Prinny while painting those within the royal circle. That information was given to someone who intends to kill Prinny. We have his confession.'

Her breathing became more rapid as she processed what he had told her. 'He asked me to sit for that portrait. He said it was because only I...' She stormed past him and grabbed the poker. 'That weasel! And to think I recommended him to friends.'

By the time she had finished stabbing the logs, they would be tiny bits of ash. At least she had got over her shock and wasn't a sobbing mess. He took a step closer just as she whirled around, waving the poker at him. He backed up just in time.

'I hope he can no longer stand this morning.' She turned back around and jabbed the logs. 'What kind of person seeks the blood of another?'

Gabriel went to step closer and she yanked the poker out of the fire.

He froze.

'He should be punished for this,' she said through her teeth.

'He will be. Once we have captured whoever is responsible for this, Manning will face trial. You should know that he was coerced into giving away the information. If he did not oblige, members of his family would have been maimed.'

'He still should have found a way to get out of his predicament.'

'Sometimes that's not always possible.'

'I don't believe that. If you think clearly, you can always find a way.'

It was hard to imagine what it would feel like to be sheltered from the ugliness in the world. 'Put the poker down, Olivia. You have successfully reduced the logs to ash.'

She narrowed her eyes at him and hung the poker on the rack. Dusting off her hands, she turned her head towards his desk. 'Why do you keep your desk locked? Is that where you hide your secret papers?'

He knew she would never have simply forgotten all that she suspected. Taking off his ring, he adjusted it so it formed the key to his desk. Her surprised expression brought a smile to his lips. 'Open it and you will see,' he said, handing her his ring.

She crossed the room as if she were heading to her own execution and pushed the chair away from his desk. The key stalled momentarily in the lock before giving way with a click. There was a slight hesitation before she cautiously slid her hand inside.

There were only three things Gabriel kept in that drawer. Apparently she had no interest in the pistol. She took out the stack of papers, but once she saw they were blank she returned them to the drawer. Then she removed the small box and placed it on top of the desk. She stared down at it as if it would devour her where she stood.

'Open it,' he commanded softly into her ear.

Holding her breath, she raised the lid and picked up the lover's eye. It took a moment before she almost dropped it.

'I had Cosway paint it from your wedding portrait. The jeweller who set it brought it to me the day after Nicholas was born. I wore it for a year before I realised there was no hope for reconciliation between us. It sat there unopened for years until yesterday when I found you in my study. Now you have uncovered the secret of my locked drawer.'

She looked back at the small gold brooch in her hand. 'You wore this?'

'Every day for a year.'

'How did I not notice?'

'You barely looked at me and even if you did, you

would not have seen it. I wore it under my coats. I've missed you, Livy. I hadn't realised how much until recently.'

She searched his eyes as if gauging his sincerity. Finally her lips curved into a small sad smile and she placed the pin back in the box. 'I have missed you as well.'

'I want you as my wife, in every sense of the word.'

'I want that, Gabriel, I do, but I will not take you back into my life knowing you will run to Madame LaGrange to satisfy your needs. Most women would look the other way. But I cannot. I would rather we lived here as strangers than to have a marriage like that.'

For years Madame LaGrange would trust only him with the intelligence she had gathered. She knew the danger she was putting herself in and he could not blame her for wanting to have only one person as her contact. But what if he could convince her she could also trust Andrew? Then he would no longer have to see her and there would be no danger of Olivia believing the worst. They could begin again and put the past behind them. 'I won't. You are the only woman I need. There will never be another.'

All this time he had not been alone in missing what they had. He cradled her neck in his palm and lowered his lips to hers. What had started out as a kiss of mutual affection turned into much more. He poured out everything he couldn't say to her—didn't know how to say to her—into that kiss.

As if she needed to be as close to him as he did her, Olivia worked the buttons of his tailcoat and then his waistcoat. He picked her up and settled her lovely bottom on the surface of his desk, all without breaking the kiss.

He needed her and needed to be inside of her to reassure himself she was his. The silk of her gown glided over his hands as he skimmed his fingers up her soft, warm legs. Her breath caught within their kiss as his hands moved higher and higher.

A soft knock stilled them and Gabriel looked at the door. Olivia pushed against his shoulders, but with one hand he grabbed her about the waist and the other hand remained on her thigh.

'Yes?' he called out, sounding as if he had spent the day in a loud debate within the House of Lords.

The handle of the door turned halfway before the lock prevented it from making a full rotation. 'Your guests have arrived, sir, and are waiting in the Green Drawing Room,' was the muffled reply from Bennett.

Gabriel and Olivia looked at one another in mutual confusion, until they both recalled they were having dinner with his family. Olivia pushed harder against Gabriel and this time he let her go. Stepping away from the desk, he buttoned his waistcoat and began to tidy his clothes.

'Tell them we will be there shortly,' he called to the closed door.

'Yes, sir,' was the muffled reply.

When he turned back around, Olivia was adjusting the neckline of her gown.

'May I help you with that,' he asked with a grin.

'I believe you have done enough for now.'

'I'd like to do more.' Visions of entering her were not going away. 'It is unseasonably warm this evening,' he said with an arch of his brow.

Her hand stilled from shaking out her skirts and she looked up at him. 'Perhaps we should venture out into the garden when our guests leave.'

It was uncanny how quickly she could follow his train of thought. 'Perhaps we should.' He took her hand in his and pressed a kiss to her skin. 'I haven't been in the walled garden in ages. Are we still in possession of that sun dial?'

The tip of her tongue ran over the dip in her upper lip. 'We are, but it won't be of much use in the dark.'

'It will be most useful when I bend you over it and take you from behind.'

Her brown eyes darkened and he knew she was picturing it just as he was. If he made it through dinner without dragging her out of the room and into the garden it would be a miracle.

Olivia was the first to look away as she flattened out her skirt. 'Do I look presentable? I don't resemble a doxy who has just had a tumble?'

He laughed and shook his head. 'I assure you my family will have no idea what we've been doing.'

Her eyes widened as she glanced at the door. 'Your family... Gabriel, we cannot keep them waiting.'

Grabbing his arm, she propelled him towards the door. When they reached the door, he spun her around and kissed her one last time. Then she pushed him away, turned the key in the lock and before Gabriel was able to say another word, she was practically running with him down the hall to the Green Drawing Room.

Aside from their heavy breathing from running through their house, Gabriel thought they had disguised their activities rather well. That was until his mother, Andrew and Monty turned towards them from where they had been sitting near the window. His mother's eyebrows rose into her hairline, Andrew's right brow arched with a knowing look of amusement and Monty's mouth had opened so wide he resembled a fish.

Gabriel glanced at Olivia. Not a hair was out of place. So what was causing such a reaction?

Olivia dropped his hand.

It suddenly felt cold and empty. She looked at the buttons of his tailcoat with a pointed stare and he re-buttoned them properly. No one uttered a word. The awkwardness of the moment would not do. Their family should know they had reconciled and, in a short time, so would all of London.

He tugged Olivia closer and kissed her knuckles slowly. Her eyes softened at the gesture. A discreet cough came from the sofa. When they both turned their heads, his mother smiled.

'We were beginning to worry that something was amiss with Nicholas. Now I see it was nothing dire at all.'

'Nicholas is well, I assure you,' Olivia said, tugging her hand back and walking towards his family. 'He will be down after dinner and you will be able to see for yourself.'

His mother kissed his cheek. 'It is lovely to see you, Gabriel.' Her wise eyes scanned his wife's face. 'You look well, my dear. I dare say you have a bit of a rosy glow. Are you well?'

'Yes, I am. Thank you. I just had a bit of difficulty with my gown this evening and Gabriel was kind enough to wait for me.'

'He did,' his mother said, eyeing her son from his shoes to his cravat as if she were looking for a strand of Olivia's hair on his clothing.

'I thought it would be the proper thing to do. We did not anticipate it taking as long as it did.'

'I suppose that comes with age,' Andrew mumbled through a smirk.

'What was that?' their mother asked, narrowing her eyes at his brother.

'I said it must be difficult to gauge,' he replied, looking at Gabriel with laughter in his eyes.

His mother glared at Andrew and Gabriel was certain, if his brother had been sitting closer, she would have rapped his knuckles with the fan she was tapping against her thigh.

'I understand dinner is ready to be served,' Olivia said, her gaze narrowed on Andrew as well. 'Andrew, would you please escort me to the dining room?'

Bowing to Olivia, Andrew flashed her a devilish smile as if he was preparing to charm his way out of trouble. 'Of course, the honour is mine, sister dear.'

'Monty, some day Andrew will find a bride and you will not have to walk into dinner alone,' Olivia said sweetly.

'And when will that be, Andrew?' his mother prodded. 'Each day I move closer and closer to my grave.'

'You are not even sixty years of age, Mother. I believe you are far from your grave.'

'I hope she isn't bookish,' Monty interjected from the back. 'I should hate to be forced to talk about literature or some other nonsense when we are together.'

'What would you like to discuss?' Gabriel asked.

'I don't know. Olivia is easy to speak with. Perhaps, Olivia, you know someone just like you that you could introduce to Andrew.'

'There is no one else like Olivia,' replied Gabriel, turning his head and catching her eye. 'Besides, the only lady Andrew would find interesting would need to have extensive knowledge of pugilism and ale.'

'Oh, dear Lord, I think I feel faint,' his mother said.

'At least she will probably be of a hardy stock,' Olivia interjected over his mother's shoulder.

'That sounds perfect to me,' Monty said. 'Do find her soon, Andrew, or I might be married before you.'

'That suits me, brat. Why don't you find a lady and keep out of my affairs.'

'Affairs?' Olivia asked in a conspiratorial whisper. 'Are you having an affair?'

Andrew cleared his throat. 'That is not what I meant and you know it. Do not encourage them. I thought I was your favourite?'

'You are.'

'But you told me I was your favourite brother,' Monty said petulantly.

'And you are as well.'

'You cannot have two favourite brothers,' he replied.

'I am a woman. Of course I can.'

'That does not make any sense.'

'The longer you are around women, the more you will see it makes perfect sense, brat.'

They reached the smaller dining room used for intimate meals. The conversation around the table was lively and pleasant. Knowing he would spend more evenings like this made Gabriel smile.

His mother wiped her mouth delicately with her napkin. 'So, I understand Mrs Siddons will be coming back to the stage at Drury Lane. With your appreciation of the theatre I imagine you will be attending, Olivia.'

Olivia's smile brightened the room. 'Yes, I've been looking forward to tomorrow night for quite some time.'

'I know Prinny adores her performances,' his mother continued. 'Goes on about them for days. I expect he will attend.'

'We had discussed it just the other day,' Olivia said smiling, as if she was recalling a rather pleasant conversation. Then her brow creased and her expression darkened. 'However, he has been suffering terribly with the gout. I do not know if he will attend.'

Gabriel did not miss Andrew's side-glance at the mention of Prinny attending the theatre. If Olivia knew he had been planning to attend the theatre, had she discussed it with Mr Manning? Did anyone else know of Prinny's partiality for Mrs Siddons?

'I will go with you.' Gabriel knew full well his statement sounded like a command.

Everyone at the table turned to him in surprise.

He kept his eyes focused on Olivia. 'I think it is time we announce our reconciliation.'

'You do?'

'I do. I can think of no better way to do so than to arrive together to a performance a good portion of London will be attending.' He raised his brow expectantly for her agreement.

Her smile warmed him. 'I would like that.'

'Excellent. Would anyone else like to accompany us?'

Andrew began to say something when he suddenly looked down towards his leg and let out a muffled cry. Their mother, sitting next to him, smiled sweetly.

'Did you want to join us, Andrew?' Gabriel asked.

His brother shook his head, while he sunk his teeth into his lower lip.

Gabriel turned to Olivia. 'It appears it will just be you and I.'

Chapter Seventeen

Gabriel was finishing up reviewing a speech Lyonsdale was preparing to give to the House of Lords and anticipating an exceptional evening with his wife when Bennett knocked on the door to his study. A letter had arrived. Gabriel was tempted to put it aside when he noticed the hand that had addressed it. He knew that writing. Closing his eyes, half in exasperation, half in dread, Gabriel broke the seal and read the words that were written for his eyes only.

Bile rose in his throat.

It might have been from the exotic scent of the paper, although it was more likely from the request made by Madame LaGrange to see him. As usual, her timing was impeccable. But Gabriel knew if she was contacting him, it must be urgent.

He hadn't yet determined how he was going to convince her to trust Andrew with her communications in the future. If he had, perhaps he could have sent his brother to meet her. But he could not send Andrew to her without her permission. There was no doubt in his mind, if he did, she would sever her ties with him and refuse to provide any more information. He would have to go to her.

He threw the note into the fireplace and watched it burn. Glancing at his watch, Gabriel calculated how long it would take him to reach her establishment, meet with her and return home. If he left quickly, he should be back in enough time to escort Olivia to the theatre and no one would be the wiser. Leaving word with Mr James as to his location, Gabriel instructed him to contact Andrew should he not return home in three hours.

He took his own horse, which would be faster to manoeuvre through the streets of Mayfair. In no time, he was in front of Madame LaGrange's nondescript white house on the edge of the fashionable district. Even though it was late afternoon, the entrance hall was filled with shadows from the clouds outside. He walked by the empty gaming rooms and saloons where gentlemen could relieve themselves of large amounts of cash in a rather short amount of time. At least no one was here to carry tales of his visit to her private suite of rooms.

Rapping his knuckles on her door, Gabriel was met with a muffled command to enter. The same exotic fragrance from her letter drifted through the tastefully furnished sitting room that served as her office. She was seated at her escritoire near one of the windows. Her blonde head was bent over a ledger while she scratched her pencil along the page. She was a very beautiful woman. He assumed her to be around his age.

Gabriel strode past a small grouping of chairs, till he stood a few feet from her. This was a woman who did not stop what she was doing for any man—even one with his prestigious title. Running his thumb along the smooth brim of his hat, he waited for her to finish her calculations. It did not take long before she placed her pencil down, closed the ledger and turned to him with a friendly smile.

'You look well, Winterbourne. It has been a while.' Her voice was like fine brandy, warm and velvety.

'Eight months and twenty-seven days.'

'How ridiculously precise of you,' she replied, as amusement tugged at her full lips. 'What a lovely coat. Such an exceptional fabric.' She ran her graceful fingers down his right sleeve and rubbed the superfine fabric at his cuff. 'Still fond of Mr Weston's work, I see.'

'I am, but I do not believe you invited me here to discuss my tailor.'

'No, I did not. You might find what I have to tell you more interesting. Would you care to have a seat?' she asked, gesturing to a nearby delicate chair. 'I am pleased you were able to arrive so quickly.'

He took a seat and adjusted his cuffs. 'You indicated it was urgent. I saw no reason to delay.' He didn't want to be rude, but he wished he could forgo the pleasantries and return to Olivia. Being here always brought back memories of the night Nicholas was born. How he wished he could have sent Andrew...

She leant her arm on the escritoire, her keen gaze sweeping over his face. 'There is something different about you.'

'I am the same man I was when my father introduced us.'

She didn't appear convinced, but knew enough not to pursue the subject. 'Very well, what I have to tell you concerns the Prince Regent.'

Gabriel's heart kicked up speed. Would he finally have information that could be used to track down whoever wanted Prinny dead?

'One of my girls had worked for a time as a seamstress at Drury Lane. A certain gentleman had made her acquaintance there and last night he sought her out here. When they were together in her room, he began to question her about the theatre, back entrances, closets near the boxes and the like. She mentioned it this morning during breakfast. I didn't think much of it at the time, but then later today I read in the papers that *Douglas* is opening tonight at Drury Lane and the Prince Regent is expected to attend. It might not mean anything, but I thought it might be relevant.'

She was right to bring it to his attention. The coincidence was too great. And Gabriel did not believe in coincidences. Was it possible they were planning to kill Prinny tonight in Drury Lane? Eighteen years ago, an attempt was made on King George's life in that very theatre and Gabriel's father had been one of the men to interrogate that gunman.

'Do you know this gentleman's name?'

Madame LaGrange nodded thoughtfully. 'He's a Frenchman by the name of Comte Antoine Janvier.'

Oh, hell! Were all the men in Olivia's circle traitors to the Crown?

The hair on the back of his neck rose. The Frenchman who'd spent countless hours in his wife's company, who had been in his very home, could be the man who wanted Prinny dead. Their friendship had to have been orchestrated. He must have been using his friendship with Olivia to get closer to Prinny. But why would he want him dead?

'Do you know of him, Winterbourne?'

Gabriel could only nod, still processing how close Olivia had placed herself to a dangerous man. If something had happened to her... He almost knocked his chair over as he stood.

She looked up at him and her green eyes widened. 'I was right to tell you. You believe there is a connection.'

'Yes, you were right to bring this to my attention. Janvier may just be the man I have been looking for. I cannot thank you enough.' He reached the door and spun around when she called out his name.

'Some day I may require your assistance. For a proprietress such as myself, it is reassuring to know I will be able to turn to you.'

'I would gladly assist you in any way I can. I know you continue to place yourself in great risk providing me with valuable information.'

'Betrayed men are not the most pleasant. As long as no one finds out where you acquire your information, all should be well. But, Winterbourne, you must see there is more unrest in our country than I believe you or I could stop. The streets are teeming with men and women unhappy with our government. There may come a day when what you and I do simply is not enough.'

She tilted to her head, studying him. 'I sensed when you arrived there was something on your mind. Is there something you wish to tell me?'

How was he to begin? 'While I like you and enjoy your company, I'd like you to consider using someone else as your contact.'

Her head tilted the other way and she smiled. 'You have reconciled with your wife.'

Gabriel wasn't about to discuss Olivia with her. He chose to chew his lip instead.

She stared at him for a long time before she gave a small nod. 'Very well, I will consider it. Who?'

'My brother, Andrew.'

'He has been in here. I know of the man. Why should I trust him with my life?'

'Because I trust him with mine.'

Silence stretched between them and then she turned back to her work. 'Give me time to consider it. I will send a note with my answer in five days.'

In five days Gabriel hoped all this would be over and she would not have information for him for a very long time.

During his ride back home Gabriel debated if he should warn Olivia about Janvier. She was hurt by Manning's betrayal. He couldn't predict what she would do when she found out Janvier was also involved in this plot. Perhaps it would be best to wait until he had proof of the man's guilt.

However if his instincts were correct, Drury Lane would not be the safest place tonight. For her own safety, he needed to somehow convince Olivia not to attend tonight's performance. Knowing how stubborn she could be, he knew it might not be easy. He would send word for Andrew and then pray that his wife would be reasonable.

It was to be their first public appearance together in over five years. Olivia strolled around her dressing room, studying the gowns draped over her wardrobe doors and every available chair. Most of the eyes in the theatre would be focused on her and Gabriel tonight as London speculated on their reconciliation. And what she wore would be on everyone's lips by morning. If she were forced to endure that much scrutiny, than at least she would look spectacular while doing it.

She paused before the jonquil silk gown spread across the chair closest to her wardrobe and cocked her head. The exceptional creation had exquisite draping and a scandalously low neckline. The silk was so fine that it glided across her skin like water. Her dressmaker had outdone herself with this creation and Olivia had worn it only once because she found it too seductive for the life of a chaste duchess. This might be the perfect choice to silently announce to London that Gabriel was sharing her bed once again. Her lips rose into a satisfied grin. Perhaps it would also entice her husband to draw the curtains of their box during the interval.

Then she recalled they wouldn't be alone tonight. She let out a groan as she remembered inviting Janvier to share her box for tonight's performance. At one time she intended to invite others to join them, but had forgotten.

Gabriel would not be happy. And if she were honest with herself, she would have preferred to spend the entire night alone with Gabriel. But it would be rude to rescind her invitation to Janvier. She would not do that to her friend. It was no secret how Gabriel felt about him. The best thing to do would be to tell Gabriel about their guest before Janvier walked into their box. She just needed to find the best way to tell him their special evening would include another man.

The loud knock startled her out of her thoughts. Colette made her way around the colourful confection of slippers that were scattered about the room, and opened the door. Past her maid's shoulder, Olivia spied her husband's powerful frame encased in blue and brown. She wasn't certain if she was excited to see him or disappointed that it wasn't Bennett with a note from Janvier saying he was unable to attend this evening. When their eyes met, she decided excited was closer to what she felt.

He entered the room with commanding strides and glanced around before he clasped his hands behind his back. Had he ever witnessed her dressing room in such a state? She was certain none of his garments had ever been treated so carelessly. He was the very picture of masculine elegance and, surrounded by all her finery, she couldn't have felt more feminine.

'Forgive me, I hope I am not interrupting anything important,' he said, stopping in front of her. 'I was hoping to beg a moment of your time.' He reached for her hand and circled his thumb along her palm.

'Of course, would you care to sit?' she asked, signalling to Colette over his shoulder that they were to be left alone.

He eyed the various colourful silks, muslins and satins melting over every available surface and arched his brow. 'Your dressing room appears to be occupied with colourful gowns at the moment. I imagine there is a semblance of order to them that I cannot fathom, so I shall remain standing.'

'We can easily move one. There truly is no order that must be maintained.'

The idea that her gowns were placed about the room in a willy-nilly fashion seemed to both amuse and astonish him. Looking around her messy room, he shifted uncomfortably and she brought her hand to her lips to stifle a laugh.

'I came to speak with you about tonight,' he said, rocking on his heels.

So he was eager to announce to the *ton* their reconciliation as well. 'What exceptional timing you have. I've been trying to decide which gown to wear. Perhaps you could give me your opinion.'

He lowered his gaze and began to spin his ring.

'Is something troubling you?'

He shifted his stance again. 'No, not at all. All is well.'

It was apparent all was not well and his thoughts were elsewhere. The spinning of his ring hadn't stopped and his attention was focused on her celery-green silk gown that was spilling onto the floor from the chair on her right. That wasn't a good sign. If only he would unburden himself to her... The best she could do was to offer him comfort and hope he would eventually confide in her.

Stepping closer to him, she combed her fingers through his thick hair by his temple. She thought she saw a flash of regret in his eyes, but it was gone before she could be certain. Reaching up on her toes, she brushed her lips along his cheek that was slightly rough with early evening whiskers.

'You can tell me anything,' she said, hoping that would spur him on.

He pulled her body into his. 'You are all that is good,' he replied, placing his lips to her forehead. A warm puff of his breath danced across her eyelids.

The lovely gesture touched her heart, even though unease swept through her. Hoping his warmth would ease the chill that ran along her spine, she brought his palm up to her cheek and burrowed her nose in the cuff of his coat.

Her body froze at the familiar cloying scent lingering there.

Victoria's words came back to her, echoing loudly in her head. *'Men cannot remain faithful. It is not their nature. He will never be satisfied with just your bed.'*

It had been too easy. He had agreed to remain faithful too quickly. He didn't even love her. She wanted to vomit.

Dropping his hand as if she had been burned, she stared at the traitor before her.

'How could you?' she choked out. 'My God, I am so stupid.' Covering her lips with her hand, she backed up a step.

The confused expression on Gabriel's face was not

helping the matter. Did he think she was so naïve that she would not find out?

'Olivia, I do not understand—'

A cold sweat spread across her skin. 'You went to see that harlot again. Even after you promised you would remain faithful! You went to Madame LaGrange!' She pushed against his marble-like chest with all her might.

'Olivia—'

'I smell her on you…on your coat! I will never forget that scent. It is the same horrid smell you stank of when you came to my bedside after Nicholas was born. How could you?' Her voice wavered and she took another step back, needing to distance herself from him. 'How could a man appear honourable one minute and so selfish the next? Can you honestly look me in the eye and tell me that you were not with her today?'

'I cannot.'

'My God! What is wrong with you? How many women do you need? Or is it just that you do not want me? I have heard about her. They say she does not take the men who come to her establishment to her bed except for you. Does she know that you were in my bed again? Or did you reassure her the same way you reassured me, that she was the only one you wanted? Do you offer her pretty sentiments to ensure that she is available when your needs arise?'

Her nails were cutting into her palms and she wouldn't have been surprised if they were bleeding. 'Do you have a lover's eye of her tucked away somewhere?'

'Olivia, stop.'

He went to grab her forearms, but she stepped back. 'Do not touch me! I cannot believe a word you say. I was a fool to think I could trust you. Rest assured, it will never happen again.'

He opened his mouth to continue, but she couldn't

bear to listen to any more of his lies. And she needed to stop talking before her voice would catch and he would see just how close to tears she was.

'Get out of this room, Gabriel.'

'We need to talk about tonight—about the theatre.'

Had he even heard a word she said? A bubble of laughter escaped her lips. 'Do you honestly believe I would be seen anywhere with you now? After this, the last place on earth I care to be is surrounded by the very people who probably watched you leave her house, or should I say brothel?'

'If you would just listen to me for a moment—'

'I am done listening to you, Gabriel. We have nothing more to say to one another.' Walking towards the door, so he would not see her face, she opened it with a flourish.

'We are not finished here, Olivia.'

'Yes, Gabriel. Yes, we are.'

He hesitated before giving her a quick nod and striding out of her dressing room like a man with a purpose.

Slamming the door behind him, she collapsed to the floor, silently sobbing and wondering what it was about him that made her lose all rational behaviour and slip blindly back into wanting to trust him. Now she knew for certain, she could never trust him again. This was the last time she would allow herself to be hurt by him.

Chapter Eighteen

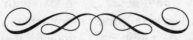

Entering his study to wait for Andrew was one of the hardest things Gabriel had ever had to do. He was fighting the need to turn around and march up the stairs to settle matters with Olivia. Things were not over between them. They couldn't be.

She just needed time to calm down. When he spoke to her next, he would find a way to smooth things over between them. At the moment Prinny's life was in eminent danger. That had to be his priority. And yet, his heart felt torn to ribbons at the pain he had inadvertently caused her. She didn't deserve this.

He sucked in a deep breath and rubbed his eyes. How could he explain this to her? He wanted to tell her why he was at Madame LaGrange's, but he just couldn't. He swore to himself he would never do something like that again. It was much too risky.

He would find another way to settle this with her tomorrow. There had to be something he could say. At least he could console himself with not having to worry that Olivia would be in danger this evening. Ignoring the burning sense of guilt, Gabriel sat at his desk to draw a sketch of Janvier and waited for Andrew.

· * * *

Olivia paced her room after allowing herself a half-hour to silently sob for the last time over Gabriel. How could she have been so stupid as to believe his sweet gestures and placating words? Was he even capable of devoting himself to only one woman? Her mother and sister had been right. Men only saw their wives as a means to an heir. They would never fall in love with them. Why would they, when men in their prominent positions could afford to have any number of women for their choosing?

He had appeared so sincere that it was easy to convince herself this time things would be different—that she mattered to him more than anyone else in the world, save Nicholas. He must have been very proud of himself that he'd duped her so easily. Obviously he had never worn that lover's eye and he'd most likely placed it in his desk drawer after he caught her snooping around his study.

Olivia stormed over to the fireplace, picked up the poker and jabbed one of the unlit logs, wishing it were Gabriel's head. She wasn't certain who she was angry with more, herself or him.

She didn't even try to hold back a loud groan as she tossed the poker aside. It landed on the carpet with a thud. Vowing to herself that she would conquer her feelings for him, she brushed her wet cheeks and rang for Colette.

She had put Gabriel behind her once before. She could do it again.

Her life these past five years had been a good one. If she wasn't already with child, she would be content with Nicholas. This room was choking her. There were too many memories of their time together here. She glanced at her bed and ran her hands over her face, uncertain how she would sleep in it again. She could no longer reside in the same house with Gabriel.

Tomorrow she would call on her sister and see if she and Nicholas could stay with Victoria until she decided where they should go. It was too late in the Season to find a house in town. Perhaps she would go off to one of the estates. Time away from Town and any reminders of Gabriel would probably be for the best. If people thought it horrid that she should avoid her commitments to steal away, that was their concern, not hers.

Just as she began scanning the walls for the artwork she would take with her, she remembered her invitation to Janvier for the theatre and threw her head back. She was swearing off men for the future. None of them was worth her time.

She knew she needed to let Janvier know that she would not be attending tonight's performance and give him a token for her box. As much as she had been looking forward to it for weeks, being surrounded by those people while feeling like she was the stupidest woman alive would be more than she could manage. She had intended to invite other friends to join them. At least she only had one person she needed to make an excuse to.

Walking through the doorway to her adjacent sitting room, she made her way directly to her escritoire prepared to write him a note. She could cry off with a headache or other such ailment. Picking up her pen, she stared at the blank paper. It lay there, mocking her.

Realising what she really needed was to get out of her house, she returned the paper to the drawer and decided to take the unprecedented step and go to his house instead.

Gabriel sat across from Andrew, resting his elbows on his desk and stabbing his fingers through his hair. His attention should be on the plans they were laying out on how they were going to catch Comte Janvier. And yet, whenever he tried to focus, his thoughts continued to turn to Olivia. Guilt was slashing his gut.

'How can you be certain that a few enquiries about Drury Lane indicates Janvier plans to kill Prinny?' Andrew asked. 'Even you have to admit, the pieces of that puzzle do not seem to fit easily together.'

Gabriel blinked and rubbed his brow, bringing his brother back in focus. 'I can't tell you for certain why I think the coincidence is too great. I simply believe it is. I believe he was looking for a fast escape or a place to hide. Why else would he be interested in the floor plan of the theatre?'

Andrew sat back and cocked his head. 'Some men might be interested in ideal locations for a tryst. Hart seems to find public venues rather stimulating. You know he is not the only one. Perhaps the Comte has plans to steal away with some fine bit of muslin.'

The image of Olivia entering Janvier's coach flashed in his mind before he quickly dismissed it. 'The man obtained the information from a harlot.'

Andrew shook his head. 'And to you that means he cannot want to lift the skirts of another? Men have been known to tup more than one woman in the course of a week.'

'Not all men,' Gabriel replied more forcefully than necessary. 'When you find the right woman for you, no other can take her place.'

Andrew stared at him as if he had spoken in a foreign language. 'Are we still discussing Comte Janvier? I have the distinct impression we have moved on and are now discussing some other annoying gentleman.'

Gabriel stood and restlessly walked around the room,

trying to pull all of his attention to the business at hand. He was having no luck.

Andrew turned in his seat and watched him. 'Would you care to tell me what is wrong? It is simply a guess, mind you, but I think the conversation has turned to you and Olivia.'

'She knows I was with Madame LaGrange this afternoon and says she wants nothing more to do with me ever again.' The words were bitter on his tongue and Gabriel wished he could have said them without hearing her own voice saying them.

'And you no longer wish to live in estrangement?'

He looked into the watchful eyes of his brother, the only person he trusted completely. 'I cannot go back to living the way we had been.'

There was a hesitation before Andrew spoke. 'I wish there was some wisdom I could impart to you right now, but I am far out of my element on this one. If you want to know who you should bet on in Friday's race or which equipage will carry you the fastest I can help you with that. I can even go a round with you when you need to attempt to beat someone to a bloody mess. However, when it comes to this…' He shook his head in pity.

Gabriel closed his eyes, to shift his thoughts away from Olivia. 'I need you to trust my instincts regarding Janvier and not make me doubt the importance of my meeting with Madame LaGrange today. The Comte wants Prinny dead. I am certain of it.'

'Very well, let's spring a trap for him tonight and then you can find a way to woo Olivia back over breakfast.'

That was what he needed. His brother's levity and confidence had him outlining his plan. 'Everyone is expecting Prinny to attend the theatre this evening. However, we both know he is still confined to Carlton House. I'll disguise myself as our Prince Regent and go to the theatre in his place. You and some of the others will mingle through the crowds and look for Janvier. Once you find him, observe him closely. The moment there is any indication he intends to cause harm, you need to stop him. And I would appreciate it if you would subdue the man before he manages to fire a shot at me.'

'I took care of the last man who shot you, I will do my best to take care of this one before it comes to that.'

Their eyes held with the weight of what Andrew had done to protect him.

'Take this sketch I drew of him. Circulate it amongst our agents so they are familiar with his face and send word to me in the royal box when you catch him.'

Andrew eyed him sideways. 'You have too much to lose here if something should happen to you. I shall play the part of Prinny and place myself in harm's way.'

Gabriel leaned forward. 'I cannot ask you to do that. This is my duty. I will not put your life in danger and risk losing you. I would not be able to live with myself if I knew I was responsible for your death.'

'You are not asking me, I am willingly volunteering.'

Before Gabriel could reply, the sound of a carriage rolling up to the house drifted in through the window and he strained his neck to peer outside. When his crest came into view, the hair on the back of his neck rose.

She wouldn't.

Flying out of his chair, Gabriel raced to the door.

'Where are you off to? Who has arrived?'

'It's Olivia, I need to stop her from leaving for the theatre.'

'But the performance doesn't begin for another few hours.'

'It doesn't matter. Our box is next to Prinny's. She is not to be anywhere near that building tonight.'

Just as he entered the hall, a vision of solemn resolve descended the stairs, adjusting her gloves. Her cool expression was focused directly in front of her, even though Gabriel was certain she knew he was standing a few feet from the bottom of the staircase.

She went to walk past him, and he reached out, holding her forearm. The warmth of her skin, exposed over the top of her glove, burn every cell of his body. Their eyes met before she arched a condescending brow.

He didn't release her. 'Where are you going?'

'I don't see how that is any concern of yours,' she replied, calmer than he expected.

'Regardless of what you believe, your welfare does concern me.'

'Then we have very different views on what that means. Release my arm, Gabriel.'

He tightened his grip. 'Where are you going, Olivia?'

'Why should it matter? Are you worried I'm heading for an assignation?'

The thought hadn't entered his mind—that is, until Olivia had just firmly placed it there. He took a deep breath and tried to force the image from his head. She cocked her head to the side as if waiting for some response. Had she asked him a question? He was so focused on getting control over the mixed emotions running through his body, he had no idea.

She appeared to continue speaking. 'Well, regardless, soon you will not have to concern yourself with my comings and goings. Tomorrow I will be leaving here with Nicholas. I find I can no longer abide residing under the same roof as you. Living apart seems a more agreeable option.'

'Olivia, do not be foolish.'

Apparently by the look on her face that was not the correct response one said in this situation.

'Gabriel, if you do not release my arm right now I will create such a spectacle that the servants and our neighbours will be speaking about it to their grandchildren years from now,' she said calmly.

Knowing her to be a woman who did not issue idle threats, he lowered his hand.

Her gaze was direct and unwavering, and her expression held no emotion. It appeared as if she had long been resigned to the fact that this would have been the outcome of their reconciliation.

His skin grew cold and clammy. He was losing her and there was nothing he could say to her now that would mend this chasm between them—unless he told her everything.

If she knew about Madame LaGrange, knew that when he was with her all he was doing was gathering intelligence, she would understand. She would see that he had never betrayed their marriage vows—not five years ago and not now. But to do that he would have to confide in her the identity of someone who worked for him. Memories of sitting in front of the fire confiding in his Uncle Peter came flooding back, making his chest ache. He swore he would never do that again with anyone.

She turned towards the door.

'Olivia—'

'I cannot do this any more, Gabriel. I have no strength left to listen to your lies.' She accepted her cloak from a visibly uncomfortable Bennett and turned towards Gabriel with sadness and resignation in her eyes. Shaking her head, she rubbed her lips together. 'You have not been a part of my life for the last five years. I shall have no problem removing you from my remaining years. And this time, I will do so while residing somewhere else. I will send word to Mr James of which of our houses I have chosen. Of course you are free to see Nicholas whenever you wish, but I will make arrangements not to be home when you do.'

Without waiting for a reply, she nodded to Bennett and walked out the door.

Ice spread through his body. She was walking out of his life and his gut was telling him it was for good. He needed to stop her. He needed to somehow fix this. And, he needed to do it now.

Gabriel took a step towards the door and heard his brother call his name, stopping him in his tracks. Demmit! Duty demanded that he go to the theatre to apprehend the Frenchman. This was what he had vowed to do. He was fighting the need to go after his wife when his father's words echoed in his mind.

'The responsibility is ours to protect the safety of our sovereign and our family. The personal sacrifices you will be forced to make will be a small price to pay for ensuring we will not endure what our friends in France had to. The lives of those you care for depend upon it.'

Living his life without Olivia was not a small sacrifice. Didn't he deserve to be happy, too?

Andrew approached his side in the empty hall. 'I can manage this for you, Gabriel. Let me impersonate Prinny. You need to trust that we can fulfil our duty even when you are not here. This operation needs to work without being solely dependent on one individual.'

Pulling in an unsteady breath, Gabriel noted Andrew's commanding stance. His younger brother, who he had teased and wrestled with as a boy, had become a formidable ally. Giving up control was not in his nature, yet

Gabriel was certain Andrew was prepared to handle such a monumental assignment.

'I assume this means you heard?'

Andrew nodded. 'I did not know what to say to you earlier, but I do know now. Listen to your instincts; they will not lie to you. Only you know what the right decision is for you. But regardless of what you decide to do, know that we will do all in our power to stop Janvier.'

Chapter Nineteen

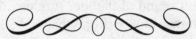

As the carriage rolled to a stop outside Janvier's town house, Olivia needed to make certain she was composed enough to hold a conversation with him without raising her voice—or throwing any objects within her reach.

Leaving Gabriel had been the hardest thing she had ever done, but she refused to be made a fool of by more of his lies. She might not have any control of his actions, but she could take some satisfaction knowing that she was the one to sever all contact. The anger she was feeling was directed at herself. He'd fooled her once, but this time she was to blame for stupidly trusting him. This time, the fault was all her own.

She had cried enough over the realisation that the man she loved would never love her in return. She was finally finished crying over what might have been. The course of her future was her own.

Placing her hand on her stomach, she took a deep breath. The air was heavy with the scent of rain. Looking out the window at the grey clouds rolling in, Olivia was grateful she reached Janvier's house before the heavens opened up and ruined her slippers. The fury bubbling under her skin was certain to spring forth with the smallest inconvenience. Janvier had played no part in Gabriel's betrayal. He didn't deserve to bear even the smallest bit of the wrath she was keeping in check.

As she walked into his home, the diamond brooch that had been affixed to her cloak fell to the floor. She took a deep breath and counted to ten. The catch had come loose and she threw it in her reticule in annoyance.

The distant sound of thunder rumbled through the dimly lit entrance hall. His grey-haired butler was just about to take her card, when the sound of approaching footsteps caught her attention. When she turned, Janvier rounded the corner dressed in fashionably tailored, black eveningwear.

She forced herself to smile at the sight of her friend. If being in his company would improve her mood, even the slightest bit, then coming to see him tonight was the right decision.

Although he appeared happy to see her, there was a brief flash of apprehension in his eyes. Showing up on a man's doorstep alone would probably warrant that reaction.

'This is a pleasant surprise,' he said.

'Good evening, Janvier. Forgive me for calling, but it was imperative I see you.' Thankfully her voice did not expose her strained emotions.

'Of course, I hope you are well?' he asked with concern.

'I am, thank you.'

He turned to his butler. 'You may leave now. I will see to Her Grace.'

The man nodded before stepping around a few trunks and heading down the hall, the sound of his footsteps growing fainter and fainter.

'May I take that for you?' he asked, gesturing to her cloak.

She allowed him to slide it from her shoulders. 'It's starting to rain,' she said, looking to break the awkwardness of the situation.

'Never a pleasant thing, however it is all too common here in England. I would offer you tea, however I suspect you would prefer a glass of claret.'

She took a deep breath and forced herself to smile. 'Thank you, I would like that.' Accepting his arm, she accompanied him to a well-appointed drawing room, styled in the fashionable Grecian manner.

The clouds outside had obscured the waning sun, leaving only the light from the fireplace and a single candelabra to cast moving shadows in the room. Walking to a table near the window, Janvier lit five additional candles. In the darkened window glass, his reflection gave away an expression of serious concern. Was it possible he was unhappy with her calling on him? She wasn't certain she could manage another rejection today.

However, when he turned to face her, his expression changed into one of welcoming interest. She shook off the foolish uneasiness and let her gaze wander from the gilt-framed landscape paintings to the marble statues resting on pedestals. If only it wasn't in poor taste to ignore him and explore his artwork.

Then she spied a rather large royal-blue Sèvres porcelain urn painted in the Empire style atop a Sèvres bisque pedestal. It was a stunning piece of craftsmanship and she wished she had time to study the intricate bucolic scene painted on it.

'That is lovely,' she commented, stepping towards it.

Janvier approached her. 'Thank you, it is a recent acquisition. Please, won't you have a seat?' he asked, gesturing to the sofa near the fire.

The gold-brocade cushions were well stuffed and she made certain to leave room next to her so that when he sat down their thighs wouldn't touch. She was being foolish. He would not try to kiss her again. She had made her feelings for him quite clear. This man was her friend. Her emotions were frayed more than she had thought to make her uneasy around Janvier.

Olivia looked into his chocolate-brown eyes that were keenly focused on her and forced herself to smile. 'I hope I have not arrived at an inconvenient time?'

'You have not. However, I must confess your arrival is a surprise. Did I misunderstand? I thought we were to meet at the theatre instead of arriving together.'

'That was our arrangement.' She rubbed her brow. 'Forgive me. It has been a trying day.'

He cocked his head to the side. 'I'm sorry to hear that. Perhaps your mood will improve tonight. I have been awaiting this evening for a long time.'

Olivia accepted the glass of claret from Janvier as he took a seat beside her. While he sipped his wine, he watched her over the rim of the crystal.

'It is an excellent vintage,' he commented, nodding towards the glass in her hand.

'I would expect no less from you.'

'Since you will not tell me what is troubling you, perhaps that wine will help return your smile.'

'Forgive me, I did not come here to dampen your evening with my mood,' she said apologetically.

'Having you in my home could never put me in an ill mood.' His grin only enhanced his handsome face.

She wished she could have unburdened herself. Being able to voice her disappointment in herself and her husband might help her straighten out the emotions that were an enormous jumble inside her head and heart. But she would not confide her secrets to someone simply because the timing was convenient.

'The wine will help,' he said, as he leaned back.

He was right. Wine would help. Only she knew she would need the entire bottle and perhaps another one as well. She brought the glass to her lips, then remembered she would need a clear head to be firm in her resolve to move out of her London residence when she returned home, so she lowered the glass to her thigh. 'This room is lovely,' she said, changing the subject.

'So this is how it is to be. I am excellent at keeping secrets. Should you choose to confide in me, I will be willing to listen.'

'I appreciate that, Janvier, I do. However, I think it best if we do not discuss it.'

'If you have not come to confide in me, what does bring you to my door? Not that I am unhappy you are here, but you can understand why I am curious.'

'I'm sorry to say I will not be able to attend the theatre this evening.'

An unreadable expression crossed his face before he took another slow sip of wine. 'I will not lie and say I am not disappointed.'

'I am disappointed as well and I was hoping to introduce you to the Prince Regent, but circumstances are preventing me from attending.'

He sat up straight, no longer appearing the epitome of relaxed elegance. 'Has His Grace forbidden you from being seen with me?'

'No, that isn't it.'

'Then help me to understand. He does not like you

spending time with me. I have seen it colour his expression when we are together.'

She shifted uncomfortably at his prodding and looked down at her glass. 'You're wrong. His Grace is not a jealous man. Of that, I can assure you.'

'You are mistaken. He is a man not accustomed to having what is his taken away.'

This discussion was pouring salt into her open wound. She needed to change the subject. She remembered seeing trunks in the entrance hall when she arrived. 'Are you leaving London?'

'I will be returning to Paris for a time to visit friends. Are you certain I cannot persuade you to change your mind about this evening?'

'I am certain, however I have no wish to deprive you of such wonderful entertainment.' Reaching into her reticule, Olivia pulled out two tokens for her box at the theatre. She held them out to Janvier. When he went to take them, she snatched her hand back.

'I have one condition. You must tell me about the performance when next we see one another.'

'Agreed.'

Clinking their glasses together, they raised them to their lips in unison. The warm spicy wine slid down her throat smoothly. There was an intensity rolling off her companion. Not for the first time since arriving here did Olivia question her decision to deliver the tokens herself.

'As you are aware,' she said, 'my box is to the left of the royal box. The hallway can become crowded with people hoping to catch sight of the royal family. It's best to arrive early, if possible, to avoid the crush.'

'The idea of becoming lost in a crowd does not distress me.'

She took another sip, this time a longer one, and she

felt her body begin to soften into the gold brocade cushion. 'I hope you enjoy your evening. Although I realise it is late, please ask anyone you wish to accompany you. There is no reason you need to attend alone.'

'That is very kind of you.'

'Have you not heard? I am all that is kindness,' she said, taking an even longer drink.

He grinned in amusement. 'I see the wine is helping. Allow me to pour you some more.'

Glancing into her glass, Olivia raised her eyebrows. When had she finished all of her wine? It was exceptional and after the day she had, she was entitled to enjoy an excellent vintage. She handed him her glass and took in his well-made form as he sauntered over to the cellaret housing numerous bottles of wine.

Her time with Gabriel was over. She would never know a man's touch again—unless, she took a lover.

Janvier had impressive shoulders, which were showcased nicely by the cut of his black tailcoat. His waist and hips were slim—much slimmer than Gabriel's more muscular form. Janvier's build was long and graceful. Gabriel's form suggested strength and power.

What would it feel like to be held in the arms of a man Janvier's size?

Just as she was trying to imagine such an encounter, he looked at her from across the room.

'I would love to know what you are thinking.'

Olivia did not want to contemplate what her expression had obviously betrayed. 'I was thinking of the wine.'

Stalking towards her with two glasses in his hands, his face became almost tiger like. 'I am certain you were contemplating something delicious. I do not believe it to be the wine, though.' Stopping in front of her, he stood there with a heated gaze looking down at her. 'I know you feel this attraction between us.'

He was attractive, but Olivia hadn't felt any desire for him. From the time he'd kissed her in his carriage, to staring into his brown eyes now, her body wasn't flush with the need to press herself against him and feel him buried deep inside of her. Those were the feelings her foolish body had only for Gabriel. She peered closer at Janvier as if she could will herself into a state of arousal.

Why couldn't he make her heart race and her body quiver in her most intimate places? If he had, she might have been able to transfer some of the feelings she had for Gabriel to Janvier. She was destined to die alone with only the love of Nicholas and, God willing, her grandchildren—but without a man's love and comforting touch.

And it was all Gabriel's fault!

The clock on the mantel began to chime and Janvier turned his head to look. In that brief instance, she studied him again.

Still nothing.

He turned back to her and again caught her examining his form. She really needed to leave before she embarrassed herself further.

'You do feel this attraction. However, if we begin exploring our shared passion now, I will miss the performance.'

Well, that was insulting. He wanted her, but not enough to give up seeing the performance of a play.

Men were toads!

This day had gone from wonderful, to horrible, to absurd in a ridiculously short period of time. She needed to leave, return to her rooms and pack her things. Tomorrow she would be at Victoria's house, where she could begin to arrange a new life for herself and Nicholas.

She picked up her reticule, looped the braided handle around her wrist and rose from the sofa. 'I shall be off.'

'Forgive me, I did not mean for you to leave immediately.' He held out her refilled glass. 'We should drink to friendship before you leave.'

She stared at the glass and imagined throwing the contents into his face. But after the day she had had, numbing herself with more wine sounded like a better notion. She accepted the glass and his watchful gaze never left her as he took a sip from his glass. Did he, too, wonder if she was planning on decorating his form with the ruby liquid?

Olivia raised her glass to her lips.

'Don't you dare drink that, Olivia,' boomed a familiar voice from the doorway.

Her hand jerked, sloshing a small amount of the red wine over the side of the glass and down the front of the skirt of her gown. Uttering an unladylike word, she placed her glass on the table.

'What in the world are you doing here?' she demanded, glaring at Gabriel.

Chapter Twenty

Gabriel had ridden as fast as he could through the streets of Mayfair to reach Olivia. She was his world and he was not about to lose her—not this time. He needed to increase Bennett's wages for his discretion during her departure and for supplying Gabriel with the address she had given her coachman. He'd assumed she would be going to her sister's house. Victoria and Olivia had always been close and he knew in his bones she would be the one person Olivia would turn to for help. But this address had been foreign to him.

When Gabriel had arrived at the nondescript town house, he had run out of the names of people he thought might occupy the building. Never in his wildest imaginings did he think his wife would turn to Janvier. It wasn't until his knock went unanswered and he picked the lock on the front door, that he realised he was in the home of the blackguard he had been preparing to apprehend that very night—a man who Gabriel had just seen place something from a small vial into Olivia's wineglass.

After following the sound of voices, he stood outside the doorway to the drawing room and listened to their unguarded conversation. A part of him wanted to storm into the room and remove his wife from this dangerous man. But this other part of him, this sick twisted part that would be bound forever by a sense of duty, wanted to listen and see if the Frenchman revealed his plans.

It wasn't until he saw Olivia raise the glass to her lips that he knew he needed to interrupt the intimate tête-à-tête before his wife was poisoned. It was taking all of Gabriel's control not to rip the man limb from limb.

'Your Grace,' said the Frenchman, his eyes narrowed on Gabriel. 'I had not heard your knock.'

'Neither did your staff.'

'My staff is now off for the evening. I'm afraid there is no longer anyone here attending the door.'

Olivia's attention had been focused on blotting up the wine from her skirt until Janvier uttered his last statement. 'You had not told me you had given your staff the night off.'

The man smiled at Olivia and Gabriel's right hand tightened into a fist.

'You had not asked,' Janvier replied with a smug smirk.

That was all it took. Thoughts of trapping the man in his plan no longer mattered. He was going to break his legs so he wouldn't have the opportunity to go to the theatre. Gabriel advanced into the room, but stopped suddenly at the sight of Olivia picking up her glass.

'I told you not to drink that.'

'As if I have any interest in what you want.' She brought the glass closer to her lips.

He snatched it out of her hand.

'I am not tipsy and that glass will not make me the least bit inebriated. Give it back to me.'

'No.'

'No?' She stood up and crossed her arms.

'Your friend put something in your glass.'

'Don't be absurd, Janvier would never do such a thing.'

'I resent such an insinuation,' the Frenchman stated, placing his own glass down on the nearest table.

'I wasn't insinuating anything. I am stating a fact that you put something into my wife's glass. What is in here?'

'Nothing but some of my finest wine.'

Gabriel held the glass out to Janvier. 'Then why don't you have a sip?' He tilted the glass and surveyed the contents. 'There isn't much left. It would be a shame to waste it.'

Olivia let out an exasperated breath. 'I have no notion of what you think you are trying to prove. Are you attempting to have me question everyone I associate with?' She took the glass from him and almost had it to her lips when he swatted it out of her hand. It flew across the room, landing with a crash and splattering the remainder of the wine around the fine furnishings and his wife.

He knew the look on her face. She was incredulous and he had pushed her too far. His gaze dropped to the reticule she was holding and he considered how heavy it might be.

She glared at him and it looked as if she might be trembling with rage. 'You have thoroughly and completely ruined this dress.'

He wanted to laugh at the absurdity of her statement, spoken through clenched teeth, but he needed to concentrate on Janvier. 'What did you put in it?'

'You believe I wish to kill her? I adore her. Why would I do such a thing?'

'Why indeed? But I did see you place something in her glass from a small vial.'

'I did no such thing.' But his eyes shifted. It was a gesture his very astute wife did not miss.

She stepped closer and searched Janvier's eyes. 'Did you?' she asked as if she could not believe her friend could be so evil.

His gaze darted from her to Gabriel and back again. A cold shiver ran along Gabriel's spine, raising the hairs on his neck. There was no telling how Janvier would react to being cornered and Olivia was standing too close to him. Her safety was paramount. Gabriel needed to distract him and keep her out of harm's way.

'Is that what you planned to use tonight to kill the Prince Regent at Drury Lane?'

He should bang his head into a wall. That was the worst distraction in the history of Britain—no, the world! His concern for Olivia had stopped his brain from thinking clearly. He knew enough not to reveal his hand too early and he had just shown Janvier all of his cards.

Olivia was about to back away from Janvier when the Frenchman spun her around by the waist and pulled her back against his front. Gabriel reached behind him under his coat and pulled out his double-barrel pistol just as Janvier removed a sharp knife from his sleeve. The silver of the blade at Olivia's throat flashed in the candlelight.

They were at an impasse. Olivia remained motionless. The sound of her breathing was as loud in Gabriel's ears as if her head had been resting on his shoulder. He needed to keep his entire concentration on Janvier to read any signs that would indicate what this man was about to do. He knew he had to block out Olivia entirely, or he risked being caught again by surprise.

'Well, it appears we are both not what the world sees. How is it you are aware of plans against your monarch?'

'I have heard rumblings.'

'I see. And those rumblings brought you to my door? Convenient.'

'Coincidence. My wife is here. I came to bring her home.'

'But that will not happen. You see, your wife will be leaving with me, or she will die because of you. If you had done nothing to cause her to arrive at my doorstep, none of this would be happening. The evening would have ended very differently.'

Guilt burned throughout Gabriel's body at the truth that was boldly stated.

'That was not poison in her glass, but something to make her sleep for hours,' Janvier continued. 'It occurred to me during our visit that I could take her to France with me as insurance, shall we say. But alas, you have forced my hand.' He wiggled the blade by her throat. 'I will be leaving with your wife now, Winterbourne, and you will remain here for three hours. Should you try and stop me, I will not hesitate to kill her.'

'I will not allow you to take her. Let her go and we can resolve this like men, not like children who hide behind a woman's skirt.'

'Should I release her, you will not let me leave here a free man. I know the penalty for what you are accusing me of and I have no intention to die now.'

Olivia tried to edge her way closer to the table with the large vase, but Janvier jerked her back. 'Do not move,' he whispered in her ear. 'I should hate to mar that pretty neck of yours.'

'You said you wanted me to go to France with you,' Olivia whispered. 'I will go willingly. There is no need for any of this.'

'Why should I believe you would do so? I thought to take you with me in the event I needed to bargain your life should my actions be discovered. And now it seems I need you more than ever. Make no mistake, I will injure you should you or your husband force my hand. And if you startle me with any sudden movements, there is no telling how much my hand will move.'

She swallowed deeply, causing Gabriel's hands to sweat as he continued to point his gun at Janvier.

'You don't even know Prinny,' she said. 'What reason could you possibly have for wanting him dead?'

'Your beloved friend has been boldly bragging about all the spoils of war he has acquired—items that rightfully belong to France and not Britain—and especially not to that fat, stupid man. He boasts how he defeated France. How he has brought down Napoleon. What is next? Will he decide to take France as well? I spit at his arrogance. We will not be subject to the rule of an idiot, forced to call ourselves British subjects. Surely you can understand how that would not be acceptable to me or any Frenchman.'

Gabriel was trying to calculate the best angle for a shot at Janvier that would pose no danger to Olivia, but he was having no luck. His heart was pounding so hard it must have been visible through his coat. There had to be a way to get Janvier to release her.

'Of course I understand.' Olivia's soothing voice broke the silence.

'How could I live with myself if I saw my family and friends harmed by British tyranny?' His gaze remained fixed on Gabriel.

'So you are doing this for your family and friends back home?' she asked softly.

'I would die for those that I hold dear,' he spat out.

'Please, do not say such a thing,' Olivia said gently. 'Surely there must be a peaceful way to settle this. Prinny is sympathetic to the Bourbons.'

In his peripheral vision Gabriel noticed Olivia slowly

and carefully opening the strings of the reticule she held down in front of her. If Janvier caught her movement, he might slit her throat. A cold clamminess crept along Gabriel's skin. Why couldn't that woman do as she was told?

'For how long will his sympathies last? With your Regent eliminated, Britain will focus inward. I do not believe his brothers have the same fascination with France. We will be free of a British threat.'

Olivia took in a shallow breath. 'I understand you are doing what you must to protect your family. That is to be commended.'

Why did Gabriel feel as if the words she spoke were directed at him? Were these to be her last words to him? He swallowed hard and forced his mind to focus on getting her free from Janvier.

'That is one of the things I admire about you,' said the Frenchman. 'You are an intelligent woman.'

'I like to believe so.'

Janvier let out a cry of pain.

He dropped his arms from Olivia as the knife fell to the ground. '*Salope*,' he growled through clenched teeth while grasping his thigh.

'You said you admired me,' she sneered back, quickly darting out of his way.

Stunned at his wife's actions, it took a few seconds for Gabriel to realise he had a clear shot at Janvier. But before he was able to pull the trigger, Olivia grabbed the Sèvres vase and smashed the man over the head with enough force to cause him to collapse to the ground. The pieces of the vase scattered around him.

She surveyed his still form cautiously. 'You don't think he is dead, do you? I find I am not bloodthirsty enough to kill him.'

All the bones in Gabriel's body disintegrated.

She was alive.

She was safe.

And she was staring at him, waiting for an answer.

Stepping closer to the motionless Frenchman, Gabriel could see what she had done to impede him. There, embedded in his thigh, sparkled a brooch encrusted with diamonds. He poked his foot into the man's side. 'He is still breathing. Do you need a moment?' Gabriel certainly felt like he did. 'Perhaps you should sit down.'

She brushed her shaking hands against her skirt, cleaning off the remnants of the porcelain vase. 'Do not concern yourself with me. Tell me what we do now.'

We? Gabriel marvelled at her fortitude. He placed his pistol back under his coat. '*We* are not doing anything. You are going to return home and I will see that he is taken into custody.'

'You would not have been able to subdue him without me.'

That was a bit of an overstatement, but Gabriel thought it best to let her feel as she did. The first time one captured a criminal it was heady stuff.

'You are not sending me home while you see this through,' she continued.

She was too stubborn for her own good. Kneeling down before her, Gabriel reached under her skirt and tore a strip off the bottom of her chemise.

She slapped his hand away. 'Was the destruction of this gown with the wine not sufficient enough that you felt a need to attack the rest of my wardrobe as well?'

Stepping over to Janvier, Gabriel rolled him over with his boot, brought the man's hands behind his back, and twisted the linen around his hands. 'It's prudent to ensure he will not get away should he wake up.'

Olivia crossed her arms. 'What do we do with him?'

'Ordinarily I would have Bow Street hold him. But I will not take the chance he has a sympathiser there. I know of a place to take him for now.'

'Richmond?' She didn't even wait for him to reply, as if the answer was a foregone conclusion. 'How did you know Janvier was planning on killing Prinny tonight?'

They were perilously close to a topic he had never wanted to discuss with her. 'I received intelligence that led me to believe it was what he planned.'

'So you arrived here to stop him.'

'No, I had no idea where he lived. The plan was to stop him at the theatre.'

'You expect me to believe you intended to give up capturing a man who wanted Prinny dead to come after me?'

'I did come after you. Why you decided to come here is your tale to tell and you will tell me, Olivia.'

'Janvier was to join us tonight to see Mrs Siddons. Since I would no longer be attending the performance, I came here to give him the tokens to our box.'

Prinny's assassin would have been sitting with them, mere feet from his intended target. Gabriel pushed his thumb against the bridge of his nose. 'I was going to impersonate Prinny tonight, but I needed to come after you so someone else has taken my place. There are people throughout the theatre looking for Janvier.'

'You will notify them the vile beast has been captured?'

'I will, but I doubt I will use those exact words. I will go myself to inform them once I have Janvier secure.'

Stepping closer to him, she rested her hands on her hips as if her small stature could intimidate him into agreeing to what she wanted. 'I will go with you.'

How she could try his patience. At least she was speaking to him. As he'd raced through the street of Mayfair to find her, he wasn't certain he could convince her to see him, let alone speak with him. It was time to tread carefully.

He rubbed his forehead and stared at the unconscious Comte. 'Why are you not hysterical? I believe most women, if a knife were held to their throats, would be a shaking, sobbing mess. But you appear to be unaffected.'

'I have had a horrid day! I am too angry at this moment to even consider crying!'

She'd saved herself and Prinny by smashing that piece of porcelain over Janvier's head. If she wasn't his wife, he would think of recruiting her. 'Very well, you will go with me to Richmond. I will take Homer and you will follow in your coach. In light of this evening's events and your actions you have every right to see this through to the end. However, I need your word that whomever you see me converse with, you will forget their identities by morning. Trusting people is not in my nature. I need to know I can trust you.'

'You're speaking of trust? Oh, that is almost too much to bear,' she sputtered. He waited for her to agree to his condition and she must have realised he would not be taking her anywhere until she gave him her promise. 'You have my word. Now, how do we get his unconscious form out of here without anyone seeing?'

'Help me empty one of the trunks in the entrance hall, then go fetch your coachman. We will strap him to the roof of your carriage in the trunk and take him to my safe house in Richmond. He will be held there under guard until his trial. By my estimates, he will swing in less than a week.'

Once Janvier was secure in Richmond, Gabriel needed to inform those at the theatre the Frenchman had been apprehended. Of course Olivia wasn't content to return home while he did that and with more coaxing on her part he let her accompany him. Strangely enough, the idea of sharing this with her was no longer terrifying.

They had not spoken one word to each other since they had left Richmond and as her carriage rolled to a stop in front of the theatre Gabriel glanced at his wife, who sat silently across from him staring out the window.

He rubbed the stone of his ring through his leather glove. 'Remember, you are to tell no one what you see tonight. Trusting you with this is harder for me than you realise, Olivia. I need you to promise that you will not tell even Victoria.'

'I understand and have already given you my word. Shall we go in now?'

Gabriel opened the carriage door and jumped down onto the pavement. Without pulling down the step he reached into the carriage, grabbed Olivia by the waist and lowered her to the wet ground.

Olivia discovered it wasn't easy to keep her cloak closed to hide the disastrous state of her gown when Gabriel took it upon himself to lift her out of her carriage. Thankfully the rain had stopped. However, the puddles that shone in the light from the windows proved a nuisance as they navigated their way along the pavement to the door of the theatre. Heads turned as they made their way inside.

This should have been a triumphant moment. This should have been the beginning of a new life together. Instead, their arrival together was a sham.

'This changes nothing between us,' she whispered to Gabriel, lest he need clarification of her feelings for him. 'I am here with you to see this through, not because I have any intention of resuming an amiable marriage with you.'

'The world does not need to know that at the moment. Our appearance together should be believable, so I suggest you smile as if you are genuinely happy to be on my arm.'

It would be a cold day in hell before she was ever happy to be with him again. Pulling from her years of experience disguising her feelings for him when they were in public, Olivia flashed him a pleasant smile. It must have been believable, because he gave a slight nod of his head and grinned at her with that annoying heart-melting smile of his.

The confines of the theatre amplified the buzzing around them, as happy voices greeted friends and audible whispers carried their names across the lobby. Aside from their unprecedented arrival together, she was certain people were questioning their lack of formal evening attire fitting such an occasion. That busybody the Duchess of Skeffington even had the gall to raise her quizzing glass at them. Thankfully Olivia's cloak was long enough that it covered her entire gown.

Olivia raised her chin and glanced over at Gabriel, who was discreetly scanning the crowd.

'Would I know any of your people? It would expedite our search if we were both looking.'

'I need to find Lord Hartwick,' he whispered into her ear.

She tried to school her features at her disbelief. 'Surely you don't mean the Earl of Hartwick?'

'The one and the same.'

'But he's—'

'An immeasurable asset in protecting the Crown.'

'Truly?'

'Truly. Now tell me if you see him.'

'Perhaps we should search the ladies' retiring room. I have seen him hovering outside of it on a number of occasions.'

'Not tonight—tonight he has a job to do.'

It was not long before they spotted the earl in his formal black evening attire casually leaning against the banister leading up to the boxes. He should have been the one to garner all the attention in the theatre with his handsome face. And yet for all his looks and charm, Olivia had no desire to wrap herself around him and get lost in his reputed skills. She glanced at the man next to her and wondered for the hundredth time what it was about Gabriel that set her body on fire—correction, *had* set her body on fire. Now he would simply be the man she'd married and once lived with.

Directing her attention back to Lord Hartwick, she watched him speak to a dark-haired woman dressed in a silvery-blue gown. Although one might think he was taken with his companion, Olivia could see his attention was on the crowd of people moving around him. Then his vibrant blue-eyed gaze locked with Gabriel's. When he shifted his focus to Olivia, he raised an inquisitive brow.

After excusing himself to his companion, Hartwick strolled up to them. 'Now I will say what everyone in this room is thinking. I am surprised to see the two of you together. Care to share?' he said with tilt of his head.

'Not in the least,' Gabriel replied.

Hartwick let out a deep chuckle and looked past Olivia to continue studying the crowd.

'We have to alter our plans,' Gabriel commented, flecking a speck from his shoulder. 'Our French friend is being detained in a safe location even as we speak. Has Prinny arrived?'

Hartwick raked his gloved hand through his hair, moving a shiny black lock out of his eyes. 'He has. Looking a tad sour, if you ask me.' He attempted to suppress a grin and then took measure of Olivia.

She shifted slightly under his piercing gaze.

'This is an interesting conversation for us to have,' he continued.

Olivia pulled her shoulders back and smiled warmly as if he paid her the nicest compliment. 'Situations have been brought to my attention due to unforeseen circumstances that required it. I assure you, I am the soul of discretion, my lord.'

He nodded slowly and tossed his head to the side to shift the lock of hair that found its way back over his eye. 'You always have been, madam. Now you know two of my secrets and I know none of yours. That does not seem at all fair.'

That small bit of information had not gone unnoticed by Gabriel, who looked down at her with a questioning gaze. There was no need to inform him she'd helped the earl avoid an unfortunate encounter with an unhappy husband by pulling him into her room at a house party two years ago.

Hartwick stepped a bit closer. 'So now I suppose you wish me to inform everyone they are no longer in search of the Frenchman.'

'That would be most helpful. I still want them to be diligent. There is no harm in remaining alert for the rest of the evening,' Gabriel replied.

Two fashionable women walked slowly past them and giggled behind their fans at Hartwick's obvious attention.

Olivia's attention wandered as she let the men discuss whatever it was men discussed when they were together. She watched the people moving up the staircase on their way to the boxes when her eyes settled on a willowy, dark-haired woman with fine features and a prominent dark brow. She was dressed in black and was not completely hidden by the moving crowd. Straining her neck, Olivia moved away from the men to get a better view of the woman's face. Some distant memory tugged at her as she tried to place how she knew the woman.

The slight pressure at her right elbow made her jump and she looked over, realising Gabriel had followed her.

'What is it?' he asked, leaning down with keen interest.

'I thought I saw someone I might have known.' She tightened her cloak. 'Shall we see how Prinny is faring, or do we need to locate more of your acquaintances?'

He led her to the stairs by her elbow. 'No, I believe Prinny will be very happy to see us. Let's not keep him waiting.'

They were granted permission to enter from the guards standing outside the royal box. As she crossed the threshold the sight of 'Prinny' in the second row of the otherwise empty box gave her pause. The man wore a wig that so closely resembled Prinny's own hair, one would think it was made from strands gathered from the Regent's own head. He was in profile, but his puffy cheeks marked him as an accurate replica of her friend.

The impostor turned his head to face them and Gabriel executed a respectful bow. It took a moment for Olivia to gather herself to curtsy. He appeared surprised to see them and eyed both of them from top to bottom before standing up and walking to the back corner of the box.

'My, this is a surprise, don't you know?' came the deep voice she knew she'd heard before.

Looking into a pair of familiar hazel eyes, she recognised Andrew at once.

'You?'

'Aye, it's me. Wot, wot? You look as if you've seen a ghost, my dear.'

It was difficult to keep a straight face with Andrew using a number of Prinny's favourite sayings—sayings Andrew would never think to use.

'You appear well,' Gabriel said.

'Prinny' smiled and patted his stomach as an array of serving trays were added to the table set out with at least ten trays of delicacies against the wall. 'The selection is impressive.' He leaned in closer and lowered his voice to a whisper. 'Do you have news for me, or is this simply a social call?'

'Our Frenchman is secured in Richmond.'

'How?'

'Imagine my surprise when I realised his house was my destination this evening.'

Andrew looked at Olivia, giving her a thorough appraisal. 'That's an interesting destination in light of this evening's plans.'

'I had nothing to do with that,' she stated firmly, looking him square in the eye.

'And yet, you sought him out.'

'To give him tokens to my box. He was to join me here tonight.' Could Andrew truly be questioning her motivation? 'Are you insinuating—?'

Gabriel stepped closer to her. 'There is no insinuation. Is there?'

Andrew shifted his gaze back and forth between them. 'If you feel there is no reason to make one.'

'There is not. Olivia is responsible for his capture.'

'And how did she do that?'

She pulled her shoulders back and raised her chin. 'With a brooch and a vase.'

Andrew jerked his head back. 'Surely I misheard.'

'You did not.'

He turned to Gabriel. 'So you do have an accurate assessment of her character.'

Gabriel crossed his arms and let out a breath. 'I told you.'

'Told him what?'

'That you have a temper.'

She pressed her lips together and gave her right glove a firm tug. 'Well, in a few short hours, Gabriel, you won't have the opportunity to witness my temper.'

He placed his hands on his hips in a commanding stance. 'That is up for debate.'

She unintentionally mimicked his posture. 'No, it is not.'

'Yes, it is.'

'No, it is not.'

Andrew cleared his throat. 'Well it was lovely chatting with you. Think I'll see what the footmen have brought me before it turns cold. Don't you know? Wot? Wot?'

They stood staring at one another, silently daring the other to move. Olivia won when Gabriel pulled her by the arm out into the hall.

'We are settling this right now.'

She tugged her arm out of his grasp. 'I am not discussing anything with you in the hallway of Drury Lane.'

'Then we will adjourn to our box, but make no mistake, Duchess, we are having this discussion.'

The riotous applause and cheering from the audience broke the silence between them as he dragged her into their box. Storming to the front, he jerked the curtains closed. Apparently he wasn't considering what people would think about the curtains being drawn in their box after they had been seen together earlier.

He advanced on her so he stood less than a foot away. 'You are not leaving me.'

Even with his noble actions, she could not forgive this last betrayal—and it would be the last. She could not endure crushing hurt like this again.

'It is obvious I am not enough for you. When I send out cards with my new address it will cease the chatter about us and everyone will know we care nothing for one another.'

All of Britain might believe that, but deep down she knew she still loved him and probably always would. Physical distance was the only solution she had to save what was left of her heart.

He grabbed both her hands, and she tried to pull away. His grasp tightened, though not painfully. 'There is no one else I need. You are more than enough for me.' He looked her in the eye. 'I have sacrificed much for what I do, but I will no longer sacrifice my marriage with you.'

'Fire! Fire!' The shout came from right outside their box.

Olivia turned towards the door and sucked in a deep exploratory breath. There was a faint scent of wood burning. They needed to leave right away.

'Andrew,' Gabriel muttered and tugged her by the hand, hauling them out into the hall.

Chapter Twenty-One

Still grasping Olivia's hand, Gabriel stopped outside their box and scanned the crowd of people stampeding past them on their way to the staircase. Panicked shouts and cries echoed off the walls as people sought out friends and family. A door diagonal from them was open and men were already forming a bucket brigade and throwing water into the smoking room.

This was impossible. He didn't even know who to look for.

Andrew exited the royal box behind two guards. His knowing gaze shot to Gabriel. He nodded in agreement that this was no coincidence. They needed Andrew out of the theatre quickly before it either burnt down or he was murdered.

A damp woodsy smell filled the hall as panicked people continued to run past them, shouting for their friends and warning everyone to run for their lives. This was a diversion. Gabriel knew it. He was just about to yell to Andrew to return to the royal box, when Olivia tugged at his sleeve.

'There she is, the woman in black. She's working with Janvier.' She was pointing to a tall thin woman with dark hair, standing thirty feet from them staring at Andrew.

Before he could ask about her assumption, the woman pulled a gun from her reticule and aimed it at his brother.

In an instant he was back in the garden in Richmond years earlier. Peter was pointing a gun at him. 'I'm sorry. I can't allow you to stop their plan,' his uncle had said, looking down at him and cocking the hammer of the pistol.

Gabriel closed his eyes at the resignation on his uncle's face, preparing for the end. The bullet ripped through his torso, taking his breath with it. Then he heard Peter cock back the hammer of the second barrel. He was aiming the gun now at Gabriel's head. Then suddenly a shot rang out and his uncle fell back. Andrew had come out of nowhere and saved him, killing Peter in the process.

He could never stand by and watch Andrew die. Jumping between the barrel of the woman's pistol and Andrew, Gabriel tackled his brother to the ground—and felt the burn of a bullet bury itself in his shoulder.

The crack of gunfire tore through the commotion in the hall, and Olivia watched a number of men tackle the woman in black to the ground. After wrestling the gun out of her hand, they held her firmly to the ground.

'*Murder, murder.*'
'*Has His Highness been shot?*'
'*We have her. We have the cutthroat.*'
'*The Duke of Winterbourne has saved His Highness.*'
'*Oh, my God, is he dead?*'

That last shout turned her legs to jelly and she looked over at the motionless form of her husband, lying atop Andrew. A stain of dark crimson was spreading near the shoulder of his coat.

Why wasn't he moving?

She ran to him, dropping to her knees just as he let out an agonised groan of pain.

'See that she is secure,' she yelled to the guard closest to her. 'And do not let them take her anywhere until you hear from His Royal Highness what should be done with her.'

Gabriel lifted himself off Andrew while clutching his right shoulder and fell back against the wall. Blood oozed through his gloved fingers. The pain must have been excruciating, if his grimace was any indication. 'Bloody hell, I hate being shot,' he gritted through his teeth.

Seeing him like this was making Olivia's hands shake. He was too young to die.

Blast him for making her feel anything towards him beside anger and betrayal. Part of her wanted to cradle him in her arms and take away his pain. Another part of her wanted to rail at him for jumping in the path of a bullet and getting shot. What was the appropriate thing to say to someone at a time like this?

'You need to find a new hobby.'

A spurt of laughter sneaked out between his clenched teeth before he pressed his lips together.

Shouting continued around them as people began to ignore the extinguished fire and focus their attention on the man who'd saved 'Prince George'.

Andrew knelt next to him, concern etched across his fake brows. 'We need to get you home.'

Olivia stood near the window of her husband's bedchamber, watching his valet dig a bullet out of his right shoulder. When had her life taken such an abrupt turn? She'd insisted they should call a physician, but Gabriel assured her Hodges would do a fine job. After what felt like an hour of digging, she wasn't certain that was the case.

Thunder rumbled and a flash of lightning exploded in the room as rain pelted the windowpanes. She rubbed the goose pimples on her arms and watched Bennett hold Gabriel's shoulder down as Hodges continued to dig at the stubborn ball of lead. Gabriel's hair was sticking up in all directions and his bare chest glistened with sweat in the glow of the candlelight. Having the bullet removed must have been incredibly painful, even with the long drink of brandy he took before Hodges began his attack. Periodically he would clench his teeth, the veins in his neck straining as he pushed his head back into his pillows. His breathing was rapid and shallow, and his left hand was clenched into a tight fist, his knuckles visibly white.

At the next burst of lightning she walked slowly over to the bed. The coppery smell of blood filled the air. 'What is taking so long?'

Hodges glanced up from his work. 'The ball is lodged deep, near a bone.' He began to dig again and Gabriel's body stiffened.

She should stroke his brow. She should hold his hand. She should do something to offer him comfort. Instead she wrapped her arms around herself, unable to touch him. 'Can't we give him more brandy, or try laudanum?'

Hodges shook his head. 'His Grace abhors laudanum. Best not to stop and just have at it.'

Gabriel squeezed his eyes shut and nodded. 'Tell me… about…the woman in black.'

He needed a distraction. That she could give. 'I saw her with Janvier once outside Madame Devy's. He had appeared unhappy that I had seen them together.'

He nodded and squeezed his eyes shut again.

There was a 'clunk' followed by the sound of the lead ball rolling around in the silver bowl. In unison Gabriel, Bennett and Olivia let out an audible sigh of relief.

'It's out,' Hodges said, releasing a breath. 'I'll stitch it up and then attend to these bloody sheets.'

A large stack of sheets had been placed under Gabriel's right shoulder. It appeared Hodges had previous experience handling situations such as this. How many times had Gabriel been shot? She recalled the scar Nicholas had found on him. Were there others?

Her thoughts turned to Andrew, who had changed out of his disguise and headed to Richmond to see to the interrogation of the woman in black and Janvier. If she hadn't spotted that woman...if she had not seen her with Janvier...would Andrew still be alive?

It wasn't long before Gabriel's wound was stitched, bandaged and the crimson sheets removed from under him. Hodges had given him another large glass of brandy before leaving the room with Bennett.

Now, they were alone.

Gabriel was taking gulps of brandy as he lay with his eyes closed, propped up by a mountain of pillows. His breathing was still erratic. Finally he handed over the empty glass and looked at her with sleepy eyes. Thunder rumbled in the distance.

'Thank you for staying.'

'Is there anything I can do to ease your pain?'

He blinked with heavy lids. 'Do not leave me.'

She wasn't sure if he meant for the time being or forever. Watching him endure the painful bullet extraction and knowing he had placed his own life before Andrew's had jumbled her emotions. And she didn't like it one bit. 'I will be here should you need anything.'

In what felt like a few short moments, his breathing was deep and even. At least he could sleep.

Olivia tried to recall the last time she had been in the very masculine room, with its forest-green walls and dark furnishings. Her gaze skimmed over his large tester bed with the silk-brocade bed hangings and settled on the two wingback chairs by the fireplace. She would guard his bedside from there.

As she rested her head against the back of the chair, her eyes were drawn to a hint of beige cloth sticking out from under Gabriel's bed. Getting down on her hands and knees, she pulled out a long rolled-up piece of canvas, tied with a black ribbon. Curious what he would keep in such an unusual location, she moved closer to the fireplace and untied the ribbon. The sight of her unfinished portrait left her breathless.

Gabriel hated the portrait. He must not have wanted anyone to find it. But why hadn't he burned it? Or shot holes through it as he had done with the candles in their ballroom?

She stood with her hands on her hips over the painting that had resulted in the downfall of two men she had considered her friends. There was a low flame in the fireplace, giving Olivia a way to remove some memories of the past few weeks. The canvas burned quickly, replacing the coppery smell of blood in the room with smoke. All that was left was ash. The portrait was gone, as if all her sittings had never happened. If only she could erase her feelings for Gabriel that easily.

Thinking about him was making her head hurt along with her heart. She needed to find something to occupy herself until morning. Then she would direct Colette to pack her things and she and Nicholas would leave for Victoria's.

It was difficult for Gabriel to open his eyes to the sound of Bennett's voice and the soft patter of rain. He stretched his legs under the piles of blankets and went to turn onto his right side. That's when the shooting pain ripped through his shoulder.

'Easy, sir,' his butler said in a soft whisper. 'Your injury is fresh.'

It was as if his mind had blocked out the events of the last few hours except for the image of Olivia at his bedside. He struggled to sit up with the aid of Bennett. 'Where is my wife?' He knew he sounded a bit panic-stricken, but at the moment he didn't care.

A terrible sense of foreboding gripped him. The pain in his heart outweighed that of his wound. He no longer believed love was purely sentimental drivel reserved for schoolboys and poets. He knew in his heart he loved Olivia. He probably always had. And she needed to know. It didn't matter the hour. He would go to Victoria's and demand to speak with her. Throwing back the covers, he swung his legs around to stand. The sudden movement made him dizzy.

'Sir, please,' Bennett begged, 'you will open your wound if you persist in moving so.'

Nothing was going to stop him from going to her. He grabbed Bennett by the arm and realised his servant was in his banyan. Bennett's astonishment at being grabbed by his employer was obvious.

'Forgive me,' Gabriel said, releasing his grip. 'Fetch Hodges, I need to get dressed.'

'But, sir, she is over there.' Bennett pointed to Olivia's huddled form, curled up in one of the chairs by the fireplace.

She was asleep—in his room—on his chair. She hadn't left him. Relief flooded his body in a rush and he was grateful he wasn't standing.

'I woke you because this letter arrived.'

Gabriel took the folded paper from Bennett, taking note of his brother's seal. 'What time is it?'

'Five o'clock. May I offer you anything? Shall we check your bandage?'

The dressing was still pristine. That was a good sign. 'No, that will be all for the night.'

His butler hesitated before leaving the room. The minute the door closed, Gabriel rubbed away tears that had been waiting to fall. She hadn't left him—yet.

He read the note from Andrew and tossed it into the fire. As the paper curled and burned away, Gabriel took a few deep breaths. It was finally over. Prinny was safe and no one had died to ensure it.

At some point during the night Olivia had changed into her nightclothes. Now she was curled up fast asleep in her dressing gown. The day had been physically and emotionally draining for both of them. Caressing her check gently, he took comfort in the warmth of her skin before heaviness settled around his heart.

Olivia blinked up at him through sleepy eyes. 'You should be in bed.'

A sad smile tugged his lips at the sound of her voice. 'I thought you had left,' he said.

'I told you, I would stay.'

Olivia rubbed the sleep out of her eyes and studied Gabriel. There was life back in his eyes and he was standing tall, not hunched in pain. She could leave him now. He was on the mend.

'When I awoke, and did not see you…' He took a deep, shaky breath, and lowered himself into the chair next to her. 'I thought you would want to know I received a note from Andrew. Both Janvier and his accomplice have been questioned. I'm certain they will be tried for treason and both hanged in the next few days.'

She sat up straighter at the news. 'What did they learn?'

'The woman who shot me has no wish to hang alone. She confessed to trying to kill Prinny and identified Janvier as the man who'd promised to pay for her passage home to France if she helped him with his plot. She shadowed the man who tried to kill Prinny the day we were returning from Mr Owen's and traced him to the Tower. At the Tower, she seduced a guard and convinced him to let her see the gunman. While there, unbeknownst to him, she poisoned that gunman's food. I'm certain in the coming days we will learn more.'

'Do they know anything of her?'

'She's an impoverished French aristocrat who has no love of the British Crown or the *ton*. Apparently she met Janvier at a coffee house, where they shared similar views.'

'Does this mean Prinny is safe?'

'For now,' he said on a sigh. 'However, a man in his position will always be a target.'

She walked to a table near the window and poured herself a glass of port. As she brought the glass to her lips, the warm rich smell held no appeal and she lowered it to the table.

'Will you not have some?' he asked with confusion. 'After this evening, I would think you might want the entire bottle.'

'I find I no longer have a taste for port.' She walked back to her chair and did not miss the sombre turn of his lips. 'I burned the portrait.'

His eyes widened and he followed Olivia's gaze to his bed.

'I found it while you were sleeping,' she explained. 'The canvas was visible from here. I burned it for you.'

'But I had no intention of destroying it.'

'You hated it.'

'I hated the fact that it would be seen by all of London. I never hated the portrait. For all his faults, Manning is a talented artist.'

'What would you have done with it?'

'I don't know, but I knew I needed to take it.' He lowered his head, noticing the scrap of embroidery near her feet. 'Is that a cat?'

'No, it's not a cat,' she replied defensively. 'It's a bouquet of flowers.'

'Oh, of course.' He looked back at the tangle of string on silk. 'I see it now.'

She stared at the mess of needlework and picked it up. With barely a glance, she tossed it over her shoulder. 'I intended to stitch flowers. I think it looks more like a dog, but I suppose a cat would be accurate as well.'

'Don't leave me, Olivia.' There was a catch to his voice.

She let out a deep breath not wanting to talk with him about her decision. 'I cannot stay.'

He leaned forward. 'You can. I can fix this between us.'

'You do not want me. There is no reason for us to live together. There is nothing to fix. I will honour my word not to reveal your secrets, but we are finished. Prinny needs you and I need you to keep him safe. You will do that for me, won't you? Make sure no harm comes to him? He may be foolish at times, but he is a sweet man.'

He reached over to take her hand, but she stood and stepped away.

'I will do all in my power to ensure his safety.'

'Do not get shot again. This should be the last time.'

'I will try my best.'

She walked to the door, needing to put distance between them or she would never leave. The sad look in his eyes had tugged too strongly at her heart. Or what was left of her heart now.

'I love you.' His voice was clear and deep.

She swung back around and stared at him. For years she had wanted him to say that to her. For years she'd wanted to say it back. But now it was too late. He didn't know how to speak the truth. And she loved him too much to be able to bear to hear him say it again.

'You don't get to say that to me,' she snapped, pointing her finger at him. 'You lost that privilege years ago when you went to that harlot's bed. That isn't love. Going back to her when you promised you'd remain faithful isn't love either. My mother and sister warned me about you. They said you would never remain faithful. Imagine my surprise when they knew you better than I did!'

He hadn't moved. He was motionless in his chair, save for his heavy breathing. 'Throw something.'

'What?'

'You know you want to. Throw something at me. Do what you must, but after you do I will have my say.'

He just didn't understand. Olivia shook her head. 'I have nothing left to give you, Gabriel. Not even my anger.'

It was as if her words had slapped him the way he reared his head back. He scrubbed his hand over his face and stood. Her husband did not want her. Couldn't he spare what was left of her heart and just let her go?

Gabriel was losing her. He could hear it in her voice and see it in her eyes. Once she walked out of his room, she would remove him from her life forever. He could not let that happen. He loved her too much to live without her.

He needed to tell her everything. His blood ran cold and his palms were sweating, but he knew there was no other way. He only prayed it wasn't too late.

'I never slept with Madame LaGrange.'

She had turned towards the door, but at his words she froze. 'Gabriel, please.'

'Hear me out. Yesterday I received a note from her, indicating that she had valuable intelligence regarding Prinny's safety. That is the only reason I went to her. She is an informant of mine. And she trusts no one else but me with the intelligence she collects.'

She turned fully to face him. 'You expect me to believe this.'

'It is the truth. Madame LaGrange provided me with the information on Janvier. That is how I knew he was behind the assassination attempt. It was an exchange of information that took place, nothing more. I never told you because I never trusted you, but I do now. I love you.' It came out as a rush, as if his soul had been waiting to say it for so long.

There was no response. Olivia just stared at him. It was gut wrenching, and he stopped breathing. It was too late. Even with his declaration she could not forgive his deception and his lack of faith in her.

He had a strong urge to rub at the stone of his ring, but his right arm was bandaged to his chest. She hadn't walked out yet. Maybe he could still reach her. 'I couldn't tell you about her years ago. We were newly married. We barely knew each other and from the time I was a small boy my father had taught me to trust no one.'

'What did you think I would do?'

'I was betrayed once by someone I held dear. That

trust cost someone their life. It's not easy to trust again when your friend's life slips away in your arms because they were shot by someone you trusted.'

'Did you receive the scar Nicholas found from the person who betrayed you?'

'I did. He intended to kill me. Fortunately he did not.'

As if it were yesterday he could feel the bullet rip into his torso again and see Peter aiming the second shot at his head. Olivia would never know that his brother had murdered their uncle to save Gabriel. She would always believe that he was killed in a robbery. Andrew didn't deserve to be looked at differently.

'Trust does not come easily to me, Olivia. I am responsible for the men and women who risk their lives every day to protect the Crown. On the night Nicholas was born, Madame LaGrange sent me a letter saying she needed to speak with me. She had worked for my father before he died so I knew this was not a social request. There was a threat against the King and she recounted what she had heard. You see, men go to her establishment and, under the influence of drink and a welcoming female, they will say things they never would in the light of day. If any of those men found out that she tells their tales her life would be in danger. A man with interest in harming the Crown would think nothing of slitting the throat of a woman who provides her services or any of the girls that work there for that matter.'

'But I smelled her on you that day. You cannot deny that.'

'She has an eye for fashionable clothes and admires my taste. In her profession she is accustomed to touching men. Her perfume might have rubbed off on me when she touched my coat or played with my cravat when she takes note of a new way to tie it. Over the years she has refused to give her information to anyone but me.' He rubbed his hand on his trousers. 'Know this—from the time I have courted you, I have never been intimate with another woman.'

'I wish I could believe you.'

The fact that she was listening to him gave him hope. 'I speak the truth, Olivia. My desire for other women stopped the moment I set eyes on you. I never strayed from our marriage vows. But my people like Madame LaGrange put their trust in me to keep their identities secret. Should I have told you and she had been killed, I somehow would have found a way to blame myself and maybe even you.' He searched her gaze. 'I never meant to hurt you, Livy. I am so sorry.'

She glared at him with angry reproachful eyes and stormed across the room, stopping in front of him. Her hands were balled into fists and he braced himself.

'For years I hated you. Years! So many times I wanted to burn the letters you wrote to me. For years I wanted to sell the jewellery you had given me. And for years I wanted to remove every scrap and shred that reminded me of a time I thought you cared for me.' She looked like she was fighting the urge to kick him. 'You let me believe all those lies. You let me hate you.'

'I had no choice.'

'But I loved you...' It came out as the faintest whisper as tears rimmed her eyes.

He closed the distance between them and with his one good arm he pulled her gently to him. She rested her head lightly against his left shoulder and he held her there, never wanting to let her go.

'It has always been you, Livy. I've never wanted anyone else.'

'Say it again.'

He looked down into her watery eyes. 'There never has or ever will be another woman for me. I have wanted only you from the moment I saw you dancing with Lyonsdale and nothing and no one will ever change how I feel about you.'

She let out a small choked sob.

'Dear God, I didn't mean to make you cry. Please, Livy, don't cry.' He was pleading with her. She was the only one in the world he would lower himself to beg. Looking into her eyes, he no longer saw anger. There was something else.

'Will you stay? I couldn't bear it if you left me,' he said.

'Will you promise to always be honest with me?'

'I will. I love you, Livy, with all my heart and all that I am, I love you.'

'And I love you. I always have.'

He had been so afraid he would never convince her to stay. Leaning closer, he kissed her. It was a soft, gentle kiss because he was afraid she would disappear before his eyes. They would start over again and this time nothing would tear them apart.

Chapter Twenty-Two

Waking up next to his wife placed Gabriel in an exceptional mood, in spite of being shot. The morning light filtered through the window of his bedchamber, casting a warm glow on Olivia's bare back. The soft, white sheet skimmed the top of her enticing backside as she slept on her stomach next to him. Her breathing was deep and steady, telling him she was sound asleep, which allowed him to look his fill.

Unable to resist, he skimmed the fingers of his left hand over her bottom. Her low groan made him chuckle.

'I pray you, I can no longer feel my legs,' Olivia mumbled into her pillow.

'I am simply touching you.'

She turned her sleepy head towards him and opened one eye. 'That was what you said last night when you somehow coaxed me to straddle you.'

'My injury prevented me from using any other position. In addition, I do not recall you complaining at the time.'

'I was being polite.'

Gabriel laughed. 'My love, last night you were everything but polite.'

'If I could move, I would smother you with this pillow. How is your shoulder?'

Thank goodness the dressing was still intact. 'Sore, but there is no blood on the bandage. That is a good indication all is well.'

She rolled onto her side, pulling the sheet up. 'You seem pleased with yourself.'

'I have a confession. I'm more pleased with you. I had forgotten that thing you are able to do with your tongue when you—'

'Yes, yes, well, we don't need to have such details this early in the morning.'

'You're becoming flushed.'

'No, I'm not.'

'Yes, you are. Let's suppose we find out how far that lovely colour travels.'

Her bare shoulders were much too tempting and the need to taste her was too great. Gabriel kissed her soft skin, trailing his tongue in circles. Within seconds he was hard.

He needed to sink into her and remind himself she would be at his side till the end of his days. Coaxing her to straddle him yet again, he claimed her lips with a searing kiss.

Yes, waking up beside his wife had its advantages.

'Tell me that you want me inside you,' he groaned against her mouth.

The crash by the door made them jump. There in the doorway, Hodges stood frozen in place with the remains of a coffee cup at his feet.

Olivia scrambled off Gabriel and took a good portion of the blanket with her.

'Does no one bloody knock in this house?' bellowed

Gabriel. 'We have a new rule. No one enters any room without knocking first!'

'I...I...I did not know. Your injury...I assumed...'

Gabriel counted to five. 'Hodges, I think it best if you left Her Grace and me alone now.'

'But I...that is to say...'

'Hodges!'

'You have callers,' his valet blurted out.

Gabriel looked over at Olivia, who was firmly wrapped in the blanket and appeared just as confused as he was. Focusing his attention back on Hodges, he noticed the man appeared to want to run out of the room but wasn't certain if he should stay or go.

'Who is here?'

With his gaze fixed on the floor, Hodges shifted in his stance. 'His Royal Highness the Prince Regent, along with Lord Hartwick. Bennett has shown them into the Gold Drawing Room and asked me to see if you were well enough to see them.'

Gabriel scrubbed his hand over his face. Tonight he was locking the door to his bedchamber and no one was interrupting them until he was good and ready to unlock it—and that might not be for days.

'Very well,' he muttered. 'Inform Colette that Her Grace is in need of her assistance and let Bennett know he is to see our guests receive whatever they wish. You can have a maid clean that up later. I will see you in my dressing room shortly. And, Hodges...'

'Yes, sir?'

'You did not burn yourself, did you?'

His valet finally met him in the eye with an appreciative glance. 'No, sir.'

Moments later the door was closed and the stillness of the room enveloped them.

'We need to get out of this bed,' his practical wife reminded him.

'I am aware of that,' he said, breathing in the faint scent of honeysuckle.

'And yet, you continue to lay there.'

He thought of how much he wanted to be inside of her. 'I don't want to leave,' he said, sounding petulant.

'Well, I don't either. However, we have no choice.' Her back bowed when he ran his thumb over her nipple. 'Do play fair, Gabriel.'

He sucked on that nipple, rubbing his tongue over it as he did so. When it hardened into a tight bud, he pulled his head away. At least he wouldn't be the only one physically frustrated while he sat enduring the presence of their guests.

Olivia had donned her nightrail and dressing gown, and was just helping Gabriel into his banyan when a muffled voice could be heard through the door to her room. They both stilled, listening to the sound.

'Mama, Mama, where are you?'

They both hurried to the door and as they stepped into her bedchamber, Nicholas walked out of Olivia's dressing room.

When he saw them, a broad grin lit his face, and he ran over to them. 'I've been searching for you, Mama. Did last night's thunderstorm frighten Papa again? Is that why you went to his room?'

The indignation on Gabriel's face made her laugh.

'Nicolas, for the last time, I am not afraid of thunderstorms.'

'But Mama was in your bedchamber. Don't fret, I won't tell anyone storms scare you. Did Mama make you feel better?' Before Gabriel could answer him, Nicholas tilted his head and tugged at his father's empty sleeve in a panic. 'Where is your arm?'

Gabriel opened the top of his banyan, revealing that his right arm was bent and tied to his chest. 'Last night—'

'It's true!' Nicholas's hazel eyes opened wide. 'You saved Prince George. I heard the servants whispering about it. Were you injured? They said it is in the papers. They said someone tried to shoot the Prince Regent, and you saved his life.'

'Where were you that you overheard all this at such an early hour of the morning?' Olivia asked.

'Near the kitchen. Sometimes when I go there cook will give me...porridge.' His expression brightened and he nodded. 'Yes, that's what I get...porridge, not biscuits or sweets. Just porridge.' He stepped closer to Gabriel and his voice turned faint. 'You are very brave, Papa.'

'I did what needed to be done, Nicholas, to save our Regent. Protecting the Crown is very important.'

Nicholas's face wrinkled with concern. 'Can I hug you? Will it hurt?'

'You will not hurt me.'

The sight of Nicholas clinging to Gabriel's waist with his eyes squeezed shut brought a lump to Olivia's throat.

'Please do not die, Papa. I need you,' he whispered.

'I have no intention of dying any time soon, Nicholas. You can be assured of that.'

Their son released Gabriel and stepped back, visibly relieved. 'That's why he is here, isn't it? That's why the Prince Regent came to call. He wants to thank you. I saw him ride up with his fine carriage with his splendid bits of blood from my window. I was coming here to tell Mama when I heard the servants talking in the hall.'

Olivia stepped closer to Nicholas and put her hand on his shoulder. 'Thank you. Your father and I have already been told. Once we are dressed, we will be able to find out what business he has in our home.'

Nicholas ran the tip of his shoe along the carpet. 'I suppose I will have to remain up here. Will you tell me what he wanted?'

Olivia ruffled his soft short hair. 'We will tell you every word.'

A short while later Olivia entered the breakfast room on Gabriel's arm and various smells from the food on the table assaulted her. Knowing Prinny and his vast appetite, she was certain he had been keeping her kitchen busy with his numerous requests.

'Ah, there you are,' Prinny said, looking up from cutting into what appeared to be a lobster cake from his seat at the table. His attention was on Gabriel's bandaged shoulder and arm, visible under the sleeve that was dangling empty at his side. He appeared to want to charge Gabriel, but then his gaze settled on Olivia. 'Good morning, my dear. Bennett did inform me you would both be down shortly. It's a pleasure, as always, to see you.'

She smiled at her friend and greeted him in return. Those were definitely lobster cakes and lobster was not on any of the menus for the week. She imagined there was a bit of an uproar going on downstairs this morning and bartering was being done with neighbouring kitchens. After extending a greeting to Lord Hartwick, she allowed Gabriel to hold her chair out for her. It was an intimate gesture Prinny did not miss.

'I say, we did not disturb your morning, did we?' he asked, picking up a glass of wine and arching his brow.

Gabriel caught her eye before focusing on Prinny. 'Not in the least. I expected to find you in the drawing room.'

'That was where your butler attempted to place us. I,

however, had a sudden desire to be in a more personal setting.' His attention was back on his plate.

The various items laid out in platters were unbearably unappetising to Olivia and she looked away to accept her cup of chocolate from Bennett.

From across the table, Lord Hartwick reclined back in his chair in a casually elegant pose, taking his coffee cup with him. There was no plate of food in front of him, as if he, too, found all this food repulsive so early in the morning.

'Prinny wanted to call hours ago,' he said, 'but I persuaded him to wait until at least sunrise before we ventured here.'

Gabriel studied Prinny over his coffee cup. 'Dare I ask what has brought you to my door?'

'Can't a man pay a call to a friend?' Prinny asked, surveying his plate and planning his next attack with his fork.

'You know you are always welcome.'

'I couldn't remain within Carlton House for one minute more. And all week I have had a craving for lobster cakes and your cook's beef with burgundy sauce. Though there is no time like the present. Don't you know? And low and behold, that talented cook of yours has managed to make me some for breakfast. Not up to her usual standard, mind you, however she hadn't much time to prepare. I expect the beef was what had remained from last night, but that sauce... I could bathe in it.'

That was the smell that was invading her nose, making her wish they were sitting out in the garden instead of this confining room. One of the footmen entered and placed a large wedge of cheese inches away from Olivia. She rubbed her stomach to settle it. Lord Hartwick's piercing blue-eyed gaze caught her eye. He tilted his head and his lips rose in a sympathetic smile.

Please let this be all the food Prinny had requested.

'I do not know if I should be insulted that you are here for my food and not for me,' Gabriel said, oblivious to her plight.

'I'd count myself lucky,' Lord Hartwick replied, taking a sip from his cup.

'Insolent pup. One day that unabashed bravado of yours will be placed in check. I just hope I am there to see it.' The prince turned his attention to Gabriel. 'I also wanted to express my gratitude to you for all you have done.' As if remembering that Olivia was in the room, he glanced at her and cleared his throat.

She caught Gabriel's eye across the table. It would have been wonderful if Prinny knew how she had helped catch Janvier and his accomplice. Suppressing a disappointed sigh, she managed to smile.

'Olivia is aware of the services I provide,' Gabriel said unexpectedly. 'She was also instrumental in foiling the plot against you. Her quick mind is what saved you last night on two separate occasions.'

Prinny's eyes widened and a smile spread across his face. 'Well done, my dear. I always knew there was something special about you.' His lips dropped from a smile to a serious line when he addressed Gabriel. 'You are not to place her in any danger in the future.'

'I have no intention of doing so. Last night was an unusual circumstance that I do not anticipate repeating.'

'Do I not have a say in what it is I am involved in?' she asked.

'No,' both insufferable men said in unison.

Lord Hartwick appeared to study her intently. 'I imagine it would be difficult to stop her should she decide to involve herself in the future.'

'Ply your charms elsewhere, Hart,' Gabriel said. 'And why are you here at this early hour? I would have assumed you would still be abed.'

'I found myself with nothing to occupy my time. An unusual occurrence. So, I decided to see if I could convince Prinny to have a go at a game of cards.'

'Nonsense,' Prinny said, cutting into the wedge of cheese.

The gesture stirred up the smell and Olivia held her stomach as it began to roll.

'Hart does not want to admit he was concerned for my wellbeing, but I saw it in his eyes.'

'Of course I am concerned for you. You are our Regent.'

'You think more of me than that and you know it.' He turned his attention to Olivia. 'Since you know of the activities surrounding me recently, you should be made aware that the artist will be spared. My understanding is that he was blackmailed. He did what he did to protect his child. I know something of the feeling one has for their offspring, therefore we shall show leniency. He will be sent to live across the ocean in America. We will not have him residing here. This will also spare a trial that might bring attention to you, my dear.' He patted her hand. 'I will have none of that.'

'That is very generous of you.'

'Wot, wot, haven't you heard? I have a rather generous disposition.'

Olivia raised her cup of chocolate to her lips, hoping the smell from the contents would drown out the horrible smell of the cheese. However, when she inhaled the scent, her throat tightened up and for the first time in many years she thought she might cast up her accounts. Looking up, she caught the narrow gaze of her husband. His attention did not waver from her, even as Prinny and Lord Hartwick continued their conversation. She knew that look. He was trying to puzzle her out. Had he witnessed her queasy moment with her cup? He arched an inquisitive brow and she shook her head to reassure him that all was well.

But just as she was beginning to feel better Prinny began to slather butter onto a lobster cake and a clammy coolness swept over Olivia's skin. If she stayed at this table much longer she was certain to make a spectacle of herself all over the floor.

She stood abruptly, startling the three men at the table. They rose to their feet and their reactions ranged from amusement, to perplexity, to concern.

'Would you excuse me for a moment?' she managed to say over the lump that had reappeared in her throat.

Prinny sat back down, eyeing his dish. 'Of course, my dear, I will be here when you return. This delicious meal will occupy me for at least another half hour.'

If one could turn green, Olivia was certain she just did. As she reached the grand staircase the rolling of her stomach had stopped and she sucked in the pure air of the entrance hall. She was so focused on inhaling deep breaths that she barely heard Gabriel's approach.

Concern was etched across his chiselled features and filled his hazel eyes. 'Tell me what is troubling you.'

The caress of his fingers along her cheek gave her comfort and she leaned into his hand. 'I find my stomach is not pleased with me this morning. All those smells mixed together were too overpowering.' She closed her eyes and took a few more deep breaths.

'I will make an excuse to our guests. You should not be forced to entertain anyone if you are not well.'

'Even if one of our guests is His Royal Highness?'

'Even then.' A gentle smile lifted his lips, and he cupped her neck with his large warm palm, seeping relief into her. 'Go to your room, call for Colette and lie down. I'm certain she can find something to ease your discomfort. I do not recall you suffering so in the past. Is this something I simply have blocked from my memory?'

She never had the urge to cast up her accounts and always enjoyed the aroma of good food—at least until this morning. Thinking back, she remembered the last time nausea overtook her.

It was when she was carrying Nicholas.

Her eyes flew to Gabriel and were met with his concerned expression.

'Tell me, Livy.'

Her legs wobbled under her and she dropped down to sit on a step of the staircase. Gabriel carefully lowered himself next to her and grabbed her hand.

'You are frightening me. Tell me.'

Excitement and fear mixed together inside of her. Only time would tell if she was correct. Taking a deep breath, she looked into the eyes of the man she loved. 'I think I know what it is that has affected me so.'

'Do I need to call for a physician?'

She shook her head and traced his wrinkled brow with her finger, smoothing out his worry lines. 'There is no need as of yet.' From the silence of the entrance hall it felt as if they were completely alone in the house. This wasn't the ideal place and time to tell him, but it was also not something she would be able to hide from him for very long, especially if the smell of food would make her ill. 'I think I am with child.'

His eyes widened, and that heart-melting smile lit up his face. 'But we haven't been trying for that long.'

'Long enough, apparently.'

He leaned over and kissed her. It was a gentle kiss—a kiss that conveyed how much he cherished her. 'You're certain?'

'As certain as I can be this early on. I only know the last time I felt this way, I was carrying Nicholas.'

He took her hand. 'It might be a girl.'

'It might. Would you be terribly disappointed if it is?'

His smile widened. 'I confess I would be rather pleased if it is. She might resemble you.'

'And we would have to continue trying to conceive a second son.'

'And there is that.'

His lips rose into that smile she remembered so well. She would love to tell him what that smile did to her, how it made her heart swell with happiness. But they had an entire lifetime ahead of them—a lifetime of smiles, and children, and love.

* * * * *

LET'S TALK

Romance

For exclusive extracts, competitions and special offers, find us online:

- **f** facebook.com/millsandboon
- **𝕏** @MillsandBoon
- **◎** @MillsandBoonUK
- **♪** @MillsandBoonUK

Get in touch on 01413 063 232